CW01507617

This is a work of fiction. Names, characters, businesses, organizations, places, events and incidents either are the product of the author's imagination or are used fictitiously. Any resemblance to actual persons, living or dead, events, or locales is entirely coincidental.

THE MYSTERY

OF

LULWORTH COVE

By

Roy J. Christie

ISBN-13: 978-1548642129
ISBN-10: 1548642126

I dedicate this book to my wife Louisa for her amazing encouragement.

CONTENTS

Chapter One

Sometimes, it's the little things that alter the course of your life, like catching the wrong bus, or helping someone who tripped and fell. Like I said, little things.

In my case, it was a call from my dentist, asking if I could come for my appointment that morning instead of the following week. As I had nothing planned for the morning, I agreed and because I agreed, my life changed forever.

Sitting in the Waiting Room, I picked up a car magazine. Inside was an ad for a classic car auction due to take place tomorrow at Biggin Hill Airport in Kent. Biggin Hill is only forty minutes from my business, which is also my home.

With my teeth nicely polished and a clean bill of dental health, I drove back to my flat above my antique shop, made myself a posh coffee and phoned my buddy Tom Cox. I mentioned the auction and said I would be going and he agreed to come along with me. We'd make a day out of it and have lunch in Westerham.

The following day, we arrived an hour before the auction was due to start. I hadn't expected it to be busy but the hanger was already crowded. People were swarming around all the exhibits - with the exception of one car. Probably ignored because it was a wreck, and calling it that was being kind. The placard on the stand informed anyone interested enough to pause, that the car was an Italian designed 1920 Bugatti. A wing dangled loosely from the main body and both headlamps were smashed. The passenger door was rusted away to almost nothing and the leather seats were ripped and worn through, but in my eyes, the car was beautiful.

Tom tugged at my arm and said, 'Come on; there's a hanger full of good stuff to see instead of studying this pile of junk.'

It was the wrong thing to say to someone newly love-struck. Like telling him that his wife is ugly and his kids are fat, and don't get him started on their buck teeth.

'Tom,' I said, 'if I bought this car, I would never lose money on it.'

He didn't reply; just stared at me as though I was insane.

Half an hour later, the auction got under way. I had no idea what price my new love might fetch, but knew my *current* bank account should be capable of providing the funds to buy two cheese rolls and two coffees when the auction ended. But! And this was a big 'But', I was here with Tom Cox, the same Tom Cox who has spent his working life happily turning brass into gold. The Tom who could retire to Utopia

2

and spend his days being fanned by faithful servants whilst drooled over by beautiful women.

And I'm his best friend. And I know he wouldn't like to see me upset if my bid failed. And I've always repaid any money I borrowed from him in the past.

In the antique business you occasionally come across a *find,* so I sometimes earn very good money. Right now though, my *business* account has twenty thousand pounds in it, which is my stock buying money. It might seem a goodly amount if you're a layman, but if you're a serious dealer, it isn't!

Things will change when the business, the building freehold and the stock are sold in four weeks' time.

Nearly thirty years have gone by since I met Tom at infant school, and we're still the best of friends. As teenagers, we took holidays together and sometimes still do, although since he married Kate, those holidays have shrunk to a few days at a time. Kate doesn't object to them though. She says that with Tom gone, she has time for herself instead of running around after him all the time.

So, returning to the Bugatti. It may be a wreck, but there's still a reserve price of £100,000 on it and if my bid is successful, Tom agreed to loan me up to £160,000, with the money to be repaid when the sale of my business is completed in four weeks' time.

I was hopping from foot to foot with excitement as I waited for the auction to begin.

Lots one and two didn't make their reserve price and were withdrawn. The Bugatti was lot five. Lots three and four took less than ten minutes and as lot five was called, butterflies wearing hobnail boots decided to go for a walk in my stomach.

I opened the bidding at the reserve price of £100,000, crossing my fingers that it would be the only bid for what was basically a wreck. I believe I'm unlucky in a few things. When I lose at golf, I usually feel that my opponent got the breaks and I didn't. It isn't something I'm proud of, but when another bidder called out £105,000, I added *Auctions* to that *unlucky* list.

Tom often lectures of the need to have a positive attitude, but I do have a positive attitude. I'm positive I'm unlucky.

So now the auction proper begins and I'm sitting on razor blades. No one has topped the other bidder's bid, so it looks like it's going to be a two horse race. My opponent, so to speak, is a studious looking guy.

The battle between us is brisk - the bids going up in £5,000 lots. My opponent is still in there at £145,000 and I'm beginning to worry. Another £15,000 and Tom's loan runs out, leaving me with the just the additional £20,000 I have in the bank. After that, I'm done for! I look across at the other bidder, willing him to, 'Stop being a prat and drop out!'

This is possibly my biggest weakness. I take everything personally, but I shouldn't. After all, he's no different to me. He isn't doing anything wrong. It's just that we both want the same car!

I raise the bid to £150,000 and with scarcely a pause, he says £155,000 and glances smugly across at me.

So, I have just the one bid left. If bidding continues as it has so far, I'll say £160,000 and if he comes back with £165,000, then it's all over bar the shouting, so I do the only thing that can possibly work. I call out '£175,000', which means that any bids will now increase in lots of £20,000 instead of the £5,000 it has been so far. So, if Studious Guy wants to stay in the game, he must now bid £195,000, which is £40,000 more than his previous bid.

He's staring at me now, probably trying to read my body language, and I grin back at him. He was comfortable with the soft shoe shuffle of £5,000 bids, but now I've changed the dance to a Quickstep and I realise from his look that he has just the one dance routine in his repertoire.

When the auctioneer banged the hammer down to seal my winning bid, Studious Guy slunk off without a backward glance. Tom, grinning widely, pumped my hand up and down; 'Bloody hell sunshine!' he said. 'I didn't know you had it in you. Maybe there's hope for you yet!'

*

I sold my house to start my Antiques business four years ago. The business is a large showroom with a one bedroom flat above that is my home. After breakfast, I walk down two flights of stairs and I'm at work. Traveling time? Around 15 seconds.

There are several valuable antiques in stock that the soon to be new owner wishes to purchase, so I'll be able to repay Tom's loan before commencing the main restoration work on the Bugatti.

Chuck Nelson is a friend of mine and I'm his young son's Godfather. He's also a top-notch car bodywork specialist, so obviously I hoped he would carry out the restoration work on the Bugatti. I rang him but was told he couldn't take the job on. He said he had a full workload for the next three months. I hadn't mentioned the car was a Bugatti, but did so on the point of ending the call.

Forty minutes later, Chuck hurried into the showroom, asking to see the car. At that point, it was under cover in the back yard. I offered him a cup of tea first, but he wasn't interested. Said to show him the car first and then we could have the tea afterwards.

In the yard, I pulled the cover off the Bugatti. Chuck's eyes widened. 'Bloody hell man!' he exclaimed. 'Of course I'll do it!'

So, I had my restorer.

Over cake and tea, Chuck explained that it would be expensive, although I could keep the cost down by doing the basics myself. 'Take out the seats, and ditch the carpets as they'll have to be replaced anyway. When you've done that, take the door panels off so they can be tarted up, but be careful with them. It ain't an easy job with an old motor like you've bought. Anyways, once you've finished, gimme a bell and I'll have the motor picked up and brought to me workshop.'

He offered a few useful tips and we made small talk over a second cup of tea before he took his leave. There was an unmistakable sparkle in his eyes as he climbed onto his runabout scooter and rode off. I finally relaxed then, knowing my treasure couldn't be in safer hands.

I planned to begin the work he'd suggested the following morning. Tom, however, warned that my yard was open to the elements and offered me the use of his double garage. He also said he would have the Bugatti picked up and transported to his place later that afternoon. I'm one lucky fella to have a friend whose generosity with his time and help seems to be boundless.

I began the work two days later, arriving at eight in the morning with a flask of coffee and a tuna and mayo sandwich for my lunch. I knew Kate would offer to feed me, but I didn't intend taking liberties with my friends' generosity.

"Morning Kate,' I said cheerily when she answered her front door in her dressing gown.

'Morning pest,' she replied. I pecked her on the cheek and she led me into the kitchen, 'Knowing you, I suppose you'll want a cup of tea before you start work?'

'Two sugars please,' I grinned, 'and don't forget to give it a good stir.'

She sighed and walked away, but she was smiling. It's lovely when you feel so comfortable with friends.

Tea finished, I began work on the car. Removing the seats wasn't as difficult as Chuck said it would be. I soaked the bolts with penetrating oil and they came undone without too much trouble, but getting the door panels off wasn't at all easy. I thought the first one would snap in two as I prised at it, but in the end, it came off without any damage.

I was working the other panel when it sprang off with a loud cracking noise, but it too was intact. A few panel clips had dropped into the bottom recess of the door and as I wriggle my fingers down to retrieve them, I saw there was an envelope laying at the bottom. Well, at that point, my pulse rate shot upwards. The car had been manufactured in the first quarter of the last century, so how long had the envelope lain there?

It took five minutes before I managed to free it, but the ink was faded and I couldn't read who it was addressed to.

I knew Tom was in his office preparing his books for the accountant, so I raced in without rapping on the door first. It's a good job some friends don't mind bad manners! Tom looked up and smiled, probably glad of the company for a few minutes. 'What! Given up already?' he said. 'I thought you'd keep at it for more than two hours.'

I waggled the envelope under his nose, 'This was wedged in the side panel of the Bugatti,' I explained. 'There's a name on it, but it's too faded to read.'

Tom gave a satisfied smile. He took a lamp from a desk drawer and plugged it into a socket. The lamp immediately emitted a strange glow. 'We'll soon sort that out, me old mate,' he said. 'This will enable us to read the writing on your envelope.'

The lamp could have come from Mars for all I knew! 'It's an ultra violet lamp,' Tom explained. 'It detects forgeries in paper currency. I use it if someone pays me in cash, just in case it isn't kosher. You can't take a chance in this day and age.'

He slid the envelope under the lamp's beam and studied the writing for a moment. I was watching intently and saw his eyes widen and my heart began to beat faster.

'What is it Tom?' I asked.

'Better take a look for yourself, me boy,' he said in an unusually quiet voice, 'just in case my eyes are playing tricks on me.'

In the glow of the lamp, the faded writing sprang to life and now I understood Tom's reaction. The decades old letter was addressed to Billy Monroe. It's a name I'm very familiar with because it's my name! I'm Billy Monroe.

Chapter Two

Dorothy Curtis had always hated her name. The Curtis part was ok. It had a nice flow to it and her 88-year-old grandmother said that as a teenager, her idol was Tony Curtis, a handsome film star - but her favourite film of all time was *The Wizard of Oz*, and Dorothy was the film's heroine.

Years later, when her daughter-in-law produced a beautiful baby girl, Grandma asked her to name the child Dorothy. With scarcely a pause, she added that she had considered gifting her money and possessions to charity when she passed on. The implication couldn't have been clearer and the new parents agreed that Dorothy would be an ideal name for their child.

The adult Dorothy took some comfort from the fact that *Lassie* was also one of Grandma's favourite films.

Dorothy's business was manic and it wasn't until the postman pushed a stack of what were obviously greetings cards through her letterbox that she remembered today was her birthday.

'Hey Dottie, apparently the Government is adding Sp – for spinster as an addition to Mrs, Ms and Miss.' This from two of her friends who had, foolishly in Dorothy's opinion, married in their teens. That was on her 28th birthday, a year ago today.

So, she was single. Surely better than rushing into marriage for the sake of it.

Plus, she didn't need the distraction of a man in her life. From what she remembered of previous boyfriends, men demanded considerable attention when she had little to spare. And for good measure, they often suggested how she could improve her Management Consultancy business. One such boyfriend supplied firewood for a living.

Dorothy headed a one-woman company, herself being the one woman. Hers was mainly a word of mouth business and the more successful she was, the more word spread and the busier she became. She knew the time had now arrived for her to employ a secretary and it was at the top of her *To Do* list.

She absolutely loved what she did and hoped to take the company to market within the next five years. No one could ever accuse Dorothy of setting her sights too low.

She checked her watch; still ten minutes before her taxi arrived. She ran a brush through her short chestnut hair, retouched her lipstick, but for some reason, men dominated her thoughts. For goodness sake! Who needed them? Most of the ones she had dated were a waste of space and she certainly didn't need a man's financial support. Her business brought in more money than most men would earn in their wildest dreams. She lived in a luxury apartment block on the fringe of Chelsea, just fifteen minutes from Knightsbridge and Hyde Park.

Kings Road shopping, Harrods department store along with some of the best restaurants in the world, what more could a girl ask for? And it was all down to *her* ability. Every bit of success generated by her and her alone. On her twenty-first birthday, there was no legacy to give her a financial kick-start. Not even a loan from the wonderful dad she adored. He could give her everything but money, but the amount of love and support she'd had from him was worth more than any amount of money. He was fifty-seven years old now - working an excessive number of hours every week in the hope of clearing the mortgage on the family home before retiring. But that wouldn't happen if Dorothy had her way. Her target was to clear her parents' mortgage on their 35th wedding anniversary. To hand over the deeds of the house and say, *'Happy anniversary mum and dad. This is to say thank you for everything,'* and as long as business continued to grow in the way it had, she knew she could do it. It was her number one target in life. The bull's-eye.

She looked in the mirror again, not particularly liking the image staring back at her. There were dark shadows under her eyes that needed to disappear. She turned away from the mirror before something else caught her eye, grabbed her purse and left the apartment.

In the lobby, Fred, the doorman rose from his seat as she approached, touching a forefinger to his peaked hat. Fred was the old fashioned type. He believed that if you had a job to do, then do it properly.

He grinned pleasantly, 'Evening Miss Curtis,' but she glowered at him in reply.

'Please, please Fred. I have asked you several times to call me Dorothy and not Miss Curtis, so why won't you? Please Fred, just for me.'

Fred faked a subdued look, 'Of course Miss Curtis, and may I take the liberty of saying how lovely you look this evening?'

Dorothy knew that had she been dragged through a hedge backwards, Fred would have still said the same thing. He certainly knew what women wanted to hear. She smiled gratefully; and so she should look lovely! Well, if not lovely, at least reasonably good. Her dress was Versace and she had spent more time than normal on her make-up.

'Of course you may say so Fred, and thank you for saying it.' She grinned and twirled around. 'So what do you reckon? Think I'll knock the guys dead at the party I'm off to?'

'If I was a young man at wherever this party is, you'd certainly knock me dead,' he answered truthfully. 'So what is this party in aid of?'

There was no enthusiasm in Dorothy's voice when she replied, 'It's one I can't get out of Fred. Not really a party actually; just business drinks in one of the Dorchester's function rooms. If I had my way, I'd go to my parents' holiday home for the weekend.'

Fred sighed enviously. 'A holiday home eh? Lucky you! And where is this holiday home? The countryside, or by the sea? I prefer being near the sea myself. Nothing beats sitting with a fishing rod and catching supper for me and the missus. Can't beat it in my book Dorothy.'

Dorothy laughed loudly. 'Aha, got you at last Fred! You called me Dorothy!'

Fred stared blankly at her. 'No Miss, you're mistaken. I definitely called you Miss Curtis. I'm sure of it!'

She grinned, shaking her head. 'I'm wasting my time, aren't I Fred?'

He lowered his eyes and said, 'I'm sure I don't know what you mean Miss.'

'So, Fred,' she continued, moving on from an argument she couldn't win, 'Mum and Dad's holiday home! As you like the sea, you would love it there. It's a big house, too large for us really, and it's situated on the coast of Dorset.' Her eyes glazed over as she thought of *Cherry Tree House* and the happy times she had spent there as a child. The area was heartbreakingly beautiful. 'It's part way up a cliff at a little place named Lulworth Cove and it's so pretty. I love it there. Whenever I think of the house, I go all squidgy inside. Do you ever get like that Fred?'

'No Miss,' he sighed, 'but I would if I owned a place like the one you're talking about.'

Dorothy knew just how lucky she was. And it was all thanks to the financial genius of her great great something grandfather. He left the house in trust for future generations of the family around 150 years earlier. On Dorothy's first visit there as a child, her mum explained how in those far-off days when the house was built in the 19th century, the family was wealthy, but something bad happened many years later and the money was lost, but not *Cherry Tree*

House. It would always be there for them to use, even when Dorothy grew up and had children of her own. By putting the house in trust, her thoughtful ancestor had made certain of that all those years earlier.

She blinked and returned to the present day. 'Even though it's a large house Fred, there's something magical about it - and it's close to the beach and just a few miles from a golf course, which is handy for dad as he loves a game of golf.'

She smiled, guessing that right now, her dad was most likely hiding somewhere at home and smoking a crafty cigarette. Dorothy's eyes shone. 'You would like him, Fred. He's a lovely man, my dad is.'

Outside in the street, her taxi driver blasted his horn to let her know he was waiting. She walked to the door calling over her shoulder, 'Night Fred, and no falling asleep on duty or I'll have to grass you up to the management!'

Fred smiled, watching until she vanished through the door. If he were ever lucky enough to have a daughter of his own, he'd be chuffed if she turned out to be like Dorothy. Absolutely chuffed.

*

I passed the letter to Tom. 'You open it,' I said apprehensively. I guess anyone would be the same. A decades old letter, seemingly to me, hidden in a foreign car manufactured almost 65 years before I was born!

'Do you think it's some sort of joke?' I asked, although I wondered what sort of joke it could be. Only Tom knew I'd be attending a car auction for the first time in my life, or that I'd buy a worn out classic car, so logically, only one answer made sense - the letter was meant for a different Billy Monroe. A Billy Monroe who made his trip to Heaven or Hell decades before I was born. Tom slid a paper knife under the envelope's fold, withdrew the letter and handed it to me. I spread it across his desk so we could read it together. It was dated May the 1st, 1925 and that made the hairs on my neck prickle. May the 1st is my birthday.

'My dearest Billy,' it began, *'how can you possibly know the joy you have brought into my life these past weeks, or how my heart soars whenever I see you. You cannot, of course, for no other human heart could possibly know the depth of my feelings for you. The way my pulse races at the merest sound of your voice. My darling, take care in your quest and return safely to me. I fear the six weeks of our separation will take the length of six lifetimes to pass, and I shall be but a distraught shell of myself until your safe return. Write to me soon my beloved, and may God speed you back into my waiting arms. My fondest love, Susan.'*

Tom faced me, grinning widely. Obviously, some sort of derogatory crack was coming my way, and of course, I was right. 'Bloody hell, whoever that Billy Monroe was, he knew how to knock the women dead! Not like modern day Billy. I've seen him in action and he's rubbish!'

I ignored the jibe. Over the many years of our friendship, I'd become used to them, although in truth, they still stung! Tom was correct though; I could use some help in the *Me Tarzan, you Jane* department.

I read the name and address aloud.

'Miss Susan Mendoza, Rose Cottage, Juniper Lane, Wooburn Green, Buckinghamshire.'

Tom scratched his head, obviously thinking, 'Wooburn Green?' He said after a moment, 'I've heard of that place Billy, although I can't think where it is.' He rummaged through a desk drawer and pulled out an AA map of the British Isles. He found Wooburn Green and spread the map across the desk. 'There it is,' he said, 'it's lovely in that neck of the woods. Probably forty miles from your place Billy.'

Well, it was certainly worth a visit to see where the romantically inclined Miss Mendoza had lived in the first quarter of the 20th century. Maybe the current occupiers knew of the Mendoza family. Maybe they even knew what happened between Susan and Billy and whether they married, assuming *Rose Cottage* was still standing of course. It may have been demolished. Whatever the outcome, it gave me a challenge for the coming weekend.

If the weekend was sunny and dry, then I'd pull the cover off my Yamaha motorbike and spin up there on two wheels. It would make a change to feel the sun on my face instead of looking at it through a car windscreen, but until then, I decided to put my curiosity on hold.

That night I dreamt of Susan Mendoza. Her brown hair was in a 1920s bob and her eyes were wide, beautiful and also brown.

*

1925; Dorset, England.

Susan Mendoza's thoughts were on Billy. She sighed and placed her embroidery to one side. With her mind elsewhere, she was making a dreadful mess of it. He had been gone for several months and she missed him dreadfully. Did other women feel as she did when separated from the man they loved? *Not much longer to wait though.* The ship was well on its way back to England and in eight days' time she would be at the Southampton docks, jammed in with hundreds of other people, most of them waiting for their loved ones to arrive.

She tried on the yellow frock bought specially for Billy's return and studied herself in the full-length mirror. She was so gaunt! And those dark hollows under her eyes weren't there when Billy last saw her. Would he still want her? She once read that some men don't like thin women. *Especially thin women with dark hollows under their eyes.*

Susan had spoken to Billy while he was away. Even primitive countries such as South Africa had telephone systems - of sorts, but they were few and far between, and calls needed to be booked days in advance.

She was surprised he hadn't received the letter she sent days before he left the country. It was probably on his hallway mat, waiting for his return. It had definitely been in the pile of letters in the Bugatti that morning, ready to post, although she had been in a hurry on that particular day. The panel on one of the doors was loose and she was late for her garage appointment to have it fixed. On the way, she stopped at a post box, grabbed the letters from the passenger seat and forced them into the slot rather than pushing them in one at a time.

On one of the telephone calls to Cape Town, Billy said he had something important to ask her when he returned to England, but wouldn't be drawn into saying what it was. His lips were sealed and only her kiss would unseal them.

Was he going to propose? She had hoped for that from the day they met. Even that early she was certain he had been chosen for her by her maker.

Just eight days of waiting left, and then – Paradise!

She left her bedroom and was half way down the stairs when her mother appeared at the bottom step. Her mother's expression told her that something dreadful had happened. Had her father been taken ill or was it to do with her sister, Celia?

'What is Mother?' she asked in a tone that conveyed her rising panic. The panic worsened as her mother dabbed her eyes with a handkerchief.

Maria Mendoza took her daughter's hands in her own and Susan said loudly, 'Has something happened to Father or Celia? Nothing could be worse than that Mum, could it?' but Maria shook her head.

'No darling, they're both fine. I'm afraid it's your young man, Billy. His ship sank in heavy seas thirty miles off the west coast of Africa. I'm so sorry my darling, but there were no survivors,' and Susan's knees buckled as she fell into her mother's arms in a dead faint.

Chapter Three

I decided to visit Wooburn Green this coming Saturday. Susan Mendoza had become my obsession, stupid really! If she were alive, she would be well over a hundred years old, but obsessions are something we have little control over and I was determined to discover more about her.

I'd planned to take the Yamaha and leave early, but the rain was non-stop. Motorbikes can be a nightmare in the rain, but by lunchtime it was sunny, so I tied a sweater around my waist, fired the Yamaha to life and roared off.

It was 2.30 as I turned into Juniper Lane. At the far end of the lane was a garden wall with red and yellow roses curling over the top of it. I drew closer and saw roses climbing up the sides of the house. I didn't need to see a nameplate. I knew I was there.

I rode the Yamaha onto the herringbone brick drive and pulled it onto the stand.

So, this was where Susan Mendoza had lived, and I was taking in the same scent she had breathed ninety years earlier. Standing there, I felt connected to the cottage. As if it was a part of me, but I knew it was the result of my foolish obsession.

I pulled off my crash helmet and gazed around with a warm feeling in the pit of my stomach. At last I was at Susan Mendoza's home. This is what I'd wanted since first reading the letter.

I strode towards the house, hoping to hear the story of Susan and Billy within the next few minutes. The front door opened and an aged woman appeared, not old enough to be Susan of course, but maybe she was Susan's daughter and I might hear how Susan and Billy's story ended. The woman shaded her eyes against the strong sunlight, 'Good afternoon young man,' she said pleasantly. 'Is there some way I may I help you?'

'If you can't, then I've had a long ride for nothing,' I said, smiling at her. I glanced around again and added, 'Well, not quite nothing. This gorgeous house and garden made the trip worthwhile.'

She smiled warmly at that, 'I'm so glad you like it,' and beckoned me towards her. 'I've been fortunate enough to have lived here for most of my life. I couldn't begin to contemplate living elsewhere, but I'm forgetting my manners! You mentioned you have had a long ride, so I assume you are not here to listen to the inane chatter of an old lady,' but she was quite wrong. That was exactly why I was at Rose Cottage.

I told her about the auction and my acquiring the Bugatti, ending the story with my finding Susan Mendoza's letter, seemingly written to me, but many years before I was born. The letter gave *Rose Cottage* as Susan's address.

She took my arm and led me through the front door of the cottage. 'This is all extremely interesting Mr -?'

'Monroe,' I said, 'Billy Monroe.'

'Mr Monroe, please come into the sitting room whilst my companion brews a nice pot of tea for both of us. Then we can discuss this letter at length. How does that sound to you? Oh, and by the way, I'm Mrs Sinclair.' She patted down her neatly kept hair, 'Perhaps, Mr Monroe, you would like a freshly baked scone along with your tea, and possibly a scoop of my homemade raspberry jam to go with it.' She smiled self-consciously; 'I'm quite famous for my jam in these parts. Everyone seems to like it.'

Having ridden forty miles in the blazing sun, sharing tea and scones with someone who might solve the mystery of the letter was an offer I couldn't refuse.

It was cool inside the cottage and the scones and tea were served by Beth - Mrs Sinclair's companion. Beth looked to be in her forties and occasionally gave me a sideways glance, possibly assessing if I was trustworthy, and who could blame her for that? She was only doing what she was paid to do. Protecting the old lady.

Mrs Sinclair asked if she could read the letter. She read it twice and my nerves twitched as I waited for her to finish. Could she know anything about Susan? She gave the letter back to me and then I told her everything. The auction, the Bugatti, how I found the ninety-years-old letter addressed to Billy Monroe, which is me. Everything.

'Well,' she said once I'd finished, 'my family moved here in December, 1927 when I was too young to know why we moved here.'

So zilch! But what I had expected? After all, it was almost a century back!

I drained my teacup and Beth, hovering silently in the background, refilled it.

But Mrs Sinclair had more to add. 'According to my father, some type of disaster befell the previous occupants of *Rose Cottage*, a death in the family or some such tragedy. It had something to do with their eldest daughter. The letter you showed me is dated the 1st of May, 1925, so possibly this Susan was the very daughter in question. I'm dreadfully sorry, but there is nothing more I can tell you.'

I slumped back in my seat, more disappointed than made sense. I'd learnt nothing of Susan Mendoza or my namesake. I had foolishly hyped myself up to the point where I was convinced I'd learn something from my visit, but apparently it wasn't to be.

'And that's all you can tell me, Mrs Sinclair?' I asked, trying not to sound desperate. 'Nothing else? Even the slightest thing would be something.'

She shrugged her thin shoulders. 'I wish I could help you more Mr Monroe, but I'm afraid I cannot. Even if there was something to tell, time has a way of eroding one's memory. Most people of my age are pleased if they can remember their own name, never mind something from so many decades ago.'

I tried not to grin, and suddenly Mrs Sinclair sat upright with a newly found inspirational look. 'My goodness Mr Monroe, I have had an idea that you may wish to consider. You could check the records at the local church. All births and deaths are registered there, at least, they are for churchgoers.' She stared critically at me, arching an eyebrow. 'Are you a churchgoer Mr Monroe?'

I go to weddings, christenings and funerals, so truthfully replied, 'Sometimes.'

The old lady moved to the large window overlooking the village, pulled the curtains to one side and pointed to the church. 'If you tell the vicar that Mrs Sinclair sent you, you will find him to be most helpful.'

'I'll do that, Mrs Sinclair. I can't thank you enough for your help and I enjoyed talking to you.' I remembered Beth just in time and added, 'And you Beth. Thank you for the delicious scones and tea.' Beth blushed a deep shade of red and I picked up my crash helmet, ready to leave, but it seemed the old lady had enjoyed my company.

'Are you off on your way so soon Mr Monroe? Most of my visitors are intrigued by the cottage, in fact, many of them ask if they may look around before they take their leave. Apart from that, I doubt the vicar will be in the church for at least another half an hour!'

I put the crash helmet back down. I didn't have to be asked twice. Just the thought of being shown around the rooms Susan Mendoza lived in was the icing on the cake. 'If you're sure you don't mind Mrs Sinclair. I'd hate to intrude.'

Over the next half an hour, the old lady showed me every room and every nook and cranny. They all seemed to have a story of some kind attached to them. She told these stories in great detail, so it was strange when she walked past one closed door without a sidelong glance. I said, 'Aren't you going to show me inside that room, Mrs Sinclair?'

She turned and looked back, as if wondering what I was talking about. 'Oh, that room! I've grown so used to walking past it, I'd almost forgotten it's there. Well, there's no mystery to it Mr Monroe, it's the library and nobody has been in there for years. Would you care to look inside?' Without waiting for my answer, she opened the door and led me into the room. I stared in amazement; it was awe inspiring - like stepping into another age, reminding me of when I visited *Raffles Hotel* in Singapore. I'd had the same feeling then as I had now. As if I'd gone back a hundred years in time. Every wall had dark wooden shelves stretching from floor to ceiling, all crammed tight with books. There must have been thousands of them.

The floorboards and the reading desk were polished dark brown, but everything was covered in a thick layer of grey dust. 'Forgive the state of the room Mr Monroe. The books came with the house but none of my family were great readers. Neither my parents nor my late husband found the slightest pleasure in reading, aside from newspapers and the occasional magazine and I'm no different. It must be a family trait. I find I never have the concentration for full-length books, only women's magazines and the occasional short story, but that is all, so this room is exactly as the previous occupiers left it those many years ago.' She gave a half smile. 'Now, my companion Beth loves to read but I don't allow her in here.' She noticed my puzzled look and spoke up in her own defence. 'She's employed as my companion Mr Monroe, and can hardly be a companion if her head is buried in a book, can she?' and I nodded in agreement, although personally, I found Mrs Sinclair's attitude selfish, but it was her business and nothing to do with me so I wasn't going to debate the point.

We left the library and moved on. Ten minutes later the grand tour was completed. Nothing had been missed. 'Well?' Mrs Sinclair asked, raising her eyebrows and obviously wanting to hear my comments on the house. We were now back in the sitting room and I picked up my crash helmet in readiness to leave. 'You have a lovely home Mrs Sinclair. You're a fortunate woman to be living in such wonderful surroundings. I envy you, I really do.'

At the front door I turned and shook the old lady's frail hand gently. Now we were back in the strong sunlight, she seemed as fragile as the bone china tea set.

I'm not sure who enjoyed themselves the most on that sunlit afternoon; Mrs Sinclair or me? I know I'd had a ball and although I'd learnt nothing of Susan Mendoza, I was glad I'd made the effort to visit *Rose Cottage*. It certainly gave me an insight into how some people live their lives.

'I've enjoyed myself so much Mr Monroe,' Mrs Sinclair said. 'Please feel free to call on me if you find yourself in the area again; I would be delighted to see you and to hear how you fared in your quest.'

I looked into those piercing blue eyes and realised she meant those words. 'And,' she added, 'you must call me by my Christian name; I insist! It's Petula. Whenever people call me Mrs Sinclair it makes me feel so dreadfully ancient.'

I suppressed a grin. Maybe when I'm heading towards triple figures, I won't feel ancient either. I took her hand in mine, 'That's fine by me, but I shall only call you Petula if you agree to call me Billy. So, is that a done deal?' and it was her turn to smile.

'I'm not sure what a *done deal* means, but I shall do that Billy; goodbye.' She looked at the Yamaha gleaming in the strong sunlight before adding, 'And *do* drive carefully on that machine Billy. People are so vulnerable on two wheels.'

I would think back on those words later.

'I promise I'll be careful,' I said, and then gave her a light peck on the cheek. It felt as if I was saying farewell to a favourite auntie. 'Goodbye for now Petula, and I will visit you again, I promise, and thanks again for the tea and the grand tour. You're very good you know. You could easily work as a tour guide. And that raspberry jam was the best I've ever tasted. Way in front of anything I've had in the past,' which was perfectly true.

I climbed onto the Yamaha and as I pulled away, gave Petula a wave. She returned my wave and walked back inside the house.

The church was deserted, so I noted the phone number listed on the board, intending to ring tomorrow. It was a church, so someone would definitely be there on a Sunday.

Chapter Four

Dorothy had correctly assessed the party. It was noisy, but with a pleasant buzz blanketing everything.

An old school-friend was also there and Dorothy spent most of the evening talking with her, although there were a lot of interruptions from men trying their luck. Well, that was something she'd neglected for the past eight months, but for a very good reason. She hadn't met a man who appealed to her. She glanced around in case she had been too judgemental, thinking a little romance wouldn't go amiss, but there was no one.

Her critical list was tough for any man to get past. Men with piercings and jewellery were nonstarters. The message they gave out was, *Look at me, don't I love myself.* Unfair maybe, but she wasn't responsible for her feelings. And if she was right, then she would always be the second most important person in the relationship.

And tattoos? It wasn't the tattoo itself that bothered her, because some were quite attractive, but they were permanent.

So, putting those things plus a few other personal dislikes into the equation, no one at the party was her type.

She waited until an acceptable time had passed and made her escape just before midnight. Back in her apartment, she sat until two in the morning watching a late movie on TV. It starred Grandma's favourite, Tony Curtis - frozen in time and every bit as handsome as he ever was. She guessed that Grandma would be sitting up in bed with a rug around her shoulders, eyes glued to the screen. Dorothy watched with a cold cloth on her forehead, hoping to subdue the red wine headache from the party.

It was three a.m. when she went to bed and she didn't stir until mid-morning.

Dorothy was having dinner at her parents' home in Ealing that evening. It would almost certainly be fish and chips, her dad's favourite meal. He could eat fish and chips for England. She visualised him in her mind's eye, leaning back in his chair, plate wiped clean and looking at wife and daughter in the hope they couldn't quite finish their own. If that happened, well, obviously as a caring husband and parent, he would feel obliged to help out.

Dorothy knew she was lucky - she had the best dad on the planet. She knew other women said the same thing, but in her case, it was true.

Five o'clock arrived and she felt better than she had earlier. At 6 o'clock, she phoned her parents. Her father answered. 'Hi sweetheart,' he said, 'is my little girl leaving yet?'

Dorothy sighed and wondered if he would ever stop calling her his little girl! She could be drawing her pension and he'd still be calling her his little girl. The truth was, she liked it! 'Yes Dad, I'll be on my way in a few minutes.'

'Good, Mum and I are both looking forward to seeing you, oh, and by the way, we thought we'd have fish and chips for a change, that's if it's okay with you sweetheart.' He followed that up by saying, 'Yummy yummy.'

Dorothy smiled. How many other fifty-seven-year-old dads would say that? She would bet everything she owned that the answer was none! He was a hopeless case.

A few minutes later she drove her little Smart car out of the underground car park and headed onto the Fulham Road. If the traffic was light, she should arrive at her parents' tree-lined home within half an hour.

Travelling home from Wooburn Green, Billy decided to avoid the motorways and take a leisurely ride skirting Greenford, and then head towards the River Thames. At that stage, he would decide whether to ride home via Isleworth or Ealing.

Fifteen minutes later he reached the iron bridge at the south end of Greenford and stopped. So, Ealing or Isleworth? He paused momentarily before kicking the Yamaha into gear and heading for Ealing.

Chapter Five

For the first week, Susan truly believed Billy would be picked up safe and well. This belief was based on her feeling that a love as strong as theirs was destined to survive. After the second week without news of any survivors, she accepted that the man she loved was gone forever. She would never see Billy again.

Susan knew that her life was now over. She would still draw breath and go through the motions of everyday life. After all, broken hearts still keep on beating, but she had a solution to end the pain that filled her being.

She rose at eight the following morning, made her bed and neatly smoothed the edges of the turned back sheet for the very last time. After breakfasting with her parents, she returned to her room and set about her plan to be with Billy again.

*

The rising sun was low on the horizon when Ola, the African fisherman, saw something bobbing in the water more than a hundred yards away. The villagers often said he had the eyes of a hawk and it annoyed Abdul, his fellow fisherman and closest friend. Ola's eyes were good, there was no doubt about that, but Abdul's pride refused to believe they were any better than his own. As Ola pulled on the rudder and pointed the boat unerringly forward, Abdul strained his eyes, but saw nothing other than the gentle waves that always followed a violent Atlantic storm.

'Your eyes are playing you tricks Ola,' he teased. 'You must stop drinking Nonie's brew before it destroys your brain. Now, will you turn the rudder back and let us catch fish, lest the village goes hungry because of your delusions?' But Ola wouldn't be deterred.

The boat glided forward and suddenly he shouted in triumph, climbing to his feet and pointing forward, 'You see Abdul? You see?'

He drew the boat alongside the body of a man. Abdul's eyes widened and the vessel canted precariously as he hurried to help his friend pull the body from the sea. Under the man's arms, a thick white ring encircled his body. Ola had never seen such a thing before. 'This must be what kept him afloat Abdul,' he said, thinking that if nothing else, the ring was something that could be of use to them in the future. The man was dead of course, his face blistered from the salt water and the sun. There was no sign of life in him, so after removing the strange ring, they would return the body to the sea. It would be pointless taking the body back to the village for burial when they were floating on one of the largest graveyards on earth.

Yet again it was Ola's keen eyesight that saw the

slight tick of a pulse at the man's neck. Thinking he may be mistaken, he lent over the body to check. 'Abdul!' he said loudly as he raised his eyes to his friend. 'This man is alive! We must hurry and get him back to the village if he is to survive.'

Abdul groaned and raised his hands in a hopeless gesture. They had already missed a day's fishing because of the storm and he thought of the rumbling bellies in the village if they missed yet another day. 'But we have caught nothing yet!' he wailed, illustrating his words by pointing to the bottom of the small boat - empty except for the man they had dragged aboard. 'Let us cast our nets at least one time. He has been in the water for so long that surely one more hour will make little difference as to whether he lives or dies.' But Ola, who had been born with a deep sense of compassion for his fellow man, ignored the pleas. He covered the blistered man with the folded fishing nets to protect him from the sun and without further ado, set the sail due East. As they moved towards the distant land mass, already covered in a heat haze despite the early hour, he pulled on the rudder and glanced across at Abdul.

'What are a few fish compared to a man's life?' he asked softly. Abdul didn't answer. He knew Ola was right and was ashamed of what he had said. It wouldn't be the first time the villagers had experienced hunger, nor would it be the last.

They took turns to carry the man through the rough tracks of the jungle, but it still took more than an hour to reach the village. They collapsed onto the floor of Ola's hut, exhausted. Ola's wife Jasmine hurried over and dropped to her knees by the white man's side, and Ola explained in breathless gasps what had happened.

She heard the clamour of excited voices from the curious villagers gathered outside the hut and as she tended to the man, she glanced up at Ola. 'You must go outside and tell our friends what has happened, lest they burst through the walls of our hut.'

Three days later, the man regained consciousness. He opened his eyes and for a while, everything blurred and danced, but gradually his vision settled enough for him to see the friendly black face of Jasmine staring down at him. She shouted excitedly, 'Nonie, quickly, come and see, come and see.'

Ola's ancient mother shuffled into the room. A miracle had given her Ola when she had seen fifty summers without child and a further thirty summers had passed since then. She was old beyond belief in a community where most people die before reaching the age of fifty. She was the only one in the small village who spoke the white man's language. Her lips smacked over toothless gums as she leant across the small cot, stroking the man's forehead and smiling encouragingly at him. 'What is your name Master?' she asked softly. 'What is your name so we may report you safe?'

The man searched through his memory banks, but they were empty. 'I'm sorry, but I haven't the faintest idea who I am.'

Nonie continued stroking his forehead and nodding understandingly. The sun could do strange things to a man's mind, and this man had been at the mercy of the sun and the sea for a very long time before he was rescued. He grabbed Nonie's arm and spoke with a trace of hysteria in his voice, 'You must help me,' he croaked. 'I cannot remember anything at all.'

*

All Motorcyclists realise they are vulnerable. I've had my share of near misses, so I approached the roundabout at a sensible speed, glanced to the right, saw the road was clear and leant the Yamaha into the turn. A little Smart car to the left raced up to the roundabout. I was already into the turn and it was my *right of way*, but the driver continued without looking or slowing down. My only choice was to grab the front brake, even though the bike was at a sixty-degree angle. The Yamaha slid from under me but instead of hitting the tarmac as I'd expected, I landed on my feet, running forward under the momentum, only stopping as I slammed into the rear of the Smart car. I slid up onto the roof with my head jerked backwards at an awkward angle.

I must have blacked out, because when I opened my eyes, probably seconds later, my head was hanging over a car windscreen and an attractive brunette was looking up at me. She had the chocolate eyes of the dream woman I had searched for since my teenage years. I grinned happily at her from the other side of the windscreen. It was an unorthodox way of finding her, but find her I had, so who cared?

My dream woman opened her side window and I knew I was about to hear the voice of an angel, probably saying, *I am so sorry, are you okay? Have you hurt yourself?* But I was wrong. 'Get off the roof of my car, you idiot,' she said harshly, and then my head filled with a mass of coloured stars and I blacked out again.

*

When I came around, a smiling black nurse explained that I was in a ward of the West Middlesex Hospital, suffering from concussion.

I had a vague recollection of being in an ambulance, dreaming of a striking brunette who for some reason seemed to hate me, but the rest was shrouded in a thick fog.

The nurse also explained that I would be spending the night in hospital, under observation in case I'd sustained any internal injuries. If everything seemed ok, Tom, whom they had contacted via the emergency number in my mobile phone, would collect me in the morning. Half an hour later, I was on the receiving end of a lecture from the doctor assigned to my wellbeing. 'You should be more careful at your age, Mr Munroe,' he lectured, and I gawped, thinking *My age! I'm thirty bloody five*, but I let the remark pass. Instead, I explained what had happened.

'It wasn't my fault Doctor, some idiot pulled straight out in front of me on a roundabout.'

'Yes, so I understand Mr Monroe, so I understand.' He tapped on my chart with the wrong end of a pencil and sighed; 'Not a man idiot though, but a female one.' He sighed loudly again before dropping into the chair by my bedside. 'However, I still consider it to be your fault. You should have learnt by now how women drive and been more diligent. I myself am campaigning for Parliament to legislate and make all women drivers display a *W* for woman sign on their cars. At least then we men can be fully prepared should a female take her eyes off the road to check her make up in the mirror.' He looked at me hopefully and raised an eyebrow. 'After your nasty experience, I'm sure you'll want to sign the petition I've started. I already have twenty signatures and it's only been running for three months!'

I was surprised to hear there were as many as twenty men with a death wish. 'It's a good idea Doctor,' I said, 'but I think I'll take a rain check on that one.' He shook his head and sighed with disappointment as he walked away.

I buzzed for the nurse and asked if she could find me a magazine to read. I was partway through a year-old copy of the *Hello* magazine when the activity in the ward increased. People suddenly arrived in clusters and took up positions around the other beds. It must be 7 pm - visiting time, although not for me of course. No one would bother visiting someone who was being discharged the following morning.

Ten minutes after the first influx of people, the ward door swung open again and a well-dressed woman wearing a wide brimmed hat walked in. She crossed to the large admin desk and spoke to the duty nurse.

I sat up sharply when the nurse pointed in my direction. The woman walked smartly across the room toward me, shoulders back and head held high. I quickly smoothed down my hair. It has a tendency to stick up when I've been lying down.

The woman reached my bed, took off her hat and fluffed out her hair. I was stunned to see it was the woman in my dream, although I had since realised that it wasn't a dream at all. I've always been satisfied with my extensive vocabulary, and gorgeous isn't a word that falls easily from my lips, but gorgeous was the only word that fitted her.

Without being invited to do so, the woman pulled up a chair and sat facing me. 'Hello again,' she said with a heart stopping smile. 'We have met, but at the time, you had your crash helmet on, so I had to ask the nurse which patient you were.'

Miss Gorgeous crossed her legs and leant forward until her face was just a couple of feet from mine. 'So,' she said cheerfully, 'how are you feeling now? A little better I hope?'

'Not really,' I lied, 'in fact I feel pretty awful. If only someone could mop my brow with a damp towel, then I'd probably feel much better, but there's a shortage of nurses, so I guess I'll have to suffer in silence.' Ms Gorgeous laughed and it was the nicest laugh I'd heard in my three and a half decades on this planet.

'Dear oh dear, poor you Mr Monroe-'

I rudely cut in and said, 'Please call me Billy.'

She huffed, but continued, 'Well Billy, I do believe you're trying to make a fool of me, although you did suffer a nasty crack on the head, so obviously can't be held responsible for what you're saying at this moment.'

So, gorgeous and a smart cookie! I sighed loudly, 'I'm afraid you have me at a disadvantage at the moment, Ms -?'

Even to me, it sounded like a line from a B movie, and I was the one who said it.

She didn't reply and embarrassment caused the

blood to rush to my face. 'What I mean is, you know my name, but I don't know yours, and apart from that, I don't have a clue why you're visiting me.' She held out her hand and I shook it, at the same time glancing at her other hand. Not a ring in sight.

'I can soon put that right Mr Monroe. I'm Dorothy Curtis.' Maybe along with her other magic, she could also read thoughts, because she added, 'That's Ms Dorothy Curtis.' I was still hanging onto her hand, trying to ignore the electricity surging through me. It was uncomfortable, but at the same time, wonderful.

Ms Curtis continued, 'And I'm here visiting you because I feel partly responsible for your being here and obviously I wanted to make sure that you are not badly injured.' She pulled her hand away and I asked, even though I already knew the answer, 'Why is that? Are you the driver of the car that pulled out in front of me at the roundabout?'

Ms Curtis smiled condescendingly, as though I was delusional. 'No Mr Monroe, I'm the person you almost hit when you decided to treat the roundabout as a race circuit. You were going far too quickly, you know. Haven't you seen those signs that read, *What's your hurry in Surrey?*'

'We were in Middlesex,' I said, to which she shrugged her perfect shoulders and frowned disapprovingly.

'Please don't be flippant Billy. It doesn't suit you at all.'

My composure was rapidly slipping away. Normally I enjoy a duel of words, but if I was going to marry this woman - and I already knew I would move heaven and earth to make that happen, then I needed to use my head and watch what I said. I made a quick count to ten to help the process along. 'So you feel partly responsible for my being here, do you?' I ventured. 'How is that Ms Curtis? Why do you feel *partly* responsible?'

I received another glimpse of the smile I hoped to see every morning for the rest of my life when I woke up. 'There's a simple answer to that Mr Monroe, sorry, I mean Billy. You see, I was on my way to visit my parents and if I'd stuck to the route I first planned on taking, then I wouldn't have been anywhere near the roundabout when you decided to speed around it.' She smiled sweetly again and added, 'I would have been several miles away.' I gawped as any man would, listening to this piece of logic. What chance do men have against this sort of reasoning? I had, of course, asked myself that question many times in the past and learnt that the only answer is - absolutely sod all. Oh, and by the way, I was travelling at 10mph when I entered the roundabout.

'And that's why you came to see me?' I asked quietly. 'To acknowledge your part in the accident?'

Ms Curtis reached into her handbag and removed a form that she handed to me. She smiled sweetly, 'Don't be foolish Billy. I came here because you scratched my car paintwork. I want you to sign this form, stating that the accident was your fault.' She removed a pen from her handbag and pushed it into my hand, indicating where she wanted me to sign. 'And once you've done that, I can make a claim against your insurance.'

Chapter Six

The villagers called the man Paul, because Saint Paul was the name mentioned mostly by the white missionary in his weekly preaching sessions a few years back.

The sessions came to an abrupt halt after he was taken by another tribe and never seen again.

Nonie was feeling smug - more than pleased with her patient's progress during the three weeks since his rescue. At last she had eclipsed that old hag Stukie's reputation. Stukie was her main rival as the chief healer in the village, but with Paul's rapid recovery, Nonie was now clearly the number one and her toothless grin was a permanent feature. However, the moment Stukie appeared, that grin became a superior smirk.

The blisters on Paul's face had healed and his strength returned, but not the memory of his previous existence. His past was as much a mystery to him as it was to the villagers, although life in the village suited him well. Since his rescue, he had formed a strong bond of friendship with Ola and Abdul and it was a good feeling. On most nights, the three of them would behave like naughty children, drinking the potent home brew that Ola's wife was famous for. Three cupfuls of the lethal fluid would reduce Ola to a gibbering idiot, collapsing into fits of laugher at almost anything. A further cupful would send him into a drunken stupor.

In just three weeks, Paul had picked up enough of the tribal language to be understood, thanks to Nonie's daily lessons. The white man was her new mission in life and she spent most of her days with him, despite receiving rebukes for neglecting her other duties.

'Are you certain you can remember nothing at all?' Abdul asked Paul one evening. It was hard for him to believe that all memories of his new friend's past life had vanished. Surely something must remain. 'You must have a woman somewhere Paul. Every man needs a woman to look after him and to warm his bed at night,' he chuckled and rolled his eyes lasciviously. 'I know I do!' But if there was a woman in Paul's old life, every memory of her had been erased.

And what if there was a woman? He was more than happy living with his new friends in the village, and although Rachael, the village chief's daughter, had given him no encouragement other than shy smiles and sidelong glances, he was sure that she liked him every bit as much as he liked her.

The accident that changed everything happened a week later. Paul was carrying water back from the river when his foot caught in a tree root. He pitched forward, smashing his head against the tree and knocking himself senseless in the process. When he regained consciousness, his head was thudding painfully. He looked at the worried black faces staring anxiously down at him. 'Ola,' he mumbled, reaching for his friend's hand. Ola hauled Paul to his feet. 'This time I really do need your help,' Paul said. 'You must help me get back to Susan.'

*

Susan had planned her suicide to the very last detail. The family holiday home at Lulworth Cove in Dorset was a few hundred yards from the rocky beach. She would walk into the sea and continue walking until the water filled her lungs. Within minutes the dreadful feeling of loss would be gone and she would be treading the same path to heaven that Billy had trodden.

But a painful month must pass before she joined Billy. Her parents' 30th wedding anniversary was three weeks away and the celebration party was already arranged. Susan did not intend to spoil that happy occasion because of her own misery and pain. However, one week after the party, nothing would prevent her from joining Billy again. She knew that he was already in that special place, waiting impatiently for her to come to his side.

*

I stared up at the lovely Ms Curtis, wide eyed with shock. Had I heard her correctly? Had she really said, 'Then I can claim against your insurance,' when I was here in a hospital bed with a thumping great headache and a bent motorcycle because of her careless driving, something she had yet to acknowledge? Somehow, I managed to keep my cool. I'd waited a long time to meet this woman and wasn't about to ruin my chances with an outburst I'd regret later.

I was, however, in a quandary. If I complied and signed her form, there would be no excuse to see her again.

'Look Doris,' I began. Of course, I knew her name was Dorothy and not Doris, but I had the beginnings of a plan forming, and this was the start of it.

Her beautiful face flushed with anger. 'Mr Monroe, my name is Dorothy. It is most certainly not Doris. Dorothy is bad enough, but Doris? That's even worse!'

I stifled a grin, 'Well Dorothy, that only proves what I'm about to say. Remember, I'm in hospital suffering from concussion. Would you really want to run the risk of my signature being nullified because of that fact? The last thing insurance companies want to do is pay out and they'll get out of it any way they can!'

It obviously made sense to her because she paused, presumably mulling over what I'd said. 'So just when do you reckon your state of mind will be beyond question Mr Monroe?' I stifled yet another grin. Most of my friends would answer, Never.

At that moment, my thoughts were along the following lines; *Careful Monroe. A horse can fall at the last hurdle, just when it seems to be home and dry.* 'If I'm fit enough, I'll be discharged on Wednesday,' I lied. Actually, I was being discharged on Tuesday, which is tomorrow. We Taurians are regarded as straightforward, but surely the odd fib is acceptable, especially when it leads to a happy ending, and surely Ms Curtis would want a happy ending, so you could say I was only lying for her benefit. That must go a long way to proving that I always think of others before myself.

'Look Dorothy,' I said casually, 'why don't we meet somewhere on Wednesday evening and I can sign your form then? Maybe in a bar, or even a restaurant? It's your call. We can even meet at a bus stop if it suits you.'

I waited with baited breath. Had I given her too many options? Please God don't let her choose a bloody bus stop, but luck was with me. Her brow creased into a thoughtful frown and she mused for a moment before answering. 'Well, some friends of mine are going to the theatre on Wednesday evening and I'm meeting them for drinks afterwards at ten-thirty. How about if we meet for a quick bite at *The Ivy* at eight-thirty? It so happens that I'm booked in there anyway and as a table for one is no different to a table for two, you could come along without causing a problem.'

I felt a surge of dismay and swallowed hard. Right answer - wrong place!

I don't visit London that often, but I do have a tendency to be star struck and often read the gossip columns, so I knew all about *The Ivy*. It's the haunt of the rich and famous and from what I've read, especially the rich! People like that prefer places mere mortals can't afford, presumably so they can eat in peace and without being overly disturbed by autograph hunters. I figured the only way I could afford to eat at *The Ivy* was to kill myself and then go with the insurance money. Or I could grovel at the feet of Thomas Cox esquire once again, always the chief helper if the Monroe budget goes awry, which isn't as often as most people seem to think. In reality, it's only around 300 days a year.

In return for Tom's financial assistance, my penance will be the usual one. I'd have to tell him all there is to know about Dorothy. How tall she is. How does she look? Is she a knockout or just nice? Weight, approximate dress size - hour glass figure or skinny and on a scale of one to ten, how did she measure up to the ultimate Hollywood sex symbol, Marilyn Monroe? All that sort of stuff – it's a Tom thing.

Back to Dorothy and *The Ivy*. I answered nonchalantly, 'That's fine Dorothy,' as though meals leading to bankruptcy are an everyday occurrence for me. '*The Ivy* on Tuesday at eight-thirty it is.'

'Fine,' she said and turned to leave. Three paces later she paused and looked back at me. 'By the way, it'll be best if you came by cab, Mr Monroe.'

I noticed a hint of a smile hovering around her mouth, '*The Ivy* is quite upmarket and has a dress code. I don't think you will be allowed in wearing a crash helmet.'

*

There wasn't a telephone within a hundred miles of the village, so it was impossible for Billy to contact Susan, or anyone else in England for that matter. And none of the villagers had even seen a car, let alone owned one, so that avenue was also closed. Billy guessed gloomily that the only way to comparative civilization would be overland on foot. 'It is not that simple my friend,' Ola warned, a grim expression etched on his face. 'To do that, we pass through some very dangerous territory. Do you remember our tale of our preacher and what happened to him?' Billy remembered only too well. It was quite amazing to think that in the supposedly civilized year of 1926, cannibals still existed.

The three friends sat around a fire on the evening following the restoration of Billy's memory. They were discussing the options open to them. After much thought, Abdul banged his hands on his knees and stood up. 'The sea,' he suggested. 'It will be less dangerous,' and after a moment's consideration, Ola clapped him on the shoulder and added his agreement.

'But we must travel by night and hide during the day,' was his only proviso. He saw Billy's puzzled look and explained, 'We have many enemies along the coast. Hostile tribes whose territory we must skirt.'

This tribal thing was just one of the vast number of things about Africa that astounded the Englishman. Different tribes were the deadliest of enemies and would think nothing of wiping out whole villages, given the opportunity.

The following evening, the whole village turned out to see them set off. To the side, Billy saw Rachael with her father. She was crying softly and he felt a twinge of guilt, but what could he do?

He hugged Nonie for several minutes before saying his goodbyes to the other villagers. Finally, he crossed to where the chief stood. He was a tall man, well over six feet and Billy looked up at him. 'Thank you for allowing me into your village and into the hearts of your people. I will miss every one of you.' He pulled Rachel to him and kissed her lightly on her cheek, 'You will make some lucky man very happy one day, but I know now that I have a woman waiting for me and she will be worried. You understand that, don't you Rachel?' She clung to him for a moment, then turned and ran back inside her father's hut.

The three men set off on their dangerous journey as darkness fell. They carried enough provisions to feed Ola and Abdul if their mission was successful and they remained alive to make the journey back home. Ola steered the boat a few hundred yards from the shore, but with nothing more than the moonlight to guide them, their progress was slow. They still managed to cover around forty miles before Abdul became anxious as dawn approached. He explained to Billy they would soon be visible from the shore. 'We must stop and hide until nightfall returns again; remember, my friend, there is danger all around us. If we are discovered by our enemies, we will be shown no mercy and our deaths will be slow and painful,' and so they dragged the boat ashore and hid with it in some dense scrub less than fifty yards from the beach. The scrub also offered protection from the relentlessly fierce African sun. They spent the hours until nightfall sleeping and swapping tales.

The following night they sailed along the coastline and when dawn approached, they again hid close to the beach throughout the hours of daylight.

There was a final night at sea before Abdul said they had reached friendly territory. At midday, they sailed into safe harbour. Abdul had been to the town before, but it was the first time that Ola had seen such an amazing place. He wandered around wide eyed at the size of the buildings and the number of people milling around. Although these people were of different colours and creeds, there was no outward sign of animosity between them. A few cars and trucks weaved through the streets, causing Ola to back away, his eyes wide with fear and his hand on his hunting knife should they came to attack him.

Billy went to find a telephone. As an orphan, there were only two people to inform that he was alive and well - Susan, the woman he loved, and his business partner.

Although the town was large, it was lacking an English Consulate, but his luck held. He met a Dutch diamond merchant who had heard of the maritime disaster. He promised to help Billy by booking telephone calls for the following evening, the earliest bookings he could get. However, there was a ship sailing for France in the morning. It was fully booked but the diamond merchant persuaded the Captain to take Billy on board. He also promised to make the phone calls on Billy's behalf.

That evening, Billy clasped hands with the two Africans who had risked their lives for him. He was safe now, but they still had the perilous journey back to their village. Billy knew he was unlikely to see Ola or Abdul again. He loved them like brothers and owed them a debt he could never repay. He clasped them too him, tears in his eyes. 'May God guide you safely home, my brothers. You and the rest of your tribe will be in my heart until my last day on earth,' and then his voice gave out and tears flowed unchecked down his cheeks. He stood on the harbour steps and watched his two friends sail the small boat out to sea, his eyes bright with the tears that wouldn't stop flowing. When they were almost out of sight, Abdul stood and gave a final wave, his broad smile splitting his face, and then they were gone, hidden by the rapidly descending darkness.

Chapter Seven

I sat in *The Ivy* and watched this slim, wisp of a woman eat her way effortlessly through the first two courses. For my own part, I pushed my half-finished main meal away; I was full to the gunnels. Dorothy stared at me, as if I'd taken leave of my senses. 'Are you ill Billy?' but I wasn't ill; I was stuffed. Not even room for an after-dinner mint. 'I'm done,' I sighed. 'If I eat one more mouthful, I'm going to explode.'

'Cool,' she said happily and plunged her fork into the steak that had beaten me. In my three and a half decades on earth, I'd never witnessed *anything* to match this, and I know people who can pack it away, although I now realised they were mere pretenders to the crown. I'm not much of a drinker either, although an expensive bottle of Chablis proved to be an unexpected blessing. Once Dorothy had polished off two thirds of the bottle's contents, she became a lot more amenable towards me. In fact, we got on so well that the purpose of our meeting - the insurance claim - was never mentioned.

When it was almost time for Dorothy to meet her

friends, she invited me to accompany her. She took herself off to the Ladies room and I asked for the bill. I checked it carefully, because even restaurants like *The Ivy* can make mistakes.

I stared wide eyed at the total, although in fairness, it was around the figure I'd guessed at. I put enough cash down to cover it, but constantly being short of money was becoming tiresome. Luckily the sale of the business was almost completed and that would take care of everything for quite a while, but until that happened, I still relied on the turnover for my income.

As I waited for Dorothy's return, I took a proper look around the restaurant. I could see why it was so popular. It really was special.

I hadn't scrutinised it earlier for a very obvious reason. Most of my time had been spent looking at and listening to the jewel in the crown opposite me.

A few minutes later, Dorothy returned. Seeing no silver plate with the Bill clipped on it, she asked, 'Haven't they brought the Bill yet?'

I grinned. 'I've taken care of it,' but she tutted disapprovingly and pulled some money from her purse.

'Thank you Billy, it's sweet of you, but I always pay my way.'

I didn't argue. I had the feeling that it would antagonise her, although splitting a bill with my date was a new experience for me. Although it wasn't a date. It was a meeting to instigate an insurance claim. Which had not been mentioned, and I'm quite certain never would be.

After we met up with Dorothy's friends, things

seemed to get even better between the two of us and they'd been going pretty well anyway. It was three in the morning when I stopped the car outside her apartment. I was shaking – too nervous to kiss her in case she slapped my face and told me to get the hell away from her, but she looked at me in a funny kind of way and whispered, 'What's the matter Billy? Aren't I your type?'

A strangled croak took the place of, *'Yes yes yes. Of course you are,'* but my face must have given my answer. She leant to my side of the car and kissed me and I felt I was floating up to heaven on fluffy white clouds.

Eventually she broke from my arms, 'How about coming up for a coffee Billy?' she asked. It sounded more like an order than a request, which was fine by me. If Cameron Diaz had appeared and said, 'Don't listen to her Billy. Come with me instead,' I'd have pushed her away without a second thought, and along with a few million other men, I adore Cameron Diaz.

Inside in the reception area we tip-toed quietly past a man in uniform, asleep in his chair. Dorothy put a finger to her lips until we were well past him. 'That's Fred,' she giggled. 'He thinks I'm wonderful.'

I whispered, 'He's not the only one.'

We ignored the lift in case the noise woke Fred and took the stairs instead. The moment we were inside the apartment, we grabbed at each other.

The promised coffee was six hours late and served along with breakfast.

What a strange life this is. Thanks to an accident that put me in hospital, I was now treading the path to Paradise.

*

The Mendoza's thirtieth wedding anniversary party at Cherry Tree House was a huge success. Fifty guests kept the hosts busy and prevented Susan from dwelling on the loss of Billy, but once the guests departed, the pain returned as strong as ever.

Lying in bed that night, she knew that at last, she could join Billy. She thought of how wonderful her time with him had been. And still would be, if only the ship hadn't sunk. She wished she had been with him. At least she would have died in his arms and they would have been together. She would have willingly settled for that! *Together forever.* It had a nice ring to it! *If only if only if only!*

'But life isn't made up of *If onlys,*' her father explained. 'It's made of joy and sadness, and, my darling girl, one never knows which of the two is coming their way.'

At the early hour of nine o'clock, the family retired to bed in readiness for the long drive home to Wooburn Green in the morning. After her parents called out their *goodnights* to her, Susan knew that it was time join Billy. She wasn't in the least afraid. The truth was, she could scarcely wait. Life had now become one thing, and one thing only. Pain heaped upon more pain. She had no second thoughts; it was the right thing to do for her.

And in any event, is there ever a good time for one to die?

She changed into the yellow frock chosen especially for Billy's return when she would have that deliciously agonising wait as he hurried down the gangplank. He would reach her side, sweep her into his arms and kiss her again and again and again until she almost fainted from lack of oxygen.

Studying herself in the mirror, she started to cry. For a moment, she saw Billy standing next to her, but she blinked and he was gone. It had been an illusion.

Susan propped the note to her parents against her alarm clock where it wouldn't be missed, then crept down the stairs and through the big kitchen where she'd eaten so many happy family breakfasts. She paused for a moment to stroke the surface of the table. 'Goodbye table,' she whispered, then her highly charged emotions took control and she began to cry again. She took several breaths to compose herself before opening the back door. She looked out to be sure it was all clear, then stepped into the chilly night air and made her way towards the shore and the grey English Channel that was waiting impatiently for her.

*

Three wonderful weeks had passed since our night at *The Ivy*.

'So when did you know I was the one?' Dorothy asked, handing me the tray of coffee and toast before climbing back into bed with me.

I turned the question back on her. 'When did *you* know I was the one?'

She slapped me playfully. 'Stop it Billy. I asked you first.'

'It was when I was hanging onto the roof of that silly little car of yours and my head was hanging over the windscreen. I saw you and I knew that you were the one. Now it's your turn Dottie, and no fibbing or your nose will grow.'

'Don't call me Dottie,' she complained. 'I reckon it was when I saw you in that hospital bed - I knew then. You looked so helpless and lost. And when I asked you to sign my form saying you were responsible for the accident, well, your face was a picture. Anyway, it was then. And I knew you were fibbing when you said you were being discharged on Wednesday. The nurse at the desk said you were only being kept in for observation and would be discharged the following morning, so I decided to engineer you into taking me out for dinner. I lied about the booking at *The Ivy,* but I reckon it worked out pretty well, didn't it?'

I still couldn't believe that this had happened to *me* of all people. If this kept up, I could probably win the jackpot without buying a ticket.

Dorothy had already met some of my friends. We had been out with Tom and Kate twice. It was obvious they liked her and I knew Dorothy liked them.

'I was thinking of asking Tom and Kate down to the family home in Dorset this coming Friday,' she said. 'We could make a long weekend of it and return to London on the Monday. Do you reckon they'd fancy that?'

Dorothy had never mentioned a place in Dorset before. I'd met her parents and they lived a modest lifestyle. Not on the breadline by any means, but surely not well off enough to own a second home.

Dorothy must have read my thoughts. '*Cherry Tree House* was bought by my great great something grandfather at the end of the 19th century,' she explained. 'It can't be sold as he left it in trust for his descendants, me being one of them.' She smiled, eyes twinkling. 'And he also left a trust fund for the upkeep of the house.'

I phoned Tom with Dorothy's invitation and he leapt at the chance. 'Kate is driving me nuts Billy. A little company will spread the misery around. Give me a break from copping the lot all the time.'

There was a noise on the phone like a door opening and I heard Kate's voice, 'Copping what all the time Tom?'

I pressed the phone closer to my ear, eager to hear my poor buddy's explanation. He's crap at getting out of these situations. Off he went, headfirst down the road to doom. 'I – er, I was just telling Billy that you hadn't quite been yourself just lately, but er, that you're all ok now and would love a weekend away with him and Dorothy.'

There was what I understand to be *a pregnant pause,* followed by Kate's sharp voice, 'Are you telling me, Thomas Cox, that you have been discussing our personal life with other people, is that what you're telling me Tom?' Even I felt nervous and I was miles away, so she couldn't get her hands on me.

Tom spluttered incoherently until Kate snatched the phone from him. 'Tom will speak to you later Billy. Right now, he and I have a few things to discuss.' The line went dead and I was left holding a silent phone.

The following morning, Kate phoned and said they'd love to join us for the weekend in Dorset.

*

Dusk was falling as Tom drove into Lulworth Cove on the Friday evening. Dorothy was out of the car in seconds. 'Quickly while there's still some daylight left,' she said excitedly. 'You must see this.'

She grabbed my hand and tugged me up the steep path to the top of a cliff. Tom and Kate followed at a slower pace. My legs felt like jelly over the last hundred yards.

'Just take a look at this,' Dorothy said, pointing down to the cove. 'What do you reckon Billy? Doesn't it just take your breath away?'

I looked at the scene below. We were so high up that I understood why I was pooped. Tom and Kate arrived then. Kate was puffing away while Tom didn't even have the breath to puff. He collapsed in a heap at my feet. 'Am I in Heaven?' he wheezed. 'Because I must be high enough!'

Kate shook her head disbelievingly, 'In Heaven? Not likely Tom. When you go, you're going down, not up.'

Dorothy nudged me and pointed downwards. Spread out before me lay a sight that I believe most people would pay to see. It was like looking at a giant apple, minus a bite where the turquoise sea had flooded in.

The sight of it made me gawp and I turned to look at the even more spectacular sight of the woman I loved. 'I can see why your many times removed granddaddy wanted a house here,' I said, slipping my arm around her waist. 'Can you imagine looking at this view every day? I mean, can you?'

By the time the four of us got back to the car, it was practically dark and we were unable to see *Cherry Tree House* clearly as we drew up outside. I grabbed the bags and walked inside, thinking that the best girlfriend on the planet had also came laden with goodies.

Dorothy went into the kitchen and placed two bags of food on the big wooden table before collapsing into a chair. She rubbed the back of her hand across her damp brow. 'I feel pooped after that journey and I don't feel up to going out to eat. I can cook something for us. I've brought enough food to feed a small army.'

'That's all very well Dottie,' I said, 'but have you brought enough to feed yourself?'

She said, 'Watch it Buster, or I may be forced to modify your features. And don't call me Dottie!' She switched on the old fashioned electric oven on to warm it up while she sorted the food out. Ten minutes later, she opened the oven door to put in eight sausage rolls. 'Just our luck Billy,' she said. 'The oven is stone cold.'

I shrugged my shoulders and wondered why she was telling me of all people? I thought the initials D I Y meant, *Don't Involve Yourself.* 'Well it's no use looking to me to sort it out,' I said, 'I'm hopeless at anything involving electricity.' But Tom - the one person even more clueless than myself - strode forward and moved Dorothy to one side.

'Leave it to me, me girl,' he said. 'If Baird hadn't invented electricity, then I would have.'

No one corrected him. I guess we all thought the same thing. Why waste our breath, but to Tom's credit he discovered the fault after Dorothy led him to the hall and pointed to the fuse board and electricity meters.

'Fuse blown,' he announced a few moments later, waving the offending item in the air for us to see. Five minutes later he pushed the newly repaired fuse back into the main board. There was a popping noise and when he pulled the fuse out again, the wire had melted. However, Tom was not deterred by a small thing such as that. 'Simple,' he announced, like the qualified electrician he wasn't, 'it just needs something stronger. The fuse wire was hanging by the meter and I used the thickest wire on the card, but it obviously wasn't thick enough.'

'You could double it up,' I suggested, 'wouldn't that work?' but he shook his head.

'Nah, let's make sure of it this time and get something *really* big.'

'Dad keeps a toolbox in the cupboard under the stairs,' Dorothy said helpfully, so Tom rummaged around in the box until he found a thick nail.

He beamed and said knowingly, 'This'll do the trick,' and as I understood nothing about electricity, I was hardly in a position to disagree with him.

Somehow, after much cussing, he managed to wedge the nail into the fuse carriage, rubbing his stomach in anticipation of the forthcoming supper. 'Yum yum gang, in a few minutes, we'll be eating warm sausage rolls, trust me.'

He gave a sort of *aren't I clever* grin and pushed the fuse carriage into the board. There was a huge explosion and his feet left the floor as he shot backwards. A lightning like flash filled the hallway, so bright that it blinded all of us for a moment. Every light in the house went out and we stood in darkness. Tom was so close that I could just about see him. His hair was standing upwards. 'Bloody hell,' he said and looked accusingly across at Dorothy. 'You want to get that fuse board looked at, me girl. I could have been a gonner.'

Kate fumbled her way across to the window and drew back the curtain. Outside was pitch black. 'All the street lights are out as well,' she said, but the crescent moon gave enough light for Tom to see three pairs of eyes glaring at him. He turned a deep shade of red.

'Hey you lot, don't look at me like that. It wasn't *my* fault. Go and take a look yourselves. That bloody fuse board is probably as old as the house.'

Dorothy sighed. In the short time she had known him, she'd already learnt that nothing was ever Tom's fault. 'There's a torch in the cupboard,' she said and he fumbled around blindly until he found it. It was one of those extra-large torches with batteries that weighed several pounds. Tom clicked it on. A powerful beam of light illuminated the hallway and we all stared in disbelief. Trapped in the beam of the torch was a young woman in her twenties, shivering uncontrollably and hugging herself in an attempt to keep warm, which was hardly surprising as she was soaking wet and her yellow dress was dripping seawater which was rapidly forming a puddle around her feet.

Chapter Eight

Tom stared at the woman. 'Where the hell did you appear from?' he asked, but Kate - a nurse before marrying Tom and taking over as his book keeper - hurried across to her.

'Who cares where she came from Tom, the girl needs our help and she needs it quickly. Dorothy, where do you keep the towels?'

In that instant, the lights came back on, flooding the hall with light. The woman stared wide eyed around her and before Dorothy could answer Kate's question, the woman said through chattering teeth, 'Towels are kept in the loft b-bedroom, in the c-corner cupboard. W-when was the d-décor changed? It wasn't l-like this yesterday.'

Dorothy removed her own jacket and placed it around the woman's shoulders. 'There isn't a loft bedroom here,' she explained softly. 'The loft is used as an office and the computer and printers are housed in there. The fresh towels are kept in the boiler room in the basement.'

Tom, seeing his chance to redeem himself, took off down the stairs and returned, clutching an armful of bath towels, puffing like an old man who had just completed the London Marathon.

Dorothy vanished for a moment, returning with underwear, jeans and a T-shirt. She took the towels from Tom and led the shivering woman up the stairs to the first floor bedrooms. Down in the hall the others heard her say, 'You can dry off in here and put these clothes on. They're mine and should fit as we're both about the same size.'

Dorothy returned to the hall and the others crowded around her. Billy spoke first. 'What did she say? We heard you tell her to put dry clothes on, but couldn't hear anything after that.'

'Well the poor thing is obviously in shock,' Dorothy explained. 'She's quite convinced that this house is hers and asked what had happened to the bedroom because it was so different, and then, when she picked up the underwear I'd given her, she stared at the thong for a moment before asking what it was.'

'D'you think she's a nutter then?' Tom asked eagerly. 'Maybe she's on the run from the local loony bin and is looking for a place to hide out.'

Kate rolled her eyes skywards; 'What are you like Thomas Cox? Fancy saying something like that about the poor girl.'

Dorothy was clearly puzzled by it all. 'But Tom has a point Kate. Maybe he's right. Perhaps we should ring the police and tell them about her. At least she'd be back where she should be, getting the right treatment for whatever is wrong with her.'

Bolstered by Dorothy's support, Tom poked his tongue out at Kate as if to say, *See!* Kate ignored him and said, 'Good idea, but let's not do that just yet Dorothy! Let's wait until she's dried off and changed into your clothes. Then, we can hear what she has to say before taking such drastic action.'

Ten minutes later the woman made her way back down the stairs. Kate had a pot of tea brewing and everyone was sitting around the big kitchen table, still discussing who this mysterious woman could be when she peeped nervously into the kitchen. Kate beckoned her towards an empty chair. The woman sat down and Kate stirred three spoonfuls of sugar into a mug of tea before handing it to her. 'Here,' she said, 'you'll feel much better with this inside you.'

The woman sipped the tea, screwed her face up in disgust and said, 'Ugh, I dislike sugar intensely,' but Kate gave her a matronly pat on the arm.

'Please try to drink it my dear. Sweet tea is the best thing in the world for shock.'

Billy glanced up at the big kitchen clock. It was eleven, so he switched on the TV. 'I just want to catch the news,' he said. 'I've been rushing about so much that I haven't a clue what's going on in the world today.'

The newsreader appeared on the screen and the colour drained from the woman's face. She leapt to her feet and the mug fell from her hand, shattering as it hit the floor. She backed away from the television set, obviously terrified.

'Turn it off!' Kate snapped. 'The poor girl is scared out of her wits!'

Billy clicked the *off* button and the newsreader's face disappeared, but the woman continued to stare wide-eyed at the silent set. 'What type of magic is that?' she whispered and they all looked at one another, now convinced that Tom's guess was correct and she was indeed an escapee from a mental institution.

Hoping to appease her, Dorothy said, 'Why don't you explain it to her Billy?'

The woman spun towards Billy and stared at him, wide eyed in disbelief. 'Your name is Billy?' she whispered.

Tom answered for him. 'That's right, my love. He's called a lot of different things, but mainly, he's called Billy Monroe.'

The woman's face turned a deathly white and she slid to the floor, unconscious.

Kate glared at Tom and hurried across to the prostate woman. 'You've done it again, haven't you?' she hissed. 'When are you going to learn?' A few seconds later, she apologised to him. 'I'm sorry Tom, you didn't do anything wrong and I shouldn't have said that. I'm just worried about this girl's state of health. There's something really wrong about all of this. Really, really wrong!'

The stricken woman groaned and with Kate's help, got to her feet staring warily at Billy as Kate picked up the chair and helped her to sit down. 'Why don't you tell us your name, my dear?' she asked gently. 'I can see that you're just as confused as we are.'

Without taking her eyes off Billy, the woman whispered, 'It's Susan. Susan Mendoza.'

The hairs on Billy's neck stood up. 'Bloody hell,' he whispered to Tom, 'Susan Mendoza is the name of the woman who wrote the letter I found in the Bugatti.'

Before they could speculate further, Dorothy leant towards them, frowning deeply. 'Now that really is odd,' she said, 'because my great grandmother had a sister named Susan Mendoza. The man Susan loved was lost at sea and apparently, she loved him so much that she drowned herself a few weeks later. However, the really sad thing was that the man called to say he was safe and well just the day after Susan took her own life.' She shook her head sadly. 'Sometimes, life is a real bummer, isn't it? It was all a long time ago though, about ninety years back.'

Susan had listened to all of this in shocked disbelief. She had always believed in coincidence, but what this woman was saying was a lot more than coincidence -- it was bordering on the supernatural. 'You mean that this woman you're talking about, this other Susan, you're saying she drowned herself in 1836?'

Dorothy flashed the others a puzzled look. 'Your maths are a bit wonky Susan,' she chided. 'If you take ninety away from 2016, it leaves you with 1926. It's 2016 now, at least it was when I woke up this morning, so the Susan we're talking about died in 1926,' and without uttering another word, Susan Mendoza slid to the floor in a dead faint.

*

Susan's *goodbye* letter was discovered by her mother the following morning. The rescue services were immediately alerted and a lifeboat launched, but a six-hour search revealed no trace of Susan, nor was her body washed up anywhere along the south coast of England during the weeks that followed.

The day of Billy's return arrived and Susan's father Samuel went to Southampton docks to meet him and report the dreadful news.

As the boat pulled into the dock, Billy scanned the crowd, desperate for his first sight of Susan in almost three months. He saw Samuel and waved franticly until Samuel spotted him and waved back. Billy rushed down the gangplank, pushing through the throng of people until he reached Samuel's side. 'It's good to see you again Sir,' he said, gripping Samuel's extended hand. 'I hoped Susan might be with you. Is she in Dorset or back at Wooburn Green?' He was hoping it would be *Cherry Tree House*, as then she would be in his arms within the hour. Samuel was strangely silent, so Billy repeated his question.

Samuel Mendoza was an important man in the city of London. He controlled boardrooms, chaired shareholder meetings and placated anxious old ladies who feared for their future should he and his fellow directors ever make a wrong move. But this was something he had no expertise in. He'd rehearsed how to break the news to the boy, but rehearsing it and telling it were two different things.

His continued silence worried Billy. Was Susan ill, or even gravely ill? Or had she had an accident? Or worse still- for people recovered from illnesses and accidents- had she found another love? If that was so, then he knew the blame was all his for leaving her alone in the first place.

Of course, that had to be it! She had another love and hadn't the courage to face him. Her father was here to break the news to him. Even now she was probably in her new lover's arms, whilst he, Billy Monroe, was nothing but a distant memory.

Samuel eventually regained the power of speech. 'We have lost her, Billy,' he said quietly. 'Our Susan has been taken from us,' and Billy's worst fears were confirmed. Susan had cast him and her family aside and gone off with this other man.

'Where exactly has she gone to Mr Mendoza?' he asked softly.

Samuel, a regular churchgoer, replied in a broken voice, 'She is in Heaven now Billy, sitting alongside Jesus,' and then he proceeded to explain to Billy all that had taken place.

Billy would have fallen had Samuel not gripped his arm and kept him upright.

*

Back at Lulworth Cove, they sat at the kitchen table along with Maria and discussed the tragedy. The first thing mentioned was that news of Billy's survival arrived the day after Susan drowned herself. It came just one day too late. Billy was angry with himself for going to a remote country such as South Africa in the first place. 'In a civilized country, I could have called at least three days earlier and Susan would be alive and with us now.' He looked at the tear stained face of Maria and shook his head, devastated by the loss and how it came about. 'I was going to ask Susan if she would do me the honour of becoming my wife, Mrs Mendoza,' he said. 'I had been thinking about it for weeks, right from when I first boarded the boat to Africa, but she died without knowing how important she was to me.'

Maria put a comforting hand on his arm. 'Oh, but she knew Billy. Susan guessed you planned to propose when you returned to England,' and just hearing that gave Billy some comfort. At least she died knowing he loved her.

A funeral without a body was not possible, but a week later a memorial service was held for Susan at the local church. Billy stared downwards during the service and whispered to Maria that he would never love another woman, but Maria knew better. At his age, what could he possibly know of these things? 'You will Billy,' she whispered. 'In the end, you will find that time takes care of everything. I'm older than you and know about these things. Of course, you will never forget Susan, but in time, her memory will fade,' but Billy wasn't in the frame of mind to listen.

'You're wrong, Mrs Mendoza. I shall never love another woman. Never!' He spoke with a force that caused the Vicar to look sharply across at them. Maria realised it best to let the matter drop, even though she felt that Billy would find love again.

*

When Susan regained consciousness, she was lying on the sofa in the lounge, certain that she was losing her mind. All the signs pointed that way. In less than an hour she had seen a man's talking head trapped inside a box with a glass front, and the Mendoza family seaside home, which she knew intimately having holidayed there every year without fail, had changed completely. And not only had it changed, but living in the house was a Billy Monroe who was nothing like the real Billy Monroe. And as if all of that wasn't enough to absorb, a woman in the house claimed the year was 2016 - the very woman now bending over her.

Susan said in a barely audible voice, 'Why are you doing this to me? Don't you people think I have suffered enough already? What do you hope to gain by all of this and why is that man over there pretending to be my Billy?'

Kate mouthed to Dorothy, '*She's in shock.*'

Billy was surprised to hear he was pretending to be himself. He wondered who his choice would be should he ever pretend to be someone different. Maybe Brad Pitt, but he quickly dismissed the thought. Brad Pitt might have almost everything a man could want, but he didn't have Dorothy Curtis, so Brad Pitt could continue being Brad Pitt, while he was happy to remain as Billy Monroe.

*

It was two in the morning when it came to me. Impossible, but the only explanation to what had happened. We knew from the letter in the Bugatti there was another Billy Monroe in 1925. And when Dorothy mentioned her great grandmother's sister Susan drowned herself ninety years back, our uninvited guest asked if that happened in 1836.

So, adding ninety years to 1836 brings us to 1926. The woman now with us believed it was 1926! Somehow, Susan Mendoza had moved ninety years forward through time.

The Susan sleeping in the next bedroom was the very same woman who had written the letter I found in the Bugatti.

Now, I couldn't sleep and waited impatiently for breakfast time to arrive. Once everyone was seated around the table, I gave a pen and paper to Susan and asked her to write her name and address on it. I hadn't mentioned my theory to anyone else and they all stared at me, but didn't comment as I waited for the result.

Dorothy and Kate probably thought I'd gone completely off my head, but there was a glimmer of understanding on Tom's face. He said, 'No way Billy, it isn't possible,' and he was right; it wasn't possible, but they said man would never land on the moon, and yet there's talk of it becoming a holiday resort in the future.

'But if you can get your head around it Tom,' I said, 'then everything that's happened since we arrived at *Cherry Tree House* begins to make sense.'

Susan hadn't yet begun to write. She was staring intently at the pen and asked, 'How am I supposed to write without an inkwell?' That added fuel to the fire for me. I'm certain the ballpoint pen wasn't invented until the nineteen forties.

'It's a special type of pen Susan,' I explained. 'The ink is contained inside it.'

She shrugged her shoulders and began to write. I suppose with all that had happened so far, she could accept almost anything as being possible.

She finished writing and handed the paper to me. I went into the hall, opened my case and removed the letter I'd found in the Bugatti. Still in the hall, I compared the two lots of writing. Now, there could be no doubt. The same loops and twirls; the same slant and if I needed further proof, the address Susan had written provided it. *Rose Cottage, Juniper Lane, Wooburn Green, Buckinghamshire.*

Back in the kitchen I said to Susan, 'You look exhausted. Why don't you go to bed and catch up on some sleep? It will do you the world of good and we'll talk some more this afternoon. Is that okay?'

The poor girl's eyes were heavy with tiredness and she seemed close to breaking point. She gave a tired smile, her way of telling me that bed would be welcome.

Dorothy took Susan up to her bedroom, returning a couple of minutes later. 'What's going on Billy?' she asked as she walked in. 'You've sussed something out, so what is it?'

So, I sat at the table and explained my impossible theory to them. They could accept it or laugh at it, but it was clear to me that the Susan upstairs had, until a few hours earlier, been living in the year 1926. Somehow, she'd travelled ninety years forward to 2016.

Chapter Nine

Susan must have been exhausted as it was seven in the evening before she reappeared downstairs.

Earlier, I thought of a way to prove that she was now in the year 2016 and while the girls cleared away the breakfast things, Tom and I walked to the local shops and bought copies of the national daily papers. I also bought the latest *Hello* magazine and a *Radio Times*, working on the basis that you can't have too much ammunition.

While we were gone, Dorothy searched the attic and found a book titled, *The Movie Stars Story*. Hopefully, the information in it would be the clincher if we hadn't convinced Susan by then. We placed everything onto the kitchen table except for the newspapers, which we read as we waited for her to appear.

'Good evening everyone,' she said quietly and Kate passed across a sandwich along with the cup of tea that she had poured for herself but hadn't yet begun to drink.

None of us wished to make the poor girl feel

uncomfortable, so we flicked through the newspapers until she'd finished eating and then Kate got things underway.

'Susan, we all realise the events of last night were a shock to you, so we talked things over and decided to clear everything up now, rather than later.'

'I wish you would,' Susan said softly, 'because my head is spinning from trying to make sense of everything.'

Kate gave Susan's arm a friendly rub. 'Right then,' she said, 'I'll start the ball rolling. I'll ask a few questions and show you some things that may freak you out, but it will all make sense once I've finished. We only want to help you Susan. Is that okay?'

Susan nodded and Kate continued, 'I'll begin by asking you what year it is.'

Without pausing, Susan said, 'That's a silly thing to ask. It's 1926 of course.'

Kate glanced at me. So, my theory was on the right track. 'Now tell me the last thing you remember before we found you in the hall last night?'

'I had walked into the sea-' Susan's voice tailed off when she saw the look of surprise on all of our faces. 'The man I loved drowned, so I had nothing left to live for. All I wanted was to die and nothing has changed; my life will be unbearable without my Billy, and I can't stand the pain that's with me every minute of every day!' She looked at each of us in turn, 'You are all nice people, so I pray none of you ever suffer it. Anyway, I had just gone under when the sea lit up like a fireball and a tremendous force pulled at me. I must have blacked out, because when I came around

I was back in the house and you were there with me.'

'You must have been in a terrible state to want to kill yourself Susan. Why would you do that?' asked Kate.

I was seeing a new side to Tom's wife. Sympathetic to everyone on the planet except my buddy.

'I already told you the reason,' Susan said irritably. 'I did it because of Billy.' She pointed an accusing finger at me and her voice rose a notch, 'I mean the *real* Billy, not that impostor over there!'

Kate ignored the remark and moved on. 'Many strange things are happening at the moment Susan. Things difficult for *all* of us to understand, so please stay calm and don't become hysterical.' Susan, obviously wondering what on earth Kate was about to disclose, nodded, which I took as meaning *Ok then,* so Kate continued, 'When the sea lit up around you, somehow you moved forward in time by ninety years. It is the year 2016 and I can prove it.'

Susan gave a half grin and rejected this out of hand. 'I may be confused, but I'm not stupid. No one can move through time. It's impossible!'

Dorothy slid the copy of *The Times* under Susan's nose and tapped the front page. 'Look at the date here,' she said and then slid the other three newspapers across in quick succession.

Susan checked the dates on all of them before looking at each of us in turn, smiling as if she knew what was going on. 'Very clever, but they don't fool me. These have been specially printed. Anyone can buy newspapers with headlines printed exactly as they want them, like, *Rudolph Valentino marries Susan*

Mendoza.' She laughed nervously, probably embarrassed because she'd linked her own name with the man who even in the twenty-first century, is still regarded as the world's greatest film heartthrob, but she had inadvertently played right into Dorothy's hands. She disappeared for a moment, returning with a book on Movie Stars and searched the pages until she found what she was looking for. She placed the open book in front of Susan, who read the words and looked up at Dorothy in astonishment. 'Valentino is dead?' she said in disbelief.

'Yes and for that matter, so is every other film star who was around in 1926.'

Susan quickly flicked through the pages of the book, whispering the names aloud. 'Fatty Arbuckle, Wallace Beery, Lon Chaney, oh God, not Charlie Chaplin.'

It was a large book and Kate cut the flow of words short. 'Every last one of them has passed on Susan.' She placed a newspaper over the book. 'Look, forget the book for the moment, will you? Why don't you read the front page of this newspaper and see if you recognize anything at all.'

Susan scanned the page and looked up at Kate. 'Iran? I matriculated in geography, but am at a loss over a country named Iran. Where is it?'

Tom was hopping from one foot to the other. I know him almost as well as I know myself. He was feeling left out of the loop and was unable to keep quiet any longer; he blurted out, 'Back in 1926 it was still known as Persia. It's just one of the many countries that have changed their names in the ninety years since then. Ceylon is now Sri Lanka; Southern Rhodesia has become Zimbabwe.'

Kate reached for the *Hello* magazine and flicked through the pages for Susan to see the sheer volume of photographs and articles. 'Do you really think we had all this printed in the short time since you arrived last night? And why would we do that? Why would we go to all of that trouble? What would be our purpose?'

'Am I in Heaven?' Susan asked, as if the thought had just occurred to her. 'Is that what has happened. That I really did drown and am now in Heaven?'

I smiled at her reasoning. I suppose that to someone whose last memory was of trying to kill herself, it was a pretty logical thought.

Kate picked up the remote control for the television. 'Now, this contraption really scared you yesterday when it was turned on, so let me explain exactly what it is and what it does.' She was careful, taking her time. Tom stood there, hoping she would make a mistake and give him the chance to show off his knowledge. I would have enjoyed that. If he believed that Baird discovered electricity, who on earth did he think invented the television?

But Kate didn't give him the opportunity to show off. She covered everything nicely and as she came to an end, Tom, now completely desperate, added, 'The pictures are transmitted via satellite and-'

Kate said sharply, 'Stop it Tom. The poor girl has enough to absorb. How can you expect someone from the year 1926 to understand about satellites? Please be sensible for once in your life.'

All in all, it took more than an hour to convince

Susan, but she finally accepted that she was now in the year 2016.

Tom and I exchanged satisfied looks, but the difficult, if not impossible job of returning Susan to her own time and her own Billy Monroe now lay ahead of us.

*

I woke up with a start the following morning at a few minutes after five. How had we managed to miss something so obvious? Even Tom, the owner of the most devious brain I've ever encountered - had failed to see it. Our houseguest was Dorothy's great great aunt! When Susan first appeared and told us her name, Dorothy said how strange that was because her great grandmother's sister was also named Susan Mendoza. Apparently, in 1926 the poor girl drowned herself following her lover's death at sea, but she hadn't succeeded, of course, because it was now clear to me that Dorothy's great great aunt Susan and the Susan now with us were one and the same person.

Trying to add it all up sent my head spinning; a gallon of information trying to squeeze into a pint pot. And the way everything appeared to be linked was creepy- like maybe my seemingly accidental meeting with Dorothy was no accident after all, but was pre-ordained. And how about the letter addressed to Billy Monroe in the Bugatti? The Bugatti had been Susan's car. Susan was Dorothy's great great aunt while I, bearing the same name as Susan's soon to be fiancé, had visited *Rose Cottage*, her old house, and afterwards, had an accident involving her great great niece on the way home. Try working that lot out. Coincidence is one thing, but this was scary stuff.

Dorothy knew none of this yet. Things had happened so fast between us that I hadn't got around to telling her about the Bugatti and the letter in the well of the car door. But the really important bit for Susan was the other thing Dorothy had said. *That the Billy Monroe of 1926 was not lost at sea at all.* He'd turned up safe and well the day after Susan drowned herself, although Susan hadn't drowned at all. She was here in the house with us, every bit as alive as I was.

So, in 1926, Billy, along with Susan's family, believed Susan was dead, whilst here in 2016, she believed exactly the same thing about Billy. Fate certainly seemed to have it in for the two lovers, and yet the only thing keeping them apart, if you dismiss the fact that by now they were all dead and buried, was a mere ninety years. Less than a blink of an eye in the time span of the world's existence.

H G Wells would have reunited them in an instant!

*

Once again, Susan slept well. Sleep was something she welcomed, it allowed her to escape the misery and pain always with her during her conscious hours.

At nine a.m., the sun emerged from the clouds and shone straight into her east facing bedroom, rousing her from sleep. She threw back the covers and walked to the window, looking out across Lulworth Cove. It was another glorious day in Dorset - at least, it was for those with something to live for.

She climbed back into bed and plumped up the pillows around her, turning everything over in her mind. Why couldn't she have sunk beneath the waves and let her life slip away? Just five minutes, that's all it would have taken for the pain to go forever.

So much for the preaching of the Bible. *Reap what you sow* it said; well, she had always tried to live a good life, giving and not just taking; always helping others if it was within her power to do so. What had *she* sown to reap this living hell? This life without the man she loved. She lay in bed feeling lower that she had ever done.

Susan had spent many hours wondering what Billy's last thoughts were before the sea took him. She liked to think they were of her. Had he been ready to propose marriage as she suspected? Somehow, she *knew* that he had.

She allowed her mind to drift into a trance like state. A kind of daydream, but unlike some daydreams, she knew that this one could never come true.

Billy was still alive and they were cycling through the lanes of Wooburn Green. He was pedalling the bicycle with her balanced on the crossbar, both of them laughing aloud whenever it wobbled precariously. Soon they arrived at the meadow next to Mr Brown's farm. The meadow was always beautiful in the springtime; one of God's green fields, covered with yellow buttercups.

Billy spread out a blanket for their picnic and they sat eating freshly made sandwiches, planning their future together, even--.

A sharp rap on the bedroom door sent the daydream scuttling away to be replaced by the clouds of despair again.

Susan straightened the bedclothes around her and called out, 'Please come in.'

Dorothy poked her head around the door,

'Breakfast is ready,' she said chirpily, 'and we have some great news for you, so the quicker you get your bum down to the kitchen, then the quicker you'll hear what it is.' That said, Dorothy turned and bounded down the stairs two at a time, unable to contain her excitement.

Susan lay back and listened to the thump thump on the stairs. It made her think of her mother. Her sweet, adorable mother. *Most unladylike Susan,* she would have lectured. *Young ladies of good breeding must walk gracefully if they hope to find a suitable husband,* and then her stomach turned over, knowing that her mother, along with Valentino and the others in the Movie book, was now dead. It was *all* so unbearable. There was no break to it; it was endless. Bad news piled on top of other bad news and so on and so on. Susan felt her head was in danger of exploding and threw back the bedclothes, put on Dorothy's slippers and went downstairs.

There was a buzz of excitement in the kitchen. Kate led her towards a chair and Susan sat down, wondering what type of news Dorothy believed could possibly be *great* to someone who now knew that everyone they ever loved was dead. She was trapped in a strange age. An age where instead of *living* their lives, people sat in front of a contraption called a television set and watched how other people lived theirs.

Kate sat on a stool next to Susan and took her hands in her own. 'I have good news for you Susan,' she was trying very hard to stay calm. 'We now know that your Billy didn't drown when his ship sank. God knows how, but somehow he managed to survive and made contact with your parents the day after you walked into the sea.'

Susan's mood lifted slightly, but was Kate really being truthful with her? It was a big step from yesterday, when they said Billy was dead, to telling her today that he was alive. But what reason would they have to lie to her? Whatever, for conformation she said, 'So you are now saying that my Billy is alive! Is that the truth? That he really, really is alive?'

'It's true Susan,' Kate said. 'Billy is alive. I give you my word.'

She turned to Dorothy and smiled for the first time since making the ninety-year journey into the twenty-first century. 'Oh Dorothy, you were absolutely right. It is the most wonderful, wonderful news anyone could give me!' She paused while she caught her breath, but then the others watched in dismay as her good mood evaporated.

'What is it Susan?' Dorothy asked in alarm. 'What on earth is wrong?'

Susan sat down again. 'Well of course I'm delighted that Billy is safe and well. Not just delighted, but thrilled as well, but don't you realise? He is back in the year 1926 while I'm trapped here, ninety years in the future. What horrible trick of fate is this Dorothy? Where is the fairness in it?' She stood up and ran from the room while the others watched helplessly. There was nothing they could say or do. It was absolutely true. Susan was now in the year 2016 and unless some sort of miracle occurred, the remainder of her life would be spent in the 21st century, while every single person she knew and loved was already dead and buried.

Chapter Ten

Susan's pain was having a profound effect on Kate, which surprised me. I was used to the Kate who constantly bit her husband's head off. She mixed a sedative and passed it to Susan who said, 'Where is the fairness?' and she was right. Where was the fairness?

With all of my self-proclaimed cleverness, I'd missed the fact that Susan was now stuck here with us while her Billy, although alive, was living in the year 1926. Or was he dead? But if he was dead, how could Susan be alive? How could someone who should be dead be with us now? Nothing made sense, so best to stick to the facts. Fact - Susan Mendoza was born in 1899, but was here with us in the year 2016, aged 27 and without a single wrinkle worth noting marring her pretty face, and despite whatever any brilliant scientist may choose to say, that was a fact!

The bottle of champagne placed in the ice bucket earlier, ready to celebrate, remained uncorked. There was nothing to celebrate. All we had succeeded in doing was to bring even more misery to the girl in the bedroom upstairs. In 1926 it had been fate keeping

Susan and Billy apart. Everything would have been fine if she had hung on in there for a little longer, but it was pointless thinking that way because she hadn't, and now she was ninety years away from Billy because of her own actions and the unfortunate girl knew it. Had she not walked into the sea that night, they would have been together.

I wanted to stretch my legs, but outside was overcast and the trees were bending in the wind, so it would be chilly outside. I decided to watch TV in the lounge instead and stretched out on the extra wide sofa with Dorothy alongside me and tucked snugly in my arms. By a strange quirk of fate, the film on TV was *The Time Machine;* H G Wells at his very best. In the film, the hero whizzed off into the future, fell in love before accidentally going back to his own time. He did, however, find a way to return to his true love again. The film ended and I said to no one in particular, 'What did you think of it?'

'I thought it was bloody good,' Tom said enthusiastically. 'Had to be true love though, because she never raised her voice to him once.'

Without moving her eyes from the TV, Kate said, 'Don't push it Tom or you know what to expect.' *Knowing what to expect* must have been grim as he made no further comment, but I detected a slight grin on his face.

Dorothy snuggled even deeper into my arms and whispered, 'Do you think we'll ever end up like that, Billy?'

'Not likely,' I whispered back, 'there's no way I would let that happen to us.'

After a while, Kate grew tired of sitting around and asked, 'Tea anyone? Served with scones, Devonshire cream, and freshly made jam. I picked some up from the farm shop earlier when I popped out for a newspaper and to stretch my legs.'

Tom was obviously still thinking about the film. He suddenly remarked, 'It's a fascinating thing, time travel. The scientists say it isn't possible-'

'Yes, but we of all people know differently, don't we?' I interrupted and he nodded vigorously.

'Too true Billy, too true. Maybe we should prove it and hand Susan over to the Government to show them it's not only possible; it's actually happened under their very noses.'

Dorothy suddenly sat bolt upright. She does that when something occurs to her. 'Look - we're all agreed that the electrical explosion brought Susan forward in time, but surely there has to be something else as well, and if we can discover what that something is, then perhaps we can replicate it and send her back to 1926? For a start, this house belonged to her family - my forefathers, and she was staying here when it happened. And now it belongs to my family, their descendants, which is a link, isn't it?'

Kate huffed, 'That's fine Dorothy, but she wasn't in the house, was she? She was several hundred yards away in the cove.'

'That's very true,' Dorothy agreed, 'but she was close by, wasn't she? Just a few hundred yards away, which could be within whatever boundaries there are to these things, but I'm sick of trying to figure it all out. The whole thing is so weird.'

A tingle of excitement ran down my spine. If Dottie was right and there is a link, then if we could discover what it is, maybe we *can* send Susan back to 1926 and her own Billy Monroe.

We moved into the kitchen, all deep in thought. Half an hour later, after the scones had been eaten and the tea drunk, Susan came downstairs to join us again. 'I couldn't sleep,' she complained. 'I am so sorry to be such a frightful bore. I must be getting on your nerves by now, constantly bemoaning my fate the whole time.'

Kate hugged her, 'Don't you dare say that. You are *not* a bore. You've had a very tough time of it and all any of us want is to help you if we can, so you are not a bore and none of us want to hear you say it again Susan.'

'How about all of us putting pen to paper and jotting down how we think Susan came to be here?' Tom suggested. 'If we discover how it happened, maybe we would find a way to get her back to her own time?'

Kate said, 'What a good idea Darling,' and Tom tore five sheets of blank paper from a pad and passed out a mixture of pens and pencils. 'Let's give it half an hour,' I suggested. 'Susan knows the 1926 end of things, which is more than any of us do.'

We sat in different nooks and crannies of the lounge to keep our thoughts to ourselves.

The minutes seemed to tick away slowly, but eventually the allotted time was up and I collected the completed sheets of paper. The top one was Susan's and I cursed inwardly. She had written just one thing, but that was all we needed.

'It was the 1st of July when I walked into the sea with the intention of drowning myself. It was close to ten-thirty at night. The newspapers I saw yesterday were dated the 2nd of July, so I arrived here on the 1st, the same date as in 1926, although I don't know what the time was here.'

We found Susan shivering in the hallway at around ten-thirty at night. Same date, same time of night. Surely that had to be it! We now had a chance to send her back to 1926 and although that chance might be a slim one, it was the only one we had.

Chapter Eleven

Three months had passed since Susan drowned herself. There had been an inquest and Susan's friends and family all gave evidence to the Coroner, stating how Billy's death had affected her. In terms of solid evidence, the coroner had been presented with the letter she left behind, along with the police report of the footprints discovered in the rear garden. Footprints pointing in the direction of the beach.

The Coroner's verdict was that Susan Mendoza took her own life while the balance of her mind was disturbed.

That evening, the coroner crept silently into his children's bedrooms, all three of them less than ten years old. They were asleep, with Benjie, the baby of the family, clutching his Teddy bear under one protective arm and sucking on his wrinkled thumb.

Joseph Wells offered his thanks to God that they were all safe and well, but the fear that occasionally haunts all parents hung heavily over him that night.

He made his way down to the lounge where his

wife was engaged in her nightly stint of knitting. She smiled up at him, 'Is everything all right dear?'

'Everything is fine, my dear,' he said hoarsely, 'absolutely fine.'

*

Samuel and Maria Mendoza sat at the dining room table in *Rose Cottage*, discussing how they should distribute Susan's personal effects in the absence of a will.

Maria was still struggling over the loss of her daughter. Losing Susan was something she would never get over. Just twenty-seven years old - a vibrant, beautiful girl. And now, Billy was safely back, alive and well, but had returned *one* day too late.

Maria held a list of her daughter's personal effects in her hand and an identical list was on the table in front of Samuel.

Samuel was a methodical man. Everything always in perfect order; every part of his life organized, every emotion carefully concealed. Although they had just lost a daughter, Maria knew he expected a stiff upper lip from her, but Samuel wasn't capable of realising that a mother would never come to terms with losing a child.

Samuel finished studying the list. There was little to consider. Not much of value to show for a short life. There had been no need. Her parents supplied whatever she needed.

Her jewellery was on the table. Maria looked at the tiny ring, found in a Fortnum and Mason Christmas cracker when Susan was five years old. She smiled softly and picked the ring up, pressing it to her face, as though part of her daughter was embedded within it. She remembered Susan's excitement as she slid it onto her tiny finger. 'This will be my engagement ring when I get big and grow up,' she announced proudly. 'Do you like it mummy?' and Maria had smiled softly, the love within filling every part of her.

'It's beautiful Darling,' she had whispered, 'just as you are.'

Maria kissed the ring and held it to her cheek. 'I shall keep this Samuel,' she said quietly as Samuel studied her, 'just as I will keep Susan's twenty-first birthday ring.'

'You should only have one. Mustn't be greedy, old girl,' Samuel teased.

'Then I shall have this one,' Maria whispered, slipping the tiny ring into her handbag.

Samuel pushed the birthday ring into her hand. 'And this one also my dear. Just my little tease; quite stupid of me really.'

He studied the other valuables. 'Most of these should go to Celia I suppose, with a few mementoes for Susan's friends so they have something to remember her by.'

Celia was their other daughter, the younger of the two. A shy, introverted girl - as plain as Susan was pretty.

There were huge tears in Maria's eyes and Samuel prayed she wouldn't lose control again. He found such things difficult to deal with.

He went back to the list and raised his eyebrows

questioningly, 'And the Bugatti, my dear? Celia is quite satisfied with her own car and most certainly wouldn't want it. Should we sell it and add it to the money put by for Celia's wedding trousseau?' He peered over the top of his reading spectacles and sighed hopelessly. 'If the girl ever marries, that is. She has shown no interest in men as of yet.'

Maria rose to her feet. 'Of course she will marry eventually,' she said, 'but it will take time. Celia is nervous of men Samuel, believing she is plain looking and they will not be interested in her.'

'But she *is* plain,' Samuel said matter-of-factly. 'Celia knows it and you should also realise that fact.'

'In whose eyes is she plain?' Maria asked sharply. '*You* think *that*, only because Susan is beautiful.' Her voice dropped as she said, '*Was* beautiful.'

Samuel said dismissively, 'Time will tell, only time will tell! However, Maria, we must stick to our task without deviating, my dear. Now, we were discussing the Bugatti and what should we do with it.'

Maria knew exactly what Susan would have wanted. 'Personally, I think it should go to Billy.' She was not a superstitious woman but crossed her fingers as she waited for the inevitable objection she knew was coming.

Samuel held his temper in check, 'My dear, we must not lose our heads in a bout of sentimentality. The car is far too valuable to give to Billy. Do you not know how much the vehicle cost me?' Maria had guessed his reply almost word for word. At heart, Samuel was a good man, but his reasoning often caused him to lose perspective.

She leant forward and took his hand in her own. 'Please dearest; this discussion is not about money. Surely it is about what our daughter would have wanted? Isn't that the very reason we are here today? To execute what Susan would have wanted?'

Samuel grudgingly conceded to Maria's wishes. He liked Billy Monroe, but the car was an expensive gift. Far too expensive in his view!

The Bugatti had been the last item on the list. In the space of half an hour, a short lifetime of acquisitions had been dispensed with.

Later, after high tea, Maria wrote to Billy. Telephoning wasn't an option. She would have broken down again, which was the last thing she wanted. Samuel was already losing patience with her. Billy would receive the letter the following morning. It read,

'My dear Billy,

Samuel and I have been distributing Susan's personal effects. We both feel that you should have her car, the Bugatti. She often told me of the happy times the two of you shared, driving through the country lanes whenever you were together at weekends.

Please do not object to this gift. I know you will protest that it is far too expensive, but it is a small sum to a man in my husband's position. The Bugatti is still at Lulworth Cove. Won't you please join us at Rose Cottage for lunch this coming Sunday and we can make arrangements for you to collect the car. Both Samuel and I would dearly love to see you again. Shall we say one o'clock?

Yours most sincerely, Maria Mendoza.'

At the bottom of the page was a postscript.

'Oh Billy, I miss her so much. I fear my heart is slowly breaking.'

*

I looked around the table. We'd gone through three bottles of wine and the cheese and biscuits, long demolished. Dorothy brushed the crumbs from her lips before smiling across at me. With the food and drink finished, now was a good time to make plans. Someone needed to get things underway and as no one else was making a move, I took it upon myself. 'So as we've all agreed on how Susan managed to travel through ninety years of time and arrive here with us, it gives us a starting point to return her to 1926.'

I smiled at her and said jokingly, 'That's if you want to go back. You might want to remain with us,' but Susan was already familiar with my sense of humour. She knew I was teasing her.

'So, me boy,' Tom began, 'you're thinking the same as me, aren't you? That if we duplicate the circumstances that brought Susan here, we should be able to send her back again. Yes?'

I stood up to stretch my legs. Ever since Susan arrived, all we had done was to sit around discussing the situation. Talk and more talk, with no action!

'Well, it makes sense to me,' I said, 'which means everything must be exactly the same as it was that night. Forgetting the year, because we can't do anything about that, we must choose a day and a month when the Mendozas are at the house -- I mean *this* house, and it must be around ten-thirty at night.'

Tom shook his head despondently, maybe doubting our plan now it had been put into words. 'Sounds Mickey Mouse when you put it like that Billy. Sort of like, *'Let's make an atom bomb. You get some gunpowder and we'll shove a fuse in it and hey presto! One atom bomb!'*

Kate agreed with him, 'Well if you want my opinion, I think we'd be wasting our time.' She gave Susan a regretful smile, 'And what's even worse, we may be getting your hopes up for nothing. You might as well face it Susan; you're stuck here whether you like it or not, and here you shall stay. We don't even possess the knowledge to fulfil the basic plan Billy put forward. No one knows when your parents were next at Lulworth Cove and neither do you.' She raised a quizzical eye at Susan, saying, 'Am I right?'

I watched the expression on Susan's face. She had no intention of being put off so easily.

'You are quite correct Kate, but my life is back there with Billy. I could not contemplate spending the remainder of my life living here in 2016. Why, it is quite dreadful.'

Unfortunately, she'd already read some examples of our yob culture in the newspapers. Read about the drunks and druggies who marred our public parks and kept normal people from using them. Maybe we should all consider going back with her. Back to when the police still had some powers, before they'd been neutered in the name of human rights. A time when victims were the issue and not the "*human*" rights of criminals who had made them victims.

'Perhaps we can discover when my parents were

next here,' Susan said hopefully. 'Maybe there are records somewhere that will tell us. We shall never know if we don't try.' She looked, eyes bright with tears. 'Please don't just give up. Please!'

Galvanised into action by the tone of her great great aunt's words, Dorothy hugged Susan and said, 'I'm sorry Kate, but I'm with Susan on this one. She is absolutely right. Whatever the outcome, we must try. It may be a waste of time, but we will have given it our best shot. We won't have to look back later and say, *if only we had tried*!'

The one thing I've always admired about Kate is that she never takes umbrage when challenged. Apart from that, I'm sure she would love to be proved wrong.

So just as Dorothy suggested, we set to and gave it our best shot. We spread out in different directions and went through the house with a fine toothcomb. Dorothy knew *Cherry Tree House* well enough and Susan knew it even better. By the time the five of us had completed our search, a team of forensic scientists wouldn't have uncovered any more than we had, which unfortunately, was absolutely nothing!

Such a simple problem, but no apparent way of resolving it.

The following morning, Tom came up with something that had been overlooked.

'What about the old lady, Petula Thingimmy? The one you visited at Susan's old home in Wooburn Green. D'you think there's a chance she'd know something?' He was talking to me, but it was Susan who sat upright.

'Am I to understand that you visited *Rose Cottage* Billy? What on earth were you doing there?'

I realised then we had never properly explained to Susan how this whole thing came about. How the letter in Susan's Bugatti had brought about my meeting Dorothy, along with everything else that had happened so far. Obviously, now would be a good time to bring her up to date her in on the story so far.

'Well, it's the reason we're all here at *Cherry Tree House* Susan. Dorothy's parents own it. It was left to them in trust by her-.' I paused, counting backwards, 'Her great great great grandfather. He was *your* grandfather Susan and in case it hasn't dawned on you yet, Dorothy is your sister's great granddaughter and you are her great great aunt.' I grinned at her wide-eyed stare. 'Spooky, isn't it?'

Susan was speechless for a moment before she said, 'Are you saying that my sister Celia has children? Why, she didn't even have a boyfriend the last time I saw her. In fact, she has never had a boyfriend!'

Poor Susan. She had last seen her twenty-three-year-old *unmarried* sister just a few days back, and yet was now confronted, in the flesh, by that same sister's 29-year-old great granddaughter. Try taking that one on-board! And how difficult must it be for someone to accept that a woman two years older than they are, is actually their great great niece?

I excused myself, went to the bedroom, found the letter from the Bugatti and hurried back into the lounge. I handed it to Susan. 'Do you remember writing this?'

Her eyes widened when she recognised her own

writing on the envelope. She removed the letter and after reading the contents, flushed red with anger and turned on me, eyes blazing like hot coals. 'I can't believe it. This letter was private. How dare you read it. How dare you!'

As well as being angry, she also appeared close to tears, so I hurriedly explained. 'Hang on a moment Susan. The letter was in your car, the Bugatti, which is now my car, and had fallen into a door well. Sometime after I bought the car, I found it.'

I took the envelope from her shaking hand and pointed at the name. 'Look at who it's addressed to. I had every right to read it because it was addressed to me, *Billy Monroe*. It was the letter that started this whole thing Susan.' I was on the point of continuing when I realised that Susan was staring at me in open mouthed disbelief.

'Are you saying that you bought my Bugatti, Billy?' and I nodded.

'Yes Susan, I bought your Bugatti at an auction. Right now, it's a wreck, but is being restored to its original condition by a friend who specialises in restoring cars.'

Her nostrils flared with anger and I found myself on the receiving end of a withering look. I saw then her startling resemblance to Dorothy.

'Restored? You have damaged my beautiful Bugatti?' Tears immediately filled her eyes. 'How could you Billy? I always kept that car in pristine condition. It was immaculate a few days ago.'

This time Tom came to my rescue. 'It may have been immaculate when you last saw it Susan, but the last ninety years have taken their toll. You shouldn't worry though. In a few month's time, it will be as it was when you owned it.'

So, I moved on, explaining events that led up to this particular moment. Yet again I had the strongest feeling that everything taking place was meant to be; coincidence is one thing, but this? This was something else! The Bugatti and the letter. Meeting Dorothy, a descendant of the letter writer's family. Lulworth Cove, where we saved the life of Susan, the Bugatti's original owner, who looked twentyish, despite being born more than 100 years ago.

Still with me? Coincidence! – No way!

But now, we appeared to have hit a brick wall.

Tom's point, however! The sweet old lady, Petula Sinclair? Maybe she was the next piece in this jigsaw puzzle, and after all, she *had* said for me to call on her at any time.

The following day, Kate and Tom returned to Kingston-upon-Thames while Dorothy and Susan, and me, of course, went to Dorothy's flat in London. Dorothy still had a business to run with masses of catching up to do, so she would get on with her business, while Susan and I would make the journey to visit Petula Sinclair at *Rose Cottage*. Depending on what we discovered from her, if anything, we would plan our next move.

*

Maria Mendoza led Billy into the garage. Both she and Samuel had insisted he accept Susan's Bugatti as a gift.

Samuel Mendoza had draped the car with the soft cotton cover made by Susan to protect her pride and joy. Maria told Billy to pull the cover off and they stood silently surveying the car. For a brief second, Billy visualised Susan behind the wheel, but he blinked and she disappeared.

The car was finished in a rich, deep red colour. 'Are you really sure about this Mrs Mendoza?' Billy asked. 'It's a valuable gift to someone who loved your daughter, but wasn't her fiancé.' He cast his eyes downwards. 'If only I'd asked your husband for her hand in marriage before leaving for Africa! At least I would have known how she truly felt about me.'

Maria slid her arm through his, wanting to end to his torment. 'My daughter loved you Billy. I can tell you with absolute certainty that had you proposed, she would have accepted. Susan repeatedly told me how she hoped you would ask Samuel for her hand in marriage upon your return from Africa.'

Hearing that was too much for Billy. His years at the orphanage had taught him the best way to survive there was to conceal his feelings, but he couldn't help himself. He began sob, quietly at first and then without control.

Maria took him in her arms and cried along with him, her grief just as powerful as Billy's. If only Susan had waited one more day, she would have had everything she ever dreamed of. *If only* the world was made of *if onlys*! If only.

Before Billy drove the Bugatti away, Maria made him promise to return to *Cherry Tree House* and join the family for the coming Christmas dinner. Whenever

Billy was around she could see her daughter in her mind's eye, happy, smiling and vivacious. Exactly as Maria wanted to remember her. She held his hand in her own and said, 'We must never lose touch, Billy. Susan would not have liked that. She would have wanted us to remain good friends.'

He smiled through still tearful eyes, 'If that is what Susan would have wanted, then that is how it shall be!'

*

Early the following morning, Susan and I left for Buckinghamshire. The weather was gloomy and overcast, but there was a feeling of excitement in the air. In the short time I'd known Susan, I had never seen her as she was now. Was it because we were about to visit what was now her old house, knowing that we may discover something there that could lead to her being reunited with *her* Billy?

Along the M40 motorway, the weather took a turn for the worst and large spots of rain hammered against the windscreen. It continued that way for the remainder of the journey to Wooburn Green.

Rolling dark clouds swept overhead as we turned into Juniper Drive and drew up outside *Rose Cottage*. Despite the gloom that accompanied the rain, the house still looked beautiful; quite exquisite. We covered our heads with our coats and on Susan's count of three, raced through the rain and up the path leading to the house. I banged frantically on the front door as the rain pelted down on us, but was suddenly gripped by a gut feeling that something was very wrong. Most people find rain depressing, so perhaps it was no more than that, but the house was unnaturally quiet and the heavy curtains were closed.

Susan seemed unaware of the atmosphere and hopped impatiently from foot to foot. 'Nothing much seems to have changed Billy,' she said chirpily, 'at least not out here,' and as I wasn't around ninety years ago to see for myself, I couldn't agree or disagree.

It was Beth, Petula's companion who eventually opened the door. She peered at me through red eyes and a spark of recognition appeared in them. 'Oh, it's you. It's Mr Monty isn't it?'

I smiled pleasantly, 'Close Beth, but it's actually Monroe. Billy Monroe.'

She had been crying and with every curtain closed, it was obvious why. Something had happened to the old lady.

'Is everything okay?' I asked before I could stop myself.

Beth sniffed loudly, all the time dabbing at her eyes with the small hanky. 'No Mr Monroe, I'm afraid it isn't. Poor Mrs Sinclair passed away last week. Her funeral takes place in four day's time.' She gave a watery smile before adding, 'She died in her sleep, you know. There wasn't a long, drawn out illness, so that's a blessing, isn't it? She was around 90, you know, so she had a very good run, didn't she?'

It was a brave effort on Beth's part, but was short lived. The weak smile collapsed and she burst into a flood of tears. 'What am I going to do Mr Monroe? I miss her so much already.'

I felt helpless; normally I'm pretty crap at handling

this sort of thing, but I pulled her to me and held her in my arms, whispering, 'There, there Beth. It's perfectly okay to be upset. After all, you're bound to miss her.'

I didn't really know what else to say. I'd met Mrs Sinclair just the once and knew nothing about her, apart from her skill at making raspberry jam and being a nice person who enjoyed company.

There was a tight feeling in the pit of my stomach, knowing we had probably wasted our time in coming here. With Petula gone, had the only path open to us ended in a dead end? However, Beth seemed to welcome the opportunity of having someone to talk to, so besides being of some comfort to her, there could still be something to be gleaned.

She patted her eyes dry and smiled bravely. 'Would you like some tea Mr Monroe and-?' She looked pointedly at Susan who smiled back.

'I'm Susan Mendoza, and yes, I would very much appreciate a cup of tea. It will be most welcome.'

Beth led the way into the lounge. 'I'll go and make the tea then,' she said. 'Shan't be a jiff; please sit yourselves down.'

Once she was well out of earshot, Susan whispered, 'Have you any idea what to do now, Billy?'

I lowered my voice; 'Tell the truth Susan; well, obviously not all of the truth or she'll think we're both potty, but as much as we can as it usually works a lot better than telling lies. In my experience, people don't appreciate being lied to.'

Beth returned carrying a tray with the tea things

rattling on it. Placing the tray on a small oak table, she asked Susan, 'Milk and sugar my dear?'

Susan smiled sweetly and replied, 'Just milk for me please,' and that's what I also got; milk, but not the sugar my taste buds always crave. Rather than make a fuss, I steeled myself and drank it as it was.

'I was with Mrs Sinclair for twenty-odd years,' Beth announced out of the blue. 'She was on her own for twenty years before that, after Mr Sinclair got himself killed when a tree fell on him. She was the kindest lady I ever met in me life was Mrs Sinclair, and that's a fact Mr Monroe.' Yet again she dabbed at her eyes with the hanky and sniffled, but now, the tears had almost dried up. She finished by saying, 'I still can't believe she's really gone, I can't.'

I stood up and placed a hand on her shoulder, giving it a comforting squeeze before saying, 'We all have to go sometime Beth, and I'm sure Petula had a good life. She seemed very content to me, and you were with her for more than twenty years, so whatever you were doing for her, you were doing it properly or she would have found someone else to be her companion, wouldn't she?'

Beth perked up a bit then, seeming to take comfort from me acknowledging that she was part of the old lady's life, and thus part of her contentment.

We chatted on, making small talk. Somewhere during the remainder of the conversation, she explained that Mrs Sinclair had no living relatives, so instead of waiting for the reading of the will, the solicitor had already phoned Beth to say the house had been bequeathed to her, which Beth explained was a huge relief because she had lived here for so long that it was more than just a house to her; it was her home.

Having unburdened herself, Beth seemed to run out of steam and eventually got around to asking why we were there. 'Did you have a special reason for calling here today Mr Monroe, or were you just passing by? I know Mrs Sinclair said for you to call in if ever you were in the area.'

I decided to be as truthful as possible. 'Well yes, actually, Beth; yes, there was a reason, I mean, yes there *is* a reason for us being here.' I glanced across at Susan, who had been more interested in looking around the room than listening to our chatter, but that was understandable. Everything was probably quite different from when she was last here ninety years ago, although for her, of course, it wasn't ninety years; it was just a matter of days.

'Susan's family used to own this house,' I explained to Beth, 'a long time ago, back in the days before Mrs Sinclair's parents bought it from Susan's great grandparents. Susan's branch of the Mendoza family came to England from Spain in 1842 (this was true. Susan had told me this during the drive to Wooburn Green), and she's really keen to write a history of the family. She's hoping there will be things in the house that will help her to do that.' I stopped as I noticed the suspicious look on Beth's face, so I spoke up again in an attempt to reassure her. 'Please don't get the wrong idea Beth. Susan doesn't want anything from the house. She only wants to look around and take some notes. This place belongs to you now Beth, and if you're not happy with us looking around, then that's the end of it. We'll finish our tea, say our thanks and leave you in peace,' but now I really *was* lying, because Susan's only way back to 1926 was if we found something in that house. Should Beth ask us to leave, it would all end there, and whether Susan liked it or not, she would live the remainder of her life in the twenty-first century.

Luckily, my explanation seemed to satisfy Beth and she smiled properly for the first time since our arrival. Her face softened and she smiled at Susan as she spoke. 'Of course Susan can look around the house Mr Monroe. Why, I just know that Mrs Sinclair would have wanted that had she still been here.' She smiled reminiscently, 'She was always one to help people was Mrs Sinclair.' As she stood up, crumbs from her dress fell and formed a semi-circle around her feet. She frowned and I knew she was making a mental note to clear the mess up after we left.

'Shall we start now,' she said, 'or would you like another cup of tea first?'

I could have drunk a teapot full of tea right then, but experience taught me years ago that once a sale is made, shut up and get on with it! 'Now will do fine Beth,' I said and along with Susan, stood up and followed Beth from the room.

*

They started at the bottom of the house and gradually made their way upwards with Beth leading them from bedroom to bedroom. Susan was in the swing of things and kept up the pretence of documenting the family history by scribbling industriously in a notebook, dragging the process out in the vain hope that Beth would become bored by it all and leave them to get on with it alone, but there seemed little chance of that happening. Beth had slipped into Petula's old role of tour guide and was enjoying herself. It gave her a feeling of pride now that others knew *Rose Cottage* belonged to her.

Susan had told Billy that the loft was where they should concentrate. Apparently, there was a hidden cubbyhole up there where her parents stored their old diaries and business accounts, along with other things that, although no longer current, could very well be needed in the future for reference purposes.

Eventually, everything had been thoroughly checked out and there was only the loft to inspect. Billy and Susan knew the biggest obstacle was distracting Beth long enough for Susan to look inside the cubbyhole. Eventually, luck swung their way as Beth solved the problem for them after Billy innocently pointed upwards. 'Can we have a look in the loft please Beth? You never know, there might be something there that Susan could use.'

Beth pulled a horrified face at the thought of such a thing. 'Well Mr Monroe, you two are more than welcome to look if you wish, but don't go expecting me to be with you. That loft gives me the willies, what with all the spiders and things that hide away in the nooks and crannies, so go up by all means, but you'll be on your own because I'll be down here out of harm's way.'

For the first time since they had arrived at *Rose Cottage,* Billy relaxed. He released the loft ladder and clambered up the steps with Susan right behind him. Although they were hopeful, they also knew they'd be lucky to find anything likely to help them in their quest, but nevertheless, the loft was their best chance, always assuming that the cubbyhole still existed. The fact that it was there in 1926 was no guarantee that it would be now. Central heating and electric lighting had been added since the house was last owned by the Mendoza family, and that type of work usually centres around the loft, so there was a strong likelihood that the cubbyhole had been removed many years back. If that was the case, there would be nothing for them to find, but it was still imperative they check it out thoroughly, for they were determined to leave no stone unturned.

They were relieved that their fears proved groundless. The cubbyhole still existed, although their elation at finding it was short lived. Nothing inside was of any use to them. No diaries or record books, just three old receipts that quite obviously hadn't even been worth the effort of picking up. The cubbyhole had been thoroughly cleared out by someone in the past.

For the first time, Billy realised that maybe Kate had been right. Thanks to everyone except Kate, Susan's hopes had been built and built, and now those hopes were dashed and she was close to cracking up. She turned to Billy, eyes bright with tears. 'I'm not at all surprised,' she whispered in a wavering voice. 'My father always was the most meticulous of men. He would never forget a place that contained important records. Never.'

Billy surveyed the cubbyhole gloomily. Nothing could help Susan now. They had nowhere else to search. Every avenue open to them had already been explored, so like it or not, the unfortunate girl would spend the rest of her lifetime ninety years ahead of everything and everyone she knew and loved. They had failed miserably, but had tried to the best of their ability.

Billy reached into the cubbyhole and retrieved the three scraps of paper that he had already glanced at. They were of no importance. Nothing more than old receipts. He shoved them into his trouser pocket and they climbed back down the ladder.

Billy was quite deflated; everything had failed. More than anything else he felt sorry for Susan. He'd done his best but still felt he had let her down.

Beth insisted on making them another cup of tea before they went on their way. She asked Billy if they were going to attend Mrs Sinclair's funeral. It seemed important to her and Billy didn't need to put his thinking cap on to guess why. Petula was around 90-years-old when she died, so most of her friends were probably already dead. It was natural that Beth would want at least a few faces in the church, so he asked for details of the service and promised they would both be there on the day.

After a further cup of tea, they said their goodbyes and headed towards Wimbledon to meet the others. It was a quiet journey. They were both peeved at how things had turned out. Billy felt cheated by their lack of success. There were no rules to this sort of thing, but he felt it wasn't fair. Everyone deserves a break occasionally.

They drove in silence until they reached the M40 motorway when Susan finally spoke, 'We failed miserably, didn't we Billy?'

He took his eyes off the road to glance at her. 'You can only fail if you don't try Susan. We just didn't succeed.'

She slumped back in her seat, not bothering to argue with this brand of logic. It was simply a play on words. However Billy chose to put it, not succeeding gave the same result as failing. Either way, she was stuck in a world without her Billy in it.

*

We had arranged to meet the others for dinner that evening at the *Dolce Vita* in the heart of Wimbledon. The restaurant was off the beaten track for all of us, decorated in the old fashioned Italian style. Men wearing Fedora hats and carrying violin cases holding Tommy guns wouldn't have looked out of place there, but the owner was a friend and the food always good. Not just good, according to Dorothy, but sumptuous.

The others were drinking glasses of red wine and waiting impatiently to hear the result of our search. My sigh as I sat down probably warned them of what was coming.

'Nothing,' I said, 'not a sausage.' It was a sad result for Susan. Only she would suffer. The rest of us could continue with our lives as normal, but we tried to be cheerful for her sake. Susan had no choice but to accept life in the twenty-first century and make the best of it. Either that or another trip into the sea, but I thought she was past that by now. And she must know that her new friends would protect and help her to move on. If there's one thing life has taught me, it's to move on and not look back. You can't change the past, only the future, and then I realised that was exactly what we were trying to do, change the past.

'What I don't understand,' Kate said as we waited for our first course to arrive, 'is why we can't just go to the house at Lulworth Cove and put a nail in the fuse again? After all, we could strike lucky. I think that we're due some luck.'

She scanned the table to see if anyone agreed with her, but Tom said, 'You're forgetting that we knocked out some of the street lights and possibly a few other things as well. If that's what always happens, then how long do you think it would be before people complained and the Electricity Board investigated? What if they fitted a new fuse board in the house? Maybe it would re-act differently to the old one and then we'd lose any chance of sending Susan back if we turned something up in the future.'

Kate sighed, pulling a face as she propped her chin in her hands. 'You're right of course Tom. I hadn't thought of that.'

Tom grinned. Brownie points from Kate were hard to come by!

It was only Dorothy, having demolished three courses in record time, who refused to accept defeat. I reckon I'm a fairly positive person, but she's in a different league to me. She is super positive. She turned to Kate. 'Look, we all know how you feel about building poor Susan's hopes up, but I really do believe that we'll find a way to send her back to her own time. Whatever the rest of you think, I *know* we will and I'm not just saying it for Susan's sake. It's something that I truly believe.'

We were all pretty bushed by then. None of us had the energy to argue the point. Nothing is as tiring as failure. We had pinned our hopes on discovering something at *Rose Cottage* and it had been a waste of time.

All except Dorothy. She was trawling through every little detail of our visit with no intention of letting things rest there. 'Now Billy, I want to be absolutely clear. There was nothing in the cubbyhole. It was empty, devoid of even dust?'

Well, finding dust would have been a result, but I realised I'd get no peace until every avenue had been explored. I remembered the three ancient receipts, dug into my pocket and placed them onto a small side table. 'Only these, you pain in the bum, nothing else.'

She snatched them up and I grinned, 'Bloody hell Dorothy, once you get your teeth into something, you don't let go, do you?'

She didn't waste breath answering - simply slid her empty dessert bowl to one side and spread the receipts on the table. Her brow furrowed as she studied the first one. I figured she had seen too many Sherlock Holmes movies for her own good. There were so many things about her that I loved.

'This one is from Fortnum and Masons,' she relayed, as if that snippet of information was the first step towards success. *'One Christmas hamper and one Turkey. Three pounds and fifteen shillings. December 23rd, 1926.'*

'My parents enjoyed the Christmas season tremendously and always asked a few friends to join them for Christmas dinner,' Susan explained.

Dorothy nodded vigorously. 'My mum and dad are exactly the same, bless them,' then placed the receipt to one side and read out the next one. *'To polish the parquet floor in the billiard room of Poole Cricket Club. £7-10 shillings.'* She looked up and said to Susan, 'It's dated the 3rd of March, 1927.'

Susan smiled once again. You could almost see her mind drift back to those happy days of the past. 'Father loved to play cricket. Whenever we stayed at *Cherry Tree House* during the summer months, he would play for the local club. He was hopeless, so I suspect that he was only chosen because he helped out with a donation whenever they were low on funds.'

Dorothy slid the receipt to join the first and picked up the last one and read it aloud, as she had with the previous two. 'It's from Brown's Garage, Swanage. It says, *To fit one new front tyre to Bugatti automobile. Four pounds and sixpence. December the 24th, 1926.'*

Tom laughed in disbelief, 'No wonder people talk about the good old days Billy. Unbe-bloody-lievable. A new tyre, supplied and fitted for under a fiver!'

'I suppose father must have used my car,' Susan said matter-of-factly. 'It can't have been mother, because she didn't drive.'

I noticed Susan now referred to her parents in the past tense, so acceptance was creeping in. It was a sad thing to witness.

Something niggled at me about that particular bill, until I realised what it was. From the things Susan had revealed about her father, he would have been too straight laced to drive around in an Italian sports car. 'Swanage?' I said. 'Isn't that fairly close to Lulworth Cove?'

'Swanage is almost on top of Lulworth,' Susan answered.

I turned to Dorothy, 'May I see that receipt please?'

I studied every detail and passed it to Susan. 'Look who it's made out to.'

She read it twice and stared back at me. I noticed for the first time that her eyes were brown, the same as Dorothy's. 'This bill is made out to Billy,' she said, not guessing why I was so excited. 'What on earth would he be doing with my car, and for that matter, why was he in Swanage? Billy lives in London.'

Susan might still be in the dark, but my very own personal Sherlock Holmes was right up there with me. When Dorothy said, 'Susan!' even I winced, while people at nearby tables frowned disapprovingly. 'Don't you see Susan? Your parents must have lent him the Bugatti. You said yourself they always invited people for Christmas dinner, so if Billy lived in London and the tyre was fitted in Swanage on Christmas Eve, then he was on his way to Lulworth Cove. Your mum and dad were spending Christmas at *Cherry Tree House* and Billy was one of their guests, which means, of course, that they were in the house on Christmas day and Billy was there with them.'

I was light headed and gripped the sides of the chair, feeling I might float away. So, we had now found a date to return Susan back to her *Billy*. Back to the man she loved and the life she was used to. Unfortunately, that date was still several months away, but none of us cared about that when a few moments earlier we'd been staring at a brick wall.

So, thanks to Dorothy's refusal to accept defeat, we were up and running again and Susan Mendoza was going back to her Billy.

Chapter Twelve

Susan and I made another trip to Wooburn Green, but for different reasons to our last visit. This time it was to say goodbye to a lady I very much liked, but only met on one occasion. A lady Susan had never met, but was also going to show her respect.

The old lady's funeral was held in glorious sunshine, but I was surprised by the number of people crammed into the church.

Beth had told us that Petula had no living relatives, so presumably everyone was there because they wanted to be - proof of the numerous friends she'd made during her many years on earth.

An old man with threadbare white hair gave the eulogy. His walking stick resting against the pulpit he was gripping for support. His eyes were bright with held back tears, but he kept himself together as he told the congregation about Petula's life. She lived in *Rose cottage* all of her life, apart from her early childhood years. When she was eight, her mother died during childbirth, along with the baby sister Petula so longed to have. Her father suffered a stroke when she was 22 and three months away from marrying the man she loved, but with the aid of a close friend and an oversized portion of courage, her father managed the trip down the aisle and gave his daughter away.

The newlyweds began their married life at *Rose Cottage* in order to care for him and when he died peacefully in 1978, Petula held his hand as he made his journey into the next world.

Fate seemed to treat Petula badly, although she never complained. She was unable to have children, and when her beloved husband John was killed in a freak accident the day before her fortieth birthday, she knew that at last fate could do no more to hurt her because the people she loved were now gone.

She had wanted to foster children, but was convinced fate would rub his hands together gleefully at this new opportunity to hurt her, so instead, she sponsored five children in Thailand, incognito, in the hope that fate wouldn't make the connection, but she never lost her faith in God and was a regular church goer.

Beth came to her in 1994, but Petula kept a barrier between the two of them for what were now obvious reasons. The old man paused in his narrative and looked to the front pew where Beth was sitting, bravely trying to hold herself together. 'She loved you like a daughter Beth,' he said, 'but she kept it a secret from you and everyone else in order to protect you, but once, she drank a little too much of her homemade dandelion wine and confessed that secret to me, so I knew, and now, after more than 20 years, you do as well Beth.'

Beside me, Susan began to cry softly and I pulled her close to me.

The old man continued, 'It's no secret that I loved Petula,' he said, scanning the congregation who were now hanging onto his every word. 'Everyone in the village knew I wanted to marry her, but she was quite direct with me and told me that no one could ever take her John's place, so I had to make do with her friendship, and I'm grateful for that.' He pulled out a large handkerchief and coughed noisily into it, at the same time, dabbing at his eyes in a way he obviously hoped no one would notice, but we all did.

He finished by saying, 'I shall miss you Petula - we shall all miss you. You were the most wonderful lady I ever had the privilege of meeting.' With that, he sniffed loudly to keep in the tears, retrieved his walking stick and made his way unsteadily back to the front pew.

I thought he made a marvellous job of it. I'm rubbish at that sort of thing. I go to talk and something inside me says, *No way matey* and robs me of the power of speech.

When the service was over, the congregation left the church and walked to the graveyard, crowding around a freshly dug oblong of ground. It was sited adjacent to a grave with a small headstone. I was curious and leant across to read the inscription, although it proved difficult because the weather had made inroads on the carving, but I managed to make out the words,

John Sinclair. Born, November 1st 1928, tragically departed this life 9th June 1972. Sleep well my darling

husband, for my heart is here with you.'

I glanced to my side and looked at Susan. She had never met Petula, but the words must have touched her as she was crying softly and wasn't by any means alone. I stood there with a lump in my throat. It was all very sad and poignant, but I guess that's how most funerals are.

Until that moment Beth had kept her composure, but when the vicar read the burial service and reached the line, *'Ashes to ashes, dust to dust...'* that composure deserted her and she sobbed uncontrollably. The elderly man who gave the eulogy detached himself from the group and hurried to comfort her, his progress hampered by his walking stick digging into the soft ground.

Outside the cemetery when the service ended, Beth, now composed, came over and thanked both of us for coming. Her eyes still red and puffy from crying.

'I'm so glad we did,' I said. 'I met Petula just the once, but I liked her the moment I set eyes on her. She was an entertaining lady.'

I stooped to give Beth a hug goodbye and as I did, her voice cracked again. 'I'm going to be so lonely without her Mr Monroe.'

There wasn't much that I could say to that, so I gave a resigned look to convey, *That's life I'm afraid* and then Susan hooked her arm through mine and we started to walk away. We had gone a few paces before I turned back to Beth, wrote my mobile telephone number on a page torn from my pocket diary and handed it to her. I asked if she would call me should she ever discover something that might help Susan with her research.

An emotional Beth nodded that she would, but I doubted we would ever hear from her again. We had already searched the house thoroughly, discovering just the three ancient receipts, but who knows? If she *did* find something, it may enable us to send Susan back to her Billy even earlier than the coming Christmas, which was still quite a while away.

*

The months leading to December passed slowly, but as the time grew nearer, the negative doubts set in. Would we succeed or fail? Our hopes were based on a weak theory that in a classroom would probably be awarded a *D minus*, but we had no other options.

Susan was staying with Dorothy until December, so I saw a lot of her. The first time I came to dinner showed how different the 21st century is to Susan's era.

Dorothy's day had been a busy one and she didn't get home until 7.15pm. She flopped into an armchair and said, 'Fancy a Chinese takeaway, you two?'

Susan stared dumbly, so I explained the takeaway business to her. She looked shocked and asked in a disbelieving voice, 'Are you saying the food is cooked elsewhere, and then delivered to your door?'

Dorothy was savouring all of this. It was like having our own equivalent of Crocodile Dundee.

An hour later, Fred the porter buzzed to say the delivery boy was on his way up.

'Forty pounds!' Susan exclaimed in astonishment after she saw me pay the delivery boy. 'But that's daylight robbery Billy! How can it be so costly? Why, that's more than a month's salary. Much more!'

Dorothy smiled across at me, shaking her head in the amused way I'd grown used to since Susan arrived in the 21st century.

'Not in 2016 it isn't Susan,' I said, grinning. 'And furthermore, it would have cost twice as much had we gone to a restaurant to eat.'

Susan said no more; merely gave me the bewildered look we had grown used to.

It was past eleven when we finished eating. With the two girls in full flow, I was lucky to get a look in. Susan pushed away her empty plate and glanced at the clock on the wall; her eyes widened and she turned to me, concerned about my welfare. 'It's already after ten past eleven. I hope you don't have too far to travel home.'

'Not really,' I answered, relaxing back in my seat. 'Caterham is probably fifteen to twenty miles from here, but I'm not driving back there tonight. Not having drunk nearly four glasses of wine.'

I left her imagination to work things out, but I'd forgotten it was a 1926 imagination, steeped in the social behaviour of the nineteen-twenties. 'So you will be staying at a nearby hotel then?'

Dorothy, probably keen to get to bed, answered on my behalf, 'Billy's staying here with us Susan, so he doesn't really care whether it's late or not.'

If Dorothy thought that was the end of it, she was wrong. 'But how can that be?' her great great aunt said. 'There are just two bedrooms here in the apartment, yours and mine, so where is Billy going to sleep?'

Dorothy nailed the matter down, 'Billy is sleeping in my bed with me Susan.'

Susan looked aghast and Dorothy explained, 'Back in 1926, most girls were probably virgins when they married, but nowadays, people who care for someone often sleep with them, and Billy says he loves me and I-' she left the sentence hanging before saying, 'Well, I quite like him, so I allow him to share my bed. Different from your day Susan, but the world moves on. Look at the price of our meal!'

'Oh,' Susan said quietly, 'I see,' although her expression indicated that she didn't necessarily agree.

The time dragged until eventually the end of November was upon us. Less than a month for Susan now. The poor girl's patience would soon be rewarded.

I felt I'd waited long enough to propose to Dottie, although it was still less than a year since my collision with her little Smart car. I had never felt this strongly about anyone before, so I made a booking at *The Ivy* where Dorothy and I went on our first date, which wasn't really a proper date.

I intended to return there and once a few whiskies were under my belt, I would propose. I was pretty certain that Dorothy's answer would be *Yes*, but you can never count your chickens with women. You may think everything is a slam dunk, but then they hit you between the eyes with a right hook that you didn't see coming. So, just in case that right hook was in the process of winging its way towards my fragile chin, I chose a table by the door so a minimum number of people would witness me legging it from the restaurant, sobbing my eyes out.

I reached out and took Dorothy's hand in my own. 'Well my darling,' I said, staring into the brown eyes that are her best feature, along with her chin, hair and cute nose, 'I have brought you here tonight for a special reason.' I took a deep breath to bolster my flagging courage, which was rapidly going downhill. It suddenly occurred to me that I could be wrong in my assumption. What if she didn't love me? Supposing I was just a fill in guy until Mr Right came along. What then? The more I thought about it, the more the idea gained strength. Sweat appeared on my forehead and I tried to push the negative thoughts away before my voice dried up. I charged on. It was the only way.

'I have something important to ask you,' I said quickly.

There - the job was half done and I could breathe again. All I needed now was a bit of encouragement to help me press on, but it didn't come. Dorothy raised her hand to silence me before I could say any more. 'No, Billy,' she said softly with eyes that were cast downwards, 'please don't say another word. I know what you're about to ask and I'm afraid that my answer is *No*. Please don't bring the subject up again. It makes me feel quite awkward.'

Well, so much for the Billy Monroe intuition system. It was obviously several notches below crap on whatever scale there is to judge these things. And! Thank God I didn't do the bended knee bit in *The Ivy* of all places. I'd have looked a right pillock.

I didn't say much after that. There wasn't much I could say, was there?

The meal continued in silence for a few minutes

until Dorothy put her knife and fork down, dabbed a napkin to her lips and stared across at me. Knowing her appetite, I thought she was going to ask for the remainder of my *Steak Diane*, but I was wrong again. Being wrong seems to be my new persona.

'I was a bit sharp with you just then Billy,' she said, although there was no trace of regret in her voice. She reached to take my hand in her own. 'It was pretty rude of me, so ignore what I said and tell me how much you want to borrow.' She paused momentarily. 'Of course, I'll need to be certain you can pay me back, but that's only fair, isn't it? Now, if Tom agrees to guarantee the loan, well of course, that would be acceptable. At least I know I'll get the money back.' Finished, she crossed her arms and smiled sweetly at me.

I could only stare in disbelief. Is this what the woman I adored thought I was about to ask? For her to lend me some money?

I felt the anger rising in me. How could she think such a thing of me? Especially after the intensity and trauma of our past months together? How could she?

Her remarks also put my back up. Kind of stung, the remnants of whatever pride I had left after the ownership of a business that just about put bread and water on my dinner table. Cheese was added as a special treat at weekends.

'Now just you hold on a minute Dorothy,' I said in a voice swiftly rising from baritone to soprano. 'You have it all wrong. I certainly don't need to borrow any-' I stopped as I saw the smile on her face and she wriggled with pleasure.

'Ah ha! Got you Billy, didn't I?' With that, she held

out her hand, palm upwards and said, 'Show me the size of the rock, baby. I'm not answering until I've seen how big it is.'

Well, so much for my people skills. I pulled the small jewellery box from my jacket pocket and passed it across the table to her.

Dorothy studied the miniscule diamond that was set in a band of white gold. If you had bad eyesight, you would only see the gold band.

It took less than three seconds before Dorothy looked at me with shining eyes. She slipped the ring onto the third finger of her left hand for me to admire. 'That'll do nicely Billy Monroe. I shall be happy to spend the rest of my life as your moll, but please be sensible and don't go telling Susan that we're now newly engaged. Right now, I think it would upset the poor thing.'

I agreed. After all that had happened to the girl, news of our engagement was the last thing she would want to hear.

'I shall wear the ring for the rest of the evening, but it'll be back in its box before I get home,' Dorothy said. I watched her studying it again, guessing she was admiring the diamond cutter's skill at cutting stones this small.

By the time the meal was finished, we had decided to announce our engagement after Christmas when we hoped that Susan would be back in the 1920s with her own Billy Monroe.

'How is the refurbishment of that car of yours coming along?' Dorothy asked as we drove back to her apartment later. I was surprised, because she had never mentioned the Bugatti before. 'I still haven't seen it, but from what Tom's told me, it sounds pretty cool. Can we have it as our wedding car Billy? Can we?'

The idea of using the Bugatti as our wedding car hadn't crossed my mind. Should we ever sell the Bugatti, at least we would have had *some* use out of it. 'I'll give Chuck Nelson a ring in the morning to hear how the car is coming along,' I promised. 'I think it must be close to completion as he's been working on it for a good few months already.'

So, at nine the following morning, I rang Chuck and explained that we hoped to use the car on our wedding day and was that a possibility? I couldn't see his grin, but I knew it was there from the tone of his voice. 'The Bugatti's looking great,' he said. 'Got a long way to go still, but that's always how it is when a job is being fitted in between others. But whatever happens, I promise it'll be ready in time for your wedding.'

*

Billy Monroe, circa 1926, was a meticulous timekeeper. To him, a person arriving late obviously felt they were more important than whoever they were meeting. But despite that, he was three hours late arriving at *Cherry Tree House* on Christmas Eve - a punctured tyre on the Bugatti being the cause. Fortunately, the manager of the garage he trudged four miles to reach, promised to telephone the Mendozas and explain what had happened, meaning Susan's father hopefully wouldn't be too angry about his lateness.

It had taken him an hour to walk into Swanage and a further fifteen minutes to find Brown's Garage. It took their driver a further hour to collect a replacement tyre from their supplier in Poole, plus another 35 minutes to fit it.

Billy banged the heavy door knocker of *Cherry Tree House* and waited, feeling more like Charlie Chaplin in *The Tramp* than a welcome guest at a rich man's house. Aside from him being filthy, there was a tear in the sleeve of the jacket. He raised his eyes skywards but stopped short of cursing his maker; the last thing he needed right now was for a bolt of lightning to head his way. Twenty seconds passed before the door was opened. Maria studied the forlorn figure standing in the porch and her heart went out to the young man. 'Hello Billy,' she said, leading him into the warmth of the hallway. At the same time, she noticed the drooping bunch of flowers he was holding.

He passed them to her. 'Sorry Mrs Mendoza; they were lovely when I first bought them.'

Maria buried her head into the flowers, breathed in their scent and smiled with pleasure. At least the boy had taken the trouble to bring flowers, something her husband rarely did. There were always other things on his mind. 'Please don't apologise to me Billy. Women *always* welcome flowers, regardless of the state they're in.'

Billy switched the *heavy* suitcase to the hand that had held the flowers and groaned with relief. Along with clothes, the small suitcase included prototype engine parts and weighed around twenty pounds, which was more than enough to restrict the blood supply to his fingers.

Maria led him to the foot of the stairs. 'The bed in your old room has been made up for you, but I'm sure you will want to tidy yourself up Billy, so I'll draw a bath for you whilst you unpack.'

As she turned to walk away, she glanced at the grandfather clock. 'Dinner will be served in an hour, so that should allow you sufficient time.' She laughed nervously. 'No doubt you will remember how strict Samuel is about punctuality at meal times.'

Whenever the Mendozas were at Lulworth Cove, they always employed a cook to prepare and serve the main meal of the day. And, why shouldn't they? Billy thought. If one worked hard and could afford to do so, then why not indeed?

In his room, he undressed and put on his dressing gown. The bath had been filled for him and he sank wearily into the hot water and let his mind daydream. Perhaps one day his income - already reasonable - would be enough for him to live as the Mendozas did, but then he remembered his reason for wanting that to happen lay at the bottom of the English Channel. *Why* hadn't he regained his memory a single day earlier? Why, why, why? He cursed aloud before realising the sound might carry to the ears of the Mendozas. He knew he shouldn't punish himself like this. It wasn't his fault that Susan was dead, and continuously resurrecting the events in his mind wouldn't bring her back. Nothing would. Lazarus was the only non-deity who had managed that, and Jesus wasn't around at the moment for a repeat performance.

*

By the time the Christmas period arrived, Susan was used to life in the twenty-first century, not that she much liked it though. The constant noise and rush. The worshipping of money and possessions and the strange way people wore their clothes with the manufacturer's logo on the outside, presumably so others would think they had good taste as the garments were expensive.

As Christmas drew closer, Susan's excitement grew daily. She *would* cross the time barrier back to her Billy. Her maker had chosen Billy as her life partner and would ensure that it happened. None of us tried to convince her otherwise. Why bring her even more misery? Susan *knew* she was going back to her Billy and wanted to look her best for the occasion, not that she'd have to try too hard. Susan would be stunning in sackcloth and ashes.

The yellow dress she had on when she arrived, soaked and shivering, had been cleaned in readiness for her return to the 20th century.

Kate and Tom collected us on the 23rd of December. After loading everything into their People Carrier for our stay at *Cherry Tree House*, there was just enough wriggling room for the five of us. Hopefully the trip back would have more room without Susan on board.

'Has anyone realised yet,' she said excitedly, 'that in eight days and twelve hours, we will all be celebrating the New Year in the same house, but it will be 1927 for me and 2017 for you?'

She was quite correct. Both Billy Mk1 and Billy Mk2 [me] would be celebrating with the woman we loved. Except Billy and Susan would be dead, or would they?

You could go nuts thinking about it.

'How do you know that you'll still be at the house on New Year's Eve?' I asked. 'You could be back at Wooburn Green by then.'

Susan shook her head, 'Father was very set in his ways. Whenever we visited Lulworth Cove for Christmas, we always remained there until after the New Year. Father insisted.'

I grinned, ready with another tease. 'Well, if that's the case Susan, then there's really no rush to send you back so early, is there? You can spend all of Christmas with us and we can send you back on the 31st. What do you think of that idea?'

'Billy!' Dorothy said sharply, although she was smiling. 'Stop being cruel to Susan and behave yourself,' while Kate huffed and gave me one of the fierce glares that always send Tom into a silent patch for a while. 'Why would the poor girl want to put up with you and Tom for any longer than she has to? The pair of you are probably the reason that she thinks this century is rubbish.'

Dorothy leant across from her seat and hugged me protectively. 'Don't be cruel to my baby,' she chided. 'It isn't *always* necessary to tell people the truth. Sometimes, it's far better to lie.'

We pulled onto the driveway of *Cherry Tree House* a few minutes later and the moment the vehicle came to a stop, Susan rushed out and waited for Dorothy to open up.

*

Christmas Eve arrived and Susan suggested going to evening mass at the local church. She seemed serene and happy in the church. 'We would always come here on Christmas Eve when we stayed at *Cherry Tree House* over the festive season,' she whispered.

I whispered back, 'How many times was that?'

'Only three or four, now shush Billy and stop talking. Please remember that we're in a place of worship.'

In my next life, I'm coming back as a woman.

The service was conducted by the Reverend Thomas Janus. He was an old man, frail to the point where I hoped he survived the ceremony. Susan nudged me in the ribs and whispered, 'His father, Hector Janus, was the vicar back in 1925. Thomas must have taken over from him. Believe it or not, I went to this one's Christening.'

'Shush,' I said. 'Remember that we're in a church.'

She dug me in the ribs and suppressed a giggle.

After the service, the vicar stood at the door and shook hands with the members of the congregation as they filed past him on their way out. We shuffled along the line, listening to what he said to others as we waited our turn. 'Goodbye Mrs Baxter, goodbye Mr Baily, how is young Rex getting on?' and so on and so on until we eventually reached him. Susan was now at the head of the queue. He studied her for a moment. 'You're new to the parish young lady,' he said as he shook her hand. 'But you are most welcome. There's always room for one more in God's house.'

Susan grinned mischievously at him, 'Thank you Vicar, but you are quite wrong about me being new to the parish. We have met before, but you probably don't remember as you were very young at the time.'

'Susan!' Dorothy chided loudly and we hurried from the church, leaving the poor man scratching his ancient head and muttering incoherently to himself.

Back at the house, we sat up until late in the evening, chatting and reliving the past few months and all that had taken place since Susan's arrival. She was sitting on a sofa next to Dorothy. I'd always known that they were similar to look at, but this was the first time I realised just *how* alike they were. The same colour eyes. Same slim build and both of them blessed with the same pert prettiness.

It was close to twelve when we called it a night and sloped off to bed, but twenty minutes later there was a soft knock on the bedroom door. Dorothy called out, 'Come in,' and Susan peeked around the door.

Dorothy patted the edge of the bed for her to sit down and Susan gave a drawn out sigh. 'I can't sleep Dorothy; I cannot stop thinking about things. Everything is swirling around in my head. Do you really think it's going to be all right? Do you?'

Dorothy gripped her hand reassuringly. 'Of course it will be,' she said, and then pointed towards the door. 'That's Billy's dressing gown hanging there. Get it and give it to him will you please?'

I stared dumbly at her, but my state of ignorance didn't last for long. 'Don't look at me like that Billy,' she chided. 'You can see that Susan needs to talk, so put this on and you can sleep in her room tonight.

Susan can stay with me.'

She was right, of course, so I slid out of the bed and Susan handed me the dressing gown, giving me a *good night* hug before climbing into my warm place.

The following morning, Dorothy told me Susan was so hyped up that it was around three before they got to sleep.

Christmas dinner was marvellous. I thought we had every Christmassy thing on our plates, but apparently not. 'Where are the chestnuts?' Susan asked. It brought home to me just how much things can change over the years. What was commonplace ninety years ago is virtually obsolete now.

The afternoon dragged. Watched kettles boil in record time compared to this. It was torture. By ten that evening, the day seemed to have lasted a week, but it was almost time. Our long wait was about to be over.

On the side table of the hall were five champagne flutes while a bottle of Bollinger's finest nestled in an ice bucket. Susan looked extremely pretty. She was wearing the yellow dress she arrived in, and Kate had spent hours on her hair and make-up. Back in 1926, if it all came off, Billy Monroe was about to get the full treatment.

The fuse for the electric oven had been removed and the wire replaced by a large nail. I shuddered, remembering the explosion the last time. There was no way on God's earth I wanted to be the one pushing that fuse in. A torch lay in readiness on the floor next to the fuse. Dorothy caught my attention and pointed to the ice bucket. 'Now Billy, open it now,' so I peeled away the foil on the champagne bottle and like the expert I like to think I am, slowly eased out the cork. It came away with the softest of *pops* and I filled the glasses. Once the bubbles subsided, I topped them up until they were full. We all chinked glasses and together said, 'Cheers everyone.'

Dorothy insisted on saying a few words as hopefully, this was the last time we would see Susan. Isn't it strange for one to say that they hoped they would never see someone again when in reality, we would all miss her. I certainly would; she had been with us for a long time and she was a sweet, good natured girl and a pleasure to be around. 'Susan,' Dorothy began, 'in the short time we have been fortunate enough to know you, we have all grown to love you.' I glanced across at Susan to see how she was taking this praise. Just as I'd expected, she was red faced with embarrassment, but nevertheless, I could see that she was pleased. 'We all realise that you're desperate to go back to your own time, and of course, we all know why. Your Billy is the reason, and I can understand that.' She slid her hand into mine and smiled. 'If I were in your situation, then I would feel the same way. I'd want to get back to my Billy. We would love you to stay because you're like family to us.' Dorothy laughed, realising what she had said. 'Well, in my case of course, you really *are* family.' At this point, she unstrapped her watch. It was a *Gucci* and Dorothy had told me once that it was the first really expensive thing she'd bought for herself when her business began to really take off. She held it out to Susan. 'Please take this. It will be something for you to remember us all by in the years ahead.'

Susan's eyes filled with tears. She stood quietly for a while. I'm not the most brilliant person at figuring out women's feelings, but I could tell she was too moved to speak. None of us spoke. Instead, we waited until she was ready, and then she unstrapped her own watch and offered it to Dorothy. 'Mummy gave this to me for my eighteenth birthday,' she said and smiled at the memory. 'It was such a wonderful day for me and I can't possibly explain how grown up I felt. It has always been my most treasured possession and nothing would have made me part with it, until now.' She moved forward and strapped it onto Dorothy's wrist before putting the *Gucci* onto her own. 'Now you have a part of me, and I have a part of you which I shall treasure 'til the day I die. I want to thank you all for the way you have looked after me and protected me over these past months. I could never have managed without your help.'

I looked across at Tom. He seemed pretty red eyed to me, which came as no great surprise. I'd been struck by a touch of the sniffles myself. Dorothy glanced at the hall clock and turned to Susan. 'It's time,' she said and one by one we all hugged our 1926 girl for the final time.

Kate dug Tom in the ribs. 'Go on then slowcoach, - get on with it,' and he picked up the fuse, opened the electric board and steeled himself for a brief moment while his courage built. I can't say I blamed him for waiting. After the force of the explosion the last time, Susan would have lived the remainder of her life with us if it had been left to me to push the fuse in, but our Tom was made of sterner stuff.

He looked across at Susan and grinned, 'Goodbye

love,' he said. 'I hope it all works out between you and your Billy,' and with that, he pushed the fuse into the board. There was an enormous explosion followed by a blinding flash and the lights went out, exactly as they had done before.

I heard Kate's disembodied voice in the darkness say, 'The street lights are all out,' immediately followed by the click of the torch as Tom switched it on. The beam cut through the darkness and rested on the spot where Susan had been standing. My heart sank at what I saw. She was still here! Still breathing 2016 air. I felt cheated, because after all those months of waiting and waiting, we had failed miserably. The searching of *Cherry Tree House*, the trip to *Rose Cottage*, the looking for clues, scrabbling around in lofts trying to find anything that would help to send Susan back to her own time; the planning and effort in trying to understand what the hell had caused her to come forward in the first place; it had all been in vain. Our supposed formula was nothing but a load of old toffee conjured up by a pair of guys who had quite obviously read too many science fiction novels for their own good.

It was my fault, I knew that much. Kate was the only sensible one. She had warned me against building up Susan's hopes on such a flimsy theory and now we had let the poor girl down. We had failed miserably.

For a moment, everyone was too stunned to speak. I'm sure that my thoughts were no different to the thoughts of the others. We stood in numbed silence and then the lights came back on. I was afraid to look at Kate. Right from the word go she'd been against this, so I knew I would have to face her anger, but what the hell; I'd done nothing to be ashamed of. I'd only ever had Susan's interests at heart. The alternative would have been to do nothing, and in my experience, doing nothing fails every time.

I scanned the hall and then scanned it with an edge of panic for a second time. My eyes swept from end to end, side to side and for some strange reason, even up to the ceiling and a cold feeling clamped around my heart. For a moment, I was afraid my legs would go from under me. I looked at the others and whispered, 'Where is Dorothy?'

Chapter Thirteen

Just as before, the flash momentarily blinded Dorothy. She rubbed her eyes to clear her vision, but without success. Multi coloured stars danced before her eyes.

'That was *some* explosion Tom!' she said. 'Even louder than the first one. All I can see are stars. Did it work? Has Susan gone?'

Silence was her answer, and then she heard footsteps close by.

'Who the blazes are you, young lady, and what the devil are you doing in this house?' It was a voice she didn't recognise, a man's voice, and whoever he was, he sounded angry.

What was going on? There were just the five of them in the house, Dorothy was quite certain of that. Once again she rubbed her eyes and her vision finally cleared. A man in his late fifties was standing in the doorway. Not a pleasant looking man by any means - slightly overweight, medium height, greying hair and a ruddy complexion. A ridiculous bristling moustache concealed most of his mouth, the kind she was sure went out with the arc. He must have walked into the house at the very moment Tom pushed the fuse into the fuse board.

He wore one of those disgusting tweed suits with a matching hairy waistcoat beneath the jacket. Before she could reply, a pleasant looking, much younger man joined him along with an attractive, fiftyish woman.

Dorothy's chin tilted defiantly upwards. How dare he, a total stranger, come into her family's house with these other people and have the nerve to speak to her in that way.

'I am Dorothy Curtis,' she informed him in a deliberately haughty voice, 'and for your information, whoever you are - I am the owner of the house you are now standing in, so perhaps it is *you* who should tell *me* exactly who you are, and what you are doing on my property.'

She saw the younger man run his finger nervously around his collar. He really was quite good looking, and then she saw a magnificent Grandfather clock standing in the space occupied by a Queen Anne chair a few moments ago. While she was puzzling over the appearance of the Grandfather clock, the tweedy man, unmoved by her words and still full of his own importance, took a step towards her. 'How dare you ask me who I am, you impertinent young madam. Why, I've half a mind to call the local constable and have you arrested.' He paused momentarily before adding, 'In fact, that is precisely what I shall do.' He cut such a comical figure that Dorothy was unable to stop herself from smiling.

What a pompous fool he was.

Obviously lost for words, the man turned to the younger man. 'Billy, would you be good enough to go and make the call on my behalf? The operator will put you straight through. If my memory serves me correctly, Amanda Jenkins should be on duty tonight.'

Dorothy's mind was buzzing. Billy! Billy? How many Billys were there, for goodness sake? But this particular Billy made no attempt to move. Instead, in a calming tone, he said to the pompous older man, 'Maybe you should be hear what this lady has to say before taking the drastic step of calling the constable, Mr Mendoza, and then, should you still feel it necessary, I shall be pleased to make the call on your behalf.'

Dorothy's heart missed a beat and she stared at the two men in shock and disbelief. Had her ears played tricks on her? First Billy, and now, Mr Mendoza. Was she asleep and trapped in a bad dream? And then, like the proverbial ton of bricks, it hit her. It was *she* who had made the 90 year journey back in time, and not Susan. She recoiled backwards because the full implications of this didn't bear thinking about, but couldn't be avoided. Just like Susan, she too had lost the man she loved.

The room began to spin as everything swirled around in her mind. All she had tried to do was help a poor lost soul, and this, this was her reward, and then she remembered the old saying: *No good deed goes unpunished.*

The spinning grew faster, all the time gathering momentum and Billy, seeing what was about to happen, caught Dorothy just in time as she continued the family tradition and fell into his arms in a dead faint.

*

Tom threw his arms in the air in despair. 'Well, it's bloody obvious even to someone with a brain the size of a pea that Dorothy has gone back instead of Susan,' he said. 'So now we are well and truly totally fucked!'

'Thomas!' Kate said loudly. 'For goodness sake, don't use that type of language. Remember that Susan is still here,' but she could have saved her breath. Susan still hadn't realised what had happened and Tom's outburst went completely over her head.

Billy stared at the empty champagne flutes. There wasn't a word in the dictionary that encompassed the dread and despair - the fear and terror that he now felt. Barely fifteen minutes had passed since they were celebrating and now, there was nothing to celebrate. Things had actually become even more desperate. And as for the worst scenario, well, it didn't bear thinking about, although he had no choice because his brain wouldn't allow him not to. Bile flooded his stomach and he was close to throwing up. He stared at Tom as he put his fears into words. 'We don't actually know that Dorothy has gone back to 1925. All we know for certain, is that she isn't here. She could be anywhere in time.' His hands went up in a hopeless gesture. 'We've dabbled in things we know nothing about Tom. Dorothy could have gone back to yesterday and we would know nothing of it, even though she was with us, because our memory is of yesterday as it was.' He paused and his head drooped as the vastness of what could have happened hit him. 'For all we know, she could be in the Stone Age, running for her life from some sort of Dinosaur.' His stomach flipped at the thought and his voice became a whisper. 'She could already be dead Tom. I could have lost her forever.'

*

It had taken Susan this long to realise what had happened. Dorothy had gone in her place. She went to Billy and wrapped her arms around him, hugging him. 'She's safe Billy,' she whispered. 'Whatever you may think, and I can understand you thinking the worst, I know that she's back with my Billy, I know she is, and all the while she's with him, he will protect her, just as all of you have protected me for almost six months. Our task now is to discover why she returned in my place and why I was left behind. There has to be a reason Billy, it's only logical,' but Billy was too devastated to think about logic. All he knew was he had lost the woman he loved, and then it dawned on him; this shouldn't come as a surprise. He had always known he wasn't entitled to Dorothy. She'd been his by a fluke. He knew his own capabilities and couldn't ignore that men cut in his mould do not win prizes like Dorothy. This was how it was always meant to be. This whole *coincidental* thing that Dorothy often talked about wasn't coincidence at all. It was preordained. Some greater power was controlling this and he was never going to get her back. Some dreams simply do not come true and he'd been an idiot to believe otherwise.

*

When Dorothy regained consciousness, she was

lying on a couch in the day room.

Dabbing her brow with a damp cloth was the fiftyish woman. The man she realised was Susan's father, Samuel Mendoza, seemed calmer than earlier. Maybe even a little concerned.

'Welcome back,' the woman said. 'I'm Maria Mendoza and these two men are-'

'I know who they are,' Dorothy interrupted. 'Your husband Samuel and Susan's friend, Billy Monroe.' The damp cloth had done its job well. She felt much better and sat upright, smiling apologetically to the woman. 'I'm sorry; interrupting before you finished was rude of me.' She turned to the older man and said, 'And I'm sorry we got off on the wrong foot Mr Mendoza, but you will understand the confusion once I've explained things to you.' She turned to Billy, 'And if you're as nice as you are to look at, then I can understand why Susan loved you so much.' She blushed at her words! Whatever would these people think of her?

The room was quiet as they awaited her explanation, but she must tread carefully because these people believed Susan died six months ago.

Maria was surprised when Dorothy had mentioned Susan's name. She thought she knew all of Susan's friends, but obviously not. 'So, you knew our daughter?'

Dorothy smiled. 'Yes, I did, I mean, I do. She's a wonderful girl Mrs Mendoza. The nicest I've ever met.'

Maria glanced at her husband. 'Then you haven't heard the dreadful news,' she said quietly. 'We lost our daughter in July of this year. It's been the worst year of our lives.'

Dorothy wasn't sure how she should respond. She couldn't just announce that Susan was alive, but had to start somewhere, but where?

In the meantime, Maria was surprised at her lack of *any* reaction to the news of Susan's death.

Dorothy sighed and began, 'Mrs Mendoza, will you please tell me what you think of my clothes, my shoes and my hairstyle.'

Maria blinked in amazement. Was the girl insane? She had chosen to ignore Susan's demise and was more concerned with her own appearance.

Samuel and Billy exchanged glances, also puzzled at this woman's behaviour. For the moment, Maria decided it best to comply with the young woman's request.

'Your clothes are very nice my dear, and your hair, quite lovely, but did you not hear what I said? That my daughter Susan is dead.'

'I heard you,' Dorothy said quietly. How did one tell bereaved parents that the child they grieved for was not dead? More to the point - tell them without causing them a possible heart attack? Not by blurting it out, that was obvious.

'This is so difficult for me,' she began, 'but whatever I might say, please don't think I'm some kind of fruitcake, because you will understand very shortly.'

Billy looked at Mr Mendoza and silently mouthed, 'Fruitcake?'

Mendoza shrugged his shoulders. Apart from the obvious, he didn't know what *fruitcake* meant either.

'Mrs Mendoza, I shall word my question differently. What about the *style* of my clothes and the style of my hair? Please say what you think of the style?'

Maria studied Dorothy once again, still half convinced the girl was deranged. 'Unusual,' she eventually replied, 'if that's what you wanted to hear, my dear. The style is very unusual, quite different to what I am used to.'

'So if I told you I was from another period in time and not from 1926, and that I'm dressed fashionably for the time I'm from, you would at least give me a chance to explain everything, because my clothes should be some proof that I'm telling the truth. You would give me a chance to explain everything, wouldn't you?'

Maria glanced across at Samuel who nodded almost imperceptibly, indicating she must humour the girl. *Not from 1926 but from another period in time! Pah! What stuff and nonsense!* So he would be making that telephone call after all, but to the local hospital and not the police station. 'Excuse me for a moment young lady,' he said and rose to his feet, but Dorothy, having witnessed the silent exchange between husband and wife, guessed his intention. She reached for his arm and stopped him, giving him what she hoped was a reassuring smile. 'You can telephone the mental hospital in a few moments if you still want to Mr Mendoza, but before doing that, I'd like you to hear what I have to say. That's all I ask, and then, if you still want to phone them, please be my guest.'

Samuel sighed and sat down again, prepared to continue this charade for no more than a further five minutes. He folded his arms across his chest and Dorothy realised that whatever she said would be of no consequence, but continued undaunted. She *would* find a way to make him believe her!

She turned to Maria. 'Mrs Mendoza, of course I heard what you had to say about Susan's death. You may not believe it, but I know a lot more than any of you about what happened to your daughter on that fateful night. July the first or second, I believe.'

It failed to register that Dorothy had given them the correct dates and Samuel bristled indignantly, 'I doubt that young lady; how could you possibly know more than my wife and I about our daughter's demise? Stuff and nonsense my girl, stuff and nonsense!'

Dorothy sighed with exasperation. He was the most irritating person she had ever encountered! 'If you give me a moment Mr Mendoza, you might be convinced by what I have to say.' She glanced at the younger man and then back at Mendoza. 'Now, Billy here took off to Africa and his ship sank on the return voyage home. Is that correct?'

'Yes, but this is common knowledge young lady,' Samuel snapped. 'Common knowledge, which means everyone knows this much, so your saying it proves nothing.'

Dorothy continued as though he hadn't spoken, 'Susan was really cut up when she heard the news. In fact, she was devastated. She loved Billy and wanted to marry him, but now that he was gone, she had nothing left to live for and planned to take her own life.'

Samuel raised his eyes skywards, wondering what this twaddle was leading up to. He said, 'Pray continue young lady, but a little faster, if you can.'

'Do any of you know what Susan was wearing on that awful night?' she asked.

Maria's eyes filled with tears. 'How could we? They never found my baby's body.' Her voice sank to a whisper, 'What she was wearing never entered my head.'

'How about the yellow dress she planned to wear especially for Billy's return?' Dorothy offered. 'Could that have been what she had on?'

The hairs rose on the back of Maria's neck. 'How on earth could you know about the yellow dress?' she whispered. 'Only Susan and I knew what she planned to wear when Billy's ship arrived at Southampton.'

'And yet I do,' Dorothy said, 'so why don't you check in her wardrobe to see if the dress is still there?'

Maria declined out of hand. 'I cannot bring myself to go into Susan's room, young lady. I have not been in there since that terrible day. Can you not imagine how I would feel with the memories of my daughter surrounding me?'

Billy was intrigued and leaned forward interestedly.

And there was something else. Although her manner was completely different to Susan's, had not Samuel or Maria noticed the startling resemblance she bore to their late daughter? He stood up and said, 'I shall be happy to look in your stead, Mrs Mendoza.'

While he was gone, the others waited in an

awkward silence. He returned, holding a dress that he passed to Maria for inspection. 'This was the only yellow dress in the wardrobe Mrs Mendoza. Susan often wore it.'

Dorothy knew it couldn't be the dress, because Susan was wearing it when Tom pushed the fuse in. Even now, Susan was in the house they were in, wearing the dress in question but separated from them by ninety years.

'No Billy, that isn't the one,' she said gently. 'You know the one I'm talking about Mrs Mendoza. It has lace trim and is square cut around the neck.'

Maria Mendoza's background was a genteel one. From a young age, she was taught to always remain ladylike and had lived her life by those rules, until this moment.

She leapt to her feet, her voice at a pitch never reached before, 'Just exactly who are you, young lady?' and then her face reddened, realising how aggressive she must have seemed.

Dorothy smiled softly at this woman who was one of her own ancestors, and a seemingly nice one at that. 'Please be patient Mrs Mendoza; I'm almost finished now.' She wanted to blurt out that Susan was alive, but knew this was the only sensible way. 'After Billy's ship went down off the African coast, Susan waited for over three weeks before walking into the sea, and why was that? Why not drown herself straight away instead of waiting that long?'

Samuel decided to stop to this once and for all. 'Because her depression grew as time went on, that is why! In the end, she was unable to stand it and did away with herself. Any fool can see that and you should be able to as well.'

Dorothy winced at the jibe but continued, 'You're quite wrong Mr Mendoza, there was a reason for her delay, and that reason was your thirtieth wedding anniversary. She didn't want to spoil that occasion for you, so waited until it had passed.'

It was too much for Samuel; he could contain himself no longer and leapt to his feet. 'What poppycock and nonsense! I refuse to listen any further to this rubbish.'

Maria placed a hand on his arm. 'Please calm down dear. We have listened this far, so why not be patient and let the girl finish?'

Samuel gave a loud, 'Harrumph,' shrugged his wife's arm away and sat down.

Now the dress had been dealt with, Dorothy held out her wrist to show them Susan's watch. 'Do you recognise this watch Mrs Mendoza?' She slipped it off and gave it to her. Maria's complexion drained of all colour. It was Susan's watch. Not a shadow of doubt in her mind, for they had taken long enough choosing it. The jeweller in the shop went into great detail, explaining that just ten of the watches had been made, and the exclusivity factor cemented the choice for the pair of them. Even the blustering Samuel was shocked into silence as he looked at the watch.

Maria held it to her cheek, eyes full of tears. 'This watch was my baby's,' she whispered and Dorothy took Maria's hand and held it softly.

'I know Mrs Mendoza, Susan told me you gave it to her for her eighteenth birthday,' and Maria's fragile resolve gave way and she began to cry.

Dorothy knew she almost there now. 'I would like to summarise everything I've told you so far. I've told you which dress Susan was wearing when she walked into the sea and explained why she waited so long after Billy's ship sank before doing it, and now I've given you her watch, which she would never normally part with. And although you do not yet believe me, I've also explained that I come from a different period in time, which is extremely hard for you to accept, and I can understand that. In your shoes, I'd find it difficult as well.'

Maria no longer knew what to think. What would the girl come out with next? 'Are you an Angel?' she whispered and Samuel's patience finally ran dry.

'Poppycock Maria,' he exploded, 'it's obvious that this, this, *person* has found our daughter's body and is looking to turn it to her advantage in some way. Can you not see it woman?'

Dorothy sighed with exasperation and turned to confront him. She held her arms up in a gesture of surrender. 'You win, Mr Mendoza, I give in. It was your daughter's dead body that told me about your thirtieth wedding anniversary, and for good measure, her body also told me about the watch and who bought it for her. It told me the significance of the yellow dress she was wearing when she walked into the sea to drown herself. Why, it even told me what it was bought to celebrate. Any fool could work that lot out.'

Mendoza was stunned into silence. Dorothy said quietly, 'Mr Mendoza, the only reason that I know all of these things is because your daughter told them to me.' She turned away from him and back to Maria, knowing the time was as right as it would ever be. 'I'm sorry I've been so long winded in telling you all of this, but I did it because I felt I had no other choice. Mrs Mendoza, your daughter Susan is not dead. She is alive and I should know as I've spent the past five or six months with her in the year 2016.' She turned to Samuel, whose jaw was now hanging loosely, 'I know it's unbelievable to you, but she is there right now Mr Mendoza. It was Susan who was supposed to return here today, not me, but something must have gone wrong and it was *me* who came back and not Susan. She is trapped ninety years in the future, just as I'm now trapped in what for me is the past. Now we must work out how to get the two of us back to our respective times.'

There was a soft thud from behind her and she turned to see Maria Mendoza spread-eagled on the floor in a dead faint.

Chapter Fourteen

Kate was fussing around like a mother hen. I watched as she made mugs of hot chocolate for everyone. The others sipped away appreciatively, but not me. I was working hard at being miserable, beating myself up the way people do when they know they have messed up big time. The woman I loved was gone and I would never see her again.

Why the hell hadn't I left things alone? Why am I always trying to sort other people's lives out? It's not as if I'm the most qualified person to do that job. What I do best is to fail miserably and this was one more example. Susan was in the same boat as me - separated from the person she loved, but at least she knew he was safe, which was more than I knew about Dorothy. Okay, so Susan wasn't able to share her life with the man she loved, but she'd eventually get over him, just as I knew I would eventually get over Dorothy. By that, I mean the pain would gradually subside. After five or six years, it would be down to a dull ache, although I didn't want the dull ache! I wanted the full, undiluted pain because it proved that

I'd once had a *real* love that wasn't simply continuous lust. I wanted the pain because it meant I was thinking about her, and thinking about Dorothy was the next best thing to being with her.

Tom, tired of sipping his hot chocolate, buried his lips in the froth, took a huge gulp and hollered out in pain. Kate glared in disgust but he ignored her. 'I know just how you feel Billy,' he said with a heavy sigh. 'I never told you this before, but I once had me a pooch and when it ran away, I was absolutely gutted - absolutely, so you're not alone in your grief. I know what sort of hell you're going through now.' Just to cheer me up further, he added, 'I never did get that dog back.'

Even Kate, who knew what a weirdo he could be, stared at him in disbelief. 'God Tom, you are the strangest person I've ever come across. Sometimes when I'm tidying up at night, I think about you and wonder if you come from the same planet as the rest of us. Like Superman from Krypton, but without his muscles.' She turned away and busied herself at the sink, stopping occasionally to look at Tom and shake her head.

Superman without the muscles leant towards me. 'She's got no soul that woman,' he whispered. 'She's always been like that Billy, but she's never known the sense of loss we share.' There can't be too many Toms in this world.

Susan put down her hot chocolate, 'We must formulate a plan Billy. I've been reviewing things and if my conclusions are correct, there isn't much time if we are to get Dorothy back.'

Tom drained his drink and put the mug down. 'So tell us your conclusions Susan,' he said softly.

'Firstly, we must take a positive outlook,' she said in a school-marmish way. 'That is extremely important in all things in life.'

I hid a smile - this from a woman who recently tried to kill herself. 'Go on Susan,' I said. 'Explain to us just why we don't have much time.'

'Well, we were on the right track in what we did, that's obvious as Dorothy is no longer with us.'

'Okay,' I said. 'True, but why don't we have much time?'

'Because if my parents being here *is* part of the formula, they shall be returning to Wooburn Green on New Year's day and we have no way of knowing when they'll next be here. So, if we intend to do something, we have five days remaining to plan it.'

I perked up hearing that; I'd forgotten there was a short time left to reverse Susan and Dorothy's place. But why had Dorothy gone while Susan remained? That was the big question.

Tom stretched and yawned. 'I'm knackered! Can we get some kip before trying to think of a plan, please?'

'Tom is probably right,' Kate said. 'Plus our subconscious may come up with the answer while we're asleep. Why don't we go to bed with a pencil and paper nearby to jot down any thoughts that wake us during the night? Then we can talk again in the morning. How does that sound?' Without waiting for an answer, she made a fast exit with Tom at her heels.

Susan came across and slid her arms under mine, giving me a hug. 'I know you think this is my fault. If I had accepted my lot, Dorothy would still be here, but I truly believe that things will eventually work out Billy.'

Not wanting Susan to feel guilt ridden, I rubbed her head affectionately. 'Don't be silly, I don't blame you at all. There is nothing wrong with wanting to spend the rest of your life with someone you love.' I glanced at the kitchen wall clock; it was late! 'Anyway, if you wish to stay beautiful, then get some sleep right now, and that's an order.'

'I'm not beautiful,' she said, walking towards the door.

'Yes you are,' I replied, 'and don't argue with your elders.'

I slept restlessly that night, staggering downstairs feeling rough. Once we'd finished eating, Kate cleared the dishes and sat down again. 'So, did anyone's subconscious help out during the night?' But when we all shook our heads, she said, 'Mine neither.'

Tom looked at Susan. 'You can be the big chief now. We're all at your command, so have you worked anything out yet?'

Susan blushed with pleasure, 'Gosh, I've never been a leader before. Thank you so much!' She studied us, like a General surveying his troops. 'We have five days in which to do something. If Dorothy *is* with Billy and my parents, by now she will have convinced them I am alive and that she is from the year 2016, although Father will still be sceptical! So, our priority is to discover why Dorothy returned in my place. Until we know that, any one of you could find yourself back in time when we try again.'

I was treated to that lovely smile of hers and for a moment, it was as though Dorothy was back with me. 'Hopefully Billy,' she said, 'it would be in the year 1926, if that did happen again.'

'That's all very well for you to say Susan,' Tom said, 'but have you come up with any ideas why Dorothy went back instead of you? Because I sure as hell haven't!'

Susan lowered her eyes. 'Me neither Tom. I'm still working on that.'

'Maybe it was because you and Dorothy are so alike that whatever causes it got confused and made a mistake,' Kate ventured and Tom's jaw dropped in amazement. He stared at her with exaggerated disbelief.

'This,' he said disdainfully, 'is a woman who bets on a racehorse because the jockey is wearing the prettiest colours. Naturally, she always loses!"

Kate glared at him, muttering something about once having a third place.

While this banter was taking place, I was working on what *had* gone wrong. As Susan said, we could go no further until we knew that one detail, but everything had been the same. Everything replicated exactly. Same time of night, same room. No chances taken that might lead to failure. Susan wore the same dress, shoes and underwear that she had on when she arrived in July. Nothing had been overlooked, nothing at all - and then I realised. 'The watch!'

I turned to her. 'Don't you see Susan? You and Dorothy exchanged watches just before Tom put the fuse in. She, and not you, was wearing the watch that you had on when you first arrived here. That *must* be it!' I turned to Tom, excitement spilling from me. 'What do you reckon? Do you think that could be the link?'

I don't know why I bothered asking him. Even when he agrees he feels duty bound to put a damper on my enthusiasm. 'Oh well, that's just great Billy, isn't it? So, once we get the watch back from 1926, we're in business again. It should be a piece of cake; after all, it's only ninety years away!' He looked at each of us in turn, defeat written all over his face, 'So, do any of you have an idea how we can get it back, because I'm bloody sure I don't.'

But Susan spoke up, 'But I do,' she smiled.

*

Dorothy came to the last part of her story, 'And just before Tom pushed the fuse in, I gave my watch to Susan to remember me by.'

Samuel Mendoza sat in dumbfounded silence, because this woman, who had appeared from nowhere, was actually telling the truth. Samuel's life had been built on logic, and listening to someone who claimed to have moved through time was not logical; and if it wasn't logical, then it wasn't possible. However, Dorothy knew far too much about Susan and the Mendoza family for *all* of her tale to be a fabrication. For the moment, he decided to accept her story and delve deeper when the time was right.

'So was that when Susan reciprocated and gave

you her watch?' Maria asked.

Listening to Dorothy's explanation had uplifted her. If it was the truth, then her daughter was still alive!

Dorothy smiled softly, remembering the poignancy of the watch exchanging ceremony. 'Yes Mrs Mendoza, that's exactly what happened. Your daughter strapped it onto my wrist and I remember her words as she fastened the buckle. *Now you have a part of me and I have a part of you which I shall treasure until the day I die.*'

Through the whole of this Billy had been silent, but now he spoke, 'So the last thing you remember was the explosion and flash as the electrical fuse was pushed in?'

'Yes, and the next thing I heard was Mr Mendoza's voice. The flash left me unable to see properly for a few moments, so it took a while to realise what must have happened.'

Maria leant forward - a different woman to the one Dorothy had first seen. 'From what you have told us,' she said in a quavering voice, 'it appears that the journey through time can only be made once, and if that is so, then I shall never see my daughter again.' She sighed heavily but still managed a weak smile. 'Well, at least we know she is still alive. That's some consolation of course. As a mother, I can accept that and be happy.'

Maria's words confirmed what Billy had been thinking but was afraid to put into words. Despite the many months since losing Susan, the ache in his chest was still tearing him apart.

'Maybe you are correct Mrs Mendoza,' Dorothy said with a wan smile. 'Maybe the journey can only be made once, but personally, I don't reckon that's the case and I hope you're wrong, because if not, then it won't just be Susan who's stuck in the year 2016; I'll also be stuck here in 1926 and will never see my Billy again. No, I reckon there's an explanation as to why this last attempt went wrong, and if I'm right, then you *will* see Susan again and I shall get back to my own time and *my* Billy.'

Mother, father and would be fiancé leant forward and waited for Dorothy's revelation. She smiled widely at them. 'It's simple really; it's all about the watch. Susan's watch is the key to this. Think about it. We did everything exactly the same as before. We were very careful about that. The exchange of watches was the only unplanned thing, and that happened before any of us had time to think about it and realise the possible danger.' She waggled her left wrist in front of them. 'This is where it was until I handed it to you Mrs Mendoza, and I'm the one who came back because of it. It *has* to be the watch!'

*

'We get the watch back because Dorothy will be wearing it when we bring her back to 2016,' Susan explained. 'Then we transfer it from her wrist to mine, and once Tom does his fuse bit again, then I shall return to my own time.'

Tom ran his finger around the inside of his collar, obviously not keen on doing the fuse bit yet again, and who could blame him?

'But what if you're wrong? What if she isn't

wearing the watch?' Kate said, a worried frown spoiling her face. 'Let's take the best scenario and assume she *is* now back with Susan's family and not lost somewhere in time as Billy suggested earlier. They could have recognised the watch and taken it from her.'

'Father may well have done that,' Susan said, 'but Mother would have returned it to Dorothy had she asked for it.'

'Which she will have,' I said, 'And she'll have a contingency plan as well - I know my girl, she'll have already figured it all out, you can bet your bottom dollar on that.'

Kate filled the kettle. 'Tea anyone?' she asked and we all nodded *Yes*.

Hot drinks and food seem to be her answer to all types of crisis. Probably why Tom's trousers stay up without the need for a belt or braces.

So, we drank tea and tossed ideas around, but there was nothing more to discuss because I knew that at 10:30 on New Year's Eve, Dorothy would be in the hallway with Susan's watch strapped to her wrist, waiting for Tom to perform his conjuring trick with the fuse board and bring her back to me. And in case we hadn't time to send Susan back that night, she would have instructed Mr and Mrs Mendoza to be standing by on another occasion. All of which meant the woman I loved would be locked in my arms in five and a half days' time. Hopefully, that is! We weren't experts and had already discovered to our cost that things can go wrong. My heart sank at the thought. If Dorothy was thirty thousand miles away, I could cover that distance in what? Maybe, a year and a half? I might be a few inches shorter and walking on stumps instead of feet. I might even be a trifle pooped, but I could do it. But she wasn't thirty thousand miles away. She was almost thirty thousand days away, and the fastest jet plane known to man could fly forever without knocking a single one of those days off.

*

I never realised five days would pass so slowly. We dined out twice and I made Spaghetti Carbonara twice. That's about the limit of my cooking skills.

New Year's Eve arrived and the four of us went to the cinema. We watched an old movie called *Man on Fire* that everyone agreed was excellent, heading home at 6pm.

I had a knot in my stomach that I didn't mention it to the others. I'm sure Susan felt the same way I did.

Four and a half hours to go and hopefully, a return to heaven for both of us.

*

Playing cards on New Year's Eve did little to speed things towards the evening deadline of 10:30. Eventually, Dorothy tossed her cards to one side and walked in circles, grumbling that, 'This is such a waste of time!'

The others said nothing. They appreciated how difficult it must be for her.

She stood up, stretching. 'I can't concentrate at all, and I'm letting poor Billy down.' Billy was her partner - their opponents - Maria and Samuel.

No one was playing well. Maria and Billy were too excited at the prospect of seeing Susan again. Even Samuel had the stirrings of excitement within him. Dorothy had put into words what they all felt.

With the cards boxed up and put away, the two women busied themselves laying out a cheeseboard with a selection of biscuits and two types of pickle. On a sideboard was a large iced cake, intricately decorated with the message, *Welcome back Susan.* Alongside the cake were five cut glass champagne flutes, ready to be filled when the time was right. Dorothy looked gloomily at the flutes, thinking, *I've already done this once,* but in the end, there had been nothing to celebrate. She guessed what the others in 2016 were thinking. Not too much excited Billy, although she was certain his heart would be beating at an alarming rate, and Susan? Well, she would be visiting the bathroom every fifteen minutes or so. Cool and calm Kate would be as cool and calm as ever. She would want nothing more than for everything to turn out right and for everyone to be happy.

When the clock showed 8:30, Dorothy, sighed with relief. In just two hours, she would in the arms of the man she loved. Two hours equated to 120 minutes. She paused for a moment as she converted it even further - 7,200 seconds and began to count silently in her head, *one, two, three-*

*

Tom suggested we stop to eat after the cinema. I welcomed the idea, thinking it would pass the time until 10:30 arrived. Most restaurants were fully booked, it being New Year's Eve, but we found a pasta and pizza place and promised to leave by 9:30 as they were fully booked after that. It wasn't a problem to us, not with our time schedule.

Pasta and pizza, Indian and Chinese food, all were relatively new to Susan. In 1926, England was still in its roast beef and two vegetable era.

Tom looked anxiously across at me, 'Do you think it will work this time, Billy?'

I smiled to reassure him. 'Of course it will, Tom. After all, it worked the last time. It went wrong only because we screwed up the formula.'

By then, I believe there was no doubt in our minds that Dorothy would come back to us. We knew why we had failed the last time, so there was no reason for her not to be back.

My mind was sorted out now and I'd returned to my optimistic ways, even planning ahead and thinking where we should go skiing the coming March.

Susan crammed an unladylike forkful of Cannelloni into her mouth and said, 'This food is lovely. Absolutely delicious.'

I couldn't resist teasing her. 'How would you know? It reaches your stomach before your taste buds have a chance to do their job.'

Kate rubbed Susan's shoulder affectionately. 'Leave her alone Billy,' but it was all small talk, spoken to use up the remaining time.

We left the restaurant at 9:20. The journey back would take fifteen minutes, leaving almost an hour to prepare and say our farewells to Susan. And then, the woman I loved would be back with me!

We reached the entrance to the private road leading

up to the house. There was heavy cloud and the moon was hidden from view, meaning it was pitch black with only the car headlamps to light the way ahead. As Tom turned into the road, a figure - seemingly from nowhere, appeared, waving a torch from side to side and barring the way. It was a uniformed policeman and he didn't have to say anything; I instinctively knew we were stuffed! He was around 21 years old; probably fresh out of Police College.

Tom lowered the window and the policeman poked his head into the car, a rueful expression on his young features. 'Sorry to bring bad news to you folks,' he said, 'but there's an escaped prisoner on the loose and somehow, he managed to get himself a gun. He's trapped in the house, which is now surrounded, but it could take a while for us to persuade him to come out.'

Of course, it went without saying that the house he was speaking of was our house. The house with the fuse board, Dorothy's only means of returning to 2016.

After tonight, there was no way of knowing when she would be in *Cherry Tree House* again.

I knew then that I would never see her again. I'm an optimist - not a defeatist by any means; but along with being an optimist, I'm also a realist, and there comes a time when you instinctively know you must accept what fate has mapped out for you, and for me, that time had arrived.

I realised, to my shame, that until now I had only been thinking of myself.

I turned to Susan who was sobbing inconsolably.

She took my hand and gripped it tightly. 'We've lost them both Billy, haven't we?' and I looked away, not wanting her to see my eyes brimming over.

Somehow I managed to whisper, 'Yes Susan, this time, we really have lost them forever.'

*

Dorothy looked at Susan's watch, now back on her wrist in readiness for her journey through time. 'One minute to go,' she said excitedly, bouncing up and down on the balls of her feet. She crossed to Billy and hugged him tightly. 'Now remember what I said. Once I've returned to 2016, if there's enough time left then we'll send Susan back almost at once, but if not, then we'll do it tomorrow, but she will be back, I promise you, she will be back. But if she doesn't make it tonight, please don't get all morbid. It'll only be because we're too close to the time limit, or at least, what we believe to be the time limit, and after what happened the last time, we won't be taking any chances.' She let go of Billy and turned to Maria. 'I know how Susan is. She'll be beside herself with excitement, waiting to see you again.' She took Maria's hands in her own. 'It's all she ever spoke about.' Finally, she turned to Samuel and gave him a broad smile. 'You haven't figured it out yet Mr Mendoza, I know you haven't, in fact, it's only just occurred to me, but the truth is that you're my great great grandfather. Hard to get your head around, isn't it? I'll bet that not too many people in the history of the world have ever met their great great grandfather. It's a shame that your daughter Celia is away in Italy, because although I know she isn't married yet, she's my great grandmother and I would love to have met her before I went back.'

Samuel had not yet realised any of this and was staggered by the information. 'My word,' he said and Dorothy prodded him in an unladylike way.

'It makes you go all squidgy inside, doesn't it?' Samuel wasn't certain what squidgy meant, but said *yes* anyway.

Billy looked at his watch and turned to Dorothy, 'Time to get in your place,' he said, not wanting her to miss the time slot through idle chatter. He wanted Susan back, and the sooner, the better. Dorothy moved to the spot where Susan had appeared in 2016. She stood still with her feet together. 'Goodbye Great Great Grandma and Grandpa,' she said cheekily and waited.

It was an hour later before the floodgates opened and she sobbed uncontrollably. She had kept a positive attitude and counted so much on getting back, but failing now was more than she could bear. Billy moved forward and took her in his arms. He held her tightly to him, stroking her hair and whispering softly in her ear at the same time. 'We will find a way Dorothy, I promise you. You *will* be back with your Billy, just as I will be with Susan. I don't know how or even when, but we *will* find a way to send you back to your own time.'

Chapter Fifteen

It was two in the morning before the escaped prisoner finally gave himself up. He'd be going to hospital and not jail, if I had got my hands on him.

One of the policemen explained that someone at the station read through the prisoner's file and discovered that this violent man was actually afraid of the dark. Armed with this information, the local electricity board was instructed to cut off the supply of electricity to the house.

Minutes later, the prisoner came through the front door with his hands held up in surrender. By the time the power was restored, we all got to bed at around three o'clock. Despite the late hour, with all that had gone wrong, there was no way I could sleep. After a fruitless hour of trying, I went downstairs to make a hot drink.

Susan had beaten me to it. I sat next to her and took a sip from her mug of hot chocolate. 'What, you too?' I said tiredly.

'Me too,' she answered, her eyes bright with tears.

'What are we going to do Billy?' and as the tears began to flow, I saw a helplessness about her that really got to me. I had no answers for her though.

'God knows, Susan, I know that I don't. Everything we try seems destined to fail. In the end, it all gets to you and you begin to think that it isn't worth the effort of trying again.'

She stopped crying and looked at me sharply. 'So you're giving up then are you?'

I banged my hands on my knees and stood up, saying, 'No way José, no way!'

She gave me a strange look. 'Why did you call me José? That isn't my name,' and I couldn't help but grin. We were back to the 90-year time difference again.

'It's just an expression Susan,' I explained. 'Roughly translated it means, *not on your life.*' And then, just like that, I was raring to go. It's strange how a few hours can change your outlook. I know what I said earlier, but that was then and this is now. I would never give up! We found a way once, so we could find a way again.

The two of us nodded off in the kitchen until the sound of footsteps on the stairs woke the pair of us.

Kate and Tom trundled into the kitchen and stared in surprise. 'Bloody hell me boy, did you wet the bed again? Your mum told me you were always doing it.'

'No she didn't! Don't tell lies!' I snapped, but he grinned happily. Humiliation was his game and he was good at it.

Kate tutted. 'Honestly Tom! What a thing to say,' so I explained quickly in case a domestic was brewing.

'Neither of us could sleep, so we had a mug of hot chocolate and were going over our next move, but nodded off without intending to.'

Tom shook his head, 'There is no next move Billy; putting it bluntly, we're fucked.'

Kate obviously agreed because she didn't reprimand him for swearing in front of Susan. Instead, she rummaged around in a kitchen cupboard, found a frying pan and asked, 'So, have either of you come up with *anything*?'

Seeing the frying pan, I said, 'I'll fill you in over breakfast; you do the cooking while I make the coffee and toast.'

I got the coffee mugs from a cupboard and Kate pointed towards me, 'Will you look at that, Thomas Cox! Some men don't mind helping with what you call *women's work!*'

Tom sat down to read yesterday's papers yet again, 'Thanks mate,' he muttered under his breath.

Fifteen minutes later we were eating bacon, eggs and fried tomatoes along with a stack of toast. Susan effortlessly cleared her plate before making short work of the last four slices of toast, but I was stuffed. I pushed my plate away and opened up the subject of our next move and my conclusions. 'I know Dorothy. She'll guess we attempted to bring her back last night, but that something went wrong. Knowing how her mind works, she will assume that we'll try again tonight.'

I looked at the others; none of them disagreed, but they remained silent. 'Well say something,' I said sharply. 'Is it agreed? Shall we give it another go?'

In unison, they said, 'Agreed.'

I suddenly remembered what day it was, 'Oh, and by the way,' I smiled, 'Happy New Year to all of you.'

We stayed in the house for the rest of the day, either watching DVDs or listening to CDs, but even so, it was a long day for all of us. The time seemed to drag by.

The evening eventually arrived and Kate cooked spaghetti soaked in a red wine and herb sauce. Afterwards, we chatted to pass the remaining minutes until Tom, who had been clock watching for the past half hour, glanced again at the wall clock and stood up. 'It's 10:20,' he said, 'time we were in our places, folks.'

In unison, we moved into the hall. I didn't know what to expect now. After yesterday and its disappointment, I couldn't bring myself to truly believe it would be successful this time. Some things simply aren't meant to be! Dorothy was far too good for me. She was a real go-getter, whereas I, without the help of Tom Cox, would now be living in a bedsit - sharing with a stranger in the same dire circumstances as me, and everything that had happened so far was nature's way of rescuing Dorothy from my clutches!

Tom got the torch from the cupboard in readiness, handing it to me while he fitted the nail into the fuse holder. After two nerve shattering explosions, he was apprehensive about doing it for a third time. He looked hopefully at me and asked, 'Do you want to do this bit Billy?'

Not wishing to even remotely build up his hopes, I said, 'I'd sooner eat dogs' poo.'

'This is so bloody unfair of you,' he snapped, 'after all, it's your girlfriend that we're trying to bring back,' but unfair or not, he screwed his eyes into tight little slits, stretched out his arm and pushed the fuse in.

This time, I was sure the walls rocked with the force of the explosion. The light was so bright, it seared through my closed eyelids. Seconds passed and then I swallowed hard to clear my ears, rubbed my eyes and clicked on the torch, but there was nothing for me to see. No Dorothy, no lost love, nothing, and now, not even hope. Only the realisation that I would be spending the rest of my life without her.

*

Dorothy's face was contorted by anger and she was close to tears. 'I don't care if it does turn out to be a waste of time,' she shouted at Samuel, her eyes blazing. 'It's only one day, that's all. Surely *even* you can sacrifice one day for the chance of getting your own daughter back.'

Samuel curbed his own rising anger. He'd had the temerity to deny Dorothy's request to remain at *Cherry Tree House* for an extra day in order to try once again, and now he was bearing the brunt of her response. He was a calm man who could handle most things in life, but a hysterical woman wasn't one of them. If his dominated wife ever realised that fact, then her married life would be very much easier.

He held up his hands - a gesture of defeat, speaking quickly to stem Dorothy's anger. 'One more attempt,' he sighed impatiently, 'and then, do I have your promise that will be the end of it, young lady. Is that agreed?'

Relief flooded through Dorothy. 'Yes, yes - that will be it! You have my promise,' but she had crossed her fingers as she said it, so it could be broken and her conscience wouldn't bother her.

Samuel might have missed seeing this, but Maria hadn't. She smiled softly across to Dorothy, the message *Well done!* made very clear by the expression on her face. If this attempt should fail, there would be other times, whatever Samuel chose to think now. Now that she knew Susan was alive, she would never stop trying to get her back.

So, once again at 10:30, Billy, Samuel and Maria stood in the hall waiting as Dorothy took her position on her spot.

It was eleven o'clock when at Samuel's insistence they gave up and went off to their beds. Dorothy lay awake for several hours wondering why Billy hadn't tried again, and puzzling over what could have happened on New Year's Eve that left her stranded in a different era. He loved her and would want her back - she was positive of that, so it wasn't worth wasting energy thinking about it, but nevertheless, why was she still here? What had happened that stopped it taking place? After all, the process wasn't exactly rocket science. Along with Billy and the Mendozas, all she had to do was stand in the hall at 10:30 p.m., while 90 years forward, Kate, Susan and Billy had to do the same while Tom pushed in the fuse.

It was the lack of communication that was the problem. If they could strip that one problem away, then everything would become easy, but how was it possible to communicate, when 90 years separated them? They couldn't, it was impossible, but her being here in the first place was also impossible, wasn't it? Dorothy knew then there was only one way forward. She must set her mind and cast all other thoughts aside other than discovering a way of contacting them. It was the only answer. She must find a way to bridge more than 30,000-day gap. That was the key to everything, and if she could find that key, then finding a way back would automatically follow. If she failed to succeed, she would be a wrinkled old woman by the time her Billy was born.

Either that or dead!

*

On the first night of the year 2017, Billy lay awake, wondering, just as Dorothy had, what had gone wrong. The escaped prisoner was just bad luck. A chance in several million, but this evening - what had on earth had happened this evening that caused them to fail? He'd been certain Dorothy would be in tune with his line of thinking, and would be waiting in the hall for him to bring her back.

But like many other seemingly complicated things in life, the answer was a simple one. The oversized wall-clock in the kitchen, which they automatically relied on for the time, was powered by the main electricity supply. With the power turned off by the supply company the previous evening, the clock stopped, automatically restarting again when the supply was reconnected 35 minutes later. Without any of them noticing this, it had actually been 11:05 when they made their attempt at bringing Dorothy back, and not the 10:30 they believed it to be. With the clock so prominent, none of them bothered to check the time by their watch.

Samuel Mendoza would broach no further argument from Dorothy, so when he insisted that they stopped this rubbish and retire to their beds, she ran up the stairs to her room at 11:00 on the verge of tears. So, at 11:05, when Tom and Billy tried to bring her forward in time, the hallway was empty, with Dorothy no longer in her place as she waited to be returned to the future. They had missed her by five minutes. Three hundred seconds was the scant amount of time that had kept Billy from the woman he loved.

*

With Dorothy trapped in another time, I needed to invent a story explaining her absence to her parents. The truth was obviously out of the question. I asked Kate and Tom to come with me to add weight to the story I'd decided upon.

I explained that their daughter was on an archaeological dig in central Africa. That she was holidaying in Morocco when the invitation came, so cut short her holiday and set off with the other *diggers*. Dorothy promised to send them a card if anyone able to post it passed through the site of the dig.

'And send me one as well,' I said hopefully. 'I'll be lost until she gets back.'

I noticed Tom's disapproving look and guessed I'd be lectured later on, although I hadn't a clue why.

Kate did her bit by saying she had been with Dorothy in Morocco when it happened.

I breathed a sigh of relief when I saw that between us, we had convinced them.

Mr and Mrs Curtis thanked us for coming and I promised to stay in touch.

We left and as expected, Tom's lecture was immediate. 'For God's sake Billy! Why did you add the bit about you being lost without Dorothy? You had already sold the story to them, so once you've sold - stop selling.' He huffed impatiently. 'You've got a lot to learn, me boy. No wonder you've never made any real money!'

The following week I bought some plain post-cards and Tom, a gifted forger, wrote them out and signed with Dorothy's signature - copied from a letter in her business records. The cards conveyed simple messages such as, '*Having a wonderful time, Love you both and hope you're well.*' I had the task of having them posted from Africa. Not difficult when one of your acquaintances is an airline stewardess.

*

Nothing happened over the following months, but without Dorothy having a means of communication, nothing could. For the moment, she could only accept her lot. She had settled into 1926 better than expected, although Billy was always in her thoughts. As for her business? Well, she started from scratch once before and could do it again. That wasn't the important thing, Billy was.

August and the Mendoza family were taking a four-week vacation at *Cherry Tree House*. Celia had long since returned from Italy, and despite Dorothy's resolve to find a way back to her own time, for the moment, her only choice was to accept her lot.

She knew Billy would be trying to find a method

of getting her back to him. It was just a matter of time before one of them found the solution.

Only a few years in age separated Dorothy and Celia and as the months passed, they became close - even more than friends, although Dorothy sometimes smiled to herself, thinking it must be the first case in history of a great granddaughter being older than her great grandmother.

Although Dorothy's knowledge of twentieth century history was weak, there were obvious things that she explained to her new family. Important things, such as the coming Wall Street crash, but Samuel Mendoza smiled condescendingly when she spoke of World War Two. 'Germany is on its knees Dottie. Are you seriously saying that in just 12 years' time, they will be strong enough to battle the rest of the world and almost win? What rubbish my girl! You have obviously been misinformed.'

Dorothy cringed, not at his scepticism - she'd learnt to accept that - no, it was whenever he called her Dottie, as if *Dorothy* wasn't bad enough! She tried to get her own back by calling him Pops, but that ploy backfired on her. Samuel Mendoza - the Chairman of a multi-million pound company and trustee of the financial wellbeing of thousands of shareholders and pompous to a ridiculous degree - delighted in the name Pops, to the point where Celia now used it.

'Well, Pops,' Dorothy said through gritted teeth, 'six million Jews were exterminated by Hitler. I would think that even you would agree that it's a huge amount of misinformation.'

Samuel gave one of his rare laughs. 'Now Dottie, be

reasonable my dear. Are you seriously trying to say that that jumped up little German fellow who recently published his ridiculous book, *Mein Kampf,* is going to lead Germany into battle against the rest of the world?'

'Yes,' she sighed, knowing she was wasting her time by even discussing it. His mind was already closed. 'The rest of the world Pops, apart from Japan and Italy, because they will both be fighting on his side.'

Samuel slapped his knees and roared with laughter.

Dorothy was not used to people doubting her to this degree. Her temperature soared, but then she thought of something that wouldn't resolve the argument there and then, but would very soon. She asked, 'What date is it today?'

Samuel looked at the top of his newspaper and said, 'It's the 3rd of August, Dottie. Why do you ask?'

'What if I told you that Rudolph Valentino will be dead in less than three weeks' time. What would you say to that Pops? Would you still insist I was talking rubbish?'

Samuel continued reading, a sure sign he had grown tired of the discussion. 'A ridiculous statement for you to make Dottie,' he said airily. 'Why - how old is the fellow? Twenty-nine? Thirty?'

'He's actually thirty-one,' Dorothy, a lifelong movie buff, explained. She stored this type of information the way a squirrel stores nuts for the coming winter.

'Well there you are then,' Samuel said, 'Dead at thirty-one. Ridiculous!' He turned a page and sighed impatiently, 'Now will you please stop chattering as I find it difficult to concentrate with this chit chat going on.'

Twenty-one days later on the 24th of August, Samuel glanced at the newspaper headline and stared across at his wife who was arranging flowers freshly picked from the garden.

Dorothy was in her room, feigning a headache. She had been waiting for this day, savouring her forthcoming victory.

'Good God Maria,' Samuel said, almost in a state of shock, 'that fellow Valentino, the one that Dottie mentioned a few weeks back, well, he has gone and died, exactly as she said he would.'

He made no reference to it when Dorothy entered the room an hour later, but she hadn't expected him to, nor did she want him to. Just knowing he knew was enough, but he never again questioned her knowledge of the future and Dorothy remained silent on the subject. In his own way, he was a goodhearted old chap and humiliating him was pointless.

When Samuel left the drawing room, *The Times* went with him and the radio was switched off all day.

He is so funny, Dorothy thought. Why did some people find it impossible to be wrong? What was the big deal?

Their first Sunday in Dorset had been spent at the cricket club, where Samuel played for the local team. He was immaculately dressed, his whites giving off an almost ethereal glow and the creases in his trousers sharp enough to cut butter. He looked the part of a cricketer more than any other team member, but was proof of how deceptive appearances can be. To classify him as a poor batsman would be paying him a compliment, and with his ever-increasing girth, he was far too unfit to be of much use in the field.

Maria, Dorothy and Celia watched his brief turn at the stumps and listened with concealed humour when he recounted his own exploits after the game ended. 'Close call that,' he said as he tucked into a plateful of salmon and cucumber sandwiches. 'Scraped home by three runs.' He brushed crumbs from his moustache before taking another mouthful of sandwich, then added nonchalantly, 'Of course, you realise the team would have lost without my four runs.'

How could they forget? He'd strode manfully towards the wicket, the last man in. The opposition fast bowler thundered down towards him at an alarming rate and hurled the cricket ball forward at a speed guaranteed to hospitalise anyone foolish enough to get in its way. Samuel cringed as the ball hurtled towards him; he shut his eyes and shoved the bat in front of him, hoping it would act as a shield and save his life. The ball struck the edge of the bat with a resounding **crack** and shot off sideways towards the boundary. The nearest outfielder should have easily stopped the ball, but as he ran forward, an undone shoelace tripped him and he sprawled headlong. Unimpeded, Samuel's ball trickled over the boundary with an inch to spare, giving him the first *four* of his cricketing life. His glory was short lived as he was clean bowled by the next ball.

Their leisurely chat was interrupted by a man's voice from behind them, 'Samuel old chap, aren't you going to introduce me to your lovely family?'

Dorothy's intuition was one of her greatest assets. She knew without the slightest doubt that she would dislike the owner of the voice. There was something insidious in its tone. Along with Maria and Celia, she turned to look at the speaker. He was around 35 years old, tall, at least six feet, slim waisted but muscular and with a boyish mop of carefully groomed fair hair above a quite handsome face. She disliked him on sight.

'Ah, yes, but of course,' Samuel said, although introducing this particular man to his family was the last thing he wanted to do. However, good manners must prevail. 'May I present my wife Maria, my daughter Celia and my niece, Dorothy Curtis. Ladies - this is an acquaintance of mine, Mr Digby Jones.'

Dorothy immediately picked up on the fact that Samuel had said *acquaintance* and not friend. That alone spoke volumes. Digby Jones stepped forward and taking Maria's hand, held it to his lips. 'And which are you, young lady? Celia or Dorothy?'

Dorothy disliked him even more. Maria was still an attractive lady, but nevertheless, looked close to her age and could never be mistaken for a woman in her twenties. Dorothy spoiled the man's toady remark by saying, 'She is Dorothy, Mr Jones, and I'm her Aunt Maria. We are so pleased to meet you.'

He was completely thrown by this and for a moment, was unsure how to respond.

Samuel smiled inwardly. He had seen Digby's act many times before, but had never seen anyone demolish it the way Dorothy had. He didn't like the fellow at all and thought, *Well done Dottie. Very well done indeed!*

Digby Jones had the good grace to redden slightly and smiled at Dorothy. She knew from the ice in the eyes above the smile that she had made an enemy for life.

As always, politeness left Samuel with no choice other than inviting Jones to join them. Dorothy was as disappointed as Samuel when Jones nodded his handsome head, saying, 'Thank you Samuel. I shall be delighted to.'

He moved to Celia and repeated the hand to lip procedure with the words, 'And you, of course, are Celia.'

Celia blushed a deep shade of red. She was a shy girl without her sister Susan's prettiness and with little experience of men. She stared at the ground and mumbled, 'Yes,' in a quiet voice.

Digby Jones turned his attention back to Dorothy, ready to fire his own salvo and unbalance her with his next remark. 'Well, you must forgive me for saying it, but beautiful though you are, for a moment I almost believed you. After all, you do look almost old enough to be their mother, but not quite.'

'I say old chap, steady on,' Samuel spluttered, but Dorothy ignored the insult. The opinions of toads such as Jones mattered not one iota. Let them cross swords with her at their peril. She smiled graciously. 'Actually Mr Jones, you would be surprised at how young I am. Why, I'm probably young enough to be your great granddaughter.'

Samuel flashed a warning look while Maria laughed uncomfortably. She understood only too well what was taking place between Dorothy and Digby Jones.

A three-letter word summed it up. War.

For the rest of the afternoon, Jones clung to the family like a limpet. Maria was more than a little perturbed, watching Celia respond to the man's attentions. She would speak to the girl later, warning her of the type of man Jones was.

Eventually, the sun dipped and the two teams and their families took their leave.

Digby Jones watched the three women and Samuel climb into the Rolls Royce. He would be travelling home in a tiny Austin car, borrowed from his uncle and deliberately parked a mile from the cricket ground. A Rolls Royce might be a car to be seen in, but a tiny Austin most definitely was not!

One day in the future, he intended to be driving a Rolls Royce. Just a matter of time - a matter of finding a woman from the correct background. Correct, of course, meaning wealthy.

The Rolls pulled away and Jones watched, sure of what would happen next. The car had covered twenty odd yards when Celia waved to him through the rear window. Digby Jones waved back and then began the long trudge to his uncle's vehicle. But he whistled happily as he walked and a satisfied glow filled his belly. Perhaps *his* day was about to arrive sooner than he had dared to hope. Much, much sooner.

Chapter Sixteen

Back at his uncle's tiny terraced house, Digby Jones, unable to afford the whisky he felt he deserved, sat drinking tea as he planned the first move in his new campaign. He had waited a long time for this opportunity and wasn't about to let it slip through his fingers. With Digby's handsome features and good physique, women had always been attracted to him and he'd had several chances in the past, but always the girl's father proved to be a man of straw. But this time it was different. Samuel Mendoza's wealth was beyond question and Digby had no intention of making a mess of things. He knew that time was running out for him. The bathroom mirror revealed that information free of charge. Fresh lines on his face warned that there weren't many years before the ravages of time made inroads on his good looks.

Digby never sold himself short. He knew he appealed to certain women in a rakish sort of way, but the things he said sometimes worked against him. The incident with Maria Mendoza earlier was a prime example. He knew, even as he put her hand to his lips that he was about to say the wrong thing, but the words spilled out anyway.

And that interfering cow of a girl, Dorothy, made the incident far worse. He paused for a moment, thinking back. Dorothy Curtis! Interfering she might be, but a real woman if ever he'd seen one. Oh, to have her tied down on his bed, begging for mercy as he slaked his lust on her again and again. He could teach that clever bitch a lesson.

Just thinking of that scenario stirred his loins, but he forced himself to get his thoughts back on track. Campaigns weren't won by sexual fantasies. They were won by careful planning and attention to detail. He'd stumbled at the winning post too many times to allow it to happen again.

*

The night of the cricket match, Celia had difficulty sleeping - difficulty doing any of the things she normally did. Ten pages remained of the novel she was reading, but it stayed in the bookcase. The piano was silent and the woollen jumper she was knitting lay on the sideboard, untouched.

A heavy sleeper, Celia remained awake into the early hours of the morning, her head full of delicious daydreams with Digby Jones in all of them. The feeling she had in the pit of her stomach was new to her. Apart from Jed, the gardener's assistant back at *Rose Cottage*, she hadn't had a crush on anyone. She was just fourteen then and foolishly revealed her feelings to her father. Samuel spoke to the gardener that same day and Jed never came to *Rose Cottage* again. Celia had no intention of being taught the same lesson twice. Her feelings would remain private.

Her heart raced when she studied the slip of paper Digby secretly passed to her that afternoon. On it was a telephone number that – should she live to a hundred, she would never forget. Celia held the paper to her cheek before ripping it to pieces and flushing them down the WC.

Written next to the number had been the message, '*I must see you again. I beg you to call me between 10 and 11am on Friday,*' but could she wait that long, or would her heart burst with excitement first? It had pounded in her chest since setting eyes on Digby. It was still pounding now. As a young girl, she had dreamt this was how it would be.

Celia knew Digby felt the same way, or why had he given her the note?

She was more alive than at any time in her life. The world had become fresher, bigger, more exciting! At last it had happened for her, and no one could spoil it because no one would know. It would be her secret. She would tell no one, not even her newly found relative Dorothy with whom Celia shared everything.

*

Celia rang the number at one minute past ten and Digby grabbed the receiver on the second ring. 'Please say it is you Celia,' he said breathlessly, 'for I cannot wait another second to hear your voice.'

This was music to the inexperienced ears of Celia. Her wildest dreams never included such words and she asked meekly, 'Is that Mr Jones?'

'It's Digby, not Mr Jones.' He sighed rapturously.

'Oh my sweet Celia, thank you for calling. Thank you, thank you! My mind has been consumed with thoughts of you. Utterly, utterly consumed.'

Celia had never expected to hear such words. She said meekly, 'You wanted me to call?'

'More than anything!! Tell me Celia, for I must know. Do you feel the way I do? It's like nothing I have experienced before. I cannot sleep since meeting you. Cannot eat, cannot work and cannot think straight. My mind is constantly filled with a vision of you.'

Celia felt light headed, not realising Digby had spoken those same words to so many different women that he could have repeated them in his sleep.

Not one of Celia's daydreams could match these words spoken by Digby. Her heart pounded in her chest. 'Yes Digby, it is so. Since meeting you, I can no longer think straight.'

Digby relaxed and put his feet on his desk and studied his fingernails. So, Celia Mendoza was already his for the taking! 'I must see you again Celia,' he said breathlessly, 'and soon. Even today, if it is possible.'

Celia was stunned. She hadn't expected this urgency! This wonderful man didn't just want to see her again; he needed to see her *today*! Her heart raced, knowing it was possible. Dorothy and her parents had gone to Weymouth for the day but she had cried off, feigning a migraine, knowing Digby expected her to call.

Samuel explained that they were dining out that evening and wouldn't be home before nine. Celia almost cried with excitement, knowing she would have hours alone with Digby. 'Do you know our address at Lulworth Cove, Digby?'

He replied negatively and she directed him to *Cherry Tree House.*

His uncle had chosen that day to go out in the car and Digby pondered on how to overcome that problem. It would look bad if Celia discovered he didn't own a car, but she played into his hands, 'Best not to come by car,' she said, 'someone could mention seeing it to my father.'

Digby said a taxi would get him there within the hour and set about prising open his uncle's savings box. He reached the house fifty minutes later and when Celia opened the door he gave a huge sigh of relief and pulled her to him, smothering her face and neck with kisses. 'Thank God,' he whispered. 'At last my search is over. Here in my arms is the woman I have spent my life searching for.'

A lesser man would be embarrassed to say such things. Would have thought he might be laughed at, but Digby's performance was a practiced routine, perfected on a multitude of women over the past fifteen years. The early rough edges of the act were as polished as pebbles on a beach, worn smooth by the surging ocean.

He swept Celia into his arms, carrying her into what he correctly guessed to be the lounge. Gently, he laid her onto a couch and before Celia could utter a word, once again proceeded to smother her face and neck with kisses. Eventually his lips found hers and they kissed passionately.

Celia could scarcely breathe. Her heart was

pounding and there was a strange feeling deep down in her lower stomach that she hadn't experienced before. How could she tell him this was the first time she had been kissed this way by a man? That she had never even held a man's hand before? Surely he would laugh at her.

'I, -I-, Digby, I-' but he held a finger to her lips to silence her.

'Please say nothing my darling,' he whispered, 'for I know you are going to tell me that I must cease and that you never want to see me again.' He could scarcely suppress a grin as he worked through act one of his routine. 'But I warn you that should you do so, then I shall stand on the lines at the nearest train station and wait for the express to end my misery. You see Celia, already I know that I cannot live without you.'

It was ham in its crudest form, but to Celia, who filled her time reading romantic novels, they were words lifted from the pages of a book. And his threat to end his life rang true, for her very own sister Susan tried to do exactly the same thing. To end her life because the man she loved would never be by her side. She caught her breath and said softly, 'I would never send you away Digby, never!'

He sat up and took her hands in his own, shaking his head and smiling in amazement. 'To think of my wasted years searching everywhere for true love, when all the time you, my darling, were here in Lulworth Cove.'

Celia reached up to stroke his face. She kissed his cheek and softly caressed it. It had happened. At long last a man had fallen in love with her, and not just any man, but one who could have any woman he wanted, and yet had chosen her. '*Cherry Tree House* is our holiday home,' she said, 'which is probably the reason we have never met before. Our proper home is in Buckinghamshire.'

Digby stood up and paced around the room, running his fingers through his hair in distress. 'What on earth am I thinking of Celia? Your father would never accept me as a suitor.'

Digby wasn't a stupid man. Despite Mendoza's politeness to him a few days back, he knew the man despised him. He looked at Celia sadly. 'You see my darling, he and I fell out over a business deal a year ago. It was a complicated thing that I won't bore you with, but I'm afraid that with my superior business skills, I got the better of him. I wish now that I hadn't, for he has never really forgiven me. Although he is always amicable towards me, because of what happened, he would never allow me to court his daughter.'

There was no hesitation in Celia's reply, 'Then he shall not know,' she declared firmly. 'It will be our secret until the time is right Digby, and then we shall face him together.'

Digby suddenly let out a small gasp and his hand went to his forehead in a gesture of despair. 'My God Celia, but it has only sunk in this very minute. Did you not say that this is your holiday home? When are you leaving? How much time will we have together? Oh, Celia, what am I to do when you return to Buckinghamshire?'

Celia had never had a boyfriend of any description. Never even been alone with a man, other than her father and some of his elderly business associates. The poor girl was no match for Digby's combination of expertise, charm and seduction. By lunchtime, clad only in her underwear, she lay in her bed alongside his naked body. His hands slid upwards beneath her slip and glided across her small round breasts. Her heart fluttered in her chest with the excitement of it all. This was what she had always dreamt of. Always wanted, but now that it was happening she was afraid and felt she should stop him, but at the same time was desperate for him to continue.

One of his hands moved downwards and slid inside her lace knickers and she gasped with the sheer thrill of it. But when he turned to slide on top of her, she panicked. 'No Digby, we must not do this, for I am not protected.'

But he whispered reassuringly, 'If that is your only concern my love, then you must not worry, for I cannot have children until I have a simple operation, so it is quite safe my darling.'

The lie floated so smoothly from his tongue that she believed him implicitly. He moved his body downwards and in one swift movement, thrust upwards and was inside her. He moved slowly back and forth, thinking of her father's millions. This was not an act of love as far as he was concerned; this was simply a necessary job to guarantee his future. If he successfully impregnated this woman, there could only be one outcome. Marriage, and along with it, everything he had ever desired. Money, admiration from his fellow man, and power.

Celia was frightened that she would disappoint him. She moved along with his rhythm and clawed at his back, the way heroines in novels always did and he cried out with feigned ecstasy. As he reached his climax, he grunted, filling her with his seed and Celia's gasp of pleasure was real. She was completely out of her league. Outgunned, outmanoeuvred, in love and determined that her father wouldn't spoil things for her.

She had known Digby for a matter of days, but if she had to choose between him and her father, then it was the man lying alongside her who would win.

*

'When can I see you again my darling?' Celia whispered into the telephone. 'Have you forgotten that I'll be returning home to Buckinghamshire in less than two weeks?'

The words registered, but Digby was desperate to see if the horse carrying the bulk of his savings had won its race. He continued reading the sports page of the newspaper, frowning with annoyance as he scanned the racing results. The stupid animal had lost by a length, leaving him with less than the price of a good meal to keep himself alive for the remainder of the week.

'Digby? Are you still there?' Celia asked anxiously, and he pulled his thoughts back to the woman who was now his guarantee of a luxurious future.

'Sorry my love, I would love to see you today, but it's impossible to come to your house as your parents will be there, and my idiot of a business partner has gone to Manchester for the rest of the week, inadvertently taking the keys to the safe with him.' He gave a baleful sigh, 'I always keep my funds in the safe. It's the only way that I can get insurance on large amounts of money.'

'We could meet at your house,' Celia said hopefully and Digby studied the peeling paintwork and damp patches all around him. Even a Plain Jane like Celia would send him packing if she saw this dump.

'Not possible I'm afraid my love. I'm having the place completely redecorated and there are workmen everywhere. The house is so large that they will be here for the remainder of the year.' He sighed theatrically. 'I can't imagine why I bought it in the first place. What on earth does a bachelor like myself want an eight-bedroom house for? I must have taken leave of my senses.'

Celia checked again to be certain no one was close by and said, 'I'd love to see the house Digby. It sounds wonderful!'

'It is wonderful, and you shall see it my love, but not until the work is completed. I'm afraid we're at an impasse. What do we do now?'

'A hotel?' Celia said hopefully. 'There's always that option.'

'You are such a naughty girl,' he admonished. 'You weren't listening when I said my money is in the company safe and Frank is now in Manchester with the safe keys in his pocket.'

'Then I shall pay,' Celia declared. 'I have over six hundred pounds that I've saved from my allowance. We can use that.'

Digby listened in disbelief, looking at the four walls around him. Six hundred pounds would buy three hovels like this one, and yet she had managed to *save* that much from her allowance? How much could the allowance be? He replied, 'I am sorry my love, but I couldn't allow that. I want to see you so badly that it hurts, but cannot have a woman paying for my pleasure.'

He capitulated on the third, *Please Darling* and arranged to meet her at the local hotel in two hours' time.

He was already in the hotel room waiting when Celia arrived. She was red faced with embarrassment when she addressed the manager, 'I have a business meeting with a Mr Jones. Would you be so kind as to direct me to his room please?'

The manager grinned, indicating that he knew exactly what type of business it was and said, 'Of course Madam.' Over the years, Jones had many such business meetings, all with young women and it was always the young women who settled the bill afterwards. He pointed along the dark corridor towards the stairs. 'Mr Jones is waiting for you in room 101 on the first floor.'

Celia hurried away from the desk and a few moments later, rapped softly on the door of room 101. Digby answered, naked except for the towel around his waist. The towel dropped to the floor as he pulled her into the room. Within seconds she was on the bed and he was smothering her with kisses as he removed her clothes. 'Quickly my love, I must be inside you this very moment,' and thrust inside her with a force that made her cry out in pain. He shuddered dramatically and let out a long, ecstatic sigh. 'We are one now, my darling,' he whispered, 'and if I should die at this very moment, then I would die a happy man with no regrets.'

Celia blinked back the tears of happiness as he began to move his hips in a steady rhythm, pacing himself until after a few minutes, he knew she was as close as he was.

Were other men like him, he wondered. It was the thought of her dowry that had brought about his erection - certainly not the woman beneath him.

He increased his speed smoothly, like a horse moving from a trot to a gallop - and as he reached the final stretch, saw that she was with him all the way. He let out a soft, deliberate moan as he released his sperm into her, praying that it would find its target and end his financial worries forever.

Celia's nails had dug so deeply into his shoulders they had drawn blood, but Digby felt it was a small price to pay for the many benefits he would receive.

Afterwards, Celia lay in his arms with a warm glow in the pit of her stomach, profusely thanking her maker for sending this wonderful man to her. When they were married, as they would be after she proved Digby was an honourable man to her father, then Digby would have the operation enabling him to father a child and they would raise their own family.

Digby's thoughts went in an entirely different direction to Celia's. He lay there wondering how many times he must endure sleeping with this plain little bitch before she became pregnant, thus putting him on an irreversible path to great riches, but he need not have worried. Nature had ensured his mission was accomplished on that first afternoon at *Cherry Tree House*.

*

Digby was stretched out on his uncle's rickety old sofa with a pile of unpaid bills scattered on the floor around him. He wondered how long he must endure this when the telephone rang, it was Celia. 'Darling, something has gone wrong. My period is late. This has never happened before, never! I am obviously pregnant darling. Whatever was wrong with you must have healed without the need for surgery. Oh, Digby, what are we to do?'

She had been back at *Rose Cottage* for almost a week and this was the first time she was alone and could call him.

Digby's worries melted away. He grabbed a handful of outstanding bills and tossed them into the air, knowing his problems were almost over. 'Digby?' Celia said. 'Did you not hear what I said?'

He calmed himself and settled down, 'So you're late are you Darling? Well, you mustn't worry about it. You were a virgin when we first made love and strange things can happen to a woman in the following months. A doctor once explained to me it's nature adjusting itself. As I've explained, I need surgery to become a father. You cannot be pregnant, it's impossible.'

Hearing this, Celia relaxed and spoke softly into the mouthpiece, 'When can meet again Digby? It seems an eternity since I last saw you.'

'No can do my love,' Digby answered. 'Frank has

gone off with the safe keys yet again. I despair of the man. Much more of it and I'll be giving him his marching orders.'

'But how can you?' Celia asked. 'You said he was your partner.'

Digby laughed derisively, 'And so he is my love, but very much a *junior* partner. All the money in the business is mine. The poor chap was penniless when he came to me. Took me for a bit of a chump I suppose, but that's my trouble. I've always been too soft with people like Frank. I think, *there but for the grace of God, go I,* but this stupidity has to stop or I'll have no option but to send him on his way. Thanks to him, we shall be apart for a while longer and that's all there is to it.'

'Darling, please don't be stubborn,' Celia pleaded. 'Come to Buckinghamshire by train and I shall pay for it at this end.'

'Sorry Celia,' Digby replied in a no-nonsense tone, 'but my mind is made up on this issue. No, no, no, no, so please don't mention it again or I shall be very cross with you.'

Celia began to cry; not pretend tears to get her own way, but genuine tears at being deprived of seeing the man she was so utterly besotted with. 'Please darling,' she cried. 'I want to see you. I can b-book a hotel room and you can stay overnight so that I can also see you the f-following day as well.'

He smiled at how easily he had achieved success with this woman. He graciously capitulated. 'All right, all right,' he said, 'I'll come by train, only will you please stop crying? This is extremely selfish of you my love. You must know how much it hurts me to hear you crying when I'm unable to comfort you,' and so they arranged to meet the following afternoon and ended the call.

Digby whistled jauntily as he threw the bills into the rubbish bin. Ten minutes later he flicked through the pages of the newspaper until he reached the horse racing section and studied the odds on the following day's runners.

Chapter Seventeen

The following month Celia missed her second period and told Digby her doctor would visit *Rose Cottage* to examine her. 'I know I am not pregnant darling,' she said, 'you have assured me of that. This is to be certain there is nothing wrong with me. After all, one can't be too careful in matters of one's health.'

They were in the hotel that was their regular weekly meeting place. Digby was aghast, knowing the doctor would immediately discover her pregnancy and feel duty bound to inform Mendoza of her condition. Abortion was illegal in England and led to prison sentences, but millionaires? Well, millionaires would be able to circumnavigate minor irritations such as that. However, once the initial three-months of Celia's pregnancy passed, then any attempt at abortion would endanger her life, and Samuel Mendoza would never take that route.

Digby squared his shoulders and sat up in the bed. With four weeks left before his luxurious future was assured, it was time to be authoritative. 'Now listen to me Darling,' he began in a tone broaching no argument from her, 'I've already explained what my doctor friend said, and he is one of the country's top gynaecologists. When a girl is a virgin, many strange things happen after she's lost her virginity. These things can, and do last for a few months and undoubtedly, that is the case here. And have you considered the consequences of your doctor consulting you at the house? Unless the man is completely incompetent, he will discover you are no longer a virgin. How long would it be before he informed your father? Five minutes? Ten at the most, I would think.'

Celia flushed with embarrassment. 'How stupid of me Digby; I am so, so sorry! Please don't worry. Dr Lawrence will *not* be coming to the house, nor shall I visit his surgery.'

Digby relaxed, thinking this was easier than shelling peas. He drew back the bedclothes and slid onto Celia. 'Right then my darling, now that has been settled, are you now ready for a second helping?'

Celia smiled and drew him into her. 'Always, my love, always.'

*

We were in a meadow, watching the sun dipping low in the sky. I looked at Susan and again saw her startling resemblance to Dorothy. Now, thinking of the woman I loved, I said softly, 'I wonder what Billy and Dorothy are doing right now.' Whenever we spoke of them, we usually said, *right now*, even though 90 years separated us.

We always assumed they were following a parallel path to ours, but with 90 years between the paths.

I found it easier to assume that Dorothy was living with the Mendozas and not lost somewhere in time. Susan squeezed my hand, 'Whatever they're doing, my Billy will protect Dorothy the way you're protecting me.' She kissed me on the cheek. 'And thank you for that, but I know we will eventually find a way for us girls to return to our own time and to our own *Billy Monroe,*' but her words couldn't lift my desolate mood. If anything, the reverse applied. I wanted to feel Dorothy's lips on my own; wanted to hold her in my arms again - I'd settle for that at the moment.

Tom and Kate returned from their hike in the nearby woods and obviously recognising my low mood, asked, 'What are you two talking about?'

I let out a long sigh, 'Oh, just the usual - talking about Dorothy and Billy.'

Tom held out his hand and hauled me to my feet. 'Something will break soon me old mate,' he said. 'I can feel it in my water,' but he had been saying that for months now and the only thing close to breaking was my spirit.

*

Dorothy was awake at four in the morning. She must persuade Samuel to sell *Rose Cottage*! What an idiot she'd been. Some things can be overlooked without bad consequences, but this wasn't one of them and she realised that they were almost out of time. 'You have to sell *Rose Cottage* Pops,' she said urgently at the breakfast table. 'Sell it immediately, and not just to anyone but to someone named Sinclair.'

Billy, spending the evening with the Mendozas, stared at Dorothy, thinking the stress of her situation had caused her to take leave of her senses, while Maria, busy knitting a cardigan, dropped a stitch and put the knitting to one side, knowing she had no chance of giving the job the necessary concentration. 'What on earth are you talking about my dear?' she asked, thinking that of all the strange things Dorothy had said during her time with them, this was the strangest. 'Why should we sell our home Dorothy?' she asked. 'Do you not realise that Samuel and I love it here at Wooburn Green? We thought you did too, but we were obviously quite wrong!'

Despite the urgency of the situation, Dorothy smiled inwardly. How could she *ever* explain to these lovely people the difference between life in a sleepy Buckinghamshire village compared to the manic hustle and bustle of 21st century Chelsea? But Maria had been correct in her assumption. She did love living in Wooburn Green, but in a different kind of way. 'I worded that really badly,' she said, 'so let me explain exactly why it is that you must sell *Rose Cottage*.

'My Billy visited here last year - that's 2016 I'm talking about when I say *last year*, and it was owned by an old lady who was born in the nineteen twenties. Her father bought the house in 1927 from a Mr and Mrs Mendoza - a couple devastated by the loss of their daughter. A couple who couldn't bear to live here any longer because the memory of their daughter was in every room.'

Billy grinned and chipped in with, 'Her would-be fiancé was also rather cut up about it you know,' and Dorothy smiled softly at him.

'Of course you were silly. We all know that. It's been as tough on you as it has on anyone.'

'I understand what you're saying Dorothy,' Maria said, 'but now that we know our Susan is safe and that one day, hopefully, we shall have her back here with us, then surely we have no reason to sell the house. No reason at all.' She let out a soft chuckle. 'I'm sorry but it sounded so ridiculous when you said an old lady who was born in the nineteen twenties. Right now, that old lady is just a little girl of six.'

Even the normally dour Samuel smiled at this piece of information.

'Well then, how is this for a reason to sell *Rose Cottage*,' Dorothy continued. 'As you know, I believe that Susan isn't here with you now because of the formula. The two of you and Billy here have to be at Lulworth Cove at 10:30 at night, and Susan and the others in 2016 must be in the house at the same time. Well, not the same time, but you know what I mean by that. Ninety years on, but the corresponding date and hour must be the same.'

Samuel had long since put his newspaper to one side. He leant forward interestedly. 'Then if that is so, we shall stay at *Cherry Tree House* permanently and wait in the hall every night at 10:30. I'd be prepared to do that if it gets our Susan back, Dottie.'

Dorothy smiled. He had changed so much since the day she first arrived. Should they succeed in bringing Susan back to 1926, she would find a very different father to the one she had last seen.

'I'm sure that you would Pops, but Tom can scarcely blow the electrical supply every night, because it shuts down the power in the surrounding area. It wouldn't take long before the electricity company investigated if that kept on happening. Supposing they changed the electrical set up. We would never get her back then.' She paused, adding sadly, 'And I'd be stuck here and could never return to my real life.'

Maria's brow furrowed, 'Would that be so terrible my dear? Don't you like being with us?'

Dorothy took the older woman's hands in her own. 'Of course I do, silly. You surely realise that I love both of you and shall miss you terribly when I do get back to my own time. It's important to me that you know that.'

Samuel gave a loud *Harrumph,* grabbed the newspaper and concealed his blushing face by holding it out in front of him. Dorothy smiled. Sometimes he was so sweet but whatever happened, his code dictated that a stiff upper lip prevailed at all times.

She turned to Billy. 'And I shall miss your friendship too, Billy. You're a nice guy, but just as you miss Susan, I miss my own Billy and want to be with him, so although I do like it here, I like my own time even more. Anyway, enough of all that. Let me tell you why you must still go ahead and sell, just as you did before, well, not actually before because you haven't done it yet so it can't be before, but very soon.' She huffed, shook her head and her brow creased. 'Isn't this time thing difficult? I think it's a real bummer!'

But Samuel smiled, 'Please continue Dottie. Both Maria and I understand exactly what you mean.'

'You sold this place to Petula Sinclair's father and Petula was still living in it up until she passed away last year. In her will, she left *Rose Cottage* to Beth, a woman who had been her companion for over twenty years. Now, I know that Beth loves it there,' she smiled and shook her head, 'I mean *here*, and intends to see the remainder of her days out here. Anyway, this is the point! After my Billy first visited *Rose Cottage*, he told me that the library was never used. Petula had explained to him the reason why. Apparently, neither she nor her parents were avid readers, so the library was unused. She said it wasn't even kept dusted. Now, this is the interesting part; she also said that Beth loved to read but wasn't allowed in there.'

She paused momentarily and Samuel leant forward, his brow furrowed, 'Where is this leading Dottie?'

'It's leading to getting Susan back Pops. I know that if I inherited this house and loved reading, one of the first things I'd want to do would be to look in the very room I'd been banned from, namely, in this case, the library, and I'll bet that Beth is no different. So, all we have to do is leave a list of dates somewhere in the library and Beth *must* find that list eventually and contact my Billy. Then we have only to visit Lulworth Cove on every one of the dates until eventually, I, wearing the watch, will be pulled forward in time. Then I'll give the watch to Susan and she'll return to you the following evening.'

She studied her small audience but could read nothing in their expressions. 'So what do you reckon?' she asked anxiously, 'Does all of that make sense to you?'

It certainly did as far as Billy was concerned. She could see that from his enthusiastic nod, although he was becoming so desperate to get Susan back that Dorothy was sure even if she'd said, *Let's try and build a time travel machine,* he would have agreed!

Samuel stood up. Without making a single comment, he walked into the hall, picked up the telephone and dialled the operator. He asked her to ring a number and when the connection was made, said, 'Henry! Glad to find you still alive and kicking old chap. Look Henry, I have decided to sell *Rose Cottage* and want to know the best way to go about it... You can? Wonderful old chap. Maria and I will expect you at eight this evening. Oh, and there is one other thing. A minor detail, but an important one. The house must be sold within a month... Yes old chap, I do understand that it will be a difficult task, but I shall be prepared to almost give it away if I have to. Look, I shall say no more for the moment; we can discuss things in greater detail this evening.'

He returned to the lounge wearing a wide smile and knowing that the others would have heard his side of the telephone conversation. 'Well, that should satisfy even you Dottie. It's all arranged. Henry is a good man and will have things underway by the morning. I'm aware that we only have weeks left, but his contacts are excellent and I'm quite certain he will successfully find a buyer for *Rose Cottage*. The thing we must do now is to sort out exactly what dates we can be at *Cherry Tree House.* The sooner we do that, the quicker you shall return to your own time and the quicker Maria and I will get our daughter back.'

They spent the remainder of the afternoon going

through Billy and Samuel's dairies and logging the dates they could make themselves available to be at Lulworth Cove.

'We could spend the Christmas week there,' Dorothy suggested. 'That's the sort of date Billy and Tom would take a chance on, even if they didn't know whether we'd be there or not.'

Samuel said, 'Good point Dottie,' and meticulously added the coming Christmas dates to the list.

Billy left the house at eight and Dorothy walked outside to the drive with him. The Bugatti was parked by the entrance with the bodywork highly polished. It gleamed in the moonlight. She looked at the car with unconcealed admiration and said, 'Wow! It was nothing like that when I last saw it. I wonder if my Billy has had it restored yet - although I don't reckon it will look this good, no matter how well it's been done.'

'You never know,' Billy said as he kissed her lightly on the cheek and gave her a farewell hug. 'Who knows? It may look even better.' He drove off with a wave and Dorothy stood and waved back until he was out of sight.

'He's so nice,' she said to Maria when she was inside the house again, 'as is my Billy, but there the similarity ends. This Billy Monroe is thorough and meticulous, whereas mine, well let's just say that he's a very different kettle of fish!' She thought of all the jobs he left unfinished and smiled, promising herself that if only she could get back to him, she would never let it annoy her again.

Henry, the man Samuel telephoned earlier, arrived just after eight. The weather had changed for the worse and the air had a winter nip to it. Henry hurried in through the front door, rubbing his hands together to warm them. 'Sorry I'm late old chap,' he apologised and Samuel shook his hand warmly.

'Think nothing of it Henry. It's kind of you to come at such short notice.'

'What are friends for?' Henry said, removing his scarf and topcoat. Samuel led his friend into the warmth of the lounge. They were of similar age and the new arrival had an effervescent personality that Dorothy warmed to. Without knowing anything about him, she thought if anyone could sell *Rose Cottage* in the few months remaining of 1926, it was Henry. He was so different to Samuel that she wondered how they had become friends in the first place.

He departed at 9:30 and had scarcely driven away when another car pulled up in the drive. They heard the front door open and a moment later, Celia walked into the lounge. Samuel glanced at his pocket watch. 'You are late young lady! You are perfectly aware that your time is 8:30,' but before she could reply, Digby Jones appeared from behind her. Had the King of England walked in, Samuel would have been less surprised.

Dorothy saw the self-satisfied smirk on the man's face and was puzzled. Like the rest of them, she hadn't a clue why he was with Celia.

'What the blazes are you doing here Jones?' Samuel asked in far from friendly manner. Celia slipped her hand into Digby's and faced her parents. She could scarcely speak, she was so nervous, but Digby squeezed her hand encouragingly.

Dorothy's stomach flipped over. She instinctively knew what was coming. She stared at Digby, forcing him to meet her eyes but he quickly looked away again. Dorothy shuddered. Watching this loathsome creature squeezing Celia's hand was like watching a thirsty man milking a cow. She waited with revulsion. If her guess was correct, this man was one of her ancestors and it was his blood that flowed in her veins.

'Father, Mummy,' Celia said falteringly, 'Digby and I have something important to tell you.' Dorothy caught Digby's eye again, only this time he didn't look away. His eyes held hers and the triumphant smirk played openly on his lips.

Without a word, Dorothy stood up and left the room.

*

The wedding was arranged for the coming January and Samuel and Maria Mendoza were now extremely glad to be leaving Wooburn Green. 'We shall need to move far away from here now,' Samuel explained to his wife. 'Somewhere such as Cobham or Weybridge in Surrey will be ideal, for people there will never know our daughter's secret. They will assume she has been married for some time.'

True to Samuel's expectations, Henry found a buyer for *Rose Cottage* in less than a week, which was hardly surprising as it was priced at twenty percent below its true value. 'The chap who wishes to purchase it seems quite genuine,' he explained when he called at the house to give Samuel all of the details. 'He is from central London, but his wife is in poor health and they are quite desperate to get away from the smoke and grime of the city and into the fresh air of countryside. *Rose Cottage* will suit them admirably.'

'And this man's name is?' Samuel waited expectantly and Henry smiled.

'It's Weaver. A lovely man. You will quite like him Samuel, for he is a thorough gentleman.'

Dorothy caught Samuel's eye and shook her head, mouthing the word, 'No' in his direction. Samuel didn't ask any questions or even pause for a moment to consider what Henry had said. He simply said, 'I'm sorry old chap, I know that you have worked hard to find a buyer, but I'm afraid this Weaver fellow simply won't be suitable.'

Henry was astounded; his jaw dropped. 'Not suitable,' he spluttered in astonishment. 'What do you mean, not suitable. For God's sake Samuel, you haven't even laid eyes on the man yet. On what grounds can you possibly say he isn't suitable?'

Samuel sighed heavily; he felt more than a little foolish, but despite that he could hardly reveal his true reason - that the house could only be sold to a person bearing the surname Sinclair. 'I'm sorry Henry, it may appear strange to you, but I can assure you that I do have my reasons. I'm sorry, but you will have to find another buyer.'

Any further conversation was stopped by an urgent knock on the front door. Samuel hurried to answer it and was confronted by a smartly dressed couple. A young girl stood between them. The man was red faced with embarrassment at his intrusion and said in an apologetic voice, 'I'm so sorry to trouble you Mr Mendoza, but my daughter is quite desperate to use the lavatory. Would you mind terribly?'

Samuel stared at him as though he were an escaped lunatic on the run. 'Who the devil are you sir?' he asked sternly. 'Do you make a habit of knocking on doors to ask if you may use someone else's lavatory?'

His words caused the man to turn an even deeper shade of red. 'I'm John Weaver,' he explained. 'Henry said for us to stay outside in the car until he'd obtained your permission for us to look around the house. We've studied the outside and it's quite beautiful, but we had hoped to look inside to be absolutely certain that it is suitable for our needs before buying it.'

Samuel cursed Henry under his breath. Now, he personally would have the unpleasant task of telling the Weavers that the house couldn't be theirs, but in the meantime, politeness must prevail. He stepped aside and said, 'Of course, of course old chap. Please come on in. I'm sorry, but Henry hadn't mentioned that you and your family were waiting outside.' He stood to one side and beckoned the three of them inside out of the cold.

As they walked into the hall, Dorothy appeared from the lounge to use the telephone. 'These are the Weavers,' Samuel explained to her and Dorothy smiled a hello to them, thinking they appeared to be nice people and it was a shame that such a cosy little family unit would never own *Rose Cottage*.

The little girl tugged at her mother's skirt and said, 'Quickly Mummy. I can't hold on much longer.'

'Where exactly is the lavatory?' Mrs Weaver asked, looking around and Samuel pointed to a door in the corner. Mrs Weaver took the little girl's hand and hurried towards it. 'Sometimes, Petula,' she scolded, 'you can be such a nuisance,' and as Dorothy heard the name, she smiled with sheer relief. Petula Sinclair, *nee* Weaver. She should have realised earlier that Sinclair was the old lady's married name.

Dorothy went to bed that night with a feeling of immense relief and a warm glow in the pit of her stomach. For the first time, she truly felt that everything was actually on course.

The sale was rushed through and the Weaver family moved into *Rose Cottage* on the fifteenth of December 1927. On the hall table, they found a bouquet of flowers for Mrs Weaver and a bottle of champagne alongside a card from Samuel and Maria wishing them the same happiness that they themselves had whilst living at Wooburn Green.

*

With his future assured, it wasn't long before Digby became his usual arrogant self. He dropped the façade and Celia, who until now could do no wrong, discovered that she could do little that was right. She guessed, quite incorrectly, that Digby was worried about money. She knew it was her fault. She was the cause! He had spent far too much time away from his business in order to be with her, and because of that - because of her selfishness in wanting to see him, he had failed to notice that his unscrupulous partner was stealing from the business, sending the firm into bankruptcy. Everything he owned in the world had gone, including, Digby explained, the eight bedroomed house that he had spent a small fortune on renovating. All of his possessions were now in the hands of the Official Receiver.

Celia was unable to help him with money as her six hundred pound savings had long ago melted away, ably assisted by Digby Jones, but she knew that when they were married and her father had taken him into the business, things would settle down to normal and he would become his former loving self again.

She was unaware that there never had been a business, or a partner, thieving or otherwise. Nothing but an ordinary job from which he'd been dismissed for constantly taking time off, along with bad timekeeping and other extremely serious but unproven things. Celia only knew that she had put the poor, wonderful man under so much strain, and yet even when he discovered she was pregnant, he had acted in the noblest of ways, like the gentleman he was, promising to stand by her. Judging by the horror stories she had heard over the years, there weren't many men who would do that.

*

Furious didn't do justice to Samuel Mendoza's reaction when Celia revealed to him that she was pregnant. Later that evening, with Digby Jones gone from the house and Celia tucked up in her bed, frightened, but at the same time deliriously happy, Samuel and Maria sat facing one another in the lounge, still in a state of shock - Samuel even more so than his wife.

Celia, of all people! Their little girl who had reached the early years of her twenties without ever having a boyfriend - pregnant!

Maria picked up her knitting and began to click away. 'These things happen Samuel,' she said softly, hoping to calm him down, but by then acceptance was already settling in with him. He filled his pipe with tobacco and tamped it down over and over again before putting it to one side and lighting a cigar instead. 'I know that my dear,' he sighed. 'I'm not a fool, and this is the nineteen twenties. A far racier time than the days when we were courting, but to become pregnant by that fellow Jones of all people. Why, the man is nothing more than a fortune hunter. A thorough scoundrel, and now he has achieved his aim at our family's expense. Like it or not, the bounder is about to become our son-in-law.'

After a few moments, when the only sound in the room came from the clicking of Maria's knitting needles, Samuel banged his hands on his knees in sheer frustration and stood up, sending a flurry of cigar ash everywhere. 'By God, but he had better be good to our Celia or I shall show the fellow what for! One wrong move and I shall thrash him to within an inch of his life.'

Maria kept her head down to hide her smile. Of course, she knew that Samuel meant every word he'd said, but she wasn't sure how he'd manage to thrash a six foot 36-year-old man when he couldn't even manage to climb the stairs nowadays without pausing on the top step to catch his breath.

Chapter Eighteen

The four of us were clothes shopping in the Kings Road, Chelsea. It was my idea, but I never mentioned why I'd chosen this particular location. They probably assumed it was to make a change from the shopping centres of Kingston and Shepherds Bush.

The truth was, this neck of the woods made me feel closer to Dorothy.

Winter was around the corner so the pavement cafes were only for the very brave. 'Coffee and cakes anyone?' I asked as a Starbucks came in sight, adding, 'My treat.'

As we sat down, my mobile phone rang. It was a woman whose voice I didn't recognise. She asked, 'Have I got the right number? Is that Mr Monroe?'

'It is, what can I do for you?'

'We have met, Mr Monroe. I'm Beth Reynolds, Mrs Sinclair's companion. Perhaps you remember me?' I sat bolt upright in my seat. The others, realising that the call must be about something important, all stared, waiting for a clue. I mouthed, '*It's Beth.*'

There could only be one reason why the woman was phoning me. She had discovered something in the house. I tried to remain calm and said, 'Of course I remember you Beth. Have you found something that will help Susan with her family history?'

Susan moved closer to me; close enough to also hear what Beth was saying. 'Well yes, Mr Monroe, I have and it's all very strange if you ask me.'

Well, whatever it was probably wouldn't seem strange to the rest of us. My fiancé was trapped 90 years back and the beautiful woman next to me was chronologically in excess of 100 years old. 'What have you found Beth?' I could hear a thump thump and realised it was my own heartbeat.

Beth continued, 'It's a diary Mr Monroe. A 1926 diary - that is what I have found.'

I held onto the table in case I fell. Was this what we had been hoping for? Could the diary contain information that would bring Dorothy back to me?

'And what is it that you think is strange Beth?' I asked as calmly as I could.

'Well, I didn't know what it was at first Mr Monroe, because it was covered in a thick layer of dust, although that's understandable because I found it in the library, and I don't know if Mrs Sinclair ever told you, but no one has been in there for years. She never went near there herself and although I love reading, I was forbidden to go into the room. She was lovely, Mrs Sinclair was, but she could be a bit on the selfish side sometimes. She said I could hardly keep her company if my nose was stuck in a book.' Beth sighed reminiscently. 'I do miss her, Mr Monroe,' and I wanted to scream down the phone, '*Get to the bloody point woman before I have a heart attack and peg it.*' However, I managed to remain calm.

'I'm sure you do miss her Beth. After those many years together, it wouldn't be natural if you didn't. So, what was it about the dairy that you found strange?'

'Well, there was a note inside it telling the finder to contact you Mr Monroe, and once that was done, to hand the diary over to you.'

My high spirits instantly vanished. The diary was obviously meant for the other Billy Monroe, but Beth couldn't know there was another Billy Monroe, not unless Petula told her after my first visit. I stopped speculating; I was jumping to conclusions.

I waited for her to continue. 'Well Mr Monroe, you gave me your mobile number in case I thought of anything that would help Miss Susan?'

'I remember Beth. That's how you were able to get hold of me now.'

'Well, it's true that I kept your number logged in my computer, but I didn't need to look in there for it.'

'Come on now Beth?' I sighed. 'You must have looked it up. How else could you have got in touch with me?'

'Exactly Mr Monroe! How else? Well, how can a note that mentions your name and mobile phone number be hidden inside a 1926 diary that's covered in years of dust when mobile phones weren't invented until the 1980s? How can that be possible Mr

Monroe?'

*

'My daughter tells me that your business has gone under,' Samuel said. He was sitting at the dinner table, directly opposite Digby. He wasn't being unkind by raising the subject, because like it or not, the man would soon be family and would be responsible for Celia's welfare and happiness.

'That is correct sir,' Digby said, pulling a wry face. 'I trusted my partner implicitly, but unfortunately, he repaid that trust by running off with the company funds, which sent it into liquidation.'

Samuel listened intently to the explanation, even though he knew the story was a fabrication. As Jones was about to become his son-in-law, he had been thoroughly checked out.

'Jones was fired from his job with a small building firm for absenteeism,' his investigator told him. 'Apparently, they were pleased to see the back of the man. Money had gone missing and although they were certain that Jones was the culprit, it was impossible to prove.'

With *Rose Cottage* now sold to the Weavers, the Mendoza family had moved into *Cherry Tree House* while the search continued for a suitable residence in the Cobham area of Surrey. The journey from Lulworth Cove to the City of London was lengthy and laborious, so during the week, Samuel often stayed at his club in London, returning to Dorset on Friday evenings. The current conversation was being conducted at Lulworth Cove. 'And exactly where do Bailey and Bailey, the builders, fit into things?' Samuel enquired and Digby turned a deep shade of pink, but said nothing further.

Samuel wasted no time in waiting for an answer that would never come. He ended Jones' discomfort by saying, 'I have a position in the firm for you my boy, should you want it. We'll start you off just as my father started me off; on the shop floor learning the ropes, and as long as you make good progress, I shall see to it that you are put on the board within eighteen months. As my son-in-law, you will find the financial arrangements more than adequate, but never make the mistake of taking me for granted Digby. Son-in-law or not, that would be a foolhardy thing to do.' He smiled across at Jones, something he found painful with this loathsome man, but he had his daughter to consider and had promised Maria he would make the effort.

Celia squeezed Digby's hand under the table. Everything was just as she had hoped it would be. Her father would soon discover what an asset her fiancé was to the business.

The meal finished and Digby said his goodbyes, kissing his future mother-in-law on both cheeks and shaking Samuel's hand before leaving. Celia walked out to the driveway with Digby. His uncle's faithful Austin was parked a few yards from the front door, completely dwarfed by Samuel's gleaming Rolls Royce. While Celia was looking back at the house, Digby ran his car key along the side of the Rolls, leaving a wide groove in the paintwork.

'How dare your father talk down to me like that?' he hissed when she turned towards him. 'Why, for two pins, I would have told him what he could do with his job, the patronising old bastard.'

'It's just his way,' Celia said soothingly, but Digby rounded on her with a ferocity that took her breath away. It was a side of him she had never seen before. This wasn't the Digby she knew. This was a different man!

'Then just you see that it doesn't happen again,' he barked, 'because if it does, then baby or no baby, I shall be off!'

Stunned, Celia took a step backwards, eyes now swimming with tears. 'Please don't say such things darling; I know you're angry, but I couldn't bear it if you left me.' But there was more chance of hell freezing over than his threat being carried out. Celia Mendoza was Digby's ticket to the good life and it was a one-way ticket. There were no stepping off points along the way.

*

Tom hammered the car down the M40 motorway as if our lives depended upon it, only slowing when we were about to pass a roadside speed camera. We reached *Rose Cottage* in record time and as Tom stopped on the drive, we all ran from the car. Obviously, whatever message the dairy contained was most likely for Susan or me.

When Beth had mentioned my mobile number was in the diary, it was obvious it contained a message from Dorothy.

Beth was surprised to see four people standing on the doorstep, but I explained how we'd been shopping together when she phoned and immediately set off for Wooburn Green. I swept my hand around, making the introductions. 'This is my friend Tom Cox and his wife Kate, and you remember Susan, of course?'

Beth asked if we would like some tea and scones and we accepted her kind offer, but more than anything, we wanted to see the diary.

Beth led us through to the lounge, with Tom and Kate taking everything in as they followed along behind. The place was beautiful and Kate was forthcoming in her admiration. 'I absolutely love your home Beth; it is one of nicest I have ever been in.'

Beth smiled with pride. 'It's very pretty, isn't it? I realise that someone from my humble background is lucky to own such a house, but the truth is that I'd much sooner Mrs Sinclair was still alive and it belonged to her.' She sighed, looking sadly across at me. 'I do so miss her Mr Monroe.'

'I'm sure you do Beth,' I agreed, remembering how protective she had been towards the old lady during my first visit to *Rose Cottage*.

Beth sat us down before she vanished into the kitchen. We all sat in silence with one thought. *What is in the dairy?*

Beth returned within five minutes carrying a tray with the tea things on it. She placed the tray on the coffee table and said, 'Shan't be a jiffy, I'll just get the scones.'

Kate reached for the teapot, 'And I'll pour the tea.'

Beth, halfway through the door, stopped and frowned. 'Thank you for the offer, but please don't. It wouldn't seem right, having guests pour their own tea. I can't think what Mrs Sinclair would have said if

I allowed that to happen.'

We were obviously privileged guests as the scones arrived with a pot of Petula's finest raspberry jam. 'I still have thirty jars left in the pantry,' Beth explained with a reminiscent smile lighting her face up. 'She loved making her jam, did Mrs Sinclair.'

Kate spread the jam and bit into her scone and gave a satisfied sigh. 'Well, we are very lucky Beth. It is absolutely delicious. Probably the finest I have ever tasted.'

Once we were finished, Beth cleared away the cups and plates. By then, our curiosity was stretched to the limit, but a few seconds later, she returned, holding what could be the most important book I'd read in my entire life. 'Would you like to see the diary now, Mr Monroe?' she asked, passing it to me without waiting for an answer.

The other three crowded around as I opened it, ready to inspect the contents, but Beth still delayed things. 'Well, you see, I've been gradually cleaning up the library whenever I have a bit of spare time,' she explained. 'Even though Mrs Sinclair provided for me in her will, I couldn't just waste my life and sit about the house all day. I think we're all put here on this planet to help one another, so I spend most of my time with disabled children.' Her eyes lit up. 'It's ever so rewarding you know. But I only found the diary because it's bound in red and yet it was in the blue bound section and stood out like a sore thumb.'

I felt a surge of pride at my Dorothy's inventiveness. I'd mentioned last year that the library hadn't been used at all since Petula's parents bought

Rose Cottage, and Beth wasn't allowed in there while Paula was alive. However, she could obviously use it when the house became hers and was bound to eventually spot the different colour. Until then, the dairy was in a safe place.

I opened it and looked on the first page and in Dorothy's handwriting was a list of dates with the words, *Love you* written alongside.

I stood for a moment, fighting back the tears.

Tom put an arm around my shoulder and gave it a quick squeeze. 'See!' he said with a grin, 'I told you she'd be ok, didn't I?'

I suppose that's just *one* of the reasons why he's my best buddy. I thought it was a really nice thing to do.

Bearing in mind that Dorothy had no idea when the diary would be found, the dates covered the next ten years. Seeing those dates proved she was still determined to get back to me, and when she did - and now that I had some dates to work on at last, I knew for sure she would - well, I didn't want to hang about. Marriage and lots of little Dorothys and Billys running around under our feet would be the order of the day.

The first two dates had been and gone. The third one mentioned was the coming Christmas day, which was the day we planned to try anyway. I was so scared that things might go wrong again and said as much, but Susan was of a different opinion.

'It will be fine this time Billy. We have both served our penance and I know that everything will work out for both of us.'

I looked at her, seeing only a peaceful smile and

shining chocolate brown eyes. If Susan was right, there were just two weeks remaining before Dorothy was back in my arms, and when she was, I was never going to let her go again - never.

*

The newly engaged couple were out for lunch along with Dorothy, Billy and Mr and Mrs Mendoza. They were at the Ritz Hotel in London's Piccadilly.

Digby leant back in his chair with an air of arrogance. 'Lovely place this,' he said as he pounded the butt of his cigar into an ashtray. 'I used to come here all the time whenever I was in London.' He pointed towards an empty table, sited in what was undoubtedly the prime position in the restaurant. 'Gordon, the Maître d', always kept that table over there for me.'

Dorothy looked across at Billy and raised her eyes skywards. He merely grinned in reply. 'Very nice too, Digby,' she remarked dryly. 'It's good to have friends in high places.'

Digby allowed himself an exasperated sigh. 'I suppose so,' he said with the winning smile that always turned Dorothy's stomach. 'But when people run around you all the time, it can be a trifle off putting. Other diners wonder who you are and constantly stare the whole time.'

The truth was that he had never set foot in the place before, but had read in *The Times* of Gordon's retirement earlier that year. The man had risen from the lowly position of kitchen porter to the dizzy height of maître d' in his 51-year career at the Ritz. At that moment, the recently departed Gordon's replacement led a couple past the staring eyes of other diners and on towards the very table mentioned by Digby. He seated them with great pomp and without turning, held his hand at shoulder height and snapped his fingers. A waiter hurried to the table, carrying an ice bucket containing a bottle of champagne. The maître d' half bowed deferentially to the couple before moving away, leaving other diners glancing curiously, obviously wondering who the couple could be. Unfortunately for Digby, he was not familiar with the phrase, *Quit while you're ahead.* 'You see what I mean about people staring?' he said to no one in particular. 'It's just as I said. Jolly off putting.'

'Yes, I'm quite certain that it is,' Samuel said impatiently. Digby's constant posturing over the past weeks was beginning to grate heavily on his nerves.

As the maître d' glided towards his position near the restaurant entrance, he had to pass the Mendoza table. Dorothy beckoned him over and Digby instantly froze in panic. The interfering bitch had caused him great discomfort on several occasions in the past with her smart mouth.

'Excuse me, but who are the two people you led to the table just now?' Dorothy asked as the maître d' reached her side. 'I'm sure I recognise the gentleman. His face is very familiar.'

'That, madam, is the Crown Prince of Sweden. He is here in London with his wife for a short visit. That particular table is kept exclusively for the use of foreign royals.'

Having answered Dorothy's question, the maître d' nodded politely to her and moved on. In unison,

Dorothy and the others turned to look at Digby whom they all knew was not, and never had been, a visiting foreign royal. His colouring now resembled an over-ripe plum. He quickly stood up, proclaiming that he must visit the gentlemen's room and vanished rapidly. 'He's just trying to impress you Daddy,' Celia explained, even though Samuel had made no comment. 'He means no harm, but he desperately wants you to admire him, the way he admires you.' She reached over and placed her hand on top of Samuel's. 'For my sake, please be patient with him.'

'I'm sure your father understands,' Maria comforted, 'but it really is a pity that Digby can't be himself instead of indulging in this constant pretence the whole time. It's so unnecessary.'

It was 20 minutes before Digby arrived back at the table. They soon discovered that his earlier experience had taught him nothing. 'Sorry for the delay,' he said, 'but some poor blighter had drunk far more than was good for him and passed out right in front of me. I loosened his collar and sat him upright, just in case he was sick and choked on his own vomit.' He misinterpreted the looks of disbelief from the others and added, 'It happens you know. It was lucky for the chap that I was at hand to help him.'

Samuel shook his head sadly, whilst Dorothy and Billy simply stared wide-eyed at one another, both of them too stunned for words.

They took coffee in the lounge and afterwards, strolled down to Trafalgar Square and continued on to the embankment of the River Thames.

As Dorothy and Billy walked arm in arm ahead of

the others, she looked up at him, excitement almost written on her face. 'It's going to happen soon Billy, I can feel it, I really can. Christmas day is my guess, and then I shall be back in my own time and you will be with Susan.' She smiled sadly. 'Although I'm really going to miss all of you, you know that, don't you?' and he nodded.

'Yes Dorothy. I know that. And we shall miss you, but I hope it happens soon.' He gave her a meaningful stare. 'It's getting difficult.'

She knew exactly what he meant and squeezed his hand. 'As it is for me Billy. Funny old world, isn't it?'

With Christmas almost upon them, the evenings were drawing in, meaning it would be dark before five. Billy was returning to his residence in Fulham, but the others were staying at the Ritz and would be returning to Lulworth Cove the following morning.

They reached Cleopatra's Needle and Billy and Dorothy paused, leaning against the iron railing as they looked out across the river. He let out a long sigh. 'Well, it's been a wonderful day, but I have work to catch up on, so I'm afraid that it's back home for me.' He stepped to the kerb and signalled a taxicab.

Digby, ten yards behind and still walking had heard his words and said softly to Celia, 'What a pity that he doesn't take that bitch with him,' but it was unfortunate for him that the wind whipped across the Thames and carried his words to Billy's ears. Billy covered the distance between himself and Digby in just a few seconds. He stopped in front of Digby, sheer menace radiating from his eyes.

'You may very soon be part of The Mendoza

family, Jones,' he spat out in words that were easily loud enough to reach Samuel and Maria's ears and cause them to stop walking. They listened in surprise as Billy continued, 'but if I ever hear you talk about Dorothy in that way again, then I warn you that I will not be responsible for my actions.'

Digby, by far the bigger man of the two, was caught completely unawares. He was more than three inches taller than Billy, outweighed him by at least forty pounds and was used to throwing his weight around, but with his goal of lifetime riches within his grasp, he wasn't sure how he should react to this. He stood speechless while Billy walked past him and up to the Mendozas. 'I apologise for my outburst Samuel,' he said, his voice still shaking with anger. 'I would like to thank you both so much for your hospitality and I'm sorry to have spoiled a perfect day by abusing it. I can only hope that I will still be welcome at *Cherry Tree House* on Christmas Day.'

Samuel smiled and clasped Billy's hand between his own. 'You will be my boy. You are family as far as Maria and I are concerned and shall always be. Now, your Taxicab driver is getting a trifle impatient, so may I suggest that you climb in and return to Fulham.' He looked at Maria and his eyes twinkled. For him, Digby's humiliation was a perfect end to the afternoon.

The evening was uneventful after that episode, although Digby Jones seethed inwardly at his own lack of activity in the confrontation with Billy. The more the time ticked away, the greater the humiliation he felt, but apart from manfully puffing out his chest and saying to Celia, 'Lucky for Monroe that he left when he did,' he remained uncharacteristically silent for the remainder of the evening. Silent he may have been, but the cauldron was bubbling inside him and it wouldn't take much to boil over.

*

Since Petula had passed away, it was obvious that even with charity work taking up much of Beth's time, she was a very lonely woman. She had never married, so with the code of morals I was certain she lived by, it was safe to assume she had no children. The woman can't have been 50 years old and yet she wasn't really living at all. She was simply seeing out the passage of time until her own time on earth was over and she would be reunited with Petula again.

Kate must have felt as I did, because she brought the subject up when we were enjoying Sunday lunch in an ancient pub at Bletchingly in Surrey. 'Shall we ask Beth to join us when we go to Lulworth Cove for Christmas?' she suggested. 'Otherwise, I think the poor woman will be stuck in *Rose Cottage* on her own, and surely Christmas should be spent with other people.'

Susan nodded her agreement. 'That is such a lovely, kind idea Kate,' she said. 'I wish I had thought of it. After all, if it hadn't been for Beth, we would still be hoping for something to happen at Christmas, instead knowing we can now *make* it happen.'

So, after phoning Beth to say that we were on our way to visit her, we piled into Tom's MPV. Bletchingly is around a mile from the M25 motorway and we reached *Rose Cottage* in just over an hour.

It would have been pointless telling Beth over the phone what we had planned for her. Knowing how she was, she would have thought she was getting ideas above her station. It would need our collective efforts to persuade her to spend Christmas with us in Dorset.

Without Dorothy's presence, her business virtually collapsed, but thanks to Tom's generosity, she still had her apartment. He had paid the mortgage repayments on her behalf, dismissing his actions with the words, 'Will you stop going on about it Billy. We all know I can afford it. In any case, Dorothy can pay me back when she's up and running again, so I'll probably have my money back inside a year.'

As Tom brought the MPV to a halt at *Rose Cottage*, Beth appeared at the door. Knowing we were coming, she had made a real effort with her appearance, even wearing a little make-up. I found it quite touching. It was raining and she held the door open as we raced from the car into the hallway. I made sure I was the last, in deference to the girls and Tom made sure he was first!

'Tea?' Beth asked, closing the door behind us; we all smiled in unison. 'And scones?' she added - we smiled even more. What with everyone wanting to say their piece, it took an hour to relay the details of all that had happened that July night of the previous year. *The oven wasn't working so Tom put a nail in the fuse and there was a huge flash of light and then we saw Susan. She had come forward from 1925 etcetera, etcetera.*

'So I'm afraid we lied about Susan's reason for visiting here before,' I apologised as we finished the tale, 'but we didn't really know you then Beth, and you would have thought we were crazy. Susan just wants to go home to her mum and dad and the man she loves.'

Beth sipped her now cold tea. 'That's quite a story Mr Monroe, and it's so farfetched that it must be true, but you were right to wait before telling me. I wouldn't have believed you if you'd told me earlier.'

'So you'll spend Christmas with us at Lulworth Cove will you?' Kate asked, and Beth nodded.

'Too true I will. I'm not missing out on a piece of excitement like this,' she said with and a distinct tinge of excitement in her voice. 'To actually witness someone travel through time! What on earth would Mrs Sinclair have said? So, *Yes*, Mrs Cox, I accept your kind offer. I shall gratefully spend Christmas with you at *Cherry Tree House*. The place sounds wonderful. Now, did I ever mention how…' and she went off on one of her verbal rambles again. Who cared? She was coming and that was the main thing.

Mission accomplished.

Chapter Nineteen

Every passing day saw Digby revealing more of his true self to Celia. As her pregnancy progressed, his confidence in a secure and rosy future grew, although he constantly complained about his position in her father's company.

'Why the hell do I have to wait seventeen months before his lordship puts me on the board of directors? For God's sake Celia, I'll be his son-in-law in a short time. Where is the man's sense of family?'

'He simply wants to be certain you will be able to cope when the time comes,' Celia said, hoping to placate him. 'I know it's a terrible bore for you darling, but Father says you have to learn the ropes first. Don't forget, that is the way he started.'

'You would side with him, wouldn't you, daddy's little darling,' Digby sneered spitefully. 'Well, in case you have forgotten, in a few weeks' time you will be my wife, and as my wife you would do well to remember that your loyalty should be to me and not to that fat pompous pig.'

Celia's eyes filled with tears. She didn't want to cry but couldn't help herself. Every morning she suffered from sickness and was generally feeling run down. She found Digby's behaviour difficult to cope with. 'Please don't talk that way about daddy,' she whispered. 'Please darling.'

'And that's another thing I can't stand,' Digby raved, his temper finally getting the better of him. 'Stop calling me darling all the time. If I really am your darling, then do something about that bloody father of yours and get me on the board now.'

Celia sobbed even more and Digby grabbed his coat, glaring at her. 'For God's sake, not more tears? Where the hell do they all come from? I've had enough of this for one evening. I shall see you tomorrow, and get to work on that father of yours. I'm warning you, if things don't happen soon, there won't be a wedding. Do I make myself clear, *darling*?'

The frightened expression on her face told him that, yes, he had made himself very clear indeed. To be a single mother in 1926 England would be the end of life with any kind of meaning for her. She would be ostracised by everyone, and the child would carry the stigma of being a bastard from cradle to grave.

Digby slammed the door behind him and a few moments later, Celia heard the new car her father had supplied him with start up and drive away. He had already complained that the car wasn't good enough for his future position as the Chairman's son-in-law.

Sitting in the lounge, Maria had heard every word that came from the study where the two supposed lovebirds spent their evenings. She turned to her husband, horrified by Digby's last words. 'Do you think he means it Samuel? That there may not be a wedding? What are we to do? If that were to happen, what on earth will our friends think?'

Samuel, never one to normally bring work home with him, put down the Auditors Report he was studying. 'That freeloader?' he said caustically. 'Leave the feathered nest? No chance of that happening old girl. No Maria, I'm far more concerned with his treatment of our daughter. I can't allow it to continue for any longer and shall have a word with the fellow tomorrow. Try and talk some sense into him,' but his words did little to reassure his wife. She felt that Digby Jones definitely had the upper hand in the matter.

The following morning, Samuel summoned Digby to his office. There was a bounce to Digby's step as he entered the room. He hadn't expected Celia to have spoken to her father in such a short time, but she obviously had. It reinforced his view that women must be treated firmly if one wanted something done. Anything else would be taken by them as weakness.

'Sit down Digby,' Samuel instructed as he studied the man who had found a way into his family and his business. The man was like a shiny apple -- good to look at, but one never knew if there was a maggot in its centre, although in Digby's case, Samuel knew only too well there was.

Digby smiled across the desk at him and asked, 'What did you want to see me about Samuel?' The smile was now a smirk as he waited for the good news to fulfil his dreams. He believed he deserved every reward he got, having to sleep with a plain bitch like Celia, a woman who should pay to share a bed with a man like him. The lies he'd had to whisper in her ear, such as *Beautiful*, when boring was more fitting. She was obviously stupid to have believed every word he said. Surely she knew he was lying, after all, she saw her reflection in the mirror every day.

In his mind's eye, he visualised his new business cards. *Digby Jones, Director of Operations*. No point in having too many printed though! The old man couldn't go on for ever. A few years down the line and the business cards would read, *Digby Jones, Chairman*.

'Well, Jones,' Samuel began, and Digby wondered why it was now *Jones* and not *Digby?* 'You may not realise it,' Samuel continued, 'but my wife and I can hear every word that falls from your foul mouth when you share the study with my daughter.' He paused, gaining some satisfaction as he saw Digby's jaw drop. 'And so, having listened to yesterday's disgraceful tirade, regretfully, I must send you on your way. The wedding will be cancelled, Celia will be instructed not to see you again, and your position here is terminated forthwith.' He opened a desk drawer and extracted an envelope, which he held onto for a moment before sliding it across the desk to Digby.

'In there is a cheque which I believe is more than generous. Certainly far more than you deserve. Now, please leave your car keys on my desk, you are dismissed. Goodbye Jones; we shall not be meeting again.'

A stunned Digby slid open the unsealed flap of the envelope and peered inside. It contained a cheque for five thousand pounds, a huge sum of money in 1926, but nevertheless, somewhat short of the million that he'd expected to be in possession of within the next ten years or so.

Samuel extracted a Cuban cigar from the box on his desk, clipped off the end and lit it. It was a job that if done properly, took almost a minute. He completed the little ceremony and looked up. Digby was still sitting there, although the old Digby seemed to have disappeared. In his place was a Digby who was slack mouthed - rather like a fish out of water, gasping for air.

'Did you not hear me Jones?' Samuel asked, concealing a satisfied smile. 'You are dismissed. Take the cheque and leave.'

Digby opened his mouth to speak, although all that came out was a single word, 'But-' and then, silence.

Samuel sat back in his chair and drew on his cigar. 'You wish to say something Jones?'

'But – you c-can't do that,' Digby stuttered.

Samuel replied matter-of-factly, 'I think you are rather missing the point Jones. Surely I already have.'

Digby was finally regaining some sort of control over his faculties. 'But my child, Celia's child, will be born a bastard.'

Samuel let out a long sigh. 'Yes Jones, I know. Unfortunately, the child will take after its father from the moment it enters the world. Now, unless you have something further to add to that pearl of wisdom, I have a busy schedule ahead of me and must get on with it.' He looked down and began to write on a blank sheet of paper. Without looking up he held his hand

234

out and said, 'The car keys please Jones,' but at last, the full implication of what was happening descended upon Digby and his temper flared.

'Do you really think you can buy me off with a meagre five thousand pounds, you fat old bastard?' he raged.

Samuel listened to the outburst nonplussed and replied, 'You may leave the cheque behind if you so desire Jones. The choice is yours, otherwise, take it and leave my office forthwith!' but Digby remained where he was.

'I shall drag your name through the mud, Mendoza. Tell people that your daughter is nothing but a slut who dropped her underwear to anyone who had the stomach to shove his penis inside her. Tell them that after discovering she was pregnant, she had been with so many men that she hadn't a clue who the father was.' His breathing became laboured as he warmed to his own words. 'I shall explain that I had a drunken fling with her, and let's face it, it would have to be a drunken fling for me to bed that plain looking bitch of a daughter of yours.'

His words finally got to Samuel. He rose to his feet, his face flushed with anger. 'Instead of hurling insults Jones, you would be better to state what it is that you want? That way, we can end this matter now and get on with our respective lives.'

Digby's breathing returned to some sort of normality. 'Very well then Samuel. I want things to be as they were. The marriage to go ahead, but instead of waiting eighteen months, I want a directorship now. In return, your grandchild will have a name, and your daughter will have a husband, because whether you like it or not, you and I both know that without me, she will end up as a lonely spinster.' He couldn't resist being spiteful and added, 'She is so plain that surely no one else would want her.'

Samuel kept his temper, 'Well, Jones, I have an alternative. The wedding will go ahead, but you will separate after a few months and divorce on the grounds of your adultery, which can, of course, easily be arranged. Celia's child will then have a father, and you will be richer by 50,000 pounds.'

It was an offer that was staggering in its magnitude. Fifty thousand pounds would mean never having to work again for the rest of his life, but to Digby, it didn't even warrant a consideration. A lifetime of marriage to Celia, or at least until the old man died and he had taken control of the company - that was the ultimate prize he sought.

To have people fawn over him. To be given the best table at restaurants. To be on every society guest list. These were the things Digby craved for. 'I'm sorry Samuel,' he smiled, 'but I'm afraid that is a long way short of what I want. I may not want Celia; in fact, I don't want her and never have done, but everything is out in the open now and you and I no longer need to pretend to one another. The truth is that for me, she was merely a means to an end, and that end is a lot more than 50,000 pounds. Like it or not, Celia will become my wife.'

Samuel raised an eyebrow. 'And what if Celia doesn't wish to become your wife? What then Jones? Do you hope to force her up the aisle at gunpoint?'

Digby laughed at such a ridiculous suggestion. 'Don't be stupid Samuel, it doesn't become you. We both know that the girl is besotted with me.'

'Then let us ask her what she wants, shall we,' Samuel said, and turned toward the door of his private toilet. A door that was slightly ajar. 'You may come out now my dear,' he said, and the door swung open and Celia stepped into the room.

*

We arrived at Lulworth Cove fairly late on December the 23rd. It was a Saturday and being the Christmas period, the traffic on the roads had been nightmarish. Although we collected Beth at 4pm, it was gone ten when we arrived at the house.

'Too late to eat out,' Kate informed us, 'everywhere around here stops serving at 9:30, but I've brought some sausage rolls with me, so I'll pop them into the oven for ten minutes.'

She was back from the kitchen a few moments later, laughing. 'Guess what?' she said.

Tom and I replied in unison, 'The oven isn't working.'

'You have it in one,' she smiled. 'I think it must have fused again.'

We all stared at Tom, but he shook his head emphatically. 'No way! Don't any of you even bother to ask. Anyway, sausage rolls taste much better if they're eaten cold with a dab of brown sauce,' and to prove his point, he grabbed one and took a huge bite from it. The rest of us followed suite. When there were just crumbs left on our plates, Beth announced that she had also brought some food with her, and Tom said, 'Scones,' and of course, he was right.

There were six bottles of white wine in the cellar. Four bottles later, Kate was having trouble with her words, so we decided it was a case of bed for all of us.

*

Billy gave the Bugatti a final polish before straightening to take the kinks out of his back. If things worked out as planned, then Susan would be back with him on the 26th and he was determined that her pride and joy should look its absolute best for her. That's if Susan ever did come back, because counting the dates Dorothy had written in the dairy she left in the library of *Rose Cottage*, this would be their fifth night time vigil, so one could never count success as a certainty. He offered a silent prayer to his maker to make it fifth time lucky.

Dorothy was polishing the inside of the car and smiled through the windshield at him and he returned the smile. She was a fantastic woman and sometimes he panicked a little, wondering if with her twenty-first century perception, she could read his thoughts. If she ever told him that she could, it would be the most embarrassing moment of his life.

He spoke loudly so she would hear him, 'Do you think it will happen this time Dottie?' and she gave him a faux snarl.

'Don't call me Dottie or I'll be forced to modify those handsome features of yours, Billy Monroe.'

He grinned and she smiled light heartedly back at

him. 'And yes, it will happen this time. I'd bet my last cent on it - that's if I actually possessed a last cent.'

He didn't agree though. She may be convinced, but he wasn't.

Dorothy put the polishing cloth down. 'Don't you see Billy, even if they haven't found the diary yet, Susan and Billy will know we'll be at *Cherry Tree House* during the Christmas period because that's when it happened the last time. I'll bet my old grandma's woollen drawers on it!' She coloured up. 'Gosh, where on earth did that come from?' but Billy laughed and put her at ease.

'Don't worry Dottie. I think my grandma also wore woollen drawers.'

He sighed heavily. The waiting had taken its toll and she saw lines on his face that weren't there a few months back. 'Do you really think it will be okay this time?' he asked yet again.

Dorothy pushed back the wedge of dark hair that flopped across his eyes and said, 'I *know* it will Billy.'

The thing Billy found difficult to handle with Susan away and Dorothy here with him was a simple one. Dorothy was *so* like the woman he loved, which meant... but he always refused to let his mind wander beyond that. Thoughts like that constituted the grossest disloyalty, making him ashamed of himself for even thinking them. All he wanted was for Susan to come back and for Dorothy to return to her own time - and the sooner, the better before he made a fool of himself. He loved Susan, and that was that!

He quickly changed the subject, 'What time is this Jones fellow due to arrive?' he asked and Dorothy's mood sank at hearing the hated name.

'Never - at least, that's what I wish. How on earth a nice girl like Celia ever became involved with a self-centred pig like him, I just don't know. But in answer to your question, Pops said that Digby will be here in time for Christmas Dinner at four o'clock and will be leaving at eight.' She raised her eyes Heavenwards. 'Which means we will have to endure him for four hours - that's 240 minutes which converts to--'

But he cut her short, 'There is no need to go on Dottie, I understand completely. You don't like the man and neither do I, but we can endure him for that amount of time and as long as he really is on his way by eight, we have nothing to worry about. However, just like you, I cannot understand why Celia is still involved with him. Obviously, she wants a father for her child, but she would be better off with a child born out of wedlock than being married to a man such as Jones.'

Dorothy smiled sadly, thinking how the nation's standards had altered so dramatically in just a few decades. 'In my time, Billy, people think nothing of it and in parts of England it's almost fashionable to have illegitimate children. If you're a single mum, the Government house you, feed you and give you spending money, all of which means you never have to work in your life. But here in 1926 it isn't acceptable. Celia would be treated like a leper and her life would be hell. But you are forgetting that she'll be rid of him for good in a few months' time. Once they're married and the baby is born, Jones has agreed to a divorce shortly afterwards. He conceded that to Samuel once Celia told him in no uncertain terms that it was his only option. Otherwise he'll walk away with nothing.'

Billy grinned and shook his head at Dorothy's naivety. He might not understand women, what man did, but he certainly knew men. 'All well and good as long as he keeps his side of the bargain, but remember we are talking about Digby Jones here and I don't trust him one iota and neither should Samuel or Celia, nor you for that matter Dottie.'

Dorothy huffed impatiently and put her hands on her hips. 'What a thing to say Billy! Of course Celia doesn't trust him - not after hearing the awful things he said in her father's office that day, but remember, if he goes back on his promises, he'll be the one who loses out because he won't get the £50,000 Samuel has promised him. He really will end up with nothing.'

'And will no doubt drag Celia's name through the mud if that happens,' Billy said gloomily. Dorothy linked her arm through his and led him towards the house.

'Come on! Snap out of it for goodness sake. We're more or less finished here and the car looks as if it has come from a showroom, so let's go inside and join the others. Once you get a glass of bubbly inside you, you'll soon cheer up, I guarantee you will.'

*

In his small room, Digby studied himself in the mirror. New suit, new shoes and an incredibly handsome man wearing them. These were the things he saw reflected in the mirror.

Thanks to some major grovelling on his part, for which Mendoza and Celia would pay dearly at a later

241

date, Digby still had his position at the firm along with the company car, and whatever Mendoza and his daughter thought, he intended to keep them. When it came to deviousness, they had just about half a brain between them and neither of them was a match for what he was planning.

He put on his topcoat, left the house and climbed into the car. A car that would be replaced by a Rolls Royce in a few months' time when he had his directorship, because whatever Mendoza had planned, that was all the time it would take. Of course, Mendoza wasn't aware of that yet, but he soon would be.

Digby smiled into the car's rear view mirror. '*My justice is swift and my sword shall smite mine enemy,*' he said aloud to his reflection. His original mission had been successful; Celia was pregnant and his marriage to her was almost imminent. Time for him to move on. Step one was completed and step two would soon be under way, and then - father and daughter would rue the day they humiliated him.

Chapter Twenty

Between them, Kate and Beth cooked a magnificent Christmas meal. The remaining three of us watched as they engaged in almost open warfare to establish who could mother us the most. Beth seemed determined to oust Kate from the position she'd held since our first weekend at Lulworth Cove. Maybe it had to do with Beth looking after Petula for more than two decades. Or maybe she felt Kate was doing work that was beneath her.

After our feast, we watched a film chosen from the DVDs I had brought with me.

Bridget Jones' Diary beat *Love Actually* by one vote. At 9:50, with just 40 nerve racking minutes remaining before our attempt to bring Dorothy back, most of us were chewing our finger nails. Beth was fine, but she wasn't involved.

My pulse was banging in my ears as I repeated a silent prayer, over and over; *Please, please let it work. Please let it work.*

I wasn't built for this kind of thing. All I wanted

was the woman I loved back in my arms, *forever and ever, until death us did part*!

I figured it wasn't much to ask; I could hardly be accused of being greedy.

Kate suggested *Scrabble* as a means of taking our minds off things and passing the time, so we set the board out on the big kitchen table. I could scarcely concentrate, but the game did give me moments of respite. Moments when I became so engrossed that for a few minutes, I managed to forget all about the deadline.

After around 25 minutes of play, Kate thumped the table hard and glared across at her innocent looking husband. 'That isn't a word Tom, you cheating little toad. Where did that warped mind of yours dream that one up from?'

He stared at his wife with a hurt expression that I was growing quite used to seeing. 'It most certainly is a word my beloved. Please don't condemn it because you have never heard of it. You and I both know that your knowledge of the English language has always been rubbish.'

'So shall we put it to the test then, shall we?' Kate said, rubbing her hands together in a way that suggested Tom was about to get his comeuppance. She looked at each of us in turn and asked, 'Have any of you heard of *Pirryisnton*?'

The other two women shook their heads but I decided that the time had come for us boys to stick together. If we had done that more often in the past, it might now be a man's world instead of a woman's.

I bowed my head in case my face betrayed me, 'I

have, Kate,' I said. 'As a matter of fact, I've actually heard it quite a few times over the past year.'

Kate gave me the evil eye. 'Well that's lucky then, isn't it? Quite handy that you can back up your best friend. So, in that case, you will be able to explain to the rest of us simpletons just exactly what the word means then, won't you Billy?'

I didn't hesitate. 'It means to miss an extremely short putt at golf,' I explained, congratulating myself on my fertile imagination.

Kate's brow furrowed as she looked questioningly at Tom for confirmation. Tom could beat a lie detector hands down. He didn't bat an eyelid. 'Well done Billy, your answer is very close, but not quite correct. No, Pirryisnton actually means to miss two short putts on consecutive holes. You often hear some of the blokes in the clubhouse saying, after a game, "Trevor had a Pirryisnton. It happened on the fourteenth and fifteenth. I know he was my opponent, but I felt really sorry for the poor bugger."'

Kate huffed disgustedly. 'Don't swear Tom, and don't think for one minute that you're getting away with that pathetic story, you no good cheat.' She turned to Susan and asked, 'Is there a dictionary in this house?'

Susan shrugged her shoulders. 'Well there was 90 years back, but I can't say if there is now.'

'I saw one a while ago,' Beth piped up. 'It was on one of the shelves in the lounge. It was the biggest dictionary I've ever seen; at least four inches thick, that's how I noticed it in the first place.'

Tom gave her a *Why don't you mind your own business*

sort of glare and Kate turned to him with a triumphant gleam in her eye. 'Go and get it will you please darling? We can check out *Pirryisnton* and if you are correct, then quite naturally, I shall apologise for ever doubting you in the first place,' although her expression said there was more chance of hell freezing over than that happening.

'Sorry my love,' Tom said and a pained expression swept across his face and dulled his eyes, 'but I hurt my leg earlier and I'd sooner rest it for a while if you don't mind.'

Beth stood up and walked towards the door. 'I'll go and get it Kate,' she said helpfully, but returned a minute later wearing a puzzled look. 'Now that is very strange. The dictionary is gone, but it was there earlier, I know it was. Either that or I've become stupid!'

Along with the others, I looked at Tom. He was sitting down but appeared to be taller than usual. About four inches taller.

Kate also must have noticed this sudden increase in height. 'Stand up Tom,' she said and he grimaced.

'But my leg, my precious! I could do permanent damage if I put any weight on it.'

She stepped forward menacingly, 'And I'll do permanent damage to your neck if you don't. Now, Tom Cox; *stand up!*'

Reluctantly, he got to his feet, revealing a thick book on the seat of the chair. His eyes opened wide in innocence. 'Well, fancy that,' he said, 'I can't imagine how that came to be there.'

Kate grabbed hold of the book and looked at the

rest of us, victory etched on her face. 'How very surprising folks. We have found the missing dictionary. Somehow, it managed to get off the shelf in the other room and find its way under my husband's bottom.'

Tom squared his shoulders manfully and met Kate's eyes. He didn't flinch, 'I know what you're thinking my love, and understand why, but I promise you that when I sat down, I had no idea the book was on the chair.'

Kate ignored him and hastily thumbed through the pages towards the letter P. She had just started checking through the *Per* section when I glanced at my watch. We'd been so engrossed in our game of Scrabble that we had all forgotten about the time.

It was almost 10:30! Here we were arguing about a bloody game and close to missing the objective that had consumed us for a year.

I leapt up in panic. 'Quickly, everyone into the hall or we'll miss the deadline.'

Everyone rushed into the hallway, but not before I saw Tom pause to mess up the letters on the Scrabble board. He noticed me watching and gave a sheepish grin.

Luckily, he had prepared a spare fuse earlier so we were ready to go. He grabbed the spare and pulled the oven fuse from the board. I looked frantically at my watch again and said, 'Ten seconds to go,' and silently counted them off. 'Now Tom,' I shouted and he screwed his eyes and pushed the fuse in.

Nothing happened! No explosion that scared the pants off you. No brilliant flash of light. Nothing. For some reason the old formula had failed.

My heart was in my boots. Surely this couldn't happen. Not now. Not after all the months and months of Susan and me waiting and hoping - waiting and praying. I looked helplessly across at Tom and as I did, I spotted the nail gleaming across the terminals of the fuse that was still in his hand and I realised what had happened.

'Tom! You've put the same bloody fuse back into the board,' I screamed. 'Come on, shift your bum before the timeslot runs out.'

He pulled the oven fuse from the board and to make absolutely certain there'd be no mix up again, threw it to the floor and shoved the specially prepared fuse into its place. I can't describe the relief as the familiar tremendous explosion rocked the hall, followed by a lightning type flash that frightened the living daylights out of everyone, and then - total blackness as the lights went out. You could have heard a pin drop as I glanced through the window and saw the streetlights were now out, just as they were on the other occasions.

I couldn't see Susan - not even her outline, but felt her hand reach for mine and grip it tightly. My breath was coming in rasps and my pulse was through the roof. I wondered if anyone's heart had ever exploded, because mine was heading that way. I tried to speak but couldn't even whimper. Somehow, God knows how, I got myself under control. 'Turn on the torch Kate,' I said in a shaky voice. I had never been so nervous in the whole of my life. If Dorothy wasn't there, I'm not sure I could take it. Everyone has a breaking point and I knew I was pretty close to mine.

I screwed my eyes shut, terrified of failure. 'Please be there baby,' I whispered under my breath. 'Please be there,' and then I heard the click of the torch as Kate switched it on. I counted to three, opened my eyes and followed the beam of light as it cut through the darkness, lighting up the corner of the hall.

*

Digby left *Cherry Tree House* an hour later than planned. At first, Samuel wasn't too bothered by the delay as there was plenty of time before Dorothy's deadline for returning to her own century. But at 8:55, without Digby showing the slightest sign of leaving, Samuel moved things along. He retrieved Digby's topcoat from the cloakroom and returned to the lounge, holding it ready for him to slip into. 'Sorry old chap,' he said, 'but there are certain Christmas traditions still to come. Traditions that are purely for family, you understand?'

Digby looked pointedly at Billy who was not family either, but had not been asked to leave. Samuel glanced at Billy before saying, 'However, I should like you to remain for a while Billy, as there are several things I need to discuss with you.'

Digby seethed at being left out of these so called family traditions. It could be something as simple as pulling a few Christmas crackers, but he was entitled to be there! His anger was made worse by Monroe being asked to stay.

'Things to discuss!' What nonsense! Monroe would never be family, whereas in a matter of weeks, he, Digby Jones, would become the son-in-law and heir apparent to the Mendoza Empire and the fortune that

came with it. However, he showed the opposite of his feelings, saying, 'But of course, Samuel. I completely understand.' He knew he had bridges to rebuild, so it made sense to do things the easy way. He was also attempting to worm his way back into Celia's affections and had been attentive to her the instant he arrived at *Cherry Tree House*. Whatever plans he had to deal with Mendoza, it was better if one had things given to them, rather than acquiring them by other means, although he still intended to take his revenge.

Digby had travelled a few miles from Lulworth Cove when the devious side of his brain whirred into action. Why had Samuel had been so keen to get him away from the house? Surely not for the exchanging of presents along with silly Christmassy attestations of love for one another? A man like Mendoza would never be that trivial. There had to be another reason. There was something going on and instead of discovering what it was, he was driving away from it. He spun the car around. When the house came into view, he eased the car into a copse of trees just outside the grounds, opened the car door, climbed out, closed the door silently and crept onto the grass alongside the drive, first checking that the car couldn't be seen from the house, but it was well hidden from view.

He grinned, seeing the lounge window ajar, and even from that distance, could hear the murmur of voices filtering from the room. Once at the window, he could hear every spoken word. He sat on the damp grass eavesdropping until 10:15 when Dorothy announced that it was getting chilly and closed the window.

Digby flattened himself on the wet grass but with the window closed, the voices were an unintelligible murmur.

Digby rose to his knees, completely saturated, his trousers clinging uncomfortably to him as he crawled away from the window. Once clear of the house he raced to the car, reversed out of the trees and sped away, thinking what a bonus that little visit had turned out to be. It made no difference that his spying had been cut short when the window was closed as he'd heard enough. Thanks to this information, he would very soon have a substantial amount of his own money. Not millions, which was a damn pity, because if *that* had been the case, there would be no marriage and Celia would then have to live with the shame of being an unmarried mother - and the Mendoza family, every last one of them, could go and rot in hell!

*

'Thank God that awful man has gone,' Dorothy said when Samuel closed the door behind Digby. 'How any woman could fall for his toady charms is a mystery to me.' She noticed the alarmed expression on Billy's face and her hand flew to her mouth as she remembered Celia was in the room. 'I am so sorry darling. Me and that big mouth of mine have managed to do it yet again. One day I'll learn to think before I spout off my opinions. I am so sorry. Am I forgiven?'

Celia diffused the situation as a thought occurred to her. She smiled and said, 'Of course you are! It can't be too often that a great grandmother gets apologised to by her grown up great granddaughter. Especially when that same great granddaughter isn't due to be born for another 60 years.'

Dorothy smiled and said, 'I'm going to miss you so much Celia, I really am.'

Samuel, with an unusual display of affection, came across and hugged the pair of them. 'Well my dears,' he said, 'Christmas is a time for forgiving. A time of joy and,' he hugged Dorothy even tighter as his stiff upper lip wavered and his eyes misted over. 'And sadly, my little Dottie, a time for saying goodbye.'

Maria put her knitting to one side and crossed the room to join the three of them, squeezing in between her husband and Dorothy. 'We shall all miss you Dottie,' she said in a quiet voice. 'We have all grown to love you - even this impossible husband of mine.' She nudged him in the ribs. 'Isn't that so Samuel?' and he nodded his agreement. For the first time in his life, Samuel Mendoza's voice had deserted him.

Billy was standing by the window, staring out into space. He shared their sadness, although it would be a blessing for him when Dorothy returned to her own time. Being around her was proving to be extremely difficult, and yet deep down, he was sure that he still loved Susan. The Susan who, if things went to plan, would be in his arms in a little over 24 hours. He felt the startling resemblance between the two women was the main problem, he was sure of that. Well, almost sure!

The flash of headlights grabbed his attention and he watched in surprise as Digby Jones' car pulled into the small copse just outside the grounds of the house. He turned to the others, saying, 'Digby Jones has returned and hidden his car in the trees. What do you make of that?'

They all rushed to the window and Billy pointed towards the copse. 'Look, you can see the car headlights,' and so they could, but a few seconds later the headlights went out. The moonlight was soft, but bright enough for them to see the crouching figure of Digby Jones appear from the trees and step onto the grass alongside the drive. They watched in surprise as, creeping low, he surreptitiously made his way towards the house. Celia, baffled, said, 'Why didn't he simply drive up to the house?'

Dorothy kept her eyes on the crouching figure and provided the answer. 'Because he doesn't want us to know he's here. It's my guess that our Mr Jones is on a spying mission, which is exactly the sort of thing I would expect of him.'

Samuel's face showed his anger as his colouring became a mottled red. He strode forward purposefully. 'Damn cheek of the fellow. I shall go outside this instant and confront him,' but Dorothy grabbed his arm.

'No Pops. Leave him. In fact, why don't we open the window a shade so that when he gets here, he'll be able to hear what we have to say?'

'Have you taken leave of your senses girl?' Samuel exploded, but Dorothy smiled knowingly.

'You're missing the point Pops. The only thing that Mr Digby Jones will hear is what we want him to hear,' and Samuel Mendoza's mood instantly changed.

He studied Dorothy with open admiration, 'It appears that there is a little of me in you after all Dottie. So, what is it that we want the man to hear?

*

Forty minutes later, Celia called from the upstairs window, 'He's gone. I've just seen him reverse out of the trees and drive away.'

Samuel checked his pocket watch and his eyes widened in alarm. 'We must hurry,' he said. 'It's almost time; we have just a few minutes left, so everyone move into the hall at once.'

Dorothy smiled nervously and took her position in the spot where Susan appeared on that fateful evening almost a year and a half back.

Billy moved towards her. He knew he had to say something, but one look from Dorothy stopped him and for the first time, he realised that this was as difficult for her as it was for him and somehow, that made it easier.

'Any moment now,' Samuel said having glanced at his pocket watch once again and they stood silently, nervously waiting. Dorothy looked at each of them in turn and smiled, her feelings clear to read on her face.

'Love you,' she said softly and as the words left her lips, a low rumbling noise seemed to come up from the floor and surround them. The house shook and Dorothy noticed the coat stand rocking on its spindly feet. She smiled even more and felt a warm glow grab hold of her. After a whole year of living in another time - not just another time but a completely different world, she knew that at last she was going home. Back to everything she loved - a world of Kings Road shopping and restaurants like *The Ivy*. Back to her lovely little Smart car and her flat on the borders of Fulham and Chelsea and Fred the doorman saying,

Evening Miss.

And even more important than any of those things, back to the man she loved.

It was happening this time, she could feel it deep inside, in her very core; it was really happening. The figures in front of her began to fade. Samuel had his arm around Maria. They looked both sad and happy at the same time, if that was possible. Celia had her hand raised in a farewell gesture and Billy just stared forlornly until he and the others faded away completely and were gone.

*

There was an unnatural silence and a stillness, then Dorothy said apprehensively, 'I'm still here, aren't I?' Her eyes were squeezed tightly shut, as if too scared to open them and learn the truth.

She was wearing the same clothes she wore when she vanished over a year ago and my heart pounded in my ears like a drum beat on a slave ship.

It's hard to describe how I felt as I saw her again. Relief? Joy? Exhilaration and love? Everything crammed into a single instant! I guess it's the way someone would feel having being sentenced to death, only to be granted a reprieve seconds before the lethal injection.

I threw my arms around her and said, 'No darling Dorothy, you are back where you belong, back here with me.'

Her eyes opened and then her breath came in huge, gasping sobs as she clung to me.

To the side of me I saw Tom and Kate smiling

and, unusually for them, holding hands, while Beth, who had never seen Dorothy before but knew all that had happened to date, looked disbelievingly at what she had witnessed.

A woman had materialised out of thin air in front of her. Her mouth hung open for a moment. 'My goodness, so everything you told me was true. The more I thought about it, the more I thought you were pulling my leg.' In the next breath, she dug Kate in the ribs, 'Will you just look at how like Susan she is.'

Susan had somehow kept herself under control during our moment, but now, rushed across, barely giving Dorothy a chance to compose herself. I could understand that though. The poor girl had waited a long time to hear of the person she loved. She grabbed Dorothy's sleeve, 'Did you see Billy? Is he still waiting for me? How are my mother and father? What about Celia? Is she safe and well? Please Dorothy, don't keep me in suspense. Has very much happened since I left?' The words rushed out like water tumbling over a thousand feet fall; almost too quick to hear.

Dorothy extracted herself from Susan's grip and slid back into my arms, said, 'Give me a few more seconds Susan and then I shall tell you everything there is to tell, but you mustn't worry, because Billy is still waiting for you and your family are all fine.'

Free now to give me her full attention, Dorothy kissed me fully on the lips. 'Still love me Billy Monroe?'

Although my throat had closed up, I somehow managed to say, maybe a tad dramatically, 'Until the day I die, my love.'

Dorothy squealed gleefully. 'Me too Billy,' she said. 'Me too,' and clung to me even tighter.

In deference to Susan's understandable impatience, Dorothy freed herself from my arms and turned towards the poor girl. 'Can we all go into the kitchen and sit down? I feel whacked out. Remember, I've travelled nearly 100 years in just a few seconds!'

So, we all trooped into the heart of the house. Beth filled the kettle and put it on the hob to boil as Dorothy began. 'For starters, everyone is good back in 1926 Susan, and like I said, Billy is still waiting for you, but you'll be able to see that for yourself in just a few hours' time, won't you?'

She took off the watch that was responsible for more than a year of torment and handed it to Susan. 'Let's not take any chances shall we? Put this on now before we forget. We wouldn't want to go through this lot again, would we?' and Susan smiled in that soft way of hers and strapped the watch onto her wrist. Her eyes were shining.

'No, we most certainly would not.'

Dorothy looked all around and the moment I saw her tongue brush lightly across her lips, I guessed what was coming. She grinned self-consciously. 'Any food about, is there? This time travel makes you ever so hungry.'

In unison, Kate and Beth rushed off to do battle. I looked at the woman I'd been without for more than a year and a warm glow nestled deep inside me. Nothing had changed. She was still the same Dorothy I thought I'd lost forever. My Dorothy!

We stayed up until four in the morning while she

recounted most of what had taken place in the year 1926. Endless cups of tea were made and countless scones demolished. We listened, enthralled! None of us would ever hear a story to match this one, not if we lived to be 100 years old, although chronologically, in Susan's case, she had already done that. Despite the late hour, not one of us was even remotely tired, which I guess is understandable. The excitement of Dorothy coming back home had all of us wide awake and tingling.

In the end, the only reason we went to bed was because so much had happened in the year plus, that it couldn't be recounted in one go. It needed to be broken into parts. We decided to listen to part two in the morning.

I snuggled up to Dorothy under the goose feather duvet and listened to the wind howling through the trees. Even from this distance, I could hear the waves crashing on the stony beach of the cove. I was at peace with the world now, trembling, but acting like a celibate saint, not attempting anything other than just holding her. Like most men, I understand little about women but do know that the time has to be right for them. I smiled, remembering a kitchen plaque on the wall of a gift shop. It read, *Women have to be in the mood, but men only have to be in the room.*

Well, thinking of the trauma Dorothy had suffered, I thought that maybe the time wasn't right for her, but after a few moments she whispered, 'Is something wrong Billy? Don't you want to make love to me any more?' which says a lot for my intuition.

'Are you kidding?' I said, pulling her closer. 'Prepare yourself madam. I've been waiting decades for this moment to arrive.'

*

Susan was the first up in the morning, but that was to be expected on the day she was going back to her Billy. At ten o'clock, just six hours after we'd all taken off to our beds, she brought tea to everyone's bedroom, sensibly knocking before entering.

Dorothy and I were served first, followed by Beth and finally, Kate and Tom who were in the bedroom next to ours. Through the wall we heard a flurry of movement and Kate's frantic voice saying, 'Quick Tom, hand me my dressing gown or Beth will cooking the breakfast before I can do it. I like her, but I'm not having her keep pinching my job.'

Dorothy gave me a puzzled look and asked, 'What was all that about Billy?' and so I explained about the competition between the two women.

'It's stupid really but it's been going on since we first arrived at *Cherry Tree House*. Drives you potty in the end. How in God's name can any sane person make a contest out of looking after the rest of us?'

Later, as we all sat around the big kitchen table, Dorothy dabbed at her mouth with a napkin and let out a luxurious sigh as she slid her empty plate away. The rest of us were half way through the gargantuan breakfast. Dorothy looked at Susan, her mouth set determinedly. I knew that look only too well. It came on when she was about to say something she didn't relish saying. She sighed heavily, taking Susan's hand in her own. 'Last night when I said that everything back in 1926 was fine, I'm afraid I wasn't being strictly truthful. There was something I should have

259

told you but I didn't want you to worry too much. Still, you'll soon find out when you get back, so I shall tell you now and then it won't be a shock.'

Susan wriggled nervously and Dorothy sighed again. 'There's this awful man named Digby Jones, just about the most despicable creature I've ever set eyes on in my life. The bastard is nothing more than a fortune hunter-'

'I married one of those,' Tom interrupted and Kate cuffed him good-naturedly around the head.

Dorothy smiled at them both. 'I missed you both so much while I was gone. I really did. Anyway, back to Digby Jones. The thing is, Susan, I'm afraid your sister Celia fell head over heels for him and he took advantage of her feelings and seduced her. He told her the worst lie that a guy can tell a woman - said that he couldn't have children, but all the time he was sleeping with her, trying to get her pregnant so he could marry into the family. The crafty bastard knew that if he managed that, he would be set up for life. Well, unfortunately for everyone back there, he was successful in his mission and now Celia is pregnant with his child and they'll be getting married in a few weeks' time. That's the real reason for your parents selling *Rose Cottage*. Right now, they're living here at *Cherry Tree House*, but they intend moving to Cobham in Surrey. If they do that, then no one there will know that Celia's child was conceived before she was married.'

Susan listened, wide-eyed. She also blushed a deep shade of crimson, probably wishing Dorothy had revealed this particular bit of news in private, but it was too late now. The cat had well and truly been let out of the bag.

Twenty minutes later, Susan knew everything there was to know of the Digby Jones saga. From the agreement that Samuel would pay him 50,000 pounds when he separated from Celia, right up to the previous night when they realised Jones was eavesdropping outside the window.

I thought about the 50,000 pounds and whistled through my teeth. It's still a fair amount of money even now, but 90 years ago? It was a huge fortune that would probably have bought ten mansions. I pictured in my mind's eye the modest house in Ealing that Dorothy's parents lived in. If Samuel Mendoza had that sort of money in 1926 then what the hell had happened to it in the years that followed? Where had it gone?

'So that's a full update on what you'll be going back to tonight,' Dorothy said. 'A man who adores you and can't wait to see you again; a sister about to marry the worst kind of guy in order to give a name to her child, and parents who I promise will be over the moon once you're back with them.'

Susan pulled a wry face as if she believed most of what Dorothy had told her, but not quite everything. 'Maybe Mummy will be ecstatic,' she said, 'but not my father. I know him too well. He will almost certainly greet me with a lecture about all the bother I have caused them.'

'No he won't,' Dorothy said in a sharp voice. 'Maybe the old Samuel - the one you remember would have, but you'll find him a changed man now, I promise you. This stiff upper lip thing of his got in the way in the past, but he really loves you and when he thought he'd lost you forever, believe me, it really shook him up. It made him reassess his life and his relationship with his family. To be perfectly truthful, he's become so nice that I love him almost as much as I love my own dad and shall miss him and your mum ever so much.' She leant forward, closing the space between herself and Susan. 'Do you know what he did an hour or so before I left? Go on - see if you can guess.'

Susan shook her head. She hadn't been there, so how could she know?

'He almost cried, that's what he did.' Dorothy smiled, 'How about that?'

Susan found this hard to believe. 'Are you quite certain you are talking about my father?' she replied bitterly, 'Because if what you are telling me is true, he has changed beyond all recognition. The way you describe him doesn't sound at all like my father.'

I had a warm feeling as I listened to this exchange. I could think of no reason for Dorothy to lie, so at least some good came out of an episode that shattered so many lives. Susan's life was about to become a whole lot better than it had been before her walk into the sea.

Lunchtime arrived and the two mother hen protagonists engaged in their tireless, nonstop battle yet again. Afterwards, Beth, easily the winner on this occasion, cleared the plates and began loading the dishwasher with a smug look on her face, leaving Kate muttering uncomplimentary things about her under her breath.

We passed the remainder of the day chatting idly, and then watched a couple of DVDs to pass the time. One of them, Keira Knightly in *Pride and Prejudice*, had Susan enthralled. 'I have read the book so many times and always loved it,' she said in awe, 'but *this* has made it all so real. The film brought it to life for me. I can't wait to tell mother about it when I get back.'

During the course of the afternoon and evening, it was mentioned several times that we would never see Susan again after tonight, something we were all pretty miffed about. After more than a year with us, she had become part of the family, although in Dorothy's case, she *was* part of the family. But there was nothing we could do to maintain the friendship. After all, we could hardly flit back and forth through time, and then I had an idea. An idea that would at least keep the link open between us. 'We don't know what's going to happen to the Mendoza family from 1927 until 2017,' I stated, 'but supposing something happened that we should know about. Maybe in that case, Susan could leave a message hidden where future generations would miss it, but as we had planned it, we would know where to look.' Everyone sat up. I had their interest. 'Like under the floorboards,' I suggested and looked at Tom. 'What do you all think?'

True to form, Tom immediately found fault and shook his head doubtfully. 'Yeah, well, I suppose it's a good idea, but not under the floorboards Billy. They'd have all been lifted at least twice since 1926 when the central heating and modern power supply were installed. Anything found under the boards by someone else would be put down to the ravings of a nutter and chucked away, so we need a different hiding place. You'd better forget about that one, me boy.'

'Maybe not, Tom,' Dorothy said. 'After all, there isn't a radiator, power point or even a light in the cupboard outside the master bedroom. I was always complaining about it to daddy, but nothing ever got done.' She smiled reminiscently now that he had been mentioned. 'Typical of dad. He said that it's just a holiday home and we're only here for a few weeks a year, so why bother. By the way, how did you explain my absence to my parents?' and I grinned, hoping that she'd appreciate my cover story.

I told her of our visit to Ealing and the yarn I'd spun, adding, 'I bought some cards and Tom copied your handwriting because he's really good at it, then arranged to have the cards posted from different places in Africa. It wasn't that difficult. The cards only said things like, '*Love you. Hope you're well. Look forward to seeing you both soon.*'

Dorothy grinned happily. 'Brilliant,' she said, 'what a clever fiancé I have, but weren't my parents even a tiny bit suspicious?'

Susan's head swivelled towards us even faster than Tom's. He glared at me and said, 'What's all this *fiancé* stuff. Have you been keeping things from your bosom buddy, you secretive bugger?'

Dorothy turned a deep shade of red. 'Let Billy finish what he's saying first Tom, and then we'll explain.' I looked across at Susan; she was the reason we hadn't announced our engagement over a year ago, but she appeared to be okay with the news. Probably because she knew she would be back with her Billy in a few hours' time.

I picked up my story again. 'No Dorothy, your parents weren't suspicious because I took Tom and Kate with me. They backed me up on everything I said and your parents obviously believed I was telling the truth - even though I was lying to them.' I glanced across at my back up team and grinned. 'Take a look at that honest face. Even God would have believed that particular porky.'

Tom huffed on his fingernails and buffed them on his shirt, but Kate sighed theatrically and said, 'Billy's talking about me Tom. No one in their right mind would trust you. You've lived a lifetime of deceit and lies.'

Tom grinned, 'Made us rich though, didn't it me little darlin'?' and Kate turned her face away to hide her smile and I smiled along with her. It's like being in a comedy club when you're with them; I could listen to their sniping at one another for hours without ever getting bored and it's all free. No wonder Dorothy said she'd missed them both over the past year.

'Anyway, Susan,' I said, 'what do you think of the idea of using the floorboards in the cupboard outside the master bedroom as a hidey-hole?'

She nodded thoughtfully before saying, 'I think it's a good one Billy, but I shall leave a message anyway, even if it isn't necessary. I want you all to know how things turned out for me. And I can break the time cycle of course, because I can put the message there anytime, even ten or fifteen years on, but I want you to look in a year's time.'

My friend with the devious brain leapt forward, 'Hey! We could look there now, couldn't we? After all, if that's what you're going to do, then it should be under the floorboards now, waiting for us.'

Well, it was a piece of logic that I couldn't argue with, but I could see from the faces of the others that they didn't agree with him and once I'd taken on board the ramifications, I didn't either. I shook my head vigorously, 'No Tom! It's time we realised we are dealing with things none of us understand. Things that on the surface are impossible, but we all know they aren't. For instance, try working this out. Susan hasn't even written the letter yet, but despite that, as you just said, it's probably under the floorboards right now. But what's the point of getting it? If it's good news, then that's what we expect, but if it's bad news…' I glanced across at Susan. 'How is this poor girl going to take it if she knows what's going to happen in *her* future? Hears it from herself before it's actually happened? It could mess up her life, especially if it's bad news.' And so, it was agreed that we would comply with Susan's wish and would not lift the boards until next Christmas.

So, whatever happened in the Digby Jones saga, if Susan did elect to tell us, we'd have to wait until then to find out.

Dorothy shuddered convulsively. 'Just wait until you see this Digby Jones bloke Susan. Even the very thought that he may be my great grandfather gives me the creeps.'

I smiled and puffed out my chest. 'You can only say that because you're used to perfection,' and there was a brief of pause as she reached out and touched my cheek.

'Stop it Billy,' she said. 'I'm trying to be serious here.'

'And the engagement, oh secretive one,' Tom said. He's like a bloody dog with a bone. He won't ever let go of things.

'We got engaged over a year ago,' I explained. 'We kept it quiet because we didn't want to upset Susan. It was when we thought we might not be able to send her back to her Billy and we didn't want to rub salt in the wound. That's all there was to it.'

Susan turned and stared at Dorothy. 'That was so sweet of you to do that.' She then explained why to us obviously not worldly wise men, 'When a girl gets engaged, the last thing she wants to do is keep it a secret. She wants to tell the whole world so it must have been extremely difficult for Dorothy not to say anything.'

I was pleased that Susan had taken the news so well, and also pleased that she'd now be able to go back to 1926 and tell Dorothy's news to the Mendozas. Obviously, I had never met them, but from the way Dorothy described them, I felt I knew them intimately.

I glanced at my watch and leapt forward with a start, seeing how late it was. 'Hey you lot! It's ten o'clock already. We'd better shift it and get prepared for the big moment, especially you Susan.'

By 10:28 we had all said our goodbyes to her. Without realising she was doing it, she kept touching her watch to make sure it was still safely in place, and who could blame her? She had been trapped in another world for what must have seemed a lifetime, with her wanting so badly to get back to *her* Billy and to see her mother, and especially the father Dorothy said had changed so much.

'Ready Tom?' I said, and for the first time since this whole thing started, he seemed a little hesitant about pushing the fuse in. He wriggled his shoulders nervously and held the fuse out to me, saying, 'Bloody hell Billy. I'm still shell shocked from yesterday's explosion. Be a pal and you do it. Please!'

I almost took it from him and then, possibly just in time, had a jolting thought. 'Can't do that I'm afraid Tom. Don't you see? It would be changing the formula yet again. Supposing it fails because of that?' and it took no more than a second's thought for him to agree with me.

He gritted his teeth, closed his eyes and was about to push the prepared fuse into the board when Susan cried out, 'Wait a minute Tom, - please.' She ran over and gave each of us a fleeting hug. Even Beth was included. 'I couldn't leave without doing that one more time,' she said and hurried back to her spot. There was a moment of panic as she suddenly looked at her wrist, but she was safe - the watch was still there. 'Ready,' she said and clutched at her heart, her pretty face flushed with excitement. As Tom was about to push in the fuse, she appeared to have a sudden thought and called out, 'If it works, I shall carve, *I got back safely* on the big oak tree at the end of the garden,' and before she could say anything further, the fuse was in. We heard the words, 'I will miss all of you,' just before the noise of the explosion obliterated every other sound from our ears. God, how I'd grown to hate this ceremony. The explosion alone was enough to scare the hell out of you. All it needed was for me to be afraid of the blackness that followed and I'd end up a right basket case.

Dorothy waited for around ten seconds before clicking the torch on. She directed its beam into the corner where Susan had first appeared almost a year and a half back. The space was empty. The girl we had grown to love was gone and we knew we would never see her again, but at least we knew that she was back where she truly belonged, and a lot of people in 1927 were going to be happy because of that, just as a lot of people in 2017 were also going to be happy for her, although at the same time, they would be sad.

I suppose in the end, life has to have balance.

*

Tom was a ball of energy. He has the most devious brain of anyone I know and it was chugging away once again. The lights were still out but he snatched the torch from Dorothy and said, 'Come on everyone, let's go and check the tree for Susan's message.' He headed for the door and we all followed, stumbling through the darkness trying to keep up with him.

'Slow down Tom,' Kate shouted but she was wasting her breath and he broke into a run. By the time we got to the end of the 100-yard-long garden, he'd already checked the tree and his long face told us the story. 'Susan didn't make it,' he said. 'There's nothing carved on it. Nothing at all.'

Of course, we couldn't leave it at that. The rest of us took the torch from him and had to look for ourselves. We went over the tree with a fine tooth comb, but Tom was right. There was nothing. 'Perhaps in all the excitement, she forgot,' Kate said in an attempt to raise our spirits, but she was wasting her breath. We all knew that Susan would never have forgotten something as important as that.

We said our gloomy *goodnights* to one another and the next morning at breakfast, Tom said what we were all thinking. 'I wonder where the poor girl ended up.'

I said, 'God knows. I don't even want to think about it. She could be anywhere in time. Maybe even in the future.'

'Now there's a thought,' Tom said ambiguously.

We watched TV to take our minds off of Susan and during one of the commercial breaks that showed a woman pushing a child on a swing, Dorothy smiled reminiscently; 'You know, I used to love playing in this garden when I was a kid. There was a swing on one of the trees and dad would spend hours pushing me. He was a really good dad like that.'

I immediately picked up on what she'd said, 'One of the trees? What do you mean, one of the trees? There's only one tree at the end of the garden.'

'Well, there used to be two, but Dad had the swing tree chopped down because it got some sort of disease and he was afraid it would spread to the other one.'

We all stared at her and her hand flew to her mouth. She said, 'Oh my God.'

*

Dorothy had been on the phone to her parents

for over an hour, which was understandable considering that she hadn't spoken to them for a year. The others were straining at the leash to discover what her father had to say, but curbed their curiosity and didn't interrupt her once.

She had decided to leave her pertinent question to her father until last as she didn't want him thinking that the tree was the real reason she had made the call. So far, the conversation had comprised of her adventures on her imaginary archaeological trip to Africa.

Eventually, when she felt enough time had passed, she signalled to the others that she was now going to ask about the tree and they leaned forwards interestedly.

'By the way dad, what did you do with the big oak tree you chopped down about fifteen years back?'

'That's a strange question Sweetheart,' he said, 'but we had a wood burning stove at the time, so it came in handy for that. When the stove went wonky and would have cost mega-bucks to repair, we dumped it and got an electric stove instead.'

'Did you use all the wood up?' she asked, knowing that he wasn't stupid and would realise there was something she wasn't telling him.

'Every last piece Sweetheart, every piece, now, do you want to tell your old dad what's going on?'

She tried to sound casual but wasn't sure that she'd succeeded. 'Oh, it's just that I met someone on the dig of all places. He said that he'd been on holiday at Lulworth Cove when he was a boy and had sneaked onto our swing when no one was about. He said there

271

was some carving on the tree and I was curious, that's all Pops.'

'Why are you calling me Pops, Sweetheart? You've never called me that before.'

'Haven't I?' Dorothy asked, thinking of Samuel Mendoza and smiling at the warm feeling it gave her. 'It must be something I picked up on the dig - but it's a nice name and I like it, so if you don't mind, then I'm going to call you Pops from now on.'

'Okay Sweetheart. I don't mind what you call me, as long as you call me. What did the carving say?'

'I think it was, *I got back safely,* but I could be wrong,' Dorothy said, holding her breath, afraid of his answer.

'No, sorry to disappoint you Sweetheart, but there was nothing like that carved in the tree. Maybe this friend of yours got his gardens mixed up.'

Dorothy turned to the others and her eyes filled with tears. She signalled *no* to them, although there was no need. The tears had given them the answer.

'I'd better go now Dad,' she said, afraid that her voice would let her down and he would realise she was upset. If that happened, she knew he would insist on coming down to Dorset straight away to see what was wrong. He was that sort of dad. Always had been.

'I thought I was being called Pops from now on,' he laughed. 'That didn't last for very long, did it?'

By now, tears were running down Dorothy's cheeks, but somehow, she managed to keep her voice in check and said, 'Sorry Pops, but I really do have to go.'

He said, 'Okay Sweetheart, but before you do, answer me this. This guy you met in Africa. Did he ever mention a woman named Susan?'

Dorothy thought her heart would stop beating. She could hardly get the words from her mouth. 'Why do you ask Dad - I mean, Pops?'

'Only because of the one carving that was on the tree - but if he did know a Susan, he must be knocking on a bit. Your mum and I saw the only carving on the tree when we stayed at the house as part of our honeymoon 30 odd years ago and it was old then.'

'What did the carving say?' Dorothy asked, a little too quickly. She crossed her fingers and said a silent prayer to herself.

'Well certainly not *I got back safely,* that's for sure. It started with a date and you know how good I am at remembering those Sweetheart. It said, '*December the 28th 1927,*' and beneath it was carved, '*Susan is back with Billy.*'

*

'I can't stand this for much longer,' Billy said as he paced around the hallway. 'The waiting is driving me crazy.'

Samuel put a comforting arm around his shoulder. 'We all feel the same my boy,' he said, but those words didn't help one bit. Samuel had lost a daughter - a terrible thing for any father, but if things went wrong and they didn't get Susan back, he still had his wife and Celia, whereas Susan was Billy's whole life. There were no brothers, sisters, father or mother waiting to comfort him, or even an aunt or uncle waiting in the wings.

After leaving the orphanage at the age of fourteen, there was just one way for Billy to go, and that was up. Not necessarily at the speed he'd risen at, but he'd been lucky. A classic case of being *in the right place at the right time,* that's how it had been for him. He was just another worker on the factory floor of a gearbox manufacturer when the idea came to him. A simple one really, but apparently the best ideas are usually the simplest ones. In this case, it was a steel spring that he realised could be dispensed with. He still wondered why it hadn't been spotted earlier. By slightly increasing the length of another gearshift spring, it would perform not one but two functions.

England was fighting for its very existence in the war with Germany and metal was scarce and badly needed for munitions. Apart from Billy's discovery helping the war effort, it also saved the sum of sixpence per gearbox and reduced the assembly time by four minutes.

The owner of the factory was never one to miss talent, even in one as young as Billy. He was also a kindly man who took Billy under his wing, making him a partner when he reached 21 and officially became a man. From that moment, Billy Monroe hadn't looked back.

Samuel said, 'It should be any minute now,' and Billy's thoughts returned to the present.

They stood silently and waited and seconds later a low rumbling sound began, shaking the house on its foundations, just as the previous evening.

Maria stepped forward and held the coat stand

before it toppled over, while an excited Celia gripped her father's hand so tightly that her knuckles gleamed white.

Suddenly, as though out of thin air, Susan was standing before them. For a moment, they were all too stunned to move and then Billy let out a whoop of sheer joy. He rushed over and threw his arms around her. She saw her father over Billy's shoulder and knew Dorothy had been telling the truth. This was a vastly different father to the one she had left behind. She had never seen him cry before; not even when the mother he adored passed away, but tears were streaming down his cheeks. Her mother stood next to him, crying and laughing at the same time. Maria touched her daughter's hand and said, 'Welcome back my little angel.'

Susan stared into Billy's green eyes. 'Dorothy said that you love me, Billy Monroe. Is that true?' and now she was wrapped in his arms, all his confusing fears vanished like smoke in a storm.

Billy clung to her and whispered, 'It's true, I love you Susan Mendoza, and always will,' and Susan began to cry; softly at first, but then in heaving sobs as all the worries of the past year and a half disappeared.

Samuel and Maria waited patiently. Had they not realised before that their role as Susan's protectors was over, they realised it now. Billy was the one their daughter would turn to, protecting her from the harshness of the world, but Samuel had known this day would come and was prepared for it. He also knew there was a special place for most parents in their children's hearts and hopefully, always would be.

Eventually Billy released Susan and she hugged her parents, crying but laughing through the tears, and then it was Celia's turn. Susan reached out and held her. This was the little sister she had spent her life protecting. 'I know all about Digby and what has happened,' she whispered, 'so you must not worry anymore because you have me with you now.'

Celia, who had held herself together for so long, buried her head in Susan's bosom and sobbed, clinging desperately to her.

Afterwards they sat and talked into the early hours of the morning, just happy to be in each other's company again. Most of the things Samuel and Maria had to tell Susan she had already learnt from Dorothy, whereas they knew nothing of Susan's life since Dorothy arrived a year back. Bringing with her the wonderful news that Susan was still alive.

Susan thought of all the knowledge she had gained during her time in the 21st century. 'Unbelievable things are waiting in the future Father,' she said during their discussion, and he gently stroked her arm.

'It is no longer *Father*,' he smiled. 'Dottie has given me a brand new name. It's Pops now my dear, and I have grown quite fond of the name.'

At four o'clock, just as they unanimously decided that bed had more appeal than any further talking, Billy took everyone by surprise when he dropped to one knee in front of Susan. Samuel winked across at his wife and they stepped back to give the lad more room.

Billy took hold of Susan's hand and looked at her with an expression that said everything she needed to know. 'It was my procrastinating that brought about all of this my darling. If I'd followed my instincts as well as my feelings, I would have proposed to you last year and cancelled the African trip. But by the grace of God and some help from your great great niece, you're back with me and I'm not about to make the same mistake again, and so Susan, I'm asking if you will do me the honour of becoming my wife.'

This was all Susan had dreamt of since the day Billy took her in his arms for the first time and kissed her. She suppressed a rising giggle of excitement. 'Have you approached my father in the appropriate manner?' she teased, and he nodded that indeed, he had. 'Very well then, Mr Monroe, if that is the case and my father, sorry, I mean Pops, has no objections, then I accept your proposal unreservedly.'

She smiled as she thought of how different life was in 2016 and how in that era they would be trooping upstairs together to share the same bed, but even if she had the choice, she would have still wanted it this way. She had waited this long. A little longer wouldn't be so hard to bear.

Although it was almost 4:30 by the time she climbed into bed, she lay thinking for more than an hour, far too excited for sleep after all that had happened. She would never see her friends from the future again and that was hard to accept. Already there was an ache in her heart. She would miss them terribly, but thanks to their persistence and the help they had given her, she was back where she belonged. She was home with her Billy. Home with the man she loved.

*

Digby Jones was quickly losing patience with his uncle. The man was stupid beyond belief. Digby had spent the past 30 minutes carefully explaining his plan to him, but he'd wasted his breath. All he needed was for his uncle to mortgage the house, not that the dump was worth much, but Digby's eavesdropping had given him the information that certain shares would be doubling or even tripling within two weeks, and to take advantage of that knowledge, speed was critical. It was important for him to gather in every penny he could lay his hands on, but his uncle was a stubborn old fool who flatly refused to cooperate and so far, no amount of Digby's carefully presented logic had made him change his mind. Digby decided on one last attempt before resorting to less pleasant methods of persuasion.

He slapped his hands on his knees in exasperation. 'You are not listening to me Uncle Bert,' he said wearily. 'Samuel Mendoza is a multi-millionaire. He made his money because of his knowledge and business acumen. If he says-' but Bert Jones slammed his fist on the table to stop the incessant flow of words.

'For Gawd's sake, shut it Digby and git your facts right. It was his granddaddy what made the money back in the eighteen 'undreds. All this Mr Samuel 'igh and bleeding mighty Mendoza did was to 'ave the good luck to be born his grandson. There ain't nuthin' clever in that, is there?'

Digby sighed and rubbed his hands across his face. This was madness. It was little wonder that the sole financial result of Herbert Jones' pathetic life was this squalid little house. A life where his miniscule income forced him to eat the type of food that the Samuel Mendozas of this world would never allow within a mile of their dinner plates. Pig's trotters, sheep's hearts, tripe and other unmentionables. He shuddered at the thought of any of those so-called foods ever touching his lips.

He fixed his eyes pointedly on his uncle, but this time with a steely eyed glare. He'd tried his damnedest to be nice and look where it had got him. His patience finally evaporated and he reached out and grabbed Bert Jones by his scrawny neck, dragging him forward. Bert's eyes bulged with fear as he felt the strength of Digby's grip and a trickle of urine ran down his leg. 'Now Uncle,' Digby hissed menacingly, 'it's time we stopped pissing about, so I'm no longer asking you. Now, I'm telling you, and Uncle, I would strongly advise that you make sure that *this* is what happens. Tomorrow morning, two men will arrive here with a set of documents that you will sign without complaint. One of the men will witness your signature and upon completion of the documentation, the other man will then present you with a banker's draft for 175 pounds. Do you realise, uncle Bert that that sum of money is more than someone like you could earn in two years of full time work?

'In the afternoon another man will call on you. That man is a share broker and using the bank draft you were given in the morning, you will purchase from him 39,000 thousand one-penny shares in the *Armstrong and Annis Trading Company*. The remaining twelve pounds and ten shillings will be the broker's commission. Within two weeks, those shares will be worth at least double the amount you paid for them.'

He pushed his uncle backwards into an armchair and squatted down next to him. His eyes were cold slits and they bored into Bert Jones. 'Now Uncle, that's the house taken care of, so shall we move on? I want you to tell me exactly how much you have put away in savings, and please don't lie to me Uncle, or I'm afraid that I shall have to hurt you very badly indeed.'

*

'Anyway,' Dorothy began to explain to the others, laughing so much that Billy was worried she would have a seizure. 'Before Digby reached the window and could hear what was being said, Pops explained to us that the *Armstrong and Annis Trading Company* was close to having its shares suspended for suspected illegal practices. However, once Digby was settled outside and listening, Pops came out with a completely different story and said they were about to be taken over and when that happened, the shares would double in value or maybe even treble.'

'And do you think this Jones fellow believed what he heard?' Tom asked. He knew that in the same circumstances, he certainly would have. Eavesdropping outside a window while inside, a multi-millionaire spouted on about a company whose shares were about to go up by that much. Shove a million pounds in and come out with at least two, maybe even more. Too bloody true he would.

'Oh yes, Digby would have believed it all right,' Dorothy said airily, confirming Tom's unspoken opinion. 'He was so full of his own importance that he would probably have advised some of his acquaintances to buy all the shares they could get their hands on,' but she was wrong on that particular point. Digby Jones' life plan had always been to soar above his friends - not to take them to the dizzy heights with him. 'Although anyone with any sense would surely check them out first before taking someone like Digby Jones' word,' she added.

'Yes, I guess so,' Tom agreed, 'but what about Jones himself? He was getting the tip from the horse's mouth. He would have no need to check them out and could have lost quite a lot of money if he bought them.'

Dorothy felt slightly uneasy at the suggestion, but shrugged it off. 'No Tom, not Digby. Pops had him checked out. He was more of less penniless and lived in a room in his uncle's little house. He might have been able to get his hands on a few pounds to buy some shares, but that would be all.' She looked around the table at her enthralled audience. 'The point of the exercise was to make him mad because he was finally in the know, but unable to take advantage of that knowledge because he was flat broke. He would have found out soon enough that his leg had been pulled when the company went to the wall a couple of weeks later. Gosh, I would love to have been there when he discovered that he'd been made a fool of. That would be an extremely hard thing for someone like Digby to swallow.'

*

Digby stared at the headlines of the financial newspaper in disbelief.

'Shares in Armstrong and Annis suspended as directors are investigated by Scotland Yard for massive fraud.'

The paper fell from his hands and he sat down quickly, then retrieved the newspaper and pushed it into his pocket so that his uncle wouldn't see it.

Digby was having trouble getting his breath and remained seated for a moment. There was a sick feeling in the pit of his stomach and his face reflected that feeling. It was pasty white. He drank his tea in a state of shock while he reviewed things. What the hell had gone wrong? He'd heard the words of the great financial wizard with his own ears, and people like Samuel Mendoza don't make those types of mistakes. Obviously, they made mistakes, but losing money wasn't one of them.

Digby heard his uncle moving about upstairs so left the house before he came down. It meant he'd be hanging about for an hour at the train station until his train arrived, but he could use that time to plan what he must do.

At the office, Grace, the pretty secretary Digby shared with five others, looked concerned as he walked in. 'Are you all right Mr Jones? You look ever so pale you do.'

'I'm perfectly well,' he said snootily, instantly regretting his tone. He had plans for Grace. Plans that had more to do with the bedroom than the office.

For the rest of the morning he sat at his desk, slowly stewing. He couldn't get his mind away from the newspaper headline and the more he thought about it, the more it became obvious that this was all Mendoza's fault. Uncle Bert might be bordering on stupid, but he was right in what he'd said about the man. It was his grandfather who had the business acumen. Samuel Mendoza was in the lofty position he now occupied because he was the grandson of a business genius. In reality, the man was a fool. A fool who had lost Uncle Bert his home and his savings - not that Bert knew it yet.

All morning, Digby sat at his desk thinking. He covered every angle other than the real one. The one that anyone without his vanity would have realised within minutes. That he had been duped. Taken in and made a fool of.

At two o'clock, he watched as Samuel came out of his office and made his way to the boardroom. As the door closed behind him, Digby strolled casually across to Grace's desk and asked quietly, 'What's the old man up to?'

'There's a meeting with all the directors in the boardroom,' she explained. 'It's scheduled to start at 2:30 and finish at 6:00.'

Digby returned to his desk. He'd thought about the situation until his head ached, but eventually the final piece in the jigsaw puzzle dropped into place, giving him the answer. He phoned Celia at *Cherry Tree house* and asked if she was alone.

She explained that her mother was playing bridge in Poole and wouldn't be back until seven. She didn't mention that Susan was there. Digby, like everyone apart from the Mendoza family and Billy, still believed she had died a year and a half back. 'Then I'll be with you in two hours,' Digby said, keeping his anger hidden. 'I must talk to you Celia. It's important.'

She was happy to see him. He had been his old self

with her since the awful things he'd said that day in her father's office. Later, she had virtually lied to herself in an attempt to excuse him.

Celia told Susan that Digby was coming to the house. She asked her to remain in her bedroom until he'd gone.

At the office, Digby ambled across to Grace once again and made a pretence of putting a sheaf of papers on her desk. 'I have to go out soon my beauty,' he said, glancing around to see if he was being observed. 'And I won't be back this afternoon, so be a good girl and cover for me will you? If anyone asks after me, tell them I left just a few minutes earlier. Will you do that for me?'

'I could get into a lot of trouble Mr Jones,' she said coyly and he stroked her under the chin with his forefinger.

'I'll make it up to you Grace, I promise.'

She blushed a bright pink colour. 'All right then Mr Jones, but only because it's for you.'

Digby made the tedious train journey back to Dorset, his mind turning things over and over until he was sick of thinking about it. From the station, he drove to *Cherry Tree House*. Celia waited in the doorway while Digby parked. He pushed past her into the hallway. 'I'm in trouble,' he announced. 'Big trouble and I need 240 pounds Celia.' He turned towards her. 'And I need it today, so please don't give me a hard time. I'm really not in the mood for it.'

Celia's heart sank. Despite her earlier hopes after the phone call, it was now quite obvious that nothing had changed. He was still the same Digby; a Digby about to discover she was no longer the same Celia. She had finally had enough of his self-centred ways. Everything was about him. About what he wanted, what he needed. Her wants counted for nothing. 'Well, I wish you luck Digby,' she said in a brittle voice, 'but don't expect me to help you, because I won't.'

Unfortunately, she was making her stand when Digby was totally desperate. His uncle was about to lose his life savings of 60 pounds, plus the house he'd worked all his life to pay for, meaning that Digby would also be losing his home. He had to have the money and that was all there was to it, with or without Celia's consent. It was her father who had put him in this situation and it was only fair that she should pay up.

He didn't argue, but he grabbed her by the hair and dragged her up the stairs, ignoring her screams of pain. At the top of the stairs, he pushed her into the room and she fell to her knees. For the first time ever, she was frightened of him. 'Please Digby,' she sobbed, 'remember the baby.'

'Find the money Celia,' he snapped. 'I know you have it, now get it!'

She climbed to her feet and then in one swift movement, slammed the door in his face, locking it from the inside. 'You bitch,' he roared and kicked the door with such force that the lock sprang and it flew open. Celia screamed and cowered by the bed as he stormed into the room. He grabbed her by the hair again and threw her forward. Her chin smashed into the chest of drawers and blood spurted from a deep cut that appeared below her lip. She collapsed in a heap and tried to raise herself, but was too dazed and fell back.

Digby pulled open the drawer where he knew she kept her valuables and money. His eyes widened upon seeing the neatly stacked piles of five-pound notes. He took every pile, knowing there was considerably more than he needed.

He turned to leave the room and Celia stumbled after him. 'Digby,' she cried as he reached the top of the stairs and he turned to face her. She made a pathetic lunge at him which he easily side stepped, but the momentum carried her forward and she screamed in terror as she fell headlong down the stairs. Her hands flew to her stomach in an attempt to protect her unborn child.

At the bottom, she lay motionless and Digby raced down the stairs after her. He came to an abrupt, horrified halt as he saw the pool of blood forming at her groin and shrank back in horror. Panic seized him; if she lost the baby, his future was gone. All of his hard work and planning would have been to no avail. He stooped down, gently lifted the unconscious Celia into his arms and carried her outside to the car.

The engine purred to life after one crank of the starting handle and he drove off.

Susan, still in her bedroom, heard the car drive away. The door had been ajar and she had witnessed almost everything. She was shaking with fear, ashamed of herself for not going to Celia's aid when she first heard the commotion, but what could she do against a man more than six feet tall? And braveness had never been one of her qualities. She'd always been afraid of violence, even as a little girl.

She ran downstairs to the hall, picked up the telephone and after telling the operator that her call was urgent, read out her father's number.

Chapter Twenty-One

When Celia regained consciousness in the hospital, her head was pounding and the deep cut under her chin throbbed incessantly. She turned and Digby - whose forehead was creased with genuine worry, although for completely the wrong reasons, saw her eyes open and hurried to her bedside. He bent down and gently pushed the hair back from Celia's forehead. 'How are you feeling my darling?' he whispered tentatively.

The fear in his voice wasn't playacting. He knew only too well that his whole future now hung in the balance. He took her hand in his but she snatched it away as the memory of his brutality came flooding back to her.

She could feel a dull ache in the area of her stomach and was swamped by a terrifying panic as she realised what it could mean. She spoke and her words fluttered from her lips like leaves falling from a tree in autumn. 'My baby, Digby,' she whispered, terrified of his answer, 'please tell me that my baby is safe.'

How she had worded the question brought home to him just how far down the line the relationship had gone. *My baby,* she had said, not *Our baby,* and Digby realised what a fool he'd been. All he'd ever had to do was be loving and kind to Celia. Less than a year of pretending and he would have been financially set for life. Had he done that, then losing the baby would not have altered anything. With the wedding date already arranged and Celia in love with him, the ceremony would have still gone ahead, but now? He realised that serious work lay ahead of him if he was to salvage a future life of luxury. Digby squeezed tears into his eyes, but Celia wasn't fooled by this show of emotion from a man devoid of feelings for anyone but himself. However, it gave the answer to her question and she began to cry softly. Out of this whole mess of a relationship with Digby Jones, the only good thing had been the child growing inside her.

'We have lost the baby my love,' he said in a broken voice. 'That terrible accident took our child from us. I am so very sorry. To think that a silly lovers' tiff should cause such a tragedy.' Tears flowed unhindered down his cheeks, but they had no effect on Celia. She knew they were crocodile tears that meant nothing. Instead of eliciting sympathy, they repulsed her. It was all playacting. The past months had shown that Digby Jones cared for no one but himself. She made no comment on this monster's interpretation of a lovers' tiff. Smashing her head against the chest of drawers and then stealing her money. She stared up at him and thought, *Just go Digby. Just get out of my life and don't come back.* She never wanted to speak to him again. In the short time she had known him, all he had done was to take and to keep on taking, giving nothing in return. Well, that wasn't strictly true. He had given her one thing, but now he'd even taken that from her. After today, she hoped she would never see him again.

She stared at him and he flinched, recognising the hatred in her eyes.

'Just leave Digby,' Celia said tiredly, 'get out of here and get out of my life. You have taken the most precious thing in the world from me, but in doing so, you have released me. Now, there is nothing to bond us together and I am free of your temper. Free of your constant childlike wants and demands, and because I am free, my family is also free.'

A feeling of dread engulfed Digby. The money he'd battled to gain for the whole of his adult life was about to be snatched away, unless he could work his brand of magic one more time.

'You'll feel differently in the morning my darling,' he said soothingly. 'You'll see,' but she couldn't be bothered to tell him he was wrong. She would never feel differently. Not if she lived long enough to receive the King's telegram on reaching her centenary. She felt nothing for Digby now. Not even the hatred of a moment ago. All she wanted was him gone from her life.

She spoke in a tired voice, 'Go now Digby, go before I call the nurse and have you forcibly removed.'

He stood up and left the small ward, realising that it was all over for him, although there was still the matter of his 50,000 pounds pay off money. He should still get that. He may not be a man of honour himself, but Mendoza certainly was, and he was quite sure that Celia would tell her father nothing of the events that had taken place. Even the gash on her chin would be attributed to the fall.

Now he must concentrate on the money and his uncle's house. Of course, that pokey little house was insignificant compared to the 50,000 pounds, but you could never have too much money and if he played his cards right, he could make certain that the house was left to him when the old boy died, and not to one of the other nephews.

Once outside the hospital grounds, he counted the wad of notes he'd taken from Celia's chest of drawers. He was pleasantly surprised by the amount and smiled with satisfaction. Five hundred and fifty pounds, a good one hundred pounds more than he'd guessed at.

When he walked into his uncle's tiny house an hour later, he found the old man sitting at the kitchen table with his head buried in his hands. His face was ashen. On the table was a newspaper with the tell-tale headlines.

The old man leapt to his feet when he saw Digby, his face full of rage. 'You've lost me bleedin' house, yer little bastard,' he screeched and Digby almost smiled at his uncle's choice of words. If anything, he'd always counted himself a big bastard, certainly not a little one.

'There you are uncle Bert,' he said as he tossed a pile of notes onto the table. 'Not quite as much as I had hoped for, but still a nice little profit just the same. Still a worthwhile venture, wouldn't you agree?'

Bert looked at him in disbelief. *Armstrong and Annis* had gone to the wall, so where had the money come from? He gave it no more than a second's thought before gathering up the scattered notes. He counted it into piles and grinned with delight. Two hundred and sixty-five pounds. Thirty pounds' profit in a matter of days. It was half as much as the sixty pounds he had managed to save in his working life and he still had a roof over his head and his life savings returned. Nowhere near the amount Digby had promised, but still a handsome profit.

He turned to Digby, his lined face smiling. 'Yer done well boy an' I shouldn't 'ave tore into yer like that, so I'm sorry if I upset yer. Sit down lad and I'll make yer some dinner. 'Ow does bangers, mash an' onions sound to yer?'

The following morning as Digby walked jauntily into the office building in London, he was met by two burly security guards. He knew them quite well and often enjoyed a few minutes chatting to them. 'What's up Fellas?' he asked.

Sid, the taller of the two said, 'Sorry Mr Jones, but we 'ave instructions not to let you in the building.'

Digby stopped in his tracks and his brow furrowed. 'Is this some kind of joke Sid?' he asked quietly. 'Is that what this is?'

Sid held out his hand and snapped his fingers. 'It ain't no joke Mr Jones, and I've been told to get your office key and your car key as well. Mr Mendoza has already been an' made arrangements to have the car picked up from your local station.'

Digby stood looking at them silently and then the anger boiled up inside him. Some of the people he worked with were now staring curiously at him, obviously wondering what the hell was going on. He took a pace forward. 'It's a mistake lads. I'll go upstairs and talk to Mr Mendoza now. Whatever it is, I'll soon clear it up,' but Sid's companion stepped in front of him and barred the way. He may have been the smaller of the two men, but he still stood at more than six feet, with wide shoulders, a barrel chest and powerful looking arms. His many times broken nose told Digby how the man spent his time out of working hours.

As Sid had done, he also held out his hand. 'Please, Mr Jones. Don't give us no bovver. Just give us the keys and be on yer way.'

Digby counted himself a fair judge of men. Despite the man's words, he knew the last thing he wanted was for Digby to hand the keys over. What he was really hoping was for Digby to race to the stairs - giving him the opportunity to unleash some violence.

Whatever Digby's legion of faults, he wasn't a coward, but realising he had no chance against the two of them, he reluctantly pulled the keys from his pocket and tossed them into the man's outstretched hand. The man's look reminded Digby of a dog who had had a bone snatched from its jaws. 'I'll go now lads,' he said quietly, 'but once it's sorted, I'll be back.'

The man tossed the keys across to Sid who caught them and grinned insolently at Digby. 'Sure you will Mr Jones,' he said, 'sure you will.'

Digby knew there was but one explanation for all of this. It was Celia. The disloyal cow had blabbed to Mendoza. Some women couldn't be trusted and she was obviously one of them.

He didn't return to Dorset right away. Instead, he walked the busy streets of the city, thinking and planning what his next move should be. Eventually, he walked into a stationary shop and purchased a writing pad along with a pack of envelopes.

Ten minutes later he was sitting on one of the many park benches that lined the embankment of the River Thames, writing a letter to Samuel Mendoza.

Digby screwed up his first four attempts, but was pleased with the fifth. It read,

Dear Samuel,

I am puzzled by the events taking place at the moment. I realise what a shock it must have been for you, with Celia ending up in hospital and losing the baby. No one was more devastated than I at losing the child I had longed for. I don't know what Celia has told you, but in hospital, she was quite delirious and hallucinating.

The truth is that it was just a tragic accident where she missed her footing and fell down the stairs. Had I not been there, I dread to think what would have happened to her and I do believe that it was only my quick thinking that saved your daughter's life.

Please give me the opportunity to talk to you and present the real facts of what took place. I believe you owe me that much.

Your humble servant, Digby.'

It took him fifteen minutes to walk back to the building housing the offices of the Mendoza Empire. A quick glance revealed that Sid and his companion were no longer around, so Digby walked up to the front desk and handed the letter to the receptionist.

'Could you see that this letter reaches Mr Mendoza immediately Carol. It's rather urgent, so please tell him that I shall wait here in reception for his reply.'

Carol scribbled something on a piece of paper, summoned a young lad of around fourteen years of age and sent him upstairs clutching the letter along with her note.

Digby waited uneasily, constantly glancing around and dreading the return of the security guards before he had his answer, but he need not have worried. Ten minutes later, the boy returned and handed Carol a sealed envelope. She glanced at it, passed it to Digby who hurried from the building as Sid and his companion approached.

Outside, he tore open the envelope and read Samuel's answer.

'I shall expect you at Cherry Tree House this Saturday at noon Jones where I will listen to your version of the events that led to my daughter being hospitalised. In the meantime, make no attempt to communicate with Celia or any member of my family. Should you do so, then the meeting will immediately be cancelled.

Yours, Samuel Mendoza.'

Digby set off for the railway station feeling happier than fifteen minutes earlier. He was back in the ball game and must now convince Celia that her version of events was inaccurate, obviously caused by the trauma of the fall. It would be a difficult task, but given what was at stake, he felt he could do it.

Chapter Twenty-Two

Samuel and his family, along with Billy, were assembled in the lounge. Samuel was in an exceptionally good mood, which none of the women could understand. How could he be so buoyant when within the hour he would be meeting the odious Digby Jones?

Only Billy suspected that Samuel was actually looking forward to the interview.

Samuel left the room and returned a few minutes later with a chilled bottle of champagne and five crystal champagne flutes on a tray. There was a smile on his face that his daughters found puzzling.

'What are we celebrating Pops?' Susan asked. 'Surely it can have nothing to do with Digby Jones' visit?'

Celia shuddered at the mention of Digby's name. Even with her father and Billy there to protect her, she remembered too clearly what had happened in her bedroom on that tragic day and was afraid of him. If he should lose his temper because things didn't go his way, then they could do little to protect her. Her father was no longer young, while Billy, at five feet nine inches, was considerably shorter than Digby. He was also at least forty pounds lighter.

All Celia wanted was for Samuel to give Digby some money and that would be the end of it. Money was Digby's God and as long as there was enough of it, that would satisfy him, but Samuel had already explained it would be pointless to do that. That whatever amount he gave the scoundrel would never be enough to satisfy the man's greed, and that sometime in the future he would return demanding more.

Knowing how Digby was about money, Celia couldn't disagree with her father, but would worry about that problem when it happened. In the meantime, she hoped Digby would leave with an amount large enough to avoid any unpleasantness and possible violence.

'This champagne is nothing to do with that Jones fellow my dear,' Samuel assured his daughter. 'This is to celebrate the fact that your mother and I have at last found a new home for us in Cobham.' He carefully eased the cork from the bottle, ignoring the girls' excited questions about the new house and half-filled the five flutes before lifting his own to make a toast. 'To our little family,' he said and looked directly at Susan. 'When your mother and I thought we had lost you, the feeling was far worse than I ever imagined possible. But then my little Dottie arrived, and although I confess that at first I didn't believe a word she said, I soon realised I was wrong and she had been telling the truth. My dear, losing you and then getting you back has taught me how important my family is to me.' He smiled softly across at Susan. 'Sometimes, one doesn't realise what they have until they have lost it.'

If Susan hadn't realised before that Dorothy had been right about her father, then she certainly realised it now. He was changed almost beyond recognition, so some good had come from what had happened.

Everyone raised their glass and said in unison, 'To the family,' and drained the contents. As they returned the empty flutes to the tray, Susan picked up the bottle and passed it to her father. 'Will you fill the glasses again please Pops? I wish to propose another toast.'

Samuel smiled, wondering what was on earth was coming. He refilled the flutes and Susan, just as he had done, raised hers high in the air. 'To Dorothy,' she said. 'May God always keep her safe and well, wherever she may be.'

The others followed suit, saying in unison, 'To Dorothy.'

'So tell us about the new house Mother,' Celia said as the empty champagne flutes went back on the tray. She needed to get her mind away from Digby's impending visit.

Maria smiled with pleasure, picturing the place in her mind's eye. 'It is so beautiful Darling. Quite breath-taking really. There are six bedrooms, a lounge, dining room, drawing room and study and it's situated a little outside of the town centre.'

She was pleased to be bringing at least *some* good news to Celia. Maybe it would help to alleviate the trauma the poor girl suffered at the hands of that awful man. 'But this is the part I know you will like Celia,' she added. 'The house is set in one and a half acres and has its own stables, so you may begin your riding again as soon as you feel strong enough.'

The word *stables* did all that Maria hoped it would. Celia had had a lifelong love affair with horses and the walls of her bedroom were plastered with pictures of them. She squealed with delight and rushed across to hug both her mother and father in turn, saying, 'Thank you, thank you, thank you!'

While all of this was taking place, Digby Jones was driving his uncle's tiny car to Lulworth Cove, going over his story again and again as he drove.

Yes, it was true that he and Celia had argued, but it had been no more than a trivial lovers' tiff. Surely all couples have them from time to time - why, even Samuel and Maria must have had the odd spat over the years. Digby paused and thought for a moment: with so much at stake, maybe it wasn't a good idea to point out that his benefactor had faults. He decided to replace *All couples* with *Most couples*. What was the old saying? *Never bite the hand that feeds you* and as the thought hit him, he realised once again that biting the hand that fed him was exactly what had put him in this sorry situation. Stupid, stupid, stupid! Would he never learn?

The next time he met the daughter of a wealthy man, for he knew there would be a next time, things would be very different indeed. With 50,000 pounds of his own money nestling in his bank account, minus, of course, the cost of a new car and a complete new wardrobe of clothes, he would move far away from Dorset. Maybe even as far as Lancashire where the rich Mill owners reigned supreme. Admittedly the people in the north of England spoke with an accent that he personally disliked, but that would only serve to make him stand out all the more to the ladies.

He would join a tennis club, that's if they had tennis clubs in the North, and a cricket club. He knew Northerners had cricket clubs and were fanatical about the game. Sports clubs would surely provide a plentiful supply of the type of women he was looking for. They needed just one requirement - a rich father.

Maybe he could take up polo as well, but then dismissed the idea immediately, thinking that the ultra-civilised game of Polo wouldn't have made the downmarket journey to the black pudding territory of the north.

He passed the *Five miles to Lulworth Cove* sign and pushed all thoughts of where his future lay to one side. One step at a time Digby, he told himself. First there was Mendoza and the 50,000 pounds to take care of.

So, he allowed his mind to go back to what *really* happened that day, despite whatever distortion of the truth Celia may have told Samuel. After all, she was angry and probably felt compelled to tell a few lies to her father. She had lost her child, so it was quite understandable that the trauma of this would have disturbed her mind and Digby was big enough not to hold it against her, but setting the record straight was a matter of honour. It was important that Samuel heard the *true* account of what had taken place that day.

He, Digby Jones, had tired of arguing with Celia and turned to leave. He was an educated man and knew that women's hormones were often maladjusted when they were pregnant. He guessed it was why Celia had instigated the argument. However, she must have felt angry at having the squabble cut short and completely out of character, physically lashed out at him. He, being a gentleman and incapable of striking a woman, had merely pushed her away in an attempt to protect himself.

He would explain to Samuel that his uncle had always been an inveterate gambler so it was impossible for Digby to leave money in the house and he often gave it to Celia for safe keeping. He went to her drawer and retrieved the 550 pounds belonging to him, but heard a noise from behind as he walked towards the stairs.

He turned to find Celia almost upon him. She was beside herself with rage and he instinctively moved to one side to avoid her. Had he known the tragedy that this protective movement would bring about, he would have remained stationary and borne the brunt of her rage. Moving out of the way was something he could never forgive himself for, but at the same time, he could hardly blame himself for acting on instinct. Surely it was the sort of thing anyone would have done.

The driveway to the house loomed before him and he drove towards the main door, putting the finishing touches of the story together. As he climbed from the car, Samuel opened the front door and waited for him. His face was impassive and Digby could read nothing in it. He offered his hand to Samuel, but it was ignored. He was led into the privacy of the study where Samuel indicated for him to sit down.

'Well, Jones,' he began without any preamble, 'I am quite astounded that you requested this meeting with me. What could you possibly have to say in defence of your disgraceful actions the other day?' He poured himself a large whisky without offering one to Digby and sat opposite him. 'But, I believe myself to be a fair man, so please begin your defence of your actions.'

It took fifteen minutes and Samuel remained silent and never interrupted once. Any stranger listening to Digby's narrative would have felt he should automatically qualify for heaven when he passed from this world to the next.

When his account was finished, Samuel said, 'Well Jones, I have listened patiently to what you have had to say, and now I would like you to follow me into the lounge.'

Digby guessed that Celia and Maria would be in there waiting and it was now that he would discover his fate. Would Celia still want him, thus presenting him with a life of luxury? Or would she reject him, leaving him with the considerable sum of 50,000 pounds to go on his way with. He rather fancied it would be the latter, but one could never discount the fact that Celia was a plain girl who might very well decide that Digby was the only chance she had of getting a man. Whatever, he had done all he could to repair the situation. It was pointless speculating; he would discover the outcome soon enough.

As he strode into the lounge, he blinked in surprise

as he saw Billy Monroe seated alongside Celia and Maria. What the hell was that man doing here? This concerned no one but Celia and her family and it rankled him. It was an out and out cheek, but Digby knew that he was hardly in a position to say anything.

A pretty woman he had never seen before was sitting to one side of the others. She had chestnut coloured hair and brown eyes, reminding him very much of Dorothy, that sharp tongued interfering relation of the Mendozas who, thankfully, appeared to have finally left *Cherry Tree House* for good.

Samuel sat himself down between Maria and Celia, leaving Digby standing and feeling rather like a prisoner in the dock - waiting for the jury to return the verdict. Samuel spoke to the others, 'I have listened carefully to what Jones has had to say, and must inform you that his version of the events of that day are not in any way remotely similar to the version I have already been told.'

Hearing this didn't bother Digby at all. After all, what he had told Samuel was a complete pack of lies with a few strands of truth thrown in to bind the story together. He flashed Celia what he hoped was a winning smile before turning to Samuel.

'Look Samuel, it's hard for me to refute whatever your daughter has told you. I still have strong feelings for her and have no desire to put her in a bad light in your eyes. I'm also hoping that she will continue with the wedding arrangements and become my wife. I'm aware that I'm not perfect, but I think I'm older and wiser now.'

Celia stared at him and there was real malevolence

in her expression. How she hated him! She realised then that hate was a far stronger emotion than love. 'Never!' she said, leaping to her feet. 'I may have been infatuated with you once, but now I despise you. From the moment I first met you, you have never stopped lying, from telling me that I mustn't worry, for you could not have children, to the pack of lies you are telling now. Digby Jones loves only Digby Jones. Digby Jones cares only for Digby Jones. You use people for your own ends without worrying what harm you do to them. Getting what you want is all you care about. I would never go back with you. You make my skin crawl.'

Celia slumped back in her seat, completely drained by her outburst, but Digby remained calm. 'So you still stand by the lies you told your father, do you? You should be thoroughly ashamed of yourself Celia, perjuring yourself in such a way.'

'Celia has told me nothing of what happened on that dreadful day. Nothing of the events that led to her losing the child,' Samuel remarked quietly. 'She has not said a word to me.'

Digby stared at him in utter bemusement. 'But that can't be true! She must have done so, or how else would you believe that you knew what happened on that day?'

'Because there was another person in the house at the time. It was that other person who told me what took place. Someone who had never met you, so therefore had no reason to lie.'

Digby tried to ignore the sinking feeling growing rapidly in the pit of his stomach. 'Well, whoever this person is, he is lying Samuel,' he protested loudly. 'The bounder is telling you a pack of lies.'

'It is not a *he*,' Samuel said calmly. 'The person concerned is a woman.'

'Then she is a liar. Bring her here and I shall tell her so to her face.'

'My daughter is not a liar,' Samuel said calmly and Digby stared at him as though the man was in the middle of a breakdown and had taken leave of his senses.

He huffed impatiently. 'Forgive me Samuel, but I am a little puzzled. In fact, more than a little puzzled. Did you or did you not say a moment ago that it wasn't Celia who told you?'

His temper was now growing and all thoughts of appeasing Samuel were rapidly vanishing, but Samuel remained calm. 'Nor did she, but I have two daughters Jones. It was my other daughter who imparted the events of that day to me.'

Samuel was enjoying baiting Digby in this way. He waited for the man to work it out, but Digby didn't even try. Instead, he said, 'This is ridiculous Samuel. Your other daughter, Susan, is dead. You're not making any kind of sense at all.'

Samuel got up and walked across to the woman who resembled Dorothy. 'This is my daughter Susan. For a year and a half, her mother and I thought she was dead, but she had merely lost her memory. Thank God she eventually regained it and came back to us. It was *she* who was in the house that day. It was she who heard everything.'

'Then she is a liar,' Digby roared and Billy immediately leapt to his feet.

Samuel placed a hand on his shoulder and eased him down, saying, 'Please remain calm Billy. I shall deal with this.' He stared at Digby. 'What is it that you want Jones? Everyone in this room knows that it is not my daughter, so can you cease this play-acting and simply say what is it that you want. Please explain to me why you are here?'

Digby knew then that there was only one option left open to him, but nevertheless, it was also an option that had made his efforts very worthwhile. 'I want the 50,000 pounds you promised me,' he said petulantly. 'Give me my money and you have my word that you will never see me again.'

'Then if that is what you want, I'm afraid you have wasted your time in coming here,' was Samuel's unflinching reply, 'for you will not receive a single penny from me Jones. Not today and not ever!'

Digby stomach flipped over as he heard this unexpected statement. The word of men like Mendoza is their bond. He thrust his face forward aggressively. 'Are you reneging on our agreement?' he shouted, and although Samuel realised that it was not a sensible thing to do, he smiled, amused that this abuser of women should still think he was entitled to even a single penny of payment.

'Not at all Jones,' he said softly. 'I have never gone back on an agreement in my life. I would ask you to cast your mind back to the terms of that agreement. Let me remind you of what they were.

'You would marry Celia to give her child a name,

and then a few months later you would separate and divorce. For that, you would receive the sum of 50,000 pounds, but thanks to your disgraceful behaviour, there will no longer be a child, Jones, and as you have heard from Celia, there most certainly will not be a wedding, and of course without a wedding, there cannot be a divorce. All of which means that the conditions for paying you even a solitary pound no longer exist.'

He let out a tired, dismissive sigh. 'And now Digby, I would like you to leave my house. I must warn you not to attempt to contact any member of my family at any time in the future. To do so means that I will be forced to have a restraining order put on you.' He stared at Digby. 'I hope you don't find me boastful when I tell you that I am not a man who lacks influence. I can have it done in less than a day.'

It was all too much for Digby Jones to absorb. His plans and dreams were gone and he had nothing. No future life of luxury and no money to set him up in the North of England. He leapt forward and felled Samuel with one mighty blow of his fist.

Samuel lay spread-eagled on the floor with his eyes glazed over. A moment passed and he climbed unsteadily to his feet, loosened his collar and removed his jacket, then adopted a boxing pose.

Digby roared with laughter. 'Are you squaring up to me Mendoza? Why, you stupid old fool.' His laughter vanished as he became serious; at least he would now have the satisfaction of pounding the man's fleshy red face to a bloody pulp, and there was no Sid or anyone else around to stop him. 'I'm afraid, Mendoza, that I am about to teach you a lesson you will never forget,' he said.

But a voice from behind contradicted him, 'No Jones, but I intend to teach you one.'

Digby turned slowly and found that Billy was now on his feet, standing behind him. There was no boxing pose for him; instead, he stood, arms hanging loosely by his sides. 'You intend to box me?' Digby asked and Billy merely grinned and shook his head.

'No Digby, I intend to hurt you, hurt you quite badly actually. I intend to pay back a small portion of the hurt you have caused this family.' He smiled across at Susan and added. 'I am a fortunate man, for very soon, it will be my family.'

'Well then,' Digby laughed contemptuously, 'you had better be prepared to defend yourself Monroe. I was stupid and let you off on that day by the river in London, but not this time. This time you will pay.'

Billy raised his fists and Digby slowly circled around him as he sought an opportunity to land the first blow. A blow that would finish the fight before it really began. Not that he wanted to finish it quickly. The blood was roaring in his head now and more than anything he wanted to inflict pain on someone and was grateful to Monroe for the opportunity.

Billy momentarily lowered his guard and Digby swung a looping hook at his head which Billy easily ducked under, pummelling Digby in the testicles, not once, but five or six times in quick succession.

A low moan escaped from Digby's lips and he fell in a crumpled heap with his knees drawn to his chest and his hands clutching his groin.

Billy stepped back and slapped his hands together as if dusting them off before sitting next to Susan again. He grinned at the stunned faces around him. 'Well, you learn a lot when you're raised in an orphanage,' he said chirpily. He cast a contemptuous glance at Digby's crumpled form. 'I doubt he will be making anyone else pregnant for a while,' although he had the feeling that things weren't over yet.

He waited impatiently for the several minutes it took Digby to recover and as he climbed unsteadily to his feet, so Billy rose to his. Digby raised his fists before him and asked, 'Do you intend to fight like a gentleman now?'

'Only if I'm fighting another gentleman, Jones,' Billy said, 'but not if I'm fighting filth like you.'

'Very well then,' Digby said, 'on your own head be it!' He changed his posture to a wrestler's stance with his hands claw like in front of him and made a lunge at Billy, but Billy sidestepped it easily and grabbed three of Digby's fingers, bent them back to an alarming angle and only stopped when he heard the crack of the bones snapping. Digby sank to his knees, screaming in agony. Billy grabbed a fistful of his hair and smashed his knee up into his face. Digby groaned and collapsed to the floor once again. His mouth sagged open and vomit spewed onto the highly polished parquet wood. One of Digby's front teeth was floating in the vomit. That was the end of the one-sided fight.

Samuel and Billy lifted Digby between them and dragged him outside. He was a big man and they struggled, but eventually got him into the driver's seat of the uncle's tiny car. Billy swung the starting handle and at the third attempt, the engine purred to life. 'Why don't you go on inside,' he suggested to Samuel. 'I can deal with anything else.' The temperature was close to freezing point and Samuel didn't need to be asked a second time. He hurried into the house while Billy waited for Digby to recover enough to drive.

'Time you were on your way Mr Jones,' he said cheerfully, 'and I would strongly advise you not to bother this family again.'

Digby glared with unconcealed hatred. 'You'll pay for this Monroe,' he said. Blood was now pumping down his chin. 'It might take a while, but I give you my solemn oath that you will pay.' Billy sighed and crashed his elbow into Digby's face with such force that the remaining front tooth came out. 'Don't come back Jones,' he warned, and watched as Digby drove away. He didn't go back into the house until the sound of the car engine vanished and he was certain that Digby Jones was gone.

Chapter Twenty-Three

Samuel had started the long drive from Lulworth Cove to Surrey with Billy sitting alongside him. Maria and the girls were in the rear seats. Celia was annoyingly chanting, *'I'm going to have my own stable, I'm going to have my own stable,'* until Maria said sharply, 'Oh do please stop it my dear. You are giving me a headache.'

Samuel smiled to himself. There was a time when Celia's monologue would have also annoyed him, but after Dorothy appeared explaining that Susan was alive, that side of him disappeared. He'd been given the second chance that very few people get.

Celia pouted at the rebuke but held her excitement in check.

As they approached the house in Cobham, Samuel smiled, 'Close your eyes please girls, and do not to open them until I say you may.'

Obviously, Maria had seen the house and smiled at the girls' excitement. A few moments later Samuel brought the car to a smooth halt on the driveway of the large country home.

'Remember my instructions,' Samuel warned. 'There must be no peeking,'

Billy helped the girls from the car and positioned them facing the house.

'You may look now,' Samuel said and his daughters stood in awe as they surveyed the house twenty yards in front of them. The selling agent had assured him it was built during the reign of Queen Elizabeth the first so it was almost 400 years old.

Susan said excitedly, 'Charles the Second may have hidden here whilst fleeing from the Roundheads. Just think, we could be standing on the very spot he once stood on.' She stared at the ground, as if expecting to see a plaque that read, *King Charles the Second stood on this very spot.*

'Never mind that,' Celia said. 'Who cares about some old king who has been dust for centuries? Let's get to the important bit. Where are the stables Pops?'

Samuel smiled at his daughter's excitement. She was well on the road to recovery now, although he knew she would carry the mental scars left by Digby Jones for many months to come. 'You shall see the stables shortly my dear. Everything in good time.'

He pulled his watch fob from his waistcoat and frowned. He was a man who liked punctuality. 'Where the devil is that selling agent? He should be here by now.'

There was a crunching noise from behind them and they turned in time to see the gangling figure of a man on a pushbike wobbling uncontrollably. He fell in an untidy heap at Celia's feet and his cap came off, revealing a mop of tousled brown hair in need of a trim. He looked up at Celia and smiled. 'Hello,' he said, 'you must be either Celia or Susan. If you're Susan, congratulations on your forthcoming marriage, and if you're Celia, then I'm very pleased to meet you. My name is Daniel Potter.'

'And I am pleased to meet you Mr Potter,' Celia said, confirming which of the two she was.

He stood up and turned to Samuel, 'Sorry to have kept you waiting Mr Mendoza, and you too Mrs Mendoza. My front tyre was flat and I couldn't leave until I had pumped it up. That's the third time it's happened this week - probably a slow puncture,' but all the while he was talking, his eyes kept sliding sideways to look at Celia.

'It appears you have a fan, little sister,' Susan whispered and Celia dug her in the ribs.

While they were still in the throes of inspecting the house, Celia asked Daniel Potter where the stables were.

Samuel overheard the question. 'Why don't you take my daughter to see them?' he suggested. 'The rest of us will continue looking around the house. I'm quite certain we can manage without your very able assistance young man.'

Daniel Potter immediately became tongue-tied and his childhood stammer returned with a vengeance. 'I- If you will follow me C-C-Celia, I shall be very pleased to show you the s-stables.'

Samuel looked across at Maria and she smiled softly at him. They both knew the cause of young Potter's awkwardness. He liked their daughter, it seemed. 'Do you like horses Mr Potter?' Celia asked as they walked through the grounds at the rear of the house.

'V-very much s-so Celia. I have my own h-horse. Do you mind me c-calling you by your first n-name? And would y-you please call m-me Daniel? I h-hate being called Mr Potter?'

'Not at all Daniel. By that I mean, no, I don't mind you calling me Celia.' She smiled at him. 'I love to ride, although I'm a little nervous of going out on my own in Cobham. You see, I don't know this area at all. It could just as well be the surface of the moon for all I know.'

He smiled shyly and said, 'Well it couldn't be, could it? Everyone knows t-the moon's surface is m-made of cheese.'

Celia laughed, 'Silly! Anyway, it would be marvellous if I found someone to ride with me until I learn my way around.'

'If you didn't hate the i-idea,' Daniel said, 'but I know you w-would, then I-I could ride with you, but I know you wouldn't l-like it so I w-won't mention it again.' His face had turned bright scarlet and Celia knew that he truly liked her.

Back at the house, Samuel turned to Billy and Susan after they'd inspected the last bedroom. 'Do you like the place?' he asked. 'I myself think it is a wonderful family home and your mother has said she feels the same way.'

'It's beautiful Pops,' Susan answered perkily, 'and Billy and I have already discussed moving down this way when we are married. Not exactly to Cobham, but fairly close by. This area will be out of our price range for a few years.' They stopped talking as they heard footsteps in the hallway and guessed Daniel Potter and Celia had returned from inspecting the stables. They went to meet them and Celia's happy face told Samuel everything he needed to know.

'Are you ready to continue Mr Potter?' he asked and the tongue-tied agent nodded that, yes, he was and led them from the house.

He swung a leg over the saddle of his bicycle and said, 'T-turn right as you come out of the drive and f-follow me please.' He set off, wobbling dangerously until he reached the firmer surface of the road outside.

Billy and the girls were mystified by Daniel's words and turned to Samuel for an explanation, but he merely smiled and said, 'Everyone into the car then. Chop chop.'

They soon caught up with Daniel on his bicycle and Samuel poodled behind him for a mile until the young agent turned into a narrow lane. 'I shall park the car here,' Samuel informed his family, putting on the hand brake, 'otherwise it will mean reversing out and that might prove difficult.'

He exited the car and strode off in the direction of the narrow lane with Billy and the girls following after him, wondering what on earth was going on, although Maria was perfectly aware of where her husband was going. The lane was just twenty yards long and at the end was a small, ivy covered cottage.

Daniel Potter's bike was lying on the floor and he was opening the front door of the cottage. 'This way p-please,' he called out and they hurried after him in silence. He took them from room to room until Susan could contain herself no longer.

'But why are we here Pops?' she asked. 'Are you not you buying the other house now? I thought you said you loved it.'

Samuel ignored her question and asked one of his own, 'How about this place, this lovely little cottage? Tell me my dear, do you like it?'

It was an easy question for Susan to answer. If she were to paint a picture of her perfect house, this would be it. 'It's beautiful Pops,' she said wistfully, 'simply beautiful.'

Samuel nodded to Daniel and then turned back to Susan. 'Well then, that is most pleasing for your mother and me to hear, because as of now, it belongs to you and Billy. It is a wedding gift to both of you.'

Susan and Billy were rendered speechless by the magnitude of the gift. Billy stared at Susan and she stared back before moving across to her parents. She threw her arms around her father's neck and kissed him on his cheek, then did the same to her mother, only this time, kissing her again and again. 'Thank you, thank you, thank you,' she said and reached out for Billy's hand, pulling him to join her. 'I know we shall be very happy here.'

She hadn't asked Billy for his opinion, but he didn't mind. He wanted only one thing - for the woman he loved to be happy. If she was happy, then he was also happy.

*

From his hidden spot in the trees, Digby had

watched the Rolls Royce pull away from *Cherry Tree House*. He knew exactly where the family were going and more or less how long they would be gone for. They were visiting Cobham to see the new house. He knew because Maria had been telling her daughters as Samuel and Digby walked into the lounge. In the two weeks since that humiliating and painful visit, the bruising and swelling to his face had gone down considerably, but he was still awaiting the arrival of his dentures, and despite the doctor's best efforts, he had explained that Digby's nose would never lose the new twist in it. That bastard Monroe had a lot to answer for, as did Samuel Mendoza and that disloyal bitch Celia and today, he - Digby Jones, was going to repay them all in the most terrifyingly, painful way imaginable. Celia had been disloyal to him for the very last time.

His uncle's car was hidden a mile from the house. Digby had no desire to be arrested. No desire to stand up at an inquest and confess to his wrongdoings, or right-doings, depending upon which side of the fence you were sitting. He had several things with him. An axe, a wood-saw, several pulley wheels and a large coil of rope, all purchased from a store 100 miles away in the county of Devonshire. Plus, he had an unshakeable alibi arranged following the soon to be tragic outcome of his work. He was attending a small gathering of friends in London.

He left his hiding place and walked a mile to a lane used only by persons visiting *Cherry Tree House*. It was the route the Mendoza family would take on their return from Cobham. Digby knew he had at least five hours to complete his intended work, which was more than enough time.

Removing his jacket, he put on a thick pair of gloves before scaling his chosen tree with the aid of climbing apparatus. At the top, he attached the coil of rope around the trunk, testing it several times by putting his whole weight on the rope. He smiled with satisfaction as it held firm and released the other end of the rope, watching its descent to be certain it didn't snag in any branches on its journey downwards.

Back on the ground, he used an axe to chop methodically into the base of the tree. His broken fingers jarred painfully when the blade struck home, but he ignored the pain as though it didn't exist. Despite the cold bite of late winter, within five minutes he was sweating profusely. Every swing of the axe caused a sharp pain in his battered testicles, but this reminder made him even more determined to complete his task. It was a substantial tree, the trunk being around eighteen inches in diameter and once he had cut a vee shape halfway into it, he moved to the opposite side of the cut and swung the axe at a point twelve inches higher.

After an hour of solid chopping, his shoulders were numb and his hands red raw. He took a breather for half an hour before recommencing the backbreaking work. Fifteen minutes later he was so exhausted that it was only his desire for revenge that kept him going. When the chopping was completed, he set about screwing the pulleys into the trees opposite and alongside the tree. Four pulleys later, he took the end of the dangling rope and began the task of threading it around the pulleys. It amazed him that these simple things enabled a person to move objects of many hundredweights with little effort, which was just as well in his weakened state. Finally, the trap was set and it would take very little effort to set the primed tree in motion.

He'd specifically chosen this area as Mendoza would have to crawl slowly along the narrow lane due to the potholes and tree roots snagging across the surface. The lane led only to *Cherry Tree House*. All that remained now was to settle down and wait.

Two hours passed, during which time he read the newspaper and ate the sandwich prepared at home. It was a long wait for him and revenge has little patience, but eventually there was the sound of an approaching car. It was Mendoza's Rolls Royce. In the days following Digby's humiliation at the hands of Billy Monroe, what was about to happen now was all he had dreamt of. He knew the falling tree should kill everyone in the car, but should anyone survive, he was quite prepared to finish the job with the axe. Not only prepared, but looking forward to it.

The Rolls was thirty yards from the tree when Digby moved into action. He swung his whole weight onto the rope. The tree creaked and groaned and began to fall, slowly at first, but then at speed. Anyone in its path had no chance of escaping it.

Susan heard the creaking and groaning made by the falling tree and looked up, screaming in terror, 'Pops! Look out Pops.' Billy dived over the seat, pushing the women down and putting his body across them to give at least some type of protection as the tree continued its downward fall.

Chapter Twenty-Four

I proposed the day after we rescued Dorothy from the twentieth century. I'm not an impatient person. I'd waited a whole day.

We both felt the time was now right, but Dorothy insisted on a June wedding.

'All weddings should take place in June,' she explained in her matter of fact way.

I grinned as I listened. It was like being back at school again. 'Weddings are meant to be in June, just as Christmas is meant to be in December. You wouldn't have Christmas dinner in March, would you Billy? No, of course you wouldn't.'

Apparently, I had given my answer without moving my lips.

She settled into her stride. 'If we don't marry fairly soon, then I will have to find a surrogate mother to have my children for me as I'll be an old hag, unable to carry a child of my own.' A moment passed while she allowed her words to sink in. 'So is that okay with you

Billy? Can we make the wedding this June please?'

It was a silly question. Dorothy knew I'd agree to *whatever* she wanted. No more than a second passed before she frowned, 'Answer the question Billy. Do - you - still - want - to marry me? Do you want to spend the rest of your life with me? Well, spit it out. Do you?'

'I do,' I smiled, 'more than anything else in the world,' but I also added that I was terrified of messing up. Dorothy smiled in that soft way of hers.

'But how do you reckon you can mess up? Remember Billy - I know all there is to know about you. I know your weaknesses, especially in business when you can be a total disaster, well, at least, that's what Tom reckons.'

I made a mental note to thank Tom for his input as the woman I loved continued her verbal assassination. 'But I'm not a total disaster, am I? And what do you reckon it is that makes a great team?'

'Sex and lots of holidays?' I ventured.

'Please don't joke about it Billy,' she snapped. 'This is serious.'

So, I sighed and said, 'In that case, I'd like to change my answer to *Different attributes*. Is that better?'

'That's much better, and without wanting to make you big headed, you are the most supportive person I've ever met.' She stroked my cheek, 'My *raison d'etre.*'

So, the date was set. Dorothy would walk down the aisle on her father's arm on Sunday, June 5th.

*

Over breakfast on the Saturday morning, Kate

reached across to Tom's plate and speared a piece of bacon that he couldn't finish. At the same time, she gave him a gentle reminder, 'Don't forget that you're going to collect Beth from the railway station at four o'clock; you know what your memory's like,' and I realised guiltily that our new friend had completely slipped my mind. None of us had seen her recently and it was shiningly obvious that she loved her visits to Lulworth Cove and being in our company, which was pretty handy because we enjoyed being with her.

Beth's train was on time and over our evening meal we caught up on the latest hot gossip from Wooburn Green.

'Old Bert Maple hasn't spoken to Roger Harmon ever since Roger's turnip won first prize at the village fete,' Beth said. 'They really seem to dislike one another.' Riveting stuff like that, but Dorothy listened with interest to the trauma of the village fete, and how the pastry on Mrs Higgins fruit pie had sunk so much that no one wanted to buy it and she threatened never to cook for the fete again.

We chatted into the early hours of the morning. By one o'clock Beth, who normally retired to the bedroom at 10:30, was yawning and took off to her bed.

I suppose it was inevitable that the conversation would move to 1927. 'I'd give my eye teeth to know what happened to that Digby Jones fellow,' Kate said, and for once, Tom agreed with his wife.

'Me too,' he said with a cheeky grin. 'I'd also give your eye teeth to know what happened,' and then he brought up the letter that Susan was going to hide away for us. 'I know I've said it before, but there's nothing to stop us from going upstairs and getting the letter now. It'll already be under the floorboards waiting, so what's the point of hanging on until Christmas?' and as he said those words, I realised once again that Susan's letter would have been there during the whole time she was with us, except that she wouldn't have known she'd written it. Well, Susan still hadn't actually written it then, had she? But nevertheless, it was still under the boards and had been written by her.

This time thing is really creepy. It could send you nuts if you tried to work it out. Best to accept it without making an attempt.

Dorothy answered Tom's question, 'We wait because it's what we told Susan we would do,' she said sharply. 'Look Tom, I don't want to pull rank on you, but it's my house and on this particular issue, what I say goes. *Comprende?*'

'There!' Kate said emphatically. 'Dorothy is quite right, so give it a rest Tom. You're not the only one who wants to find out about Susan you know. We all feel the same way, but we made a promise to her, and a promise is a promise, so we'll have to wait and if you dare ask again, you'll get a knuckle sandwich.'

'Ooh, good,' he said, 'you know how much I love boiled bacon.'

*

The inquest drew tremendous attention from the press as well as the locals of Lulworth Cove and the surrounding areas. Even though the Mendoza family were not permanent residents in Dorset, they were well liked. They always tried to fit in with the community and had taken part in quite a few of its activities over the years. Samuel played cricket, albeit quite badly, while Susan and Celia were active members of the tennis club. Along with most of the locals, the Mendoza family prayed at the parish church on Sundays, and when the roof of the church was badly in need of repair and in danger of collapsing, Samuel donated a substantial amount of money towards the cost of restoring it, so they were considered an asset to the community.

As the inquest date drew nearer, it was the main subject of discussion in most of the local pubs. 'Crushed to death by a falling tree,' 85-year-old Harry Watts said to his cronies. He shivered convulsively. 'That be a bugger of a way to go. And to watch the bloody thing falling on yer, knowing yer a gonner and yer can't do sod all about it…' He pulled a gruesome face. 'There's a lot ter be said for dying in yer bed maties, I'll tell yer that much.'

Everyone nodded and said things like, 'Too bloody true 'Arry. Too bloody true.'

The bar door swung open and the group fell silent as they looked to see the newcomer. It was Digby's uncle Bert. A lad named Arthur was about to call out to him but Harry dug him in the ribs and hissed, 'It ain't the time or place son.'

Bert Jones ordered a pint of bitter and leant on the bar, but nobody made a move to join him. People looked at the floor if his gaze fell on them and an uncomfortable atmosphere settled in the room. After a minute of complete silence, Bert drained his glass and left the bar without saying a word. Apart from the barman mentioning the cost of his drink, nobody spoke to him.

*

The day of the inquest arrived and the courthouse was packed to capacity. Although the Coroner speculated on the evidence, it was obvious there could be but one verdict. Nevertheless, nearly every head craned forward as he announced that verdict.

'Having listened to the evidence of the witnesses in this case, and having taken into consideration the police report and the expert testimony of the Tree Surgeon who examined the fallen tree, there can be but one conclusion for this court to arrive at.' He looked around at the expectant faces hanging onto his every word. Despite his many years of performing this task, people's preoccupation with death still amazed him.

'It is the verdict of this court that the death of Mr Digby Jones, although brought about by his own hand, was accidental and let it be so recorded.' He shuffled his papers together and as he made his exit, the buzz of multiple conversations filled the room.

As the only witnesses to the events of that fateful day, Billy and the Mendoza family were sitting in the front row of the court. With the ordeal of the inquest now over, Samuel stood up and ushered them all towards the door.

'A classic example of *As ye reap, so ye shall sow,*' he said in a low voice as they reached the chill of the outside. No one responded - not even the charitable Maria.

A band of newspaper reporters immediately

flocked around Samuel, blocking his exit, but when they repeated the same questions the coroner had asked in court, he said, 'All of you heard the evidence. The Tree Surgeon appointed by the court as an expert explained that the siting of the axe cuts into the tree had been incorrectly calculated, causing it to fall in a different direction to the one that Mr Jones had obviously planned. Because of that mistake, and by the grace of God, my family and I had an extremely lucky escape.' He looked around at the small band of men and women busily scribbling in their notebooks and added, 'And now, if you will excuse me, it has been a traumatic time for my family and we would like to put it behind us and return home.'

Not content with those words, one of the more forceful reporters stepped forward. He had an eager readership to satisfy and if that meant asking inappropriate questions, then so be it. It was second nature to him. 'Mr Mendoza, I understand that your youngest daughter was engaged to Mr Jones.' His voice was loud enough to carry above the commotion. 'Surely she must be devastated by all of this?'

But Celia spoke up for herself. Her voice was brittle, 'I'm unaware of your name sir and have no desire to know it! I am surprised that you have been callous and unfeeling enough to ignore my father's request. However, I shall answer your question. My engagement to Mr Jones had been broken off weeks before the so-called accident.' She fixed the reporter with a glare that dared him to contradict her. 'Whatever my earlier feelings for Mr Jones may have been, I can assure you that at the time of his death he meant nothing to me. Nothing at all.'

The reporter had the good grace to blush. 'Sorry Miss,' he said feebly, 'but editors don't allow us reporters to have feelings!'

Billy forced a way through the crowd to the safe harbour of the car. They scrambled inside and Samuel hurriedly drove away. After a mile or so, he said, 'Well, no surprises there.' He sneaked a glance in the rear-view mirror at Celia, concerned after the ordeal of the inquest. She was pale faced, but seemed in control of herself and he smiled; pleased with the way his girl had stood up through all of this. He was proud of the way she had handled the reporter and asked softly, 'Are you all right, my dear?'

Celia offered him a weak smile. 'Watch the road please Pops. I'm fine thank you, absolutely fine. I'm just pleased that it's all over and we can get on with our lives again. At least one good thing came out of this. The world is a better place without that monster Digby Jones inhabiting it.'

'Darling!' Maria said sharply. 'It is quite wrong to speak ill of the dead. What happened to Digby was a terrible thing,' but Celia was unrepentant and had no intention of either retracting her statement or showing remorse for having made it.

'He got no more than he deserved Mother and I'm glad that he's dead. Pops is absolutely right. *As ye sow, so ye shall reap,* and that is exactly what happened to Digby Jones. He tried to kill all of us. Not just Pops and me and, if you like, Billy, but also you and Susan as well. He sowed death, and death is what the evil man reaped, so I say - Goodbye to you Digby Jones. I mourn you not.'

The remainder of the drive was completed in silence. After the trauma of the past months, Celia wanted to move on with her life, although deep down, she knew she would carry the nightmare of her time with Digby Jones to the grave.

As the miles passed, she thought of the house at Cobham where a whole new world was waiting for her. That night she lay in her bed, restless and with many things filling her mind. Her last thought before sleep took her was of the Daniel Potter, the young agent. She had ridden with him on several occasions and his nervous stutter always made her smile. Other people might think it an imperfection, but she quite liked it. And for that matter, she quite liked him.

*

The days leading up to our wedding in June seemed to fly past on wings eager for exercise. Dorothy went off on her hen night a week before the ceremony and paid the price the following morning. 'How did it go?' I enquired casually not wanting to appear nosey.

She pulled a face, 'Don't even ask Billy. I can scarcely remember myself.'

As for my stag night, well, it didn't happen. I gave it a miss. Tom and I went for a quiet drink instead. 'Do you ever regret getting married?' I asked, and he was surprised that I'd even asked the question.

'Not one iota,' he said. 'Ignore our silly banter Billy. That's just surface stuff. I love my Kate, in fact, I'd be lost without her, and she occasionally says that she loves me, although she doesn't have to say it because I know she loves me. We couldn't have kids

Billy.' He saw my surprised look and smiled, 'Never told you that, did I? We spent a bloody fortune on specialists, but none of the treatments worked and that's what I think I've become to Kate - husband and child, all in one package.'

The wedding day - Sunday the 5th of June, arrived. The ceremony was held, not at a church, but at Kew Gardens, near Richmond in Surrey. Thomas Henry Cox was entrusted with the job of best man. He was my *only* choice, although not necessarily a wise choice. He had performed the job of the *best man* on one other occasion. I wasn't a guest at that particular wedding, so Kate felt duty bound to warn me that his speech left much to be desired.

I felt a surge of rapidly growing warmth around my collar. 'What did he say then?' I stuttered, knowing that with a few drinks inside him, Tom could start a war between two countries that had been at peace for centuries.

'Well, he'd had quite a few whiskies,' she began, taking a deep breath before continuing. 'Anyway, the bride had been engaged three times before and each time the engagement had been broken off, so what does my Tom say in his speech?' She didn't wait for my answer but continued, 'Did he say that the bride had finally found happiness - the obvious thing for a normal human being to say? No! Of course he didn't Billy. That would have been too easy. No, he said he was pleased she had found a husband at last, because everyone knew that she'd been around the block a few times.'

I went weak at the knees as I listened. Even knowing how verbally liberal he can be, I was stunned to hear this, and he's been my mate for all of my life, minus the first five years.

Kate paused for a second, probably reliving it all over again in her mind's eye. 'I did not know where to put my face Billy. The bride's father was so furious that we left early. The groom has never spoken to Tom since, and remember, Tom was his best man, so was a very close friend indeed.'

I swallowed hard, 'Maybe it would be a good idea if we didn't mention any of this to Dorothy,' I said and she nodded her head in agreement.

'Too bloody true we shouldn't mention it Billy!'

It was the first time I'd heard her swear, apart from that amorous routine of hers at *Cherry Tree House* when she was slightly more than tipsy.

And so, the big day arrived. It sort of crept up on me. Like I'd known for weeks that I had won the lottery, but today, I was being given the cheque.

Chuck was true to his word and had the Bugatti ready on time. Dorothy told me later that people were stopping in the street and staring as the car drove past them. According to her, they were paying more attention to the Bugatti than they were to her, but I doubt that. The car was beautiful, but so was she. It was probably fifty-fifty.

Sixty people occupied the seats in the room where the ceremony was taking place. At the front of the room, behind a long desk and facing the guests, was the female registrar. She obviously loved her job as she smiled through the whole of the ceremony. Behind her were exceptionally large windows giving the guests spectacular views of the gardens that people come from all over the world to see.

The ceremony began as Dorothy arrived on the arm of her father. I glanced across at him and he flashed me a quick smile. Dorothy looked stunning. The registrar asked the necessary questions and we obviously gave the correct answers and in what felt like seconds, Tom passed me the ring. As I slipped it onto my Bride's finger, one thought ran through my head. *That's it Dottie! You're my wife at last and I shall never let you go!*

The registrar said I could kiss the bride and I didn't need telling twice.

I had worried unnecessarily about Tom's speech being bad news for Dorothy, because it wasn't, at least, it wasn't for her. He was a bundle of nerves when he stood up. Perhaps he remembered what happened the last time he did this job. He glanced apprehensively at Kate, so she had obviously threatened him with something worse than death if he messed up as he did the last time.

'My friend Billy,' he began, 'is a lucky bloke. Wouldn't we all like to get a bride who looks the way that Dorothy does, but some of us aren't so lucky,' and I covered my eyes and thought, *Oh my God!*

The room went deathly quiet around him, like someone had cut the wires to everyone's voice box and not even a cough broke the awed silence. It was then that it must have dawned on Tom exactly what he'd said. He tugged at his collar and somehow, onehandedly, managed to loosen his tie and undo the top button of his shirt. The silence continued as he stood staring into space like a rabbit caught in a car's headlights, so I nudged him to continue. 'Um, er, not that I'm saying my Kate isn't beautiful,' he said quickly, 'because she is, in her own way. Well, what I mean is, after she's put a lot of makeup on, um, not that she needs makeup, but it's a big help. Well, it is some of the time, but not always.'

If he was going to carry on like this, my wedding could be a prelude to his funeral, with Kate appearing some time later at The Old Bailey on trial for his murder, so I trod on his foot, hoping to move him along. It worked! He yelled out in pain, 'Ouch Billy, that hurt that did.'

'Kate will be hurting you far more than that if you continue like that,' I hissed. The guests were waiting in stunned but excited silence for him to continue. Even the caterers stopped what they were doing and waited for the resumption of Tom's seemingly never ending stream of *faux pas*. Tom gave me a final glare and then took a huge breath before plunging back into the fray, words coming out in one long sentence, uninterrupted by normal speech pauses. 'Anyway the bride looks stunning the groom is handsome all the bridesmaids are beautiful and the food was brilliant and I love my wife very much. And Kate doesn't always need makeup honestly she doesn't and she's the light of my life.' With that, he slumped down into his seat and a round of cheering and raucous applause filled the room.

Dorothy left her place at the table and kissed him on the cheek. 'Well done Tom,' she said. 'I'm sure that Kate knew exactly what you meant. It was a really sweet speech and one that most people will never forget,' and I thought, *You're dead right there, my darling.*

No one here will ever forget that lot!

There was a disco arranged for the evening and Dorothy and I watched in amazement as Beth bopped away on the dance-floor with David, the official wedding photographer. There was a lot of eye contact between them that Tom picked up on. He grinned at me. 'Do you think she'll ask him back to Wooburn Green for tea and scones Billy?'

I laughed, adding, 'And Petula's raspberry jam, if he's lucky.'

Later, when Tom was on the other side of the room regaling some poor trapped sucker with the history of guns and bombs from the year dot, Kate told us that after he realised she was going to let him carry on breathing for a few more years, he was so encouraged by Dorothy's complimentary remarks that he asked Kate if he should forge a new career as an after-dinner speaker.

There was no real honeymoon for Dorothy and me. Two nights at The Imperial Hotel in Torquay was our ration, and then it was back to *Cherry Tree House* for the first time as a married couple. But for our wedding night we were staying at a local hotel, set into the side of Richmond Hill and overlooking a sweeping bend in the River Thames. I've seen the view from the top of the hill hundreds of times and it still takes my breath away.

As we drove away from Kew in the Bugatti, Dorothy said, 'Can I ask you something Billy?'

I grinned, replying, 'Of course you can, silly. You may ask me anything your little heart desires, Mrs Monroe.' I think it was the first time anyone had called her by her married name and she blushed and laughed at the same time.

'Let's try and hang on to the Bugatti shall we? If it hadn't been for the car, we would never have met, would we? I never want to let it go. Not ever!' and of course, I agreed because I felt exactly the same way. Everything I now had, I owed to the Bugatti.

The small cottage we recently purchased in Weymouth was still being renovated. Once the work was finished, we'd move in there and *Cherry Tree House* would again become a holiday home for the descendants of the nineteenth century tycoon, Emanuel Mendoza.

New wife. New home. New life in Dorset. As I said earlier, *My cup runneth over.*

Chapter Twenty-Five

Daniel watched Celia with open admiration. She could ride, that much was obvious. She was one of those riders who seem to be an extension of whatever horse they're astride. She sensed him watching her and turned toward him, causing him to colour up and quickly look away. 'One day Daniel, I shall be as good a rider as you,' she said and he turned an even deeper shade of crimson.

'You're already b-better than m-me,' he stammered and although she smiled at the compliment, she felt it was untrue.

One hundred yards away, standing like a sentinel on the verge of the track, was an oak tree. The locals said it was more than eight hundred years old, and if that was true, then it had taken root when Robin Hood was robbing the rich and handing the proceeds to the poor. Celia kicked her heels into the mare's flanks and shouted, 'Race you to the tree.' Daniel took up the challenge and spurred his gelding after her. The horse had the scent the chase in its nostrils and he had difficulty holding him back to ensure Celia's victory, but somehow he managed and she passed the tree two lengths ahead of him.

'Promise you didn't let me win?' she shouted.

He lied and said, 'I p-promise.'

He forgave himself for lying, telling himself that it didn't count if you loved the person you lied to, and he certainly loved Celia. Had done so since he first set eyes on her after he fell and landed in a heap at her feet. Even now, thinking about it embarrassed him. He loved spending time with her, loved the scent of her perfume and holding her foot, hoisting her onto the back of the mare and all the time knowing his feelings could never be returned. His would always be an unrequited love, for she was the daughter of a rich man, whilst he? He was the son of a gamekeeper, a man who knew his station in life and always tipped his forelock to his betters.

If only, Daniel thought, *if only*, but his dad had lectured him many times that life isn't made of *if onlys*, and that he must learn to live in the real world and accept the cards life dealt him.

Well, at least the real world contained dreams, there was that much to be thankful for, so he would have to content himself with those.

Soon, they arrived at the stables at the rear of the house. Celia had suggested that as they rode together daily, it would be better if he kept his gelding in the stable adjacent to her mare's. Daniel gladly accepted the offer. It meant he would be with her for a few minutes longer each day.

'That was fun, wasn't it?' Celia said happily, and rather than stammer an answer, he simply nodded.

After they had unsaddled the horses and rubbed them down. Daniel grabbed a pitchfork and turned over the straw in both stables and put down hay for the horses to feed on. When he finished, Celia said, 'Well, goodnight then Daniel. I shall see you at six o'clock in the morning.' As she walked jauntily towards the house, she called over her shoulder, 'Sleep tight Daniel,' and he wondered how he was supposed to do that when he couldn't stop thinking about her.

'Y-you too,' he stammered, trudging miserably to the gate, his life now ended until he saw her again in the morning.

He had just climbed astride his bicycle when Celia called out, 'Daniel,' and he turned. 'Daddy said to ask you to dinner tomorrow night. What shall I tell him?' and his life began again, ten hours earlier than normal.

He struggled to get his answer out, but somehow managed to stammer, 'T-tell him y-yes please!'

*

Double weddings are something of a rarity, and this was the first that any resident of Cobham could remember. Even 93-year-old Timothy Smith couldn't remember one, and he was famous for having been there, heard it and seen it way before anyone else. Once, when 88-year-old Dickie Tremane, thinking he'd finally got one over on Timothy, mentioned seeing a woodsman accidentally chop his own hand off, Timothy responded by spitting out a stream of tobacco juice and saying, 'I've only seen that happen twice.'

But not a double wedding - he hadn't seen that, and most definitely not a double wedding for sisters.

*

They had just driven the car onto drive of the house at Cobham when a Post Office boy pedalled up on his bicycle and handed Samuel a telegram. He told the boy to wait while he read it and then handed him a shilling, saying, 'On your way lad, there is no reply.' The boy stared wide eyed at the size of his tip and pocketed it with a happy grin. It was six times the amount he was normally given and he pedalled off while Samuel explained the contents of the telegram to Maria.

'Celia and Daniel have arrived in the Scottish Highlands. She says that the hotel and the scenery are both beautiful. She also says that Daniel's stutter is getting better by the hour.'

'And a good job too,' Maria said, smiling as her mind went back to the wedding ceremony. 'When the vicar asked, *Do you take this woman to be your lawful wedded wife*, I thought the poor lad was never going to get his answer out.' She smiled mischievously and altered the tone of her voice; 'I d-d-d-d-d-do,' she said, giving a fair imitation of her new son-in-law.

'Now, now my dear,' Samuel chastised, 'it isn't like you to be cruel.'

Maria didn't answer; instead, she linked her arm through his and walked towards the front door of the house. 'It's a trifle unusual, isn't it Samuel - a honeymoon spent horse riding in the hills of Scotland, but I can think of nothing more romantic.'

'It has all turned out rather well old girl, hasn't it?' Samuel said. 'When you think of the swine that our daughter came close to marrying. I could not be more pleased with her choice of husband. Young Daniel is fine young man and unlike some, he's a giver, not a taker.'

'Samuel, I know who you are talking about and would like to remind you that one should never speak ill of the dead,' Maria chastised.

As they opened the door and walked into the hallway, Samuel hung up his coat and said innocently, 'Did I mention any names my dear? No, of course I did not. The name Digby Jones never left my lips.'

Chapter Twenty-Six

'I love Midnight Mass at Christmas time,' Dorothy whispered.

I squeezed her hand and said, 'Me too.'

There were six of us now. Apparently at our wedding, Beth had taken the bull by the horns and invited David the photographer, for afternoon tea at Wooburn Green and things had gone from there. We took up a whole pew. People were standing at the back, down the sides and in the middle of the pews almost up to the Alter. I guess that a lot churches are that way at Christmas time.

Once the service ended, an aged and frail Reverend Thomas Janus stood in his usual place by the outsize church door, shaking worshipers' hands as they left. As we drew closer to him, I nudged Beth and said in a low voice, 'Susan went to his Christening when he was a baby.' Within a short time, we reached the Reverend Janus and he shook each of our hands in turn.

'God bless you all,' he said, and then stopped,

giving us a long, hard look. 'Weren't you with that pretty young girl who said I wouldn't remember her because I was very young when we first met?'

Tom grinned and said, 'Guilty as charged Reverend.'

'Where is the girl tonight?' he asked. 'I'd be interested in seeing her again. There were several things I wanted to ask her,' and as I looked at his frail body, I thought that if the Heaven he believed in really was there waiting for those who have been good, then he shouldn't have to wait too long before getting his wish.

Outside, Kate scowled at Tom, 'Fancy saying, *Guilty as charged* to the vicar. Honestly, you're only happy when you're showing me up.'

'Hey you two, remember it's Christmas, a time of goodwill to all men,' Dorothy lectured.

Tom turned to Kate, 'See! Even Dorothy wants you to shut up.'

Back at the house, Tom tried to speak to Dorothy, but she guessed what was forthcoming and stopped him in his tracks. 'We'll do it after our Christmas lunch Tom,' and her look warned him not to argue because he'd lose.

The floorboards would be lifted and Susan's letter - if there was one - would be retrieved at around five o'clock the coming afternoon. I could understand Tom's impatience though, because I myself was curious to discover what had happened to Celia and Digby Jones and to know how Susan and Billy had got on. Had they married? Had any children? How had the family lost their wealth? Having heard of the financial astuteness of Samuel Mendoza, I *really* wanted the answer to that question. As the floodgates opened, even more questions crowded in, but I pushed them aside and said, 'Right everyone, it's time for mince pies and brandy.'

Kate and Beth were poised, each ready to hurtle into the kitchen ahead of their rival, but Dorothy had beaten them to it. She came from the kitchen wheeling a food trolley with brandy, champagne, glasses and mince pies on it. Apparently, she had put the pies on a low oven before we left for the church.

So, we got a little sozzled and comfortable until eventually, David looked at the clock and exclaimed, 'Good God! It's three o'clock already. Time for my beauty sleep.' He turned to Beth. 'Ready for bed old girl.'

Poor Beth! Her earlier crimson colour was pale pink in comparison to the new colour brought on by his words. She sat rigid with embarrassment. 'What's up? Stuck are you?' David asked. 'Hang on and I'll help you.' He leapt to his feet, took her hands in his own and pulled her from the armchair. 'Night all, thanks for a lovely evening,' he said cheerily and led Beth away and up to the bedroom. Even prudish Kate found it amusing and laughed.

'I feel sorry for Beth,' Dorothy said, 'the poor woman hardly knew what hit her.'

'Any bets?' Tom grinned and Kate almost bit his head off.

'Don't be so disgusting Tom Cox,' she snapped.

'It is late though,' I said, having heard the clock strike three, 'so maybe we should join them.' I should have guessed my choice of words would start *him* off.

'Bloody hell Billy, six of us in a single bed would be ridiculous.'

Kate was the first person in the kitchen that morning. I was surprised. I'd expected Beth to be the first one down, proving that she didn't really want to share a bedroom with a man, but it was 11:30 before she appeared. David, on the other hand, looked a picture of happiness. He winked across at the rest of us and said, 'Morning all, and a very happy Christmas.' It appeared that his Christmas had got off to a good start.

Although Beth avoided our eyes, she seemed pretty happy to me, definitely the happiest since losing Petula.

In order to avoid the never-ending battle between Kate and Beth in the kitchen, Dorothy had opted to cook the turkey herself.

At some time during the food preparation and cooking, she pulled Beth to one side. 'We're going to lift the floorboards at 5:30 to get Susan's letter. It's going to be complicated if David is here, so can you get him out of the house for a while? Take him for a long walk or something like that. We'll tell you what we find out later on. Oh, and I'm sorry Beth, I should have asked you earlier; do you want me to get that other bedroom ready for you?'

Poor Beth wasn't much of an actress. She tried too hard to be casual. Like she hadn't really given it a moment's thought. 'Well I wouldn't want you going to all of that bother Dorothy. We're managing fine.'

Because of the silly rivalry between Kate and Beth,

every dish of food on the table was the *Crème de la crème*. By the time we'd finished eating, we were all stuffed.

At five o'clock, remembering Dorothy's request to get David out of the house, Beth said, 'Fancy a drive to Poole and a walk around the town David? Just you and me.'

'Nope,' he said, 'I'm fine right here.'

Beth saw Tom's annoyed glare. He'd waited long enough. 'Well, you might be fine right there,' she said, 'but I'm not. I need some air, so shift it.'

He obviously realised that the sleeping arrangements could easily be rearranged in a way not to his benefit. He stood and bowed in a sweeping gesture, at the same time saying, 'To hear is to obey my Queen.'

This stuff was all new to Beth and she relished it. 'We'll be at least a couple of hours,' she informed us as they left the room. The moment the front door closed, we hurried to the very top of the house and went to the designated cupboard. Tom was on his knees faster than a miser searching for dropped money. He ripped up the patch of carpet. Underneath was one sawn floorboard, held in place by six woodscrews. 'Sod, sod, sod,' he exclaimed and rushed off to get the toolbox from the hall cupboard. Five minutes later the floorboard was to one side and he was groping inside the space. After a few moments, he looked up at me, puzzled and almost angry. 'Nothing Billy,' he grated. 'Not a sausage. The bloody space is empty.'

None of us had contemplated this and I could

understand Tom's disappointment. Susan's letter had obsessed him for a year, but I knew Susan wasn't the type to break her word. 'Move over and let me have a go,' I said, but it as he had said, just an empty space.

'Let's all think for a moment before we start to get panicky,' Dorothy said, but it was all too much for Tom.

'Think?' he exploded. 'What's there to think about? Thinking won't change anything. It's bloody empty - there's nothing there!'

Dorothy ignored the outburst, 'Well Tom, Susan must have left something there or why was that floorboard lifted? Are there any pipes or cables in there?'

He looked into the void and said in a sulky tone, 'No, there isn't anything there.'

'Well then Mr Stroppy, why has it been lifted, if not for our benefit? Something was obviously left there,' I said, 'so either someone else has beaten us to it, or the letter is in there, but we haven't managed to find it yet.'

Kate sighed heavily. 'What an awful thought! If someone else has found it, then that's the end of it, but I got to know Susan pretty well and I'm guessing she would have made certain a casual searcher wouldn't find it. I think it's in there somewhere. Still under the floorboards.'

Dorothy went into a bedroom and came out holding a wire coat hanger. She handed it to Tom and pointed to the toolbox. 'Get some pliers, cut this and straighten it into a long length with a hook on the end will you please Tom?'   ·

He produced the finished article in less than a minute and handed it to her. Dorothy knelt down and pushed the coat hanger into the space. She fished around and then smiled. 'Kate's right! There's something here, I can feel it.' We heard the dragging sound of something moving and then Dorothy pulled out a lidless wooden box. Nestled in the box were two sealed letters. The years had settled a layer of dust over them. We crowded around the box. One letter had written on it, *'To be opened by Dorothy Curtis on Christmas day, 2017.'* On the other was, *'To be opened by Billy Monroe on Boxing Day 2017.'* I recognised Susan's writing.

Tom scratched his head. 'Two letters?' he said softly. I could almost hear his brain ticking over. 'That wasn't part of the arrangement.'

Although I felt uneasy because of the second letter, I said, 'Well, we only have to wait a day to open the other one. Just a day, that's all.'

Tom glanced at his watch and his eyes lit up. 'It's 5:30 now Billy. It'll be Boxing Day in 6 hours and 31 minutes time. We can open it then.'

Whoever coined the phrase, *Like a dog with a bone* got it all wrong. It should have been *Like Tom with a bone!*

'No one could ever say that you have the patience of a saint Tom, could they?' I said caustically. 'We can, but we won't,' and as I said it, I saw that Dorothy had opened the first envelope.

We all leant forward expectantly and she said, 'Why don't we go to the lounge and I'll read the letter to you in there.'

Tom agreed but said, 'Okay, but I'm just going to the loo first so I'll see you downstairs. Don't you dare start without me Dorothy or there'll be big trouble!'

She gave him a contemptuous look, 'And who's gonna give it to me Punk? You? Why, I've got nephews in nappies who could duff you up.'

'Just wait for me, ok?' Tom said, grinning.

In the lounge, I poured Brandies all round and we flopped into chairs, waiting for Tom. He was gone awhile and then we heard the sound of running feet and he hurried into the room, his face glowing with excitement. 'I looked into Beth and David's bedroom and guess what? Only one of the beds has been slept in, so they must have had it off by now.' He beamed widely like a detective who had solved a mystery.

Kate gave him a disgusted stare. 'Nothing is sacred with you, is it, you grubby minded little toad?'

He turned to me in surprise and asked, 'What did I do Billy - what did I do?'

Dorothy shook her head sadly. 'Hopeless!' she exclaimed and then turned her attention to Susan's letter and read it aloud.

'Hello again Dorothy. I'm so glad you are reading this letter at last. I realise that for you, it has only been a year since we were all together, but I'm not writing this letter a year after I came back and it is quite different for me. It's June 1942, so England has been at war with Germany for almost three years and sometimes, I struggle to remember all that happened in my time with all of you.

It is hard to believe that it's more than fifteen years since I last saw any of you. Looking back, I realise I quite enjoyed much of my time with you, but was so anxious to return to my Billy that it overshadowed everything else.

He was there waiting for me in the hallway of Cherry Tree House when I left you on Boxing Day 2016, and I was in his arms a minute later.

God, the relief! It felt wonderful and all my earlier fears disappeared in an instant.

I want to thank you so much for looking after me the way you did. There are no adequate words to express my feelings for the support and love all of you gave me for almost a year and a half.

Billy and I were married in May 1928 along with Celia and her fiancé in a double wedding ceremony. It took place in the parish church of the new family hometown of Cobham, in the county of Surrey, and by then our family had made enough new friends in the area for the church to be full.

Cobham is a lovely place, but it took a little getting used to after all our years living at Wooburn Green, however, we are all very happy here.

Sadly, I'm on my own now. My Billy was killed in action at the end of last year, but I am no longer upset in the way that I was in the beginning. Thanks to all of you, I had fifteen wonderful years with him. He was 41 when the war started and was too old to be called up, but he said it was his duty and volunteered. Of course, because of you, we already knew the outcome of the war, but he was still determined to do his bit for King and Country. I begged him not to go, but he had a great sense of duty and I couldn't budge him.

There is not a day that passes when I don't think of him. Not a day when I don't think of all of you, but I digress, because I know that you will be anxious to hear everything that has happened since my return. Well, Celia did not marry the

348

revolting Digby Jones. Because of him, she lost the baby she was carrying and immediately severed the engagement. What a horrible man he was, although I shouldn't be speaking badly of the dead. Oh yes, that must come as a surprise to you, hearing that he is dead. According to the old saying, only the good die young, but that isn't always the case, because Digby Jones is no more and I would be lying if I said it didn't please me.

After Celia finished with him and Pops refused to give him any money, he tried to kill the whole family and Billy as well, but unfortunately for him, his plan backfired badly and he died as a result of his own actions, crushed by a falling tree. I'm sure it would have been a painful death, but Digby Jones knew all about pain. After all, he caused enough of it!

Pops moved the family to Cobham more than a year before the joint weddings and Billy and I lived a stone's throw from Pops and Mother's new home. Celia's husband is a lovely chap named Daniel and your grandmother was born in 1932. She told me The Wizard of Oz was her favourite film and when she grew up and had a daughter of her own, she was going to name her Dorothy after the film's heroine. Perhaps it is not in her destiny to have a daughter, but a son instead, which would explain why it is you, her granddaughter who is named Dorothy. I know you dislike the name, but not me. Whenever I hear the name, it brings you back to me.

It was a difficult birth for Celia and left her unable to have another child, so the Mendoza blood is getting rather thin on the ground, but it's in you Dorothy, so have lots of children and keep the spirit of Pops going for many years to come. He got off to a shaky start as a father, but thanks mainly to you, he ended up as the best.

I know you often wondered how the family lost its wealth. Well, now I can tell you how it happened. Pops had invested heavily in the American stock market years before you came *into our lives, but hearing from you of the coming Wall Street Crash, he intended to sell his shares before the crash took place. Unfortunately, my lovely Pops was killed in a car accident in September 1929. By the time his lawyers had sorted everything out, it was too late. The Wall Street Crash had happened in October and the Mendoza fortune was lost. All of the insurance money was gobbled up by the personal guarantees Pops had given out, but luckily for Mother, the house was paid for so at least she still had a roof over her head. She started giving piano lessons to make ends meet and Celia and I helped out whenever we could, but the thirties was a lean period for most of us.*

Billy and I didn't have a child. I would have dearly loved a son, but Billy wanted a girl. Unfortunately, it didn't happen, but I take comfort in knowing that you, darling Dorothy, will be appearing in a little over 40 years' time. Who knows? Maybe I will still be around at that time, although I have the feeling that I won't make old bones, but let's hope that I am wrong.

When I lost Billy, Mother moved in with me. We often sit around the fireside into the early hours of the morning, talking about all of you. The others aren't strangers to her. You see, I sneaked a few photographs of you all back with me. Sorry.'

Dorothy paused there and looked at the three of us. 'So that's where those pictures of all of us in Covent Garden vanished to. Naughty Susan! I spent hours searching for them to show to Mum and Dad but without any luck, and now I know why!' She smiled softly and turned her attention back to the letter.

'So that is it, - all of the important things that have happened since my return!

I do hope that Tom and Kate are all right. They did make me laugh, the way they bickered at one another. I often wonder if you still see Beth. She is such a nice lady. Please tell her how much I miss her scones and Petula's raspberry jam.

I do wish that I had been lucky enough to meet Petula and thinking about it, I suppose I still can meet her. After all, she can't be more than 25 years of age at the time of my writing this letter, but perhaps that isn't a good idea. I have a feeling that some things are best left alone and this is one of them.

Oh, and by the way, I should mention the Bugatti. It was stolen ten years ago and was never found. Before it was stolen I was often tempted to look for my letter; the one that started it all, but I thought better of it. If I did and anything went wrong, I wouldn't be here writing to you, for I would have drowned 17 years ago in the English Channel, and your Billy would have never gone to Rose Cottage and you would not have collided with him in Ealing, so the two of you would never have met.

This time thing is so utterly confusing. Anyway, this is a fitting time to end my letter to you. It all started with the Bugatti, and that is how I shall end it. I loved that car.

All my love, Susan.'

Dorothy put the letter down. I think all of us were a bit misty eyed by then, but she was sobbing. She had known Samuel Mendoza and Susan's Billy for a whole year, whereas they were just names to the rest of us. Names that we'd grown to care about, but nevertheless, still only names.

I sat there in silence for a moment. We were all quiet. No one spoke. It was a strange thing to take on board. Dorothy was still crying quietly to herself and I put my arm around her shoulders. She snuggled her face into my chest and let out a heaving, shuddering sigh. 'They were so nice Billy. The other Billy and Pops. Pops was a bit brusque when I first met him, but it was the way he was brought up - not to show his feelings. But he changed immensely, and I know he loved me, and I loved him.' She looked up at me with those tearful chocolate brown eyes. 'Isn't it sad Billy?'

I said, because there was nothing else to say, 'It's life my darling, that's all it is, it's life!'

I could see Tom was disappointed by the contents of the letter, or rather, lack of them. 'Susan didn't say much about the war and what it was like living through it,' he said and I noticed a trace of irritation in his voice. 'I'd have thought she'd have mentioned that,' and I remembered then of his interest in wars and guns and things that blew up buildings and bridges and – unfortunately, sometimes people.

'She lost her husband because of the war Tom,' I said. 'I suppose that's why she didn't talk about it. Too many bad memories.'

Kate made us all a cup of tea and asked if anyone wanted a sandwich, but after hearing the contents of Susan's letter, not one of us had an appetite. Not even Dorothy.

We sat and watched a Christmas comedy show on the television, but none of us laughed. Collectively, we were on a real downer.

It was a blessing when Beth and David eventually returned from their trip and once she started to tell us about their drive and walk, we all cheered up a bit. By the evening, we were back to normal, all except Beth whom Dorothy had given the letter to read, having, of course, got her away from David first.

We all took off to our beds at a little after midnight, but not before Dorothy had asked Beth if she'd mind getting some more eggs from a little store that was situated a few miles away from Lulworth Cove. She explained that it was the only shop that would be open on Boxing Day, although Beth already knew that it was a ploy to get David out of the house so that the other letter from Susan could be read.

*

'The shop opens at eight o'clock on the dot,' Dorothy explained to Beth the following morning before sending her off on her errand. 'Now, are you quite certain you know the way?' and Beth nodded and gave her a proud smile.

'Like the back of my hand,' she said. Since arriving with David, she was like a different person to the one we'd known before this Christmas break and was far, far more confident. I think I've said it before. We all need to love and be loved. She turned to David and nudged him in the ribs. 'Righty ho then; are you ready?'

He stared out through the window at the drizzling rain that was like a blanket of fog, then let out a heavy sigh and looked at Beth with a grimace and pleading eyes. 'Look, I don't mind going without eggs if it means not having to go out in this.'

Beth snapped, 'Well, I do, now will you please stop whingeing and come on.'

Reluctantly, the poor guy dragged himself to his feet and shrugged his shoulders in defeat. He took Beth's hand in his own and said, 'Okay okay, I suppose the quicker we're gone, the quicker we'll be back here in the warm.'

We waited until we heard the van start up and as it pulled away, Tom swooped in on me like a hawk homing in on a field mouse. 'Quickly, open the letter Billy,' he said. 'I can't stand this bloody waiting for a second longer,' and so I pulled the envelope from my pocket and ripped it open. I didn't have a clue what to expect, I mean, what had she put in my letter that she couldn't have put in the one to Dorothy?

I said as much to the others and Dorothy tutted, 'Surely it's obvious Billy. She wrote it at a different time,' which explains why I spent so much time at school standing in the corner wearing the dunce's cap.

I slid the letter out of the envelope and as I did, something else dropped out and landed at my feet with a soft thud. Four pairs of eyes looked down in unison and the same four pairs of eyes recognised the object straight away. It was a watch, but not just any old watch. It was Susan's watch. Tom snatched it up and said, 'What the hell was that doing in there with the letter?'

Not being psychic, I shook my head. 'Search me Tom, but curb yourself for a moment and we'll soon find out; just give me a chance to read what Susan has to say.'

Dorothy gripped my hand. She was unsettled. I'd known her long enough to recognise the signs - and then I understood why. It was simple really; she knew why the watch was in the envelope.

I began to read, aloud, of course. It was a short letter, just seventeen lines to be exact, so it didn't take long.

'Billy, it is now 8pm on December the 26th 1944 and

thank God, the war will be over soon. How vile war is! Two of my friends have already lost sons. They were boys really, not men, barely eighteen years old and just starting out in life with all the good things waiting in the future for them, but now they are dead and without them, their parents might as well be dead too.

I know how much Tom is fascinated by wars; well, now he has a chance to see one at first hand because in three days' time on the 29ᵗʰ of December, 2017, I'm praying that both you and Tom will come back in an attempt to save my life. I beg you not to let me down. There is no one else who can help me now but you. You saved my life once before and by the grace of God, I hope you can do so again. If you do decide to help me, then at 10:30 p.m., hold the watch between the two of you and get someone else to push the fuse in. I know that the formula is different to how it was before, but I honestly believe that it works whenever I need help. I hope I'm correct, or all is lost. I really do mean it Billy - you and Tom are the only ones who can save me and I'm praying I can count on the two of you, but I shall understand if you chose not to come. You have lives of your own to live and responsibilities that I know nothing of. God speed both of you. All my love, Susan.'

I looked at Tom. His face was glowing with excitement. He punched his fist in the air and shouted, 'Way to go Billy, way to go,' and I couldn't help thinking that if we did as Susan asked and things went wrong for us back in wartime England, then he could be right. It would be the way to go.

I'd been dwelling on Susan's letter and had forgotten the girls were in the room; that is until Kate's voice came from behind me. 'You are not going Tom Cox, so don't even think that you are.' He turned and frowned at her, puzzled, although I don't know why. 'It's no use looking at me like that Tom,' she added, 'you're all I have in this world and I'm not prepared to have you risk our life together by going off on some silly escapade to save Susan's life, especially when she's already dead.'

So, there it was, mentioned once again. The vagaries of time travel.

'It hardly sounds like a silly escapade,' Dorothy said sharply, 'and you know Susan as well as any of us. In fact, you know her better than I do because you were here with her while I was trapped in 1926 for a whole year. She's hardly the type to beg for the boys' help unless she had no other option.'

She sighed wearily and took Kate's hands in her own. 'Look, I don't want Billy to risk his life any more than you want Tom to risk his, but Kate - remember that Susan is our friend and from the tone of that letter, it's obvious that she desperately needs our help. Desperately! And you say that she's dead, but is she? Not one of us has managed to work this time thing out. If she's dead now, then she was already dead when she arrived at Christmas time before, but she seemed pretty much alive to me then.'

I looked across at Tom. I'd never seen him so anxious. He was hopping from foot to foot and I felt that he'd go back to 1944 whether Kate agreed or not, but after all, she was his wife and obviously, it would be far better if she did agree.

'Please Kate,' he pleaded. 'I know you think that it's stupid, but I've always wanted to see at first-hand what the war was like. Unfortunately, I was unlucky and was born too late. This is my big chance.'

I stared at him in disbelief. His big chance? Not a single mention of the real issue here, namely Susan. So here was the proof finally laid bare before my eyes. Tom Cox had made a fortune over the years and yet somehow, he'd managed to do it without the aid of a brain. On a scale of one to ten, his verbal skills were somewhere between one and two, and that's me being generous because he's my best friend.

Kate's voice shot up a couple of octaves, 'But Tom, you're making the Second World War sound like it was nothing more than a game, and it wasn't Tom, it wasn't! Millions of people lost their lives in it. Millions of little tots grew up without knowing what it was like to have a father.'

'I know that,' Tom said, realising at last that the *Susan in danger* ploy was a better one than, *I want to go back and see what it was like.* 'But we can't just abandon Susan and ignore her letter, can we?'

What with Dorothy's argument and now this, Kate was wavering. Dorothy moved in for the kill, 'It's your choice Kate. Billy will be going regardless of what Tom does, and much as I'm scared for his safety, I wouldn't want it any other way, but it's your decision whether Tom goes or doesn't go. I understand your reasoning and maybe Billy can manage on his own. If not, I'll have to pray that he gets back safely without Tom's help.'

I felt a pang of sympathy for Kate. Put in that way, I guess she didn't really stand a chance. She gave a long sigh. 'Oh for God's sake Dorothy, don't you realise that I know you're right? It's me being selfish because I'm afraid, really afraid.' She turned to Tom who was still hopping from foot to foot like a child desperate to go to the toilet. 'If I say yes, will you promise to be careful Tom?' and his face lit up. I prayed that he wouldn't punch the air again and shout, *Way to go* and thank God, he didn't. So that was it settled. I was going back to 1944. I just wished I shared Tom's enthusiasm.

Shortly after that, Beth and David arrived with the eggs. This time there was no argument over who cooked breakfast. Kate was too upset, so Beth did the cooking, probably thinking Kate had finally realised her rival's culinary superiority. For the first time in living memory, Dorothy picked at her food and left most of it. 'Are you feeling all right my dear?' Beth asked with genuine concern. 'It isn't like you to leave anything on your plate. Is it my cooking? Is that what it is?' and Dorothy picked up her fork and, realising there was only one way out of this, began eating again.

We hadn't yet revealed to Beth the content of Susan's other letter, so she had no way of knowing what was wrong.

Beth and David returned to Wooburn Green the following lunchtime and we all realised now that David was a nice guy who obviously cared for Beth, and she seemed happy enough with him, so it had all the ingredients of lasting the course.

December the 29th arrived. Not one of us was in a jovial mood, not even Tom. Maybe he'd had time to dwell on it all and think of the reality of war. After all, in war films, victims get up and go home to their supper at night, but in real wars, people who are shot rarely see the light of day again.

Kate remained in her room for most of the

morning and afternoon and when she reappeared at dinner-time, her eyes were red and puffy. It didn't take a genius to figure out that she'd been crying.

Over dinner, Dorothy appeared to be upbeat, talking about her plans for the new house in Weymouth when it was finished, but I knew it was all a front and that she was really worried. I mean *really* worried! By the time 10:25 arrived that evening, I just wanted to get it over and done with.

I was scared that I would never see Dorothy again, or hold my unborn children in my arms, but most of all, scared of not being there to protect Dorothy and hold her and love her until the day I drew my last breath.

Tom and I were dressed in our plainest clothes. There were no designer labels back in 1944. We both had a hunting knife with us, so at least had some kind of protection, although whether I'd ever have the courage to stick it into someone if I had to, well, I guess that's another matter.

Dorothy was holding the fuse with the nail in it that Tom had prepared earlier. I said, 'Remember, I'll leave instructions on how to bring us back under the same floorboard as before, but the note will be pushed even further back than the box that held the other two letters. You'll need two wire coat hangers joined together to reach it.'

'When?' she asked, getting panicky. 'We haven't discussed it at all Billy. When shall I look?' and as she said it, I realised there was no need for her to wait at all. In fact, if the time thing did work for us again, then the letter was already upstairs waiting for

Dorothy to fish it out. Even though I hadn't written it yet!

I hadn't yet gone nuts, but I figured I was getting close.

I glanced at Tom and saw at once that his thoughts were on exactly the same plane as mine. The bugger was about to race up the stairs to the loose floorboard until I shouted, 'No Tom, it's almost 10:30! Leave it or we'll miss our time slot.'

I turned back to Dorothy, 'Have a look under the floorboards tomorrow evening,' I said, 'but remember, even though the formula might give a bit of leeway, I think the day of the month and the time here will still have to match those in Susan's England, so although you should get our message tomorrow, it will tell you when you have to bring us back. It could be months, but at least you'll know we're safe.'

'And what if there is no letter?' Kate asked, putting into words what I was thinking. 'What then?'

I looked across at Tom. He shrugged his shoulders in a throw away gesture. 'Then we didn't make it. If there isn't a letter, then we will have died 36 years before we were born.'

He was right of course, but unlike him, I didn't want to go back to 1944, I really didn't, but knew I had to.

Having once lost Dorothy for a whole year, I wanted a lot more time with her and wondered if this was the last time I would ever see her.

Now I'd mentioned to Tom how close it was to 10:30, Dorothy looked up at the clock for confirmation, her eyes full of tears. 'Thirty seconds Darling,' she whispered in a broken voice.

I said, 'Well then, you'd better come and give me a kiss you gorgeous creature, hadn't you?'

She ran to my arms and hugged me, tears falling in huge drops from her brown eyes and chasing down her cheeks. Kate ran to Tom and did the same thing. In all the years they had been married, it was the first time I'd ever seen them hug.

I pushed Dorothy away and offered half the watch for Tom to hold. I was having trouble keeping it together, but my bosom buddy was grinning like a schoolboy who'd just discovered the magic of girls. He took a firm grip on the watch. There was no fear in his face, only excitement. I took a deep breath and said, 'Now Darling, now,' and Dorothy gave me a brave smile before pushing the fuse in. There was the usual tremendous explosion and I felt myself being pushed violently away from my spot. The watch came out of my hand and I staggered towards Dorothy. I heard Tom's voice shouting, 'Goodbye Billy,' and then there was silence and darkness and an empty space where he had stood.

On the mantelpiece in the lounge we found a letter. Of course, it was from my greatest friend. I opened the envelope and read it aloud for the girls to hear. In my head, I heard his voice saying the words.

This is what I was born for Billy and I've never been so excited! Unfortunately though, some poor bugger has to stay behind to look after the girls, just in case things go wrong. And so, with that in mind, I held a democratic vote - me being the only voter, - and it was decided by a vote of one to nil, that you should be that poor bugger!

Don't let Kate go worrying about me because I'll be fine. As Arnold Schwarzenegger used to say in his movies, I'll be back!

Who knows? I might even make a few bob while I'm here and buy up some properties. Remember, I know all the places that escaped the bombings in the blitz, and all properties in the London area will be cheap. Remember that old saying? Make hay while the sun shines? Well, I'm going to make some hay, once I've taken care of Susan, of course!'

I paused for a moment, smiling. Did I expect something different from Tom Cox? Of course not! I continued to read.

'Please take care of Kate for me while I'm gone. There was never a woman I loved more than her, nor a friend I cared for more than you. There! You didn't think I'd get all soppy on you, did you?

Don't forget to check under the floorboards to see when I'll be coming back. There isn't much point in my sowing the seeds of a fortune in 1944 if I can't get back to spend it, is there? All the best, your mate Tom.'

Printed in Great Britain
by Amazon